THE LEGEND OF CANADA JACK

BY
JOHN R. H. TUCKER

TRAFFORD

CANADA • UK • IRELAND • USA • SPAIN

Printed in Victoria, Canada

National Library of Canada Cataloguing in Publication Data

A cataloguing record for this book that includes the U.S. Library of Congress Classification number, the Library of Congress Call number and the Dewey Decimal cataloguing code is available from the National Library of Canada.

The complete cataloguing record can be obtained from the National Library's online database at: www.nlc-bnc.ca/amicus/index-e.html

ISBN 1-4120-3142-7

This book was published _on-demand_ in cooperation with Trafford Publishing.
On-demand publishing is a unique process and service of making a book available for retail sale to the public taking advantage of on-demand manufacturing and Internet marketing. **On-demand publishing** includes promotions, retail sales, manufacturing, order fulfilment, accounting and collecting royalties on behalf of the author.

Suite 6E, 2333 Government St., Victoria, B.C. V8T 4P4, CANADA

Phone	250-383-6864	Toll-free	1-888-232-4444 (Canada & US)
Fax	250-383-6804	E-mail	sales@trafford.com
Web site	www.trafford.com	TRAFFORD PUBLISHING IS A DIVISION OF TRAFFORD HOLDINGS LTD.	
Trafford Catalogue #04-0969		www.trafford.com/robots/04-0969.html	

10   9   8   7   6   5   4   3   2

This book is dedicated to my wife Margo with love.

I would like to acknowledge the Command Post of Victoria, B.C. for the fine collection of military items shown on the cover. The owner Brent Fletcher and his colleague Mark Jackson are responsible for this artistic display.

The medal shown in the book is the medal awarded for military service in this war.

This book first appeared in weekly newspaper serialization across Canada. I have received an overwhelmingly positive response from readers of the series. Many of whom were relatives of those who had served. The readers reacted invariably with warmth and enthusiasm. Their reaction has been very gratifying to me.

This is a work of historical fiction. All the characters and events portrayed in the book are the product of the author's imagination or are used fictitiously.

However, with a few exceptions, the military units and the names of their leaders are accurate: In addition when it comes to the unfolding of the events of the battle itself every effort has been made to remain true to the historical facts, not only as to the dates of the military movements but as to their timing and character.

Needless to say, any mistakes are solely the fault of the author.

A Note To The Reader

This book is intended to serve as a memorial to those first generations of Canadians who founded Canada and all those who engaged in this battle according to their conscience and their own vision for the future of the country when it was less than twenty years old.

Many of their grandchildren and great grandchildren and their descendants are our neighbours today. Some of these have taken the trouble to contact me after having read Canada Jack serialized in newspapers from coast to coast.

For this I feel truly gratified and honoured.

John R.H. Tucker
Victoria, Canada
June 2004

PART ONE

HOME

CHAPTER ONE

THAT SUMMER of 1884 seemed the longest ever. And in the autumn the warm days crowded back the crisp cooler ones to come. The rolling hills blossomed as one grand bouquet in russet, yellow, orange and red as the trees reluctantly yielded up their summer green.

And down amongst a grove of maples only three miles from the town of Cobourg, a wisp of smoke curled up through the colorfully bedecked branches, it reached the tips of the trees and then drifted off into the early evening blue of the sky.

Jack Holden poked gingerly at the burning logs of his campfire. He busied himself getting his dinner. It was not much, a small partridge roasting on a spit and a can of beans. The bird turned over as Jack poked at it occasionally. The beans, nestled in red and white embers, bubbled and steamed.

Jack was tired. It had been a long day. He had hunted since dawn, pausing only a moment at noon, by the sun, to munch on a sandwich from his pack.

He had found a cozy sheltered break in the thick forest and had stopped for the approaching nightfall. The clearing was only ten feet in diameter. A nice spot to spend the night. Jack cleaned off a particularly flat grassy verge and with a flip rolled out his sleeping bag. He stood his rifle against a nearby tree.

He tasted the beans, then pushed them off the coals and placed them on a rock. He pulled at a wing on the partridge. It moved easily. Done, he thought, and he reached for his mess kit.

A sharp crack split the air.

Jack paused, motionless.

A scream rent the air.

He leaped to his feet, grabbing his rifle as he moved. He swiftly and silently threaded his way through the trees in the direction of the sounds. Now he heard crunching and thrashing. The sound could not be more than forty yards away.

The forest was intensely silent now, but for the sound of Jack's movements, and these were audible only to him. He moved forward stealthily.

Then he stopped. He stood for a moment and listened. To his right he heard the heavy heaving of breath, then a muttered voice. In that direction was a small hill only six feet at its height. Jack moved quietly to its crest. He paused again. Then he slowly moved his head so that his eyes came to rest on the scene below.

The hill gradually sloped down over a distance of twenty feet. At the bottom two men were locked in a fierce struggle.

Jack could see that one was slight. The other was immense. He seemed to have the power of a grizzly. Even as this thought flashed in Jack's mind, the big man picked up the smaller in a vise like bear hug. They were face to face now. Grunting and snarling like a beast, the large man tightened his grip as though to break the back of the other man.

"Drop him", shouted Jack. The sound of his own voice startled him. He has not

5

spoken to anyone for two days. He levelled his rifle steadily on the figures below.

The head of the beast snapped around, searching the rim of the forest.

Their eyes locked. A wicked smile spread across the face of the beast. He dropped his quarry. The man lay like a rag doll on the floor of the forest.

Silence reigned for what seemed an eternity. Then suddenly a knife flashed in the upraised hand of the beast and he plunged it with a thud into the chest of the inert figure beneath him.

For many seconds, Jack stood transfixed by the scene below. He had not fired. Even now his muscles refused to respond.

They gazed at one another for one infinite minute. Then the killer lunged at Jack.

With an explosion, Jack's gun recoiled. The brown derby resting on the head of the killer flipped back and tumbled into the trees. There was no time to reload. Jack wheeled and fairly bolted down the hill.

Jack was fast. He raced through the forest dodging trees as he went. He heard the crashing of underbrush behind him. He ran for his life. His encampment flashed by as he raced through the forest.

Shortly he heard a yowl and, still on the run, he cast a backward glance. The killer had planted his foot in the glowing embers. The roasting partridge seemed to take flight, the boiling brown beans spouted in an arc over the clearing.

The killer moved relentlessly, like a locomotive, crushing all in his path.

For twenty minutes Jack ran steadily. His chest ached as he panted for breath.

Darkness fell suddenly in the forest, casting shadows among the tall maples. As he ran Jack heard his own feet crunch the crisp leaves underfoot. The footsteps following him were like an echo.

The moon slid behind a heavy cloud. Utter darkness. A brook gurgled peacefully only paces away, and beyond rested a huge boulder. If I stop he may think I have crossed to the other side to hide behind the boulder, thought Jack. He wheeled left and stopped suddenly, pressing his back against the far side of the enormous trunk of a tree.

He could hear the killer as he crashed through the underbrush. He heard the chuffing of his breath. Then suddenly, silence.

Jack edged his way around the trunk of the tree and carefully peered back. He saw the killer, his chest heaving, his hand against the boulder as he looked up and down the stream. Then he held his breath and listened.

Jack thought his own breathing could be heard for a mile. He stopped until his lungs were ready to burst. Just before he released his breath, the killer moved off following a path downstream.

Jack expelled his breath and bend over, hands on his knees, breathing hard.

CHAPTER TWO

COBOURG WAS a quiet little town hugging the water-line of Lake Ontario. Settled more than a hundred years before, by United Empire Loyalist, the community had long ago shaped its habits. The Union Jack flew proudly above the red brick town hall. Commercial establishments, doctors, lawyers and the Court House occupied Main Street. The blacksmith, shoemaker and other lesser trades were one street over near the livery stable. Drays and buggies moved purposely up and down these streets and occasionally along the tree lined residential streets.

On this day a crowd had gathered at the town hall. A dray had been drawn up for a makeshift platform. It was festooned with bunting.

"Ladies and gentlemen", said the mayor, "It is not very often we enjoy the pleasure of having in our town a man so important and influential as our guest today. A former town councillor, mayor and member of the Legislature. A gentleman who served some years as a member of Parliament in Ottawa and who is now the Honorable Senator and Lieutenant Colonel Wilbert Trubshaw.

Ladies and gentlemen, a big welcome for Senator Trubshaw."

Polite applause greeted the speaker as he rose from his chair, fiddled with his watch fob and planted himself in front of the lectern. He was a man of average height but great girth. He wore a white moustache, yellowing slightly here and there. He had intense close set dark eyes. Under the autumn sun he looked hot in this three piece vested suit. But he also looked quite at ease with himself as he stood there on the platform

"It is always a great pleasure", he began, "returning to the town with a future, the great little town of Cobourg."

There was polite applause from the audience.

"I always say, the ladies in Cobourg are the prettiest ladies in all of Ontario. We gentlemen do appreciate the ladies."

Once again modest applause interrupted his remarks.

"And if you will bear with me while I make a few remarks, the ladies have prepared a fine lunch for us. We do look forward to this. Especially the apple pie. Do we not, gentlemen!"

A chuckle from the gentlemen.

"But let me get down to business. I'm not here just for the fine food, though Lord knows that would be inducement enough to come all the way down from Ottawa.

"No! I'm here at the request of my colleagues and other concerned citizens to speak to you about the crisis we face.

"Now I'm not talking about the crisis in the Sudan. I am sure Mr. Gladstone, despite his errant political beliefs, can take care of that. And I know that as good loyal citizens of this great British Empire you have sons right now standing shoulder to shoulder with General Gordon in defense of the British way of life. This is important to us all.

"I'm here about the crisis we face right here in our own backyard. I'm talking about the rebellious intransigence of the Metis and Indian tribes in our own North West Territories.

"Gangs of young warriors, as they call themselves, have been roaming the plains threatening our settlers, stealing, marauding, raping and pillaging. The administration of law and justice hangs by a thin thread. Murder has been committed. We are now threatened with outright revolt. There is talk about setting up a provisional government. That, my friends, is seditious talk."

There was a small burst of applause at this remark. But the approval was not unanimous.

"But they're starving, Guvnor," shouted a voice from the crowd.

"That simply is not true," broke in Senator Trubshaw. "This Government has provided for their every need. They want for nothing. Everything they could possibly want is provided for them by this Government."

"How about freedom, independence," heckled another voice in the crowd. "Aren't they entitled…"

"The only freedom worth having," interrupted the Senator, "is under the British flag in a dominion ruled by her gracious Majesty Victoria and with our British

Parliamentary institutions!"

Loud and lengthy applause greeted this last remark. The Senator cleared his throat and the applause died.

"I am here to tell you that, with the approval of the Minister of Militia, Mr. Carton, it is my intention to raise a company from this region. A similar effort is to be mounted all across Ontario for the purpose of maintaining or restoring order in our western territories, should the necessity arise.

"Gentlemen, Canada needs you," he finished, placing great emphasis on the last word.

Tumultuous applause burst from the throng and a military band struck up an enthusiastic march.

Recruiters opened up business at tables. Quickly, long lines of young men formed, men anxious to join the great national cause.

CHAPTER THREE

JACK HOLDEN was not yet sixteen, but he was already full grown. He had flaxen hair, blue eyes and a winning and ready smile. He was tall and lithe. His biceps and shoulders were large and muscles rippled across his bronzed chest and back. He lived with his parents. His father was the town smithy. They did not live on the fine tree lined streets with the large white clapboard houses. The family lived on the other side of the Grand Trunk Railway track; the lower part of town known to all the townsfolk, young and old, and for reasons long forgotten, as cat's alley.

There, amongst tar paper shacks, a few barns and the humble homes, stood the Holden home. Though only a log cabin, it was clean and neat and, in winter time, warm and cozy. The Steeves lived to one side of Holdens and the Garners to the other.

The kitchen garden now frosted and finished with the arrival of fall, led off to the back alleyway. But you could still see the rows of bean and tomato plants, twisted and sagging in the afternoon sun.

Piled against the cabin in neat stacks, two and three rows deep, were many cords of wood. Jack was adding to these piles now as, stripped to the waist, his muscles working in his back, he raised an axe and brought it down with a great 'thwack' on each piece of wood. His younger brother, Andrew, busily snatched each piece and neatly stacked it on the growing piles. Sarah Tuttle watched from where she sat on a saw horse.

Sarah lived on the 'right' side of the tracks with her family. Her father, J. Hiram Tuttle, was a town councillor. He was a lawyer and a man of considerable wealth. He did not approve of Jack. Sarah had been forbidden to visit down on Jack's side of the tracks, but she came anyway.

Jack and Sarah had started school together. In grade four he had been forced to kiss her lightly in a school pageant. By grade six he had managed to kiss her again. This time they were behind a hedge near the school yard. She returned his kiss with ardour and ever since the two had become inseparable companions. Sarah had pale delicate features and spoke in a small breathless voice.

Now, her eyes followed Jack's every move. She chattered while he chopped.

"Aren't you cold Jack?"

"I feel fine," he answered.

"It is fall you know. And I can see steam rising from your back. Surely you'll catch your death of cold."

"No chance. Uhh." 'Thwack' went the blade and two pieces of wood somersaulted off the chopping block.

"It feels good. Bracing. This cold air is good for you."

"You're just making that up. You're always making up things. Daddy says you could get in serious trouble one day, the way you're always dreaming up stories."

"That was no story, Sarah. It was real. It did happen. Even if your Dad and everybody else running this town doesn't believe it. It happened. Anyway I appreciate your Dad's help. I sure don't want to appear in front of Judge Bigelow."

The few weeks that had passed since the incident in the woods had been difficult for Jack. If he had been shaken by his experience that fateful night at the campsite, he was stupefied by the reaction to it in town.

What he had not reckoned on was his reputation.

Like most people his nature began to make itself known in school. While he was active in sports, lacrosse and soccer, and vigorous and athletic, he also had great imagination.

Literature lessons, especially poetry, were like a magic carpet to him. Merely to hear about 'a host of golden daffodils' and his mind took flight. Out the open window, he travelled, into the azure sky and across the yellow autumn fields to untold adventures. Tom Brown's School Days left him yearning for adventures at Rugby.

History was especially enticing. While the teacher rambled on, to the boredom of his classmates, Jack sailed with the English fleet under Charles Howard, the English Lord Admiral. On a cobalt sea, with white scudding waves below and the flag of St. George proudly flying above, he sailed into battle to defeat the Spanish Armada in 1588. He sailed with Sir Francis Drake when Drake captured the Spanish ship Rasario with her rich booty. In 1670 he sailed the Caribbean with Henry Morgan, the buccaneer. In 1777 he sailed with Captain Cook to the South Sea Islands. Only sixty-four years before, on February 6, 1819, with the legendary Thomas Stamford Raffles, he raised the flag of the British Empire over Singapore. And a scant forty-eight years before, in 1838, he fought with James Brook in his campaign through the Borneo Province of Sarawak. When Brook was hailed Rajah of Sarawak, Jack was there, at his side.

Jack was inspired by these heros of the Empire. He saw himself in these adventures. He longed for adventure of his own. He longed for an heroic life. His dreams and expectations were boundless.

His maternal grandfather, Major Harry Belshaw (the family had moved down a social grade or two since the Major) served in the 1st King's Dragoon Guards who fought alongside the cavalry under the command of Sir Colin Campbell in the battle to retake Lucknow in 1858.

Jack's head still reverberated with the sights and sounds of battle so nostalgically recalled by his aging grandfather; the roar and tumult, the confusion, the blast of cannon, the flash and clash of sabre, the acrid smell of gunpowder and the profusion of color and smells, the dead and the dying, the disembowelled shrieking horses, screaming and moaning men. All of this played out against an exotic Indian panorama of battlements, cupolas, great and small buildings and swaying indifferent palm trees. He still had his late grandfather's blue tunic and gold braid, and his white desert sun helmet. These, along with his copy of Cruchley's Map of India – The Seat of the Mutinies, were his most prized possessions.

Naturally he did not keep his dreams and plans to himself. His vivid imagination so filled his head that his thoughts spilled from his lips as naturally as water from a spout.

Jack was unlike the other boys in Cobourg.

In the Coffee Pot Cafe, however, he was not taken seriously. So skeptical were the men of coffee row, that Widow Cranshaw's barn burnt before the fire department could swing into action. Jack had spotted the fire late one night when returning home from pitching sheaves at the Updike farm. Upon seeing the flames he raced to Mr. Boulton's summer house. Coffee row also served as the town fire brigade. They would be playing cards at Boulton's. He shouted 'Fire' – 'Fire' – and then sped on to help Widow Cranshaw with her cattle. Unfortunately the alarm did not take with the fire brigade. They played on until the Town Hall bell began to peal. In a panic they raced to the scene, but the barn was already ashes.

This was the state of affairs when Jack reported the murder. Of course there was initial interest. Then skepticism took hold, and soon most everyone disbelieved Jack's story. It was with considerable trepidation, therefore, that Jack reported the murder to the local police.

"That's the full story then?" said Chief Henry Scott. He was a great husky man with a deep voice. He was chief even though the town constabulary had only one constable in the ranks. That was Constable Homer Plews. Unlike the chief, Homer was thin and short. He had no chin, but a large Adam's apple. Every time he spoke he became so nervous it rose rapidly as though it was going to strike a bell. Then he would blurt out his message.

The chief looked at Jack, waiting for his answer.

"That's it, Chief," said Jack.

"A brown derby you say."

"Yes Chief."

"And it seemed to spin off his head?"

"Yes Chief."

"Then you must have hit it."

"Yes Chief."

He pondered, "Then it would have a hole in it!" He had leaned forward as he interrogated Jack. Now he threw himself back in the chair with satisfaction.

"A clue," he said.

"A clue," he repeated. "A brown derby with a bullet hole. Many brown derbies, but only one with a bullet hole!"

"Homer, a clue," he called. "Where is that runt?" he asked, of no one in particular.

He shuffled through the papers on his desk. Then he began to make notes. He appeared to have forgotten Jack.

Jack didn't know whether to leave or to stay. Was the interview over? He thought it best to wait.

He looked about the room. It had oiled wood floors and pale green paint on the walls. He recognized the pictures on the wall. Any schoolboy would. The larger one flanked by a pair of Union Jacks was a picture of Queen Victoria seated and holding a scroll. Standing slightly to the right and behind her was Prince Albert.

How solemn, he thought. His eyes wandered. A wall clock ticked off the minutes, its pendulum moving ever so slowly from side to side, its hands pointing to 3:30 pm. On the desk sat a brass lamp with a green shade, an ink well with long black pen and a jumble of papers.

On top of these lay The Cobourg Times. Jack's eyes passed over the page, a headline stood out in bold print:

"KHARTOUM UNDER SIEGE"

Then a smaller headline:

'Gordon Virtual Prisoner --Wolsley Ordered to Sudan'

And in smaller print: "Prime Minister Gladstone has ordered General Wolsley," and here the print became too difficult for Jack to read.

Then a small headline to the lower right of the page…"Indian Warriors Off Reservations. Civil Strife Feared on Great Plains."

Jack turned his attention back to the Chief who now appeared to be asleep. Jack moved to rise.

"Just a moment lad."

"Yes, sir."

"You saw his face?" he seemed fully awake now.

"Yes sir."

"You can describe it?"

"I think so sir."

"Think so?"

"I can sir."

"Well?"

"Well, go ahead boy, describe it. Do I have to spell it out?"

"Yes sir, I mean no sir. Well sir, he had a large brown mole."

"A mole?"

"Yes sir, a mole – behind his right eye – very large and reddish brown in color."

"Anything else?"

"Well, he had 'beetle brows'."

"'Beetle brows'," repeated the Chief. He grimaced, "Mmm."

"He was tall, no moustache and he had a strange gait."

"Gait, son? What do you mean 'gait'?"

"His walk. He seemed to have a hitch in his walk. And he seemed very strong, sir, powerful. He lifted that man as though he were a rag doll."

"Homer," yelled the Chief.

"Chief," said Homer, who materialized, breathless, out of thin air, "There's trouble next door, the doc's."

"Yes, yes, what is it?"

"Somebody died in there Chief, and the doc's really upset."

The Chief paused for only a moment.

"Come along boy, I'll just be a moment."

Jack tagged along to Doc Saunder's office.

There, laid out on an examining table lay a body.

"What's the problem, Doc?" enquired the Chief.

"It's Joe Hodgins," said the Doc.

"Was," corrected the Chief.

"He mentioned to me at poker last night that he wanted to drop by for a checkup."

"I saw you two talking."

"I had lots of time today, today being Saturday and all, so I told him to come on in."

"So?" said the Chief. "Get on with it. I feel like a dentist today. It's like pulling teeth to get information. First Jack, now you!"

"Ah, well, yes, yes." The doctor stalled, embarrassed. He looked around the room for a moment, then blurted out his story. "Well the problem is, Chief, that he walked in here a well man. And everybody in town saw him walk in here hale and hearty. How's it gonna look Chief, it we gotta carry him out dead now, me being a doctor and all. How's it gonna look, Chief! It's gonna scare people – that's how it's gonna look."

"I see. You've got a problem all right."

"I just said, 'Open your mouth and say Aah,' and he opened his mouth, said 'Aah,' gurgled and flopped over dead. Heart attack."

They all looked at Joe for a moment.

"I think I've solved your problem," said the Chief. "Let's dress him up. You, Doc, splash a bit of lab alcohol on him."

Doc did as instructed, liberally applying alcohol to the deceased.

"Here, Doc, just a minute. A bit for the dear departed's pals."

The Chief took two large swallows. Then the Doc took a swig.

"Not for you, Jack. You run around to Boulton's livery stable and fetch Joe's buggy. Tell 'em to hurry. When you've got it parked out front rap on the door twice. Then hustle back to the buggy. Make sure the top's up. You're gonna drive poor drunk old Joe back home. Don't worry, I'll be there before you and warn the new widow."

Thirty minutes later three men staggered down the steps of doc's office. Just then the Speckley sisters passed as they did every Saturday at this time. The spinster sisters were on their way to do their weekly shopping.

"Drinking," sniffed one.

"Drunk they are," said the other, "especially that Joe Hodgins. Look at him. He can hardly walk."

The Chief and Doc planted Joe Hodgins in the buggy. The Chief gave the horse a slap on its hind quarter and the buggy drove off.

The interview had ended.

For three frustrating days a party of townsfolk combed the forest. Nothing was found – no body, no brown derby, no bullet holes, not even a cracked twig.

Jack was summoned for a second interview. If the last was unpleasant, this was worse. Jack was informed that a thorough search has taken place. This he knew, he had been present. He had shown the Chief and his party where to search. He was told there was no body and no derby, there had been no flight and that Jack was suspected of having manufactured the whole story.

Jack protested his innocence and reaffirmed the story.

Then he was warned. It was a serious offence to make a false statement to a police officer for the purpose of causing him to enter upon an investigation.

"But it is true," protested Jack once more.

"No, it is not," said the Chief, "and you are now warned a second and final time. A third false report and I caution you, you will be charged with public mischief. You'll go to jail."

CHAPTER FOUR

JACK HAD told his mother and father about his brush with death. He told them about the interview with Chief Scott. Jack's parents knew their son. They believed that what he said had happened, did happen. His father said, "It's over Jack. There is nothing that can be done about it. You have done your duty. If the Chief takes it no further, it is not your responsibility. You have done all you can."

"Yes, dad," said Jack. He loved and respected his parents. But somehow he felt his father had missed the point.

The weeks flew by. The family worked hard as winter approached. There was wood to split, canning to do, potatoes to put up, the endless chores of a self sufficient family making preparations for winter. Jack also worked on the Langford farm, one-half mile north of town. He loved the feel of good hard labor and helped Mr. Langford with haying and at harvest time.

October 31, 1884 arrived. Halloween had not changed for a hundred years. The moon was full. The adults of the town braced themselves. The children planned and plotted with glee.

It was midnight.

Tom Boulton was Jack's closest friend. The two had known each other all their lives. They had been classmates throughout school. Tom was several inches shorter than Jack and inclined to be slim. He was not very athletic. He had dark blue eyes and dark hair with a prominent cowlick, a stubborn tuft of hair standing at the back of his head. He had a healthy, though somewhat irreverent sense of humor and whenever mischief was found, there too was Tom.

Now Jack and Tom worked quietly in the darkness of the stable. They saddled up two of the mares.

"Have you got the pumpkin heads?" asked Jack.

"In the office."

They had planned a furious frightening midnight ride through the centre of town clad in white sheets and jack o'lantern heads.

Jack felt his way into the livery stable office. All he saw was the glint of metal and he knew. He dived for cover. He heard a swish and then 'thunk' as the knife imbedded itself in the door jamb.

"Tom, look out, there's someone in here."

All he saw was an enormous shadow. It came from nowhere and seemed to be falling directly on him. He rolled as his attacker crashed in the shadows where Jack had called out only seconds before.

Jack leaped to his feet and ran from the office.

"Run, Tom, run for your life!"

"Up," shouted Tom. He was mounted and in one motion swung Jack up behind the saddle. The horse bolted for the open door.

Moments later Jack looked back. The brown derby! He had recovered his knife and come charging through the open stable door on a horse. Tom shouted again and dug his heels into the horse urging him forward.

Jack was stunned. The killer had tried again to murder him. How had he found him? Had he learned their plans? Followed him most likely. There was no time to think. The killer was gathering momentum. He closed in.

Tom's horse fairly flew down the street of the town. Their white robes flew behind, illuminated by the full moon.

"We've got to split up, Tom," shouted Jack. "Drop me at the end of the street. I'll lose him in the cemetery."

Jack vaulted from the horse over the fence and dropped to his feet on the run. In seconds he heard pounding feet behind him. Tom's safe, thought Jack.

Once again he heard the heaving breath behind him. Jack ran up a mound of earth. He leaped a gaping grave, and landed safely on the other side. As he ran on he heard a muffled thump and then nothing.

It would be some hours before the brown derby could claw his way out.

Of course, Jack's report fell on disbelieving ears. The grave was examined. It was empty and waiting patiently for an occupant. Tom tried to corroborate Jack's story, but to no avail. It being Halloween did not help.

The Chief now promised to make good on his threat. Jack knew he had no more time. Something had to be done. Now.

The room he liked best in the cabin was the kitchen. Jack sat at the table. A huge mound of freshly baked buns, covered by a tea towel, sat on the table in front of him. His mother added to the mound from time to time, taking buns from the baking trays in the oven.

Jack took a hot bun and made a huge hole in it with his finger. Then he piled fresh butter in the hole and waited for it to melt. He bit down through the crunchy top and munched contentedly.

He remembered now how often he had snitched a hot bun from under the towel on coming home from school. His mother always reprimanded him, but secretly she was pleased.

His father sat next to the stove and watched Jack's mother moving about the kitchen doing her baking. His father was quite a bit older than his mother. Now, having heard Jack's plans to leave, he seemed defeated by the adversities of life. For an hour they had discussed Jack's future. Neither his father nor his mother had done much travelling. Both were descendants from loyalists who had fled the American revolution more than a century before. Their families had settled in the area and travelled little since. When his father had married his mother, and before he settled down to the quiet life of a blacksmith, they took a trip to Niagara Falls. That, and the adventurous travels of Jack's grandfather seemed to have exhausted the family appetite for far off places.

They seemed a little lonesome for him even now, and he had not yet left. They were worried about his future and where his travels would lead him.

It was Jack, however, who worried about the present. For a long time there had been silence in the room. Finally, it was Andrew who spoke their thoughts.

"Is that the only thing you can do?"

"I think so," said Jack. "He's tried to murder me twice now. I'll never be safe as long as he's alive. As long as I live here I'm in danger. And living at home, I put all of you in danger too. He's determined."

"But the police…" began his mother.

"No, Mom, I tried. They just refuse to believe me. Not even Tom was able to convince them. Now they're thinking of charging me with causing a false police investigation. If I go maybe I can solve both problems. It's the only answer."

"What will you do? There's no money." Her head was bowed. She was unable to look at her son.

"I've decided to enlist," said Jack. "They're raising a company to send West. Tom wants to go anyway and Lieutenant Simpson at the recruiting office said they would take us both."

PART TWO

THE ARMY

CHAPTER FIVE

AT THE edge of the city sprawled the Armoury. It was a great conglomeration of red brick buildings, towers, walls and fortifications, complete with crenelations. The entrance was comprised of two massive wooden doors. It looked, really, like a fortress.

Gathered here were many of the military elements that were to constitute the North West Field Force: the Regiment of Canadian Artillery under Lieutenant Colonel Montizambert; the Toronto Expeditionary Force under Lieutenant Colonel W. D. Otter; C Company Toronto Infantry School; 2nd Battalion, Queen's Own Rifles; 10th Battalion, Royal Grenadiers under Lieutenant Colonel Grasett; the Midland Battalion under Lieutenant Colonel Arthur T. H. Williams; the York and Simcoe Battalion and many others.

Military personnel swarmed all over the compound, across the regimental parade square and over the fields beyond. The fields had been converted into a temporary military camp; tents, barracks, drill sheds, military stores, stables and corrals were scattered everywhere.

Red tunics were to be seen throughout the camp, but so were green and purple tunics and the new and very controversial khaki uniforms. The ranks were swelling every day as new recruits were added to the already burgeoning lists. The army seemed to need everybody, from wranglers to cooks and blacksmiths, to clerks and telegraphists. Hardly a trade or occupation was overlooked.

Major General Frederick D. Middleton had been appointed commanding general of the expeditionary force.

He was of average height but an imposing figure nonetheless. He was rotund. His red tunic with gold braid, ribbons and brass buttons, always seemed about to burst. A great walrus moustache framed his ruddy jowls. He routinely wore his dress hat during his rounds in camp. It was peaked fore and aft and fine white plumage cascaded from its crown.

He was commissioned Ensign in 1842 and first saw active service in South New Zealand against the Maoris. He saw service in India, and was engaged in the suppression of the Mutiny of 1857 and 1858. As a captain he fought at Sultanpore and marched with the troops on Lucknow. He also took part in the battle for Azemghur in 1858. Under orders he led a mounted attack against the enemy. In the tumult of battle he saw his lieutenant fall. The mutinous sepoys threatened to engulf the wounded officer. Captain Middleton scooped him up and galloped out of the murderous melee. In a similar manner he saved a private under his command. For these two acts of valour he had been promoted to Major and recommended for the Victoria Cross, but for obscure reasons the decoration was never awarded.

Only the previous year he had been promoted from Lieutenant Colonel to Major General.

Though much in evidence the General was still an enigmatic figure. He appeared everywhere, had his nose into everything. He was even seen dressing down the Lieutenant in charge of the stables. He made his presence felt throughout the camp.

While the officers were familiar with his background, little was known about the General in the other ranks.

Hence the rumours flew!

One had it that the General had served as a young lieutenant with General Nolan in the Crimean War in 1855. When the infamous charge of the light brigade took place, Lieutenant Middleton was said to have been there, in the thick of it. It was common gossip that Lord Cardigan himself leaned very heavily on the advice of Lieutenant Middleton, and gave him orders to ride into the valley and there rally the few surviving troops to lead them out of range of the brutal crossfire of gun and cannon.

One aging sergeant, a veteran of the war, claimed that Middleton received a field promotion to Captain from Lord Cardigan himself for this exemplary conduct.

For a while, it seemed that stories made the rounds putting the doughty General in the centre of every skirmish and every battle of the last twenty years. Some even had him in two battles, at opposite ends of the Empire, at the same time.

Perhaps the most spectacular story about the General also raised the greatest skepticism. This concerned his alleged part in the savage Zulu Wars in South Africa five years before. A self appointed camp oracle said that it was Captain Middleton and not Lieutenant Bromhead who had led B Company, of the 2nd Battalion, 24th Foot in the famous defence of Rorke's Drift. He claimed Lord Chelmsford, the officer in overall command of British forces, had been gravely mistaken to recommend Lieutenant Bromhead for the Victoria Cross instead of Captain Middleton. At the very least the General should have been included with the eleven who did receive the honour from Her Imperial Majesty.

General Middleton did nothing to suppress the rumours or dispel the illusions. He carried on with his inspections and training.

Jack became vaguely aware of other senior officers who were present from time to time: Lord Melgund, second in command to General Middleton; Colonel Grasett; Colonel Williams and others. They were often pointed out and mentioned in conversation around camp, but they remained remote figures. Jack could scarcely recognize them and knew even less about them or their service records.

CHAPTER SIX

JACK HOLDEN and Tom Boulton fell early into army routine.

At 6:30 am reveille was sounded by the company bugler. All enlisted men, Jack and Tom included, got up, washed, shaved and made up their cots.

At 7:00 am they tumbled out of the barracks and hastened to the parade square. They formed up for roll call, then a brief ceremony as the Union Jack was raised. The salute, then dismissal for breakfast.

Jack and Tom, as was their custom, grabbed two chairs together at Baker troop's table. They wolfed down their hot biscuits, bacon and eggs and then raced back to barracks for regular morning inspection.

"Attenn...hut!" a brief command from the Sergeant and the men snapped to attention, each beside his own bed, each rigidly staring straight ahead.

The troop commander, Lieutenant John Richards, moved slowly down the middle of the barracks between the two rows of cots. He stopped here and there and spoke to a trooper or inspected kit or bed.

At the conclusion of inspection Lieutenant Richards left.

A stir sounded in the room. The sergeant wheeled on the men:

"Steady, men steady. Remain at attention."

The men settled down.

"The Lieutenant is not very pleased with conditions in here. We're falling behind the performance of Charley troop. Kit's not neat, bed's a mess. I've told you men before and I'll tell you again," he paused and tapped his swagger stick on a bed, "The blanket so tight that a coin can bounce on it."

Jack and Tom mentally moved their lips to this remark, they had heard it so often.

Then, inevitably, the demonstration. The sergeant reached in his pocket for the large penny coin, flipped it into the air. It arced up and over, then fell, without bouncing, on the nearest bed. The sergeant grabbed the bedding and ripped it away from the mattress.

"Do all these beds again." He shouted the order. Then he rapidly walked toward the far exit ripping open each bed as he went.

"Dismissed," he called. And then he was out the door.

Jack and Tom soon got to know all the men in Baker Troop. There were twenty-one of them and not all of them were Canadians.

Kurt Schmidt was from Germany. He was tall and thin. He wore his prematurely grey hair in a brush cut, exaggerating his already severe features. He easily took offense and was especially sensitive about his scar. He wore it proudly.

"It vass from duelling, you know," he confided to every newcomer. "I vass a student at Heidelberg University."

Of course he could do everything better than anyone else and was continually showing others how things should be done. He was always jumping to be the first to execute orders. He fawned unashamedly on all the officers. When they came even within a hundred feet of him, he snapped to attention with a slight bounce and a loud click of his heels.

He was also the oldest in the Troop and was fond of patronizing his comrades. He incessantly talked down to them, claimed to have served in the last Franco-Prussian War, and asserted, therefore, that he was the only veteran in the Troop. Accordingly, he was full of advice as to comportment, now and under fire. He spoke endlessly of how it felt to be "engaged in battle."

"Und sometimes I could hear the bullets vissing by mine ears. I'm tellink you zere is nossing so srilling as to be shot at vissout result," he intoned seriously.

Surprisingly, the other men in the Troop grew to like him.

Bruce "Sandy" McCallum was from Scotland. Because of his rich brogue, it was a long time before everyone understood what he said. He was constantly asked to repeat everything in English. Like so many of his race, he was fond of Robert Burns. He quoted him endlessly. It seemed the great poet had advice for every situation. McCallum was also careful with his money.

There was Tubby Mills from Ottawa whose stomach wreaked havoc on his tunic buttons; they were forever blowing off.

Langford Hughes came from Waterloo. He seemed always so lofty, so aristocratic.

Ronald Crutchley, along with Tom, was from Jack's home town. He was the undertaker's son. Like his father, he was tall and angular. Every one of his joints was double hinged. It was impossible to break his arm; it moved in any direction. He never did learn to march. To him marching was a mystery. He would pinch his eyes together in concentration as he threw left arm and leg forward simultaneously. If he gave no thought to it he was fine, but put him on the parade square and order him to march and it became an intellectual exercise demanding all his concentration. And usually with the same result; he marched in gorilla fashion – a sort of modified totter. By common consent he was hidden in the middle of the Troop during parade. He was aptly nicknamed "Crutch".

"Duffy" Durell was a small and muscular young man from Southern Ontario. He had gimlet eyes and his face was pitted with pockmarks. Despite his appearance, he was outgoing and friendly.

There was Horace Busby from Halifax, "Busby" to his mates. And "Butch" Saunders from Own Sound; and Henry Higginbottom ("Higgy") from Windsor; and "Bo" Sandford from Toronto; and Donald "Yank" Smith from New York. Yank kept to himself a great deal.

There were others both in the troop and eventually in the company that they grew to know and like.

Especially did they come to like the trust Lieutenant Richards. He was tall and slim with kindly grey blue eyes and dark hair. He was clean shaven except for a full black moustache that he had recently begun to cultivate. The Lieutenant was twenty-nine years old, but he was still a bachelor. He had been born and raised in Kingston. He attended Royal Military College there, and had become a thoroughly professional soldier. He was firm and exacting but the men knew that he made the same demands on each in his Troop, without favor. He also made them understand that no matter how hard they drilled, whether on parade or with small arms, it was for their own good. It might one day make the difference between living and dying.

And drill they did.

"Fall in!"

A great clatter of feet as the Troop obeyed.

"Rahhht dress!"

A shuffling of feet. The men shot out their right arms, fists closed, onto the left shoulder of the man to the right, and thus on down the ranks to the marker.

"Attenn...shunn!"

A 'whup' as all arms slap down and heads snap forward.

"Platoooooon, stand at....ease."

Left foot up then slammed down one and a half feet from the right foot. Hands clasped behind the back.

"Attennnn...shun! Let's try that again men, and this time I want to hear only one foot. All together." "Stand at (a long pause)...wait for it...ease!"

"Attennnnshun!"

"Ah raaaaght...turn!"

"Move to the right in columns of three...(pause)...quick march!"

"All right men, sound off!"

They chorused:

"A leff, a leff, a leff rahht leff,
A leff, a leff, a leff rahht leff."

"Sound off!" called the Sergeant.

"One, two, three, four, knock 'em deader than a door."

Then they sang:

"Peas, Peas, Peas, Peas
Eating goober peas,
Lordy how my teeth ache

18

Eating goober peas!"

The drilling went on all morning, every morning until Jack and Tom felt they could march no more, and then, after a half hour break for lunch, they were ordered on a ten mile route march with rifles and full pack.

Increasingly in the afternoon, the men were trained in military skills that they felt would be more useful at the front. They took target practise with the new breech loading rifles and with handguns. They learned semaphore flag signals for communications. They were trained in hand to hand combat and given bayonet drill.

Gunny sacks were filled with straw and suspended at a normal man's height.

"Now men, this is the enemy. You hate his guts. He's a rebel, he ain't loyal to Queen and country."

"Now, fix bayonets."

A rattle of metal as bayonets were rammed home on the muzzles of twenty-one rifles.

"Now when I holler 'charge,' I want to hear some blood curdling screams. I want you to scare them sons a bitches to death. Hear me? I want them to faint. Ah want them askeered to move. Unnerstand me?"

The Sergeant looked over the Troop.

"Now ah don't want you waltzin' in there lahk a fairy Crutchly."

Snickers rippled down the ranks.

"Shaddup!"

"Ah right…(pause)…Charge!!"

A blood curdling scream rose (amidst a few embarrassed chuckles) as the troop charged forward toward the dummies. Jack and Tom were in the vanguard.

For many weeks the training continued like this and the men soon became soldiers. They developed loyalty and discipline and obedience and their strength and military skills grew too. They developed cohesiveness and a strong esprit de corps.

Jack in particular developed great skill in shooting, especially with the six cylinder revolver. He could draw and shoot so fast that he empties every chamber before the others got off a single shot. Five out of six of his shots invariably hit the bull's eye, the other rarely missed.

Lieutenant Richards took great interest in Jack's unusual skill with a six shooter. He used every opportunity to coach Jack and help him practise and improve. While this went on, Jack developed a deep respect for the Lieutenant. The Lieutenant reciprocated with admiration for Jack's skill. A firm bond of friendship and affection grew between the two men. It was not the affection of father and son, but more that of older and younger brother.

The men in the troop had a different reaction. They were all sitting around the barracks one night, too tired out by training exercise to move.

"I don't know why you practise anymore Jack, you can't get any better."

"Yeh, Jack's so good, he's a regular Wyatt Earp."

"Hell no!"

"No he ain't, he's Billy the Kid."

"Yeh, said Tubby Mills, "The 'Canada Kid'!"

"That's right," said Tom, "Canada Jack! You're really something with those shooters, Jack. I'm glad you're on our side. I'm beginning to feel sorry for them injuns."

They all looked at Jack in silence. From that moment the nickname stuck and he was called Canada Jack.

CHAPTER SEVEN

THE DAY came when basic training ended. The entire regiment went on parade. General Middleton took the salute as Commander in Chief of the North West Field Force. Everything proceeded without flaw. After the marchpast, the troops were ordered to stand easy. The General delivered a speech, a long-winded affair complimenting the men on their state of readiness, warning them of the battles that lay ahead, advising them of the righteousness of their cause and of how proud Her Majesty would be if she could be there that day. He hinted there may be earlier action for a select few before many weeks and then dismissed them with his hearty good luck.

Jack felt good. He thought he had put the past firmly behind him. However, several weeks before, Lieutenant Richards had interrupted his small arms target practise and told him to report to the Company orderly office. After a wait of three-quarters of an hour, the orderly officer paraded him before Colonel Trubshaw.

The Colonel sat at his desk shuffling through papers. He did not look up as Jack came to a sharp halt in front of the desk.

"At ease," the Colonel said at last.

Jack complied, but still looked straight ahead.

"Stand easy son," said the Colonel.

"You have a good record here soldier. I hear you've developed into a crack shot. That's good my boy, that's good. We could do with more men with skill like that."

"Thank you sir," said Jack.

"That's why," said the Colonel without taking notice of Jack's reply, "I am somewhat concerned about this report I have received."

"Report, Sir?"

"That's what I said," snapped the Colonel impatiently. "A report. From Chief Scott and Magistrate Bigelow."

He paused as he glanced once more over the letters.

"I won't go into the details because you'll know what I'm talking about. Your motivation to join the military had less to do with patriotism than with a pressing need to leave town."

"Sir…"

"Please! I'm not finished. I want it clearly understood that you continue on probation here for the time being. Further, I will have none of that overworked imagination."

"We have a difficult enough time dealing with army scuttlebutt. You should understand that any false reporting in the army means immediate court martial! Is that understood?"

"Yes, sir."

The Colonel seemed to relent a little, now that the need for firmness had passed.

"You've done well here, Jack. There might be a military future for you if you can keep your nose clean."

"Thank you, sir."

"Baker Troop has done so well," went on the Colonel, "that I have arranged to have them assigned to my new command, the Canadian Military Rangers."

The cavalry! exulted Jack silently. He could not have wished for any better luck.

"You have had extensive experience with horses as have all of Baker Troop. You have also done well otherwise. No reason you shouldn't go with the rest of Baker Troop over to the new unit."

"Thank you sir," he said one last time and the next moment he was outside the Company orderly office letting off a real whoop.

Later he began to understand better the reason for the interview. He received his first letters at mail call.

One was from Sarah Tuttle. He tore it open and read it avidly:

'Dear Jack,

I hope you do not think me bold writing to you like this. If my father knew I am sure he would disapprove, but I simply had to write to you.

At dinner last night he was telling mother that Chief Scott and Magistrate Bigelow had sent full reports on your conduct this past year to Colonel Trubshaw. At a meeting in the judge's office the three of them decided that, however admirable it was of you to enlist, it was their duty to place your character fully on record. In wartime, they agreed, it is most important for the commander in the field to know the good and the bad. It may someday save lives. At least this is what father had to say.

This upset me no end. I dare say I ate nothing at supper that night. When Mama asked me if something was wrong I said only that I felt slightly faint and perhaps the grippe was coming on. I was excused and took myself off to my bedroom.

Jack, I do so miss you. Even the town has lost its sparkle since you left.

When I got to my bedroom I threw myself on the bed and buried my face in the pillow that I was using that early morning when you said goodbye.

Goodness, I should not be writing such things.

Take good care of yourself. I will try to write again. If you wish you may write to me at Amanda's. She has told her parents, dare I say it, that I care for you so deeply.

Let me know how I may write to you out west.

Jack, I do so want to believe that these things really happened to you. I wish somehow you could show the whole town!

I miss you.

Affectionately,

Sarah

P.S. Did you know that local hardware store burned to the ground three weeks ago. Mr. Moffatt the blacksmith must have been at work inside. He burned to death in his own building. Isn't it awful!'

Jack then opened the letter from his parents:

'Dearest Son,

Your mother and I and Andrew miss you very much. The town does not seem the same since you left.

Your mother is busy as usual. Today she finished putting up the tomato, onion and green tomato pickles. She won't admit it but she sure misses your filching from the kitchen table.

Tomorrow she's going to make us krullers. Remember how you used to break the bubbles and fill them with your mother's crabapple jelly?

Andrew is driving us all to distraction. He is so impatient for news about his brother. You must write him a long letter telling him all about your experiences. He says he hopes the war lasts long enough for him to get into it. He doesn't think, of course, about the danger this would mean for you.

Several weeks ago Moffatt's Hardware and General Store burnt down. Mr. Moffatt's body was found among the charred ruins. I think foul play is suspected. A large consignment of bolt action rifles from Smith & Wesson that the hardware received only last week was never found, not so much as a single barrel. And the ashes have been thoroughly combed through by Chief Scott and some volunteers.

Look after yourself and write soon.

Your loving mother and father.

P.S. Mr. Crutchley, the undertaker, has been seen around town wearing a brown derby. I wonder if it has a bullet hole in it. I must try to find out.'

A wave of confused emotions swept over Jack. Loneliness for the warmth and security of his home, his mother and father and young Andrew; the familiar streets and faces; the smell of burning grass in the fall.

He wondered whether the missing rifles could have anything to do with the man in the derby. If the hat had been holed by a bullet, there was some evidence the killer did exist. Jack longed for vindication. How much he wanted the whole town to know and believe the truth. But most of all he found himself longing for Sarah.

He picked up her letter once more. In his mind's eye he saw everything that happened that last time.

He was leaving town by the 9:00 am train. Her parents had refused to let him see her the day before. As far as they were concerned, his departure was better for all concerned.

In the early dawn that day he quietly climbed the maple tree outside her bedroom. He silently dropped to the verandah roof. He could see through her window. She was lying with her bare back toward him. The first rays of the morning sun, filtered by the slowly shifting branches of the tree, played across her blond hair.

He rapped ever so lightly.

She moved slightly, awake now.

He rapped once more.

She sat up now and the bed clothes fell away. One hand flew to her mouth and the other to the blankets. She motioned for Jack to open the window. It moved easily and he slipped inside.

"You're cold," she said. She could feel the frigid morning air clinging to his plaid shirt. She moved the woolen blanket around his shoulders. For a long time they whispered to each other. They had never spoken like this before. The intimacy thrilled them both. She made him promise to write and begged him to be careful. He left as swiftly as he came.

The bittersweet memory of it filled his body. He placed the letter into his kit beside his cot. He could not afford to succumb to these feelings now. I have battle to confront before I set my eyes on home again, he thought. And anyway, I may never be able to return.

CHAPTER EIGHT

ACTIVITY AT the military camp grew ever more intense. Each day Jack worked harder than the last and swore he could work no harder. Each night the members of the Troop fell into their cots as soon as all leather was polished, every button burnished. They slept immediately.

The men had been convinced that, at the very least, regular morning inspection would be dropped, leaving them an extra half-hour in bed. They had soon discovered otherwise.

Fate and the hi-jinks of Tom, however, came to their rescue.

One night they were relaxing around the barracks. It was close to lights-out. Tom, Jack, Yank, Tubby, Kurt and Duffy were gathered at the back lounging on four cots, bragging and swapping stories.

As the conversation continued Yank got up and went over to his tunic, hanging with the rest of his clothing near his bed. He reached into his pocket and withdrew a bulging napkin and returned to place it next to him on the cot. Then he reached down to his barracks box, opened it and withdrew a small jar. He placed the jar next to the napkin.

By now all eyes followed Yank, especially those of Tubby, who suspected a snack war in the process of preparation.

Yank opened the napkin to reveal five rolls that had been rescued from the supper table. Next he turned to the jar, which appeared to contain a pale, yellow-brown substance. As he forced the sealer open, Tubby could contain himself no longer.

"What's that, Yank?"

Yank looked down at the freshly opened jar.

"Gooberbutter," he replied.

"Gooberbutter? What's that?" Tubby persisted.

"Gooberbutter is gooberbutter. It's from my Aunt. She used to live in New York. Now she lives in Georgia. She sent it."

"That still doesn't answer my question," said Tubby, impatient and anxious at the same time.

"You should know what it is," Yank teased, "You've been singing about it when we march."

By now all other conversation had ended. Yank, who was usually so quiet, had finally opened up and the men were enjoying it.

Yank dipped a knife into the jar and scooped up a smooth blob which he artfully began to spread on the bread.

"That's peanut butter, Tubby." said Tom. He was eyeing the jar speculatively. "We call that peanut butter."

"Let's have some," exclaimed Tubby, reaching for a roll.

"Just a minute," said Tom. "I've got a better idea." Tubby sat back, annoyed.

"You know how every morning five of us have to do latrine detail." He was referring to latrine inspection. Each morning as part of barracks inspection the sergeant did latrine inspection. The Troop was expected to maintain the five stalls in spotless condition. Any lapse meant scrubbing the whole latrine down a second time, perhaps scrubbing the barracks floors as well. Five men were assigned in rotation to this duty and each was assigned a stall. During inspection the five were expected to stand at rigid attention, each beside his stall, while the inspection was conducted.

Suddenly Tom jumped up and grabbed the jar.

"We've got a better use for this," he called, as he ran for the latrine. The gang of them stumbled after Tom, Tubby and Yank protesting loudly.

Tom stopped in front of his assigned cubicle and slammed open the door. He paused for a moment as he studied the interior. Then before the jar could be grabbed away, he scooped out a huge handful, took a step into the stall and threw it down with a dull 'splat' next to the stool.

Then he stepped back to admire what he had done. The others jostled him to get a better view.

The following morning the inspection got underway in the usual fashion. As soon as the lieutenant left, the sergeant marched into the latrine for the inspection. The five soldiers stood rigidly to attention, each at his own stall. Their eyes were fixed straight ahead.

The sergeant stepped smartly to the first stall. He inspected first the soldier. Then at a nod the soldier, still staring straight ahead, pushed the stall door open with his right hand. The sergeant glanced inside without moving from his spot. Then he nodded once more and the door was closed.

Quickly he stepped to the next cubicle and the second soldier. This inspection, too, went off without a hitch.

Then he stepped smartly to the next cubicle. Tom had never looked so smart. The sergeant was pleased. After giving Tom the once-over he nodded for the door to be opened. Tom complied, flinging it back with military precision. All the while, of course, he kept his eyes fixed on the far wall.

The sergeant glanced inside. He was about to step away when he did a double take. Then he stepped forward and peered down at the floor. He stepped back astonished.

"What's that?" he exclaimed, to no one in particular.

"Sir!" said Tom, snapping to attention. He whirled smartly around, took one step forward into the latrine, bent and ran his finger through the pile. He stepped back, did a smart about face, coming to attention, and ran his finger through his mouth.

"Tastes like poop, sir!" he nearly shouted, maintaining all the while the finest military bearing.

The sergeant's mouth dropped, then twisted in distaste. His eyes bulged from their sockets. He fell back a step, as though about to faint.

The others in the room were about to burst.

"Ha!" barked the sergeant.

"Ha!" he barked again. He recovered his composure stepping toward tom. "You… You…in your…" he pointed with his finger at his mouth.

"Yessir!" snapped Tom, offering his finger to the sergeant, who once again fell back. "Have some."

At that they could contain themselves no longer. They burst into gales of laughter.

The sergeant soon realized he'd been 'had' and joined in the laughter.

Morning inspections ended that day.

Jack had told the others of the plans to assign the platoon to cavalry duties. This information was confirmed by Lieutenant Richards. They looked forward eagerly to the day on which they would be assigned, each of them, a horse.

The day came and Jack drew the most beautiful two year old white mare he had ever laid eyes on. She was lively, intelligent and responsive to his every command. Jack could not keep himself away from the stable. He spent every free moment fussing over her, feeding her and even talking to her.

And after a while he even thought she began to understand what he said.

He exercised her and rode her in drill. They soon became a team. He needed no saddle, no cinch, no bridle nor halter. She seemed to respond to his thoughts. She rode like the wind. Man and horse became one.

She liked nothing more than to be ridden by Jack at full gallop over the open fields without purpose. She frisked about and playfully jumped and reared. At these times she seemed to Jack a free spirit galloping above the earth. So fast was she that no other horse in the company was her equal. Many offered to swap horses with Jack. All offers were refused. It was not long before it became clear that nothing could part the man from his horse.

So swift and free was she that Jack named her Cloud.

Upon being assigned to the Rangers, the men in Baker Troop traded their red tunics for khaki uniforms. They were among the first troops to use the new uniforms.

Jack and Tom returned from the quartermaster with their arms laden. Slowly Jack pulled on his breeches. Then he put on his khaki jacket. He sat down on the bed and pulled on his highly polished brown riding boots. He stood and slipped on his brown belt. He fastened his gun to the belt, reached down and picked his khaki pith helmet off the bed, placed it on his head and pulled the strap under his chin.

Slowly Tom and Jack turned to face each other. Tanned and fit, Tom now wearing a full regimental moustache, they faced each other for a long minute. Then each broke into a foolish grin. They looked like what they were: seasoned soldiers in the North West Field Force. They were ready for action.

Long before the orders came the men were prepared to move. In retrospect it seemed inevitable. Lieutenant Richards often brought the newspapers to the barracks. They were full of news from the Sudan, but the men seized upon any scrap of news that could tell them when they would see the action they so eagerly awaited. The papers were full of that too:

DAILY INTELLIGENCER.
Belleville, Ontario
THE FIRST BLOOD
Encounter Between the Mounted Police and Rebels.
A SURPRISE AT DUCK LAKE.
Two Constables and Ten Civilians Killed.
ELEVEN OTHERS WOUNDED.
Retreat of the Police to Fort Carleton
An army to be Thrown Into the Country at Once.
The Rebels to be Put Down at all Hazards.

OTTAWA, Ont. – It is understood that the Government have received despatches from the North-West giving details of a conflict between the Mounted Police and the rebels. Capt. Crozier marched from Fort Carlton and engaged the rebels, while Col. Irvine, with his force, was crossing the Saskatchewan River. Both then withdrew to Fort Carlton. Eleven of the Mounted Police and 80 rebels were killed. The rebels are retreating westward.

The Battle.

OTTAWA – The following telegram from Lt.-Col. Irvine to the Right Hon. Sir John Macdonald, Fort Carlton via Winnipeg, was read by the Premier after recess to the House: – A party under my command has just arrived. When near Fort Carlton we found that Crozier with a party of one hundred went to Duck Lake to secure a large quantity of supplies stored there and was met by some hundred rebels, who held an advantageous position at Beardy's reserve and endeavoured to surround the police and civilians. The rebels fired first. When it became general, Crozier, owing to the disadvantage at which he was taken, retreated orderly, arriving at the fort at the same time as my party. Ten civilians of Prince Albert and two policemen were killed, and four civilians and seven constables wounded: the number of rebels killed is not known. The police and civilians acted with the greatest bravery, under a heavy fire.

THE KILLED ARE……..

Other headlines were just as lurid:

NORTH WEST MOUNTED POLICE OFFICERS SLAIN.

Cried the headlines of one.

INDIANS ON THE RAMPAGE

said another. And still others said:

RIEL RETURNS!

PRIME MINISTER DENOUNCES REBELS:

Government will not countenance sedition. Minister of Justice Speaks to Rally: Treason is hanging offence, he advises.

MINISTER OF MILITIA ANNOUNCES TROOPS ARE READY:

WELL ARMED

PARLIAMENT TO ACT!

The newspapers were full of advice to the Government, all of it of one kind: Do Something. Act!

PART THREE

ON THE TRAIL

CHAPTER NINE

BAKER TROOP had been on the move now for two weeks. The orders had come suddenly. Jack and Tom and the rest of the Troop were relaxing in the barracks on Sunday afternoon.

"Attenn…Shun!" shouted Sandy.

They all jumped to attention. Silence fell in the room.

"At ease men," said Lieutenant Richards. "Just relax, smoke if you wish."

A number of the men lit up cigars and pipes.

"Orders have just come down from General Middleton. We are to proceed West with all possible haste and as much attention as possible. The Prime Minister is quite anxious that the government appear to be doing something."

Laughter greeted this last remark by Lieutenant Richards.

"Once on the plains we are to make ourselves highly visible, provide protection to settlements that require same and enforce law and order in cooperation with the North West Mounted Police. In general we are to do everything possible to contain the situation and make preparations for the main body of troops which will follow in due course.

"We are under strict orders not to provoke the enemy prematurely. There will be time enough to engage the enemy later.

"There will also be plenty of time for questions later. For now, Sergeant," he turned to the Troop Sergeant as he said this, "see that the men and their horses are ready to embark by train at eight o'clock tomorrow morning."

"That's all men, and good luck!"

With that the Lieutenant departed. Cheers, laughter and shouting filled the barracks.

Jack, Tom and Crutch occupied two seats facing each other. They swayed with the gentle motion of the train as it rhythmically clacked its way west. The country side gradually became more gentle, the rock gave way to earth and inviting lakes as the powerful little engine poured forth steam power relentlessly.

It was now late in the evening. Jack watched through the window of the train as the silent forest slipped by. It was shrouded in darkness.

Jack could hear Bo tormenting Yank two seats back.

"Yeh, it's you Yanks causin' all the trouble, always stirring up the Indians."

"Hell no," said Yank, "we got enough trouble with our own Indians, we don't need to trouble with yours."

"What fur are your traders always comin' up fur, tradin' 'em guns an' all?"

"We ain't doing that."

"Hell, yes, you is!"

"I say we ain't!"

"What fur is Captain Howard here fur then, with his gatling?"

"Why you know as well as I do he's gonna help us. That's a mighty powerful new weapon. We can just mow 'em down."

"Yeh, sez you. I bet he's gonna sell it to the Indians."

This nagging had gone on since they had boarded the train. They all saw Captain Howard shout orders as he supervised the loading of this gatling gun.

"I'm going back to check on Cloud," said Jack as he eased himself between the legs of his companions.

Jack braced himself on the seat backs as he moved through the coach.

"See what's keeping Duffy," someone shouted to him as he made his way to the rear of the car. "He's been gone an hour. He must be sleeping with the ponies."

Jack did not acknowledge the remark. He slipped out the back door of the car and continued his trip to the rear coaches of the train.

Finally he reached the stable coach. He heaved open the door and was hit with a draft of stable smells as he entered.

The horses had been stabled facing forward to avoid losing balance during acceleration or braking.

A foot path for feeding and servicing had been retained on the right hand side. Jack now walked down to the third manger from the end, where Cloud was tethered.

"How are you girl," he said as he stroked her neck. The horse quietly whinnied acknowledgment and nuzzled Jack in his chest and arm.

"That's my girl," said Jack, "How about a nice rub down."

As Jack picked up the curry comb he had the uncomfortable feeling he was being watched. He raised has gaze. Standing only a few feet away, looking back was Duffy Durrell. He was in the last manger.

"Hi Jack."

"Hi Duff. They're asking for you back there." Jack gestured toward the front of the train. "For some reason they miss you."

They both chuckled quietly.

"I've been feeding a few oats to Yank's pony," offered Duffy. He looked vacantly around for a moment. Then he said, "Well, I guess I better be running along. Don't want the boys getting lonesome do we?"

They both chuckled again and Duffy left for the passenger coach ahead.

Jack turned his attention back to Cloud and set to work with the curry comb. He brushed while Cloud, satisfied to have her master close and stroking her, stood motionless. He finished and was about to hand feed oats to Cloud when he heard a clang at the end of the coach.

Jack looked over. He could see nothing. He could feel the rocking of the coach, but he could barely make out the motion of the next and last coach because of a thick film of grime on the window in the door.

There was no reason for anyone to be between Jack and the end of the train. The last coach contained munitions and dynamite. It was a sealed coach.

Slowly and quietly Jack made his way over to the door. He glanced out the dirty window. He could see no one.

He pushed open the door and stepped outside onto the metal platform. He saw a man straining at the coupling. He's trying to uncouple the munitions car, thought Jack. He sensed more than saw an iron bar flash upward at his head. He ducked and the bar fell with a dull clank against the metal frame of the coach.

Jack struck out at the man. He landed a heavy blow with his fist on his chin. The man staggered back.

Suddenly the man leaped on the ladder leading to the catwalk on the roof of the train. He disappeared in a moment.

Jack followed up the ladder. Once up he almost choked on the thick black smoke and ash curling back from the stack of the steam engine.

The train rocked dangerously as he blindly crawled forward. The catwalk seemed to buck and Jack carefully clutched at the boards with his left hand before freeing his right. In this fashion he made his way to the forward end of the coach.

Halfway down the next coach, Jack's right hand came down on the cuff of a pantleg. He surged upward and charged. He tackled the man about the waist and both rolled toward the front.

A fist smashed into the side of Jack's head. Stunned, he lost consciousness for a split second. He awoke rolling toward the edge of the car. His hands flailed for something to break his fall. Then he was over and falling.

With superhuman effort, Jack's fingers grasped the gutters running along the edge of the rooftop. For a moment he dangled there, his feet dancing in the window of the coach.

Slowly he eased himself up, finally swinging one leg over the edge of the roof. Painfully he pulled himself higher. He thought his finger joints would explode from the pressure. With one final heave he rolled back onto the roof, back into the choking smoke.

Confidently he began to move forward again, feeling his way. Abruptly the catwalk ended. At the same time the choking black smoke ended. Jack looked up to see the train rounding a long slow bend in the tracks.

He could also see his quarry, fully a coach away and virtually running forward. He stood and ran as fast as his shifting foot allowed. He now seemed to almost fly forward and he sensed the train begin to decelerate. Then he remembered the planned stop at the water tower to take on more water for the steam engine.

He heard a crack and a ping. He was being fired at.

In a flash he had his shooter in his hand, the attached lanyard flying. He fired.

Then he heard a crack and wood chips flew from the catwalk in front of him.

Jack dodged forward loosing a volley of shots. He saw the man pitch forward between the coaches. Jack heard a slight 'chunk' sound as the man fell under the heavy cutting edge of the wheels.

As Jack saw the locomotive chug slowly up to the tower and stop he raced forward to report to Lieutenant Richards.

The Lieutenant and many of the troopers had heard the shots. They all listened excitedly.

"There's someone trying to sabotage the train, Lieutenant," said Jack. "I just caught him trying to uncouple the munitions car. I think he's dead. At least I shot him."

"Where is he?" asked the Lieutenant, "Better search….."

Just then a volley of shots rang out and one shattered the window. Another the gas lamp on the wall.

"Ambush," shouted Tom.

CHAPTER TEN

LIEUTENANT RICHARDS deployed his troops on either side of the coaches, on the top and inside as well. A second fire fight erupted. The soldiers took what cover they could. The gunfire and shouting created an uproar.

The Lieutenant ordered his troops to advance and they moved toward the rear of the train. The munitions car had finally uncoupled. It had drifted to a stop about a hundred feet behind the stable coach. Intense cross fire broke out, most of it from the trees opposite the solitary munitions car. The fusillade stopped the advance of Baker Troop.

Then, as the shooting continued, there was a noticeable drop in the whine and ping of bullets around the troopers.

The barrage could be clearly seen now as the raiders, all mounted and in constant motion, poured round after round into the munitions car. Fire could now be seen through the windows, leaping and dancing inside.

"They can't steal it so they're going to blow it," Lieutenant Richards shouted to Tom nearby.

The fire then began to lick at the sides of the car from one end to the other.

"Down, everybody, down!" shouted the Lieutenant above the roar of the flames and shooting.

The men scurried to find cover.

"She's going to blow" began the Lieutenant again. Then his words were interrupted by a huge blast.

The whole coach seemed to rise from the railway tracks. For a moment it remained intact. Then a second blast more fierce than the first blew it to pieces, shooting shards of wood and steel in all directions.

"Jack, Jack." called the Lieutenant.

Jack looked over from the boulder behind which he had taken shelter. The Lieutenant beckoned to Jack. Dodging intense fire, Jack made it to his side in seconds.

"We have a serious problem on our hands, Jack. There's another train scheduled through here in two hours. The track's torn up. Twisted steel and material are scattered for several hundred yards up the line. We've got to stop that train."

"Yes sir," said Jack.

"We're also going to need whatever reinforcements we can get. There's a North West Mounted Police detachment and railway telegraphist about ten miles further on. I want you to ride there, as fast as you can. Warn them. Fetch help."

"Yes sir,"

"Go to it Jack. Good luck!"

Jack urged Cloud forward. He rode as he had never ridden before. He and Cloud had been lucky. They had managed to escape under a hail of bullets. Good girl, thought Jack as Cloud responded to his will once more.

For seven miles they had followed the tracks. It was night time, but the moon shone brightly. The tracks glittered toward the horizon. On they went. Jack spoke sporadically to Cloud and stroked her neck. She had worked up a real lather.

Jack knew that Cloud could not keep up this speed indefinitely. She had to be paced. He had to ease up. He also knew it could be dangerous for her if he were to stop altogether. It would do no good for the Troop if he were to lose Cloud.

He decided to pull her back into an easy canter. After a few minutes he allowed her to slow to a walk. For some minutes he went on like this.

He looked around. It was a cool clear night. He had not noticed this before. Up to his left and to his right spread back twenty feet on either side of the tracks ran the tree line. Behind it was darkness.

Cloud shuddered. Sympathetic, Jack permitted her to stop for a moment. They sat there for several minutes, man and horse, in the all enveloping silence. Then...

Jack heard the double click of a revolver being cocked. He strained his eyes in the darkness. At first he saw nothing. Then he saw the glowing of ash as someone drew on a cigar.

Jack's hand moved to pull his shooter.

"I do not advise that my friend. We have five guns aimed at you and your horse."

Slowly five mounted figures emerged from the darkness of the tree line.

"Hands up," snarled one.

Prudently, Jack raised his hands.

Jack kept his eyes riveted on the quintet as they came into view. As they moved forward, the speaker cast his cigar aside. An uneasy feeling crept over Jack. Then the dread certainty seized him: A derby!

It was the killer.

Jack kept his hands in the air. His eyes followed the riders as they came to within seven feet of him. Then they halted. Three of them kept their rifles trained on Jack, as the killer eased the firing pin forward on his shooter and returned it to its holster.

"Well bless my soul," he said, as he recognized Jack. "Look what chance has dropped into my lap. My young friend from Canada."

The six horsemen rode for many hours that night in the bright moonlight. They made camp only when the sky began to hint of the approaching day.

They drew up in a small natural amphitheatre in the terrain. Any fires in there would be impossible to spot.

Bedrolls were pulled off the horses. The horses were unsaddled, loosely hobbled and allowed to forage nearby for food.

The men unrolled their bedrolls. They used the saddles for pillows.

A campfire was quickly lit and the men set about roasting a rabbit that had been slung on the saddlehorn of one of the riders. The aroma of the roasting meat filled the air. Jack was famished and his saliva glands involuntarily watered at the smell of food.

But no food was offered to Jack. He was left alone, bound hand and foot, while the five hostile strangers first drank their whiskey, then ate and then slept.

For three days the men rode west. Soon the rough rocky terrain had entirely disappeared. The thick forest gradually gave way to grassy meadows and fields.

Jack rode with his hands bound to the saddle horn. He had been given little food and less to drink. He felt weak, exhausted and filthy. No conversation was directed his way, only sharp commands to ride harder, stay with the party, and eat up, saddle up, mount up, dismount or hobble his horse.

There was conversation between the killer and his men however. From that Jack finally learned what his true name was: Mr. Benson. No first name, only 'Mr. Benson'.

He did have a nickname, however, but it was used only behind his back by the others. They called him 'Beetle', presumably after his large and mobile eyebrows.

Jack noticed that they only called him 'Beetle' in whispers. He was soon to learn why.

Apparently "Beetle" Benson was an American, as were three of the others; Clancy, Kennedy and Roper.

These three were an unsavoury lot. Donald Clancy, short and unshaven, was filthy in the extreme. While 'Beetle' Benson was immaculate in his personal care and hygiene, 'Clance', as he was called, was the complete reverse. Jack never saw him wash. Though they passed many a stream or pond, and though they often stopped to water the horses, Clance never cleaned even his hands. He was about twenty-seven. Jack wondered if he had ever had a bath since he left home ten years before. He didn't think so since he smelt awful. He stunk so bad that the others, who were not models of cleanliness themselves, (except Mr. Benson, of course) refused to sleep downwind of him. Even the horses seemed to object to the smell. The other men swore, they made no end of fuss, unless pastured upwind of Clance.

Frank Kennedy was a sport. Like Mr. Benson he was from New York. He had a faint accent and Jack wondered if, perhaps, he had found his way into the world at some other part of the planet.

He was of average build and dark, a good looking man. He wore traditional western garb, high western boots, dark brown chaps kept in immaculate condition and a leather vest. He also sported a large walrus moustache, the ends of which he kept twisting to ensure they maintained the proper style and dash.

'Clint' Roper was from Colorado territory. He was tall, of regular build, had a clean shaven pasty face and wore the same fine western clothes that Kennedy wore.

He had a habit of poking fun at everybody and everything. There was nothing sacred to Clint Roper. After every jibe he drifted into a nervous giggle. Despite Jack's threatening circumstances, he found himself responding to the occasional humourous jibe. Once he even managed a guffaw, which caused Roper and Frank to cast him a surprised glance.

The last of Mr. Benson's men was not American but English. His name was David Ormsby Pratt. He was slim and angular. He was also clean shaven. Though he wore western boots, his concession to frontier life in the colonies ended there. He wore a squat top hat of beaver and a black frock coat. He wore no chaps. He always spoke in perfect sentences and, unlike his companions, could never be heard to mutter even so much as an oath. He tolerated Roper, but just barely, for Roper never called him by his proper name.

It was usually "Spratt" or "Jack Spratt". Jack had no idea how long the five had ridden together, but Roper never tired of tormenting Pratt and Pratt never failed to become annoyed. Perhaps that was why Roper never grew bored with teasing; he always got a reaction.

Sometimes as they rode along Roper would sidle up to Pratt and sing, just under his breath:

"Jack Spratt could eat no fat,
His wife could eat no lean,
And so between the two of them,
They licked the platter clean."

And then he would chuckle to himself.

After a week on the trail, Jack finally learned why he was being held. He also learned a good deal more.

In late afternoon, with the sun beginning to shine into their eyes from the west, they spotted a thin wisp of smoke.

As they drew nearer they found it came from the campfire of a lone frontiersman. He appeared to be a prospector. He wore a beaded buckskin jacket and trousers and a full grey-white beard. He also clenched a pipe in the right hand side of his mouth.

On the fire roasted a large bird. The man was also busy making sourdough bread from a sack of flour resting up against the open door of his tent.

"Howdy strangers," he said as they rode into his camp.

"Good day to you sir," said Mr. Benson. "May we share your fire? We don't have much time. Gotta push on. But we sure would like a good hot meal."

"Help yourself stranger," he replied. "What's mine is yours."

The prospector had turned to tend his cooking when two shots rang out. The old man stiffened up at the first, as though stretching his back and then, at the second shot, he went careening forward into the wall of the tent. In a moment they heard a rattling gurgle. Then he was silent.

Jack was so stunned at first that he thought the shot had come from elsewhere. When he looked, however, he saw a smoking revolver in Mr. Benson's hand.

"Search him, boys," Mr. Benson said as he holstered his pistol. "Rare is the prospector who doesn't have some gold in his pocket. Anyway, not enough food for seven."

With that he dismounted. The body was removed and they quickly settled in for the night.

As the embers glowed, Mr. Benson broke the silence:

"Sounded just like Miller," he said.

"Who's Miller?" Frank asked.

"Our soldier boy knows," he replied. "Don't you Jack?"

Jack looked at him, uncertain.

"You saw me kill him," he said directly to Jack.

Instantly Jack understood.

"Yes," he said, "but I never learned why."

"It's easy. He double crossed me in an arms deal," said Mr. Benson. "He and that damned fool Moffatt. I got him too, and gave him a nice cremation. Burnt all the evidence."

He paused for a moment.

"Bet you guessed that," he said to Jack.

"They searched, you know, they combed the forest for the body," said Jack, referring to the first killing.

Mr. Benson broke into hearty laughter.

"Simple really," he finally explained. "I filled his pockets with rocks and dragged him into the lake. I know he liked water."

He laughed once more at his humor and this time the others joined in.

"But why Mr. Moffatt?" asked Jack.

"I told you. He double crossed me. I had placed an order through him for 350 rifles from Remington in New York. My clients out west needed them badly. It also meant a lot of money to me. He thought he had found another dealer, but I guess he was mistaken, wasn't he boys?"

They all laughed again. After a long pause he continued: "You have no idea of the huge demand for rifles out west, Jack. Some people out here just don't like Canada. As a matter of fact most of them don't. Except for a few white settlers, that is."

"Gun running is illegal," said Jack.

At this they all burst into laughter. Jack realized that in the circumstances it was a pretty foolish thing to say. After a while he spoke again.

"What do you want with me?" Why are you holding me?"

"Well now, you might just come in handy. If we run into the army it would be nice to have something to trade, now, wouldn't it?"

"I'm a hostage?"

"You might say that, though I don't know if that's just the right word for a deserter!"

The words fell on Jack like a hammer blow. His head reeled. His mind revolted against the very idea. Never, never would Lieutenant Richards and his mates believe he had deserted them.

Never.

Mr. Benson was in a talkative mood that night. Jack learned that Mr. Benson had first broken Mr. Moffatt's neck, then stolen the delivery he had ordered, before setting the building afire.

The men who had ambushed the train were also working for him. He had hoped to multiply profits many times over by hijacking the military arms coach. Unfortunately the boys had failed. They must have been very frustrated. It was just like them to blow up the coach. Mr. Benson approved heartily. If he couldn't have the arms, then nobody should have them!

As he listened to Mr. Benson talk, Jack regretted he had told them what had happened at the ambush.

By this time Mr. Benson and the gang were well into their cups, whiskey bottles were scattered about the camp. A small sack of gold coins had been turned over to Mr. Benson after the first search of the dead man. He now had them searching for whiskey and they came up with several more bottles.

As Mr. Benson talked on, Jack learned that Mr. Benson had many clients on the plains. There was a clamour amongst the Indians and Metis to buy arms. There was revolution in the air.

On thing Mr. Benson did not make clear: whence came the money for his operations. The plains Indians and Metis did not have the funds to make these massive purchases.

Jack was prodding the slightly drunk Mr. Benson to learn more. Mr. Benson was saying it was not just the Indian nation resisting Canada, another nation was very interested in keeping the "kettle on the boil" in the North West Territories, when Jack heard the word:

"Beetle".

Dead silence fell upon the camp. Only moments before Roper had been giggling and talking to Frank. Now they both looked at Mr. Benson. Guilt was written all over Roper's face.

Jack heard a loud explosion in his left ear. Simultaneously Roper's body seemed to bounce subtly and a small hole appeared in the middle of his pale face.

"I told you never to call me 'Beetle'"! Mr. Benson said.

Roper started back for a moment and then his face fell forward as though in acknowledgment.

"Jack, you're just too obvious riding around in a uniform. Tomorrow I want you to wear Roper's outfit. He's just about your size."

And the next day, when Jack slipped it on, he found out that Mr. Benson had been right; it fit him perfectly.

CHAPTER ELEVEN

THE FOLLOWING day, Benson roused everybody early in order to get a full day of riding. They had been riding for many days with real purpose, but Jack had no idea why. For the moment his mind dwelt on other matters.

He now looked like all the others. To all appearances a desperado. His blond hair was covered with the worn sweat stained Stetson of his late riding companion, Roper. For many days now he had not shaved so his face had a good growth of stubble. He had discarded his khaki tunic and, as instructed, wore the brown leather vest over his khaki shirt. His legs were now covered with large dark brown leather chaps. On his feet he retained his own sturdy brown military boots. He carried no shooter but in every other respect he resembled the others. Cloud was saddled with a large western style saddle. In front of him on the right was a lariat. Directly behind his saddle was strapped his bedroll. Saddlebags on either side completed the picture. They carried whatever personal effects he had been able to scrounge.

The men no longer bound his hands and since the night Roper departed, the conversation flowed easily amongst them all, including Jack.

This was how, after all this time, a sort of relationship got its beginnings between Pratt and Jack.

To begin with Pratt was unlike the others in dress. His British accent seemed to separate him even more decisively. He adopted a somewhat lofty view toward his colleagues. Though he was often openly disdainful of the others he was more circumspect when dealing with Mr. Benson.

It seemed natural therefore that he and Jack increasingly brought up the rear. As they rode they talked and the more they talked, the more Jack got to know his riding companion.

David Ormsby Pratt was born the fourth son of an English Duke. Under the law of primogeniture he was not in line to succeed to the title of Duke. His oldest brother was destined for that. The estate was not large enough to provide occupation for anyone but the first son. His grades were not such as would permit him to enter Oxford, or any other university for that matter. That left Sandhurst, the military college, or the church.

Sandhurst not being as tolerant of these things as were the colonies, he was asked to resign after three months for what was decreed "complete personal unsuitability for command."

That left the church and since he was agnostic, he turned from that with distaste.

It is what he turned to that became the problem, for at age twenty-one, he launched himself in the fast set in Mayfair as a dandy and roué. Numerous letters were received by his father complaining of his 'trifling' with various ladies. Warnings only fanned the flames. He turned to gambling and was well on the way to the life of a complete wastrel when the family had had enough. He was summoned from London to the country estate. He was given a choice: to be cut off without a cent or leave for America with a promised semi-annual remittance sufficient to keep body and soul together.

To the relief of his family he chose the latter, thereby sparing them further embarrassment.

Mr. Pratt was a 'remittance man'.

Jack listened to all of this sympathetically. He listened to the triumphs and conquests, and to the adventures in the new world. He listened to it all and like all good listeners he began to earn the good opinion and finally almost friendship of the strange outlaw.

It was in this way that he confirmed their riding had not been aimless. Jack was dismayed to learn that the information he had innocently provided about the ambush was the cause of this relentless ride. Pratt refused to divulge more. When Jack pressed, he became vague and finally refused to discuss it altogether. Whether he did this out of loyalty or plain fear of Mr. Benson, it was difficult for Jack to tell.

One thing that Pratt said bothered Jack considerably. Upon first seeing Jack mount up newly attired, he had said:

"You look like one of us. I started like you, a prisoner. Look at me now."

This caused Jack considerable thought. He reviewed his behaviour with the gang over and over. He finally decided he had done nothing wrong and carried no guilt for anything done since his kidnapping.

But he resolved to escape as soon as possible and he was considerably comforted as he ran his hand down his right leg to the hard lump that was well concealed by folds in the chaps. They had ordered him to wear the chaps. Little did they know that Roper, living always in fear, carried a revolver in a concealed pocket in the chaps.

Benson had unwittingly provided the means for escape. Now Jack must find the opportunity.

CHAPTER TWELVE

JACK ESTIMATED it was about four in the afternoon. The sun was already low in the sky thrusting long shadows from the few tall pine trees here and there along the trail. They had stopped only briefly at noon. Since then they continued to ride north west.

Cloud moved forward powerfully. Her muscles rippled and her hide shone with a silver sheen in the late afternoon sun. She still moved briskly and breathed easily after the long day's ride.

Though Cloud appeared fresh the other horses did not. Jack could hear their harsh laboured breath.

He was thinking that they would soon have to stop, when Mr. Benson roughly reigned his horse over to a hard right turn. He passed between two small hills. They were no more than twenty feet high and they were covered with evergreens.

The men followed.

Jack did not know what to expect, but soon found himself winding to the left. He emerged from the grove of trees to find they had arrived in a small valley rimmed by the same small hills.

When Benson drew up, the others reigned in as well. They sat there for a moment to take in their surroundings.

One hundred and fifty feet away stood a log cabin. It was small, about twelve feet by fifteen and it had a flat roof of logs and sod. Jack could see the door from where he sat. It was not open. At the corner to the left sat a rain barrel. Midway between the barrel and the door a window stood open. The roof had been extended from the cabin to provide shade in the afternoon. Beneath the window rested a long crude bench. Opposite the cabin not twenty feet away was a water trough, next to it a hitching post.

Ten feet further on again stood two chestnut horses. They were loosely hobbled and continued to graze, indifferent to the newcomers.

"Frank," ordered Benson, "check it out."

"Yeh Boss," he said.

They all watched Frank walk his horse forward.

Mr. Benson drew his rifle and cocked it. Keeping it in his hands, he placed it across his lap. His eyes were riveted on the cabin.

Jack watched the others pull their rifles from their saddle holsters. They threw off the safety catch and cradled them across their chests in their arms.

Frank had reached the shaded porch. He dismounted. He rapped on the door. Long minutes elapsed. Jack saw movement in the window. He thought it was a face. Shortly thereafter the door was opened by a man.

After a brief conversation, Frank moved from under the shade back into sunlight. He waved at Mr. Benson.

"All right boys, we're there," said Mr. Benson.

He lightly kicked his spurs into the flanks of his horse. With a little jump forward, it started for the water trough. The others followed.

"Clance," ordered Mr. Benson. "You look after old faithful here." He gave his horse an affectionate pat on the withers, "I've got a meetin'."

With that he dismounted and walked over to the cabin.

As he reached the cabin he turned, "You boys might as well settle down. We ain't going nowhere for several days. We might as well get some rest."

Then he disappeared inside.

Jack dismounted. He quickly unfastened the cinch, removed the saddle and threw it over the hitching post. As Cloud drank hungrily, Jack gave her a quick brushing; he would brush her again at nightfall when the chill night air moved in. He stroked beneath her head and then down her neck.

"Good girl," he said, "have a good feed. We'll rest up for a few days."

Not being concerned that she would wander, he did not hobble her.

Jack sat in the shade beneath the shelter of the roof. He looked out at the horses. It was very bright beyond the shaded porch. He tilted his hat over his eyes and dozed.

He had been in this position for some time when he became conscious of conversation. It came from within the cabin. At one point Jack recognized Benson's voice.

Something about the conversation aroused Jack's attention. Was it the tone? Was it something said? Jack was wide awake now, but he did not move. He was aware that only Pratt sat next to him. The others were not around.

The voices drifted out. They must be moving about the cabin, thought Jack.

Suddenly he could hear Mr. Benson quite clearly. He must be standing right by the window, thought Jack.

"...explosion. It must have made a hell of a bang. Something to see, all that dynamite and ammunition going up at night. Damn!"

Then there was a long pause before Mr. Benson started in again.

"If it hadn't been for soldier boy we might have gotten away with it. Enough rifles and ammunition to supply every hostile Indian on the plains."

The voice drifted out, then in again.

"...do our job and make us all rich into the bargain. Would have pleased the committee too. They'll be mad as hell now."

Another long pause, then:

"Should have shot him right off, I should. Thought he might be useful though. More information. Maybe trade him to the army."

A new voice broke in: "Trade him? For what?"

"For money," replied Mr. Benson.

"For money?" another voice said. "Why would the army pay money for him?"

"The way I figure it, by now they must think he deserted. Under fire too. A hanging offence in the military."

"But I thought you said he had been ordered to make that ride."

"Of course he was, dammit, but not to ride off and not be heard from again."

"Yeh," said a voice.

"That's right," said Mr. Benson. "Think of it. He's ordered to bring help. He rides off. No report is ever made. He's never seen again. And they're under fire, man. It's a dangerous situation they're in and he's given a way out on a golden platter. They'll think he's yellow."

"I'll bet there's a reward for him."

"Now you're thinking." said Mr. Benson. "That's my point. They'll pay money for him. But still I wanted to shoot him right away. He sure messed up a great opportunity."

Another long silence. This time it was broken by one of the strangers.

"Well, what do we do?"

"You're right, we've got to act. No use crying over spilt milk. And we have no time to lose. You, Starner, warn Dumont. I don't know or care how, but warn him. Tell him what happened. We've done all we can for him. Also, warn bluecoat. He should do whatever he can to help out. Sabotage, anything."

"And you, Pepper, you'd better let the committee know. Telegraph will do. Use code. Make sure you cross the border first. Absolutely do not report from this side of the border. Too dangerous."

Odd, thought Jack, they seem to know each other well, and yet he used their surnames.

There was some further unintelligible conversation. Jack thought they must have been asking if they should make a start the following sunup because Mr. Benson suddenly shouted:

"No dammit. I mean now. What do you think this is, a tea party? It's war man! I'm ordering you to leave now!"

"Yessir," said one.

"Yessir!" said the other.

Jack heard the scuffle of feet as the two moved about making ready. Then the door slammed open and they all emerged.

As they walked toward the hitching post, Mr. Benson threw a glance back to his right. He took in Pratt and Jack lounging on the bench in the shade.

A further brief conversation while Starner and Pepper saddled up and then they were off at a gallop.

Jack had tried to take in a description of the two, but all he made out was the shocking red hair of one.

Mr. Benson turned and walked back toward the cabin. His eyes were fixed in a malevolent stare at Jack.

"How long had he been sitting there," he snarled, as he reached the cabin.

"I dunno, an hour maybe," said Pratt.

"I dunno, an hour maybe," mimicked Mr. Benson.

Then he went on, "He could hear everything we said, everything!"

"I don't think so Mr. Benson," said Pratt. His voice was shaking as he said this. He shifted uneasily on the bench.

The atmosphere was electric. Jack was now fully alert. He knew something serious was about to happen. There could be no waiting for opportunity. He would have to make his opportunity. He ran his right hand down the side of his chaps. It disappeared within the folds of leather.

"I don't think so, Mr. Benson," mimicked Benson once more.

Pratt simply looked at Mr. Benson. Jack took in the scene. The only other gang member present was Kennedy. He too was mesmerized by the unfolding scene. Even the horses had stopped grazing. They looked over to the raised voices by the cabin. Cloud, as though sensing danger for her master, walked slowly toward Jack.

"Of course he did, you useless limey," snarled Mr. Benson. "Everything! He heard everything!"

For a moment nobody moved. It was a frozen tableau.

Then suddenly Mr. Benson spat out, "Get rid of him." He motioned to Kennedy with his hand.

Then he must have changed his mind for he immediately said, "Never mind, I will. And I'll take care of you later." This last statement was flung at Pratt even as Mr. Benson went for his gun.

The blast of Benson's gun struck the bench where Jack had been seated. In one fluid motion, Jack had rolled to the ground. Up he came, gun in hand, blazing away. Two shots at Benson. With the first Benson's gun flew. At the second he went sprawling back to land on the wooden floor of the porch with a thud.

In the same moment, even as Kennedy's gun fired, the third shot from Jack's gun found its mark in Kennedy's left chest. He staggered back. A large red stain formed on his shirt and then seemed to burble downward to his belt. Then he pitched forward.

"Cloud," shouted Jack. He levelled his eyes and his gun at Pratt. For an eternity he looked into the fearful eyes of Pratt.

Then he swung onto the back of his pony and was off at a gallop.

He heard guns blazing. Bullets zipped by his head. He didn't know whose, but somehow he wanted to believe they weren't Pratt's.

Jack rode with no saddle. He brought his feet up as high as possible and bent himself flat on Cloud. He presented almost no target as the guns fired and the bullets whined past him.

Cloud had started at a gallop. Now she was fairly flying.

As Jack and Cloud entered a grove of birch trees, he could hear the dull splat of the bullets as they ripped into the bark.

On they rode. Cloud had no bit, no bridle. She needed neither. They galloped as one, Cloud instinctively followed the foot of the hills.

Another few minutes and they were free of the valley. Then the forest ended and they galloped into the open rolling plains.

The guns were silent now, but horse and rider did not slacken their pace. They rode at full gallop for the better part of an hour, Jack leading his pony by subtle caress to the neck.

They rode down valleys and up hills, through brush and bush, around thickets and through forests.

At one time Jack thought he saw two men in pursuit several miles behind. Then he lost sight of them as on he rode.

Darkness was beginning to fall. The rolling prairie was now hills and shadows, but Cloud moved on as sure of foot as though it were the brightest day.

For a while now, off to his right, Jack could just make out the dark recesses of a ravine. He urged Cloud in that direction. As he rode closer the black turned to grey. Then the grey gave way to objects as Jack rode right up to the thick trees that marked the beginning of the decent into the ravine.

Quickly, Jack rode into the ravine. Forest and darkness folded protectively around him.

Cloud picked her way carefully down through the shallow depression. Jack brought her to a halt with a whispered command.

They listened many minutes for the sound of voices and hooves. Nothing could be heard. Utter silence reigned.

Jack slipped off Cloud's back.

He stroked her neck, and she responded, nuzzling him back.

"We made it," said Jack to his faithful pony. "As surely as I stand here, you saved my life." He put his arm under her head until his hand could fondle her alert ears, and he put his own head against hers and hugged her with a silent prayer of gratitude.

PART FOUR

AMONGST THE INDIANS

CHAPTER THIRTEEN

THE BROAD plain stretched out before rider and horse all the way to the horizon. It was spring. The year, 1885.

Jack saw no fences, no roads and most of the time, not even a trail. For hundreds of miles not a single sign of civilization. Just the endless yellow turf of the plain.

As the hooves of his pony came down on the rich grassy loam it occurred to Jack that he may be seeing land that no white man had ever seen. He may be travelling over prairie that no human had ever travelled before.

The land was immense, sometimes rolling, sometimes flat, but it seemed to go on forever. The plains were sometimes interrupted by great sprawling forests of birch and poplar trees. No maples here, few pine.

He tried to imagine this empty land, the great plains, from the lake country he had left, running west and north hundreds of miles. And then what? He knew that if he travelled far enough west, many months travel by horse, he would see great mountains rear up out of the earth. He knew that as he drew closer the plains would begin to roll and he would be in the foothills, next to the mountains.

He had heard of a town in the foothills. He remembered the name: Calgary.

This brought his mind back to the present.

As Cloud walked slowly westward, Jack pondered his predicament.

It had been very real to him, the suggestion that he was now probably a wanted person. It was liable to be true. The Rangers under fire. Bullets flying. An order to bring aid. Off he goes, never to be seen again. What else would Lieutenant Richards think? Tom would never believe it, but what else could the others think?

It seemed inevitable. His spirit rebelled at the injustice of it, but deep inside Jack knew some would believe it was true.

He turned the options open to him over in his mind. He could seek out the unit. Turn himself in. He could truthfully tell them what had happened. Would they believe him? Lieutenant Richards might. But would a matter so serious as this be left to him? He did not think so. He felt sure it would be referred to Colonel Trubshaw, or even to General Middleton. Would they believe him? All his senses told him no. Too many times he had not been believed. He no longer retained the trust of youth.

And if they did not believe him, what then? Dismissal? Dishonour? Would there be a court martial or a trial?

Jack knew desertion under fire could mean execution.

Death or dishonour! To Jack, they were equally repellant.

The only option, he realized, was to accept his fate. It had been sealed by others. He had not made it. Others had.

He must put behind him all of his past. He must forget family and friends. His future lay before him, in the west. First to Calgary, then to Victoria. If his past found him there, then perhaps across the sea to a new life. Hong Kong? China? Or to the land down under, Australia?

There he could put his past firmly behind and build a new future.

For a moment he pondered the adventure that would be his. He could win a new life and with it, honour once again.

Could he, could he? Once more he was overwhelmed by doubts. A wave of nostalgia swept over him. The sounds and smells of home, the smell of fall in the air, burning grass, the crisp nights, the rustle of crisp leaves underfoot. And what of his duty to Queen and country? His comrades in arms?

Jack was confused, but three words persisted.

They echoed through his being.

Duty, Honour, Country!

CHAPTER FOURTEEN

FOR THREE days Jack and Cloud wandered aimlessly. During much of this time he thought about his recent narrow escape. He knew he had killed Kennedy. God forgive him. He had never killed another human being. He had been trained by the army to do exactly that: to kill. He had been told that it is often a case of "kill or be killed". But the memory kept forcing itself in on his waking moments and he had to admit that it troubled him.

Though he knew he had killed Kennedy, he was not so certain about Mr. Benson. He had seen him hit, but had the bullet been fatal. If the bullet had found its mark, if Mr. Benson were dead, why did this not bother his conscience like the death of Kennedy did? This was all too complicated.

He also wondered what had happened after he left. Did Pratt and Clance give chase? Were they the ones he thought he had seen after the escape?

He thrust these questions out of his mind. His stomach gnawed at him. He had eaten little for the last few days. He had managed to slake his thirst frequently, however, from the many small creeks and brooks coursing over the prairie in springtime.

Jack began to learn that though the prairie was vast and lonely it was not as empty as he first thought.

Yesterday at noon he had seen a small party of seven mounted Indians riding northerly. It was only luck that they had not seen him. He was crossing a hill when his eyes caught a glimpse of a pinto, its black and white hide standing out against the brownish yellow plain in the middle distance. Jack stopped, dismounted and after ensuring Cloud could not be seen over the crest, crawled carefully up to take a good look.

There they were, the pinto and its rider in the lead. He was followed by six other riders. It was hard to distinguish clothing but there was no doubt they were armed. The leader carried a rifle. On his back he also slung a bow. The other riders were armed with spears and bows.

For some time Jack watched the party move north. Then he slid and crawled back down the hill. He took great care all the while not to be seen.

He checked several more times. Only after he was sure the Indian party had disappeared over a distant rise did Jack mount up and move on.

Now he was less concerned with Indian plains riders than with his constant hunger. He decided he would have a greater chance of finding wild game if he travelled at the edge of a poplar forest lining the edge of a valley about two miles north and to his right.

He rode the forest line for the remainder of the afternoon. Sometimes the line would run off to his right leaving hillsides covered only with prairie turf. At these times he had a commanding view of the valley.

It seemed to stretch out for many miles. Jack thought it looked like an old river bed long since dried up. He knew there must be a creek meandering through the valley bottom. He could see the willows and scrub brush. The growth was lush and greener down there too. Jack knew he would make his way into the valley before sunset.

The valley bent to the north west now and Jack turned with it. To his left the sun was slowly setting. In the distance the hills and valleys took on a misty magenta hue, in turns darker and lighter.

The sun was sinking quickly to the horizon now. A thin spool of cloud had unravelled across the breadth of the horizon. He watched the sun quickly sink until only half remained to spin out a last few minutes of daylight. Only part of the glowing red sun could be seen behind the cloud. The cloud was white and blue and then smokey black in front of the sun. The edges of the cloud glistened crimson and yellow. Jack lifted his eyes up from the horizon. Across the great vault of the heavens spread filaments of cloud glowing pinkish and red.

Like a great cathedral, thought Jack.

Then suddenly the red ball of flame dropped beneath the horizon. Jack immediately felt the chill.

He made his way down the gradual embankment in the gloaming. After pushing his way through the trees for an hour he found himself in a natural clearing. In front of him ran a brook. To his left stood a large boulder. Beyond that again a twenty foot rise in the embankment that ran down to the creek's edge as though to nudge it further north.

He decided to stop there for the night.

Jack woke around midnight. He wondered what had caused him to wake up, for he had fallen asleep exhausted. It must have been Cloud moving, he thought.

He looked about. The recesses of the forest were dark. The moon was full, however, and despite the darkness he could see the white bark of the birch trees around his encampment. He could also see Cloud. Her gleaming white hide stood out clearly. She whinnied softly, then shuddered.

Jack paused a moment. Then he mentally shrugged his shoulders and turned over.

He was about to shut his eyes when he heard it. The sound of many drums pounding out a steady rhythm. Jack listened quietly. A hard blow followed by three quiet blows, another hard blow then three quiet blows. The beat did not vary.

For many minutes Jack listened. The beat did not stop, but continued relentlessly.

Jack picked his way through the birch trees. He quietly scrambled up the ridge. It was higher than it first appeared for each time he thought he had reached the crest he found it rose up once again.

Finally, he reached the top. It was dark yet the moon helped him find his way. He crouched down and moved forward and over the cold damp earth.

Suddenly, the ground seemed to end. He peered forward. It was pitch dark. He strained his eyes. The ridge ended abruptly, forming a cliff.

What he saw beyond stopped his heart for a moment. The forest petered out a hundred yards distant.

There, about fifty yards from the creek, sitting around a large fire were hundreds of Indians.

Jack swallowed. He could feel his still empty stomach working. He moved to the left a few feet to get a better view.

42

The Indians sat in a circle twenty feet away from the fire. Their faces glowed red in its reflection.

Three large drums could be seen in the centre upon each of which a number of men beat out the steady rhythm.

Jack could just make out the clothing of the Indians nearest to the fire. They wore leather leggings of hide. Their shirts were also of buckskin. Both were decorated with many coloured beads. Some of the men close by the fire wore resplendent feathered headdress.

I wonder if they could be chiefs, thought Jack.

A pipe slowly made its way around the circle pausing now and then for one or another in the gathering to take a puff.

Behind them in no order but all facing toward the fire were hundreds of men. He could clearly make them out. Though it was difficult to see their dress, he could see many bows and spears. Here and there, Jack could also see the glitter of rifle barrels in the moonlight.

Jack could hear the occasional voice that was raised and now and then a burst of laughter. Otherwise the scene went on for about an hour without incident.

Then without warning, one man with an elaborate headdress who had been sitting next to the fire unfolded himself and stood. He began to speak. Only snatches of what he said carried over the gentle night air. Jack could not understand but he watched in fascination.

The person speaking was tall and slim. He had a high forehead and aquiline nose. As he spoke he made subtle gestures.

Now and then the listeners reacted with a murmur or a shout. Then suddenly the speaker stopped and pandemonium broke loose. The whole multitude erupted in screaming and shouting. Then the drums began in earnest and the Indians began to dance around the fire.

Jack drew back from the cliff edge. They must be all around here, he thought.

Without further pause for reflection he pushed his way silently back to Cloud and the two retreated quietly in the opposite direction, following the creek. He took great care to remain within the protection of the forest for the remainder of the night.

CHAPTER FIFTEEN

A DAY had passed since the spectacular scene by the creek. Jack wondered what it meant. He was always very careful now to ride close to protection, remaining as near to forest edge as possible. Sometimes he travelled through the forest thinking it may be safer.

It was for this reason he found himself working his way through a sparse grove of poplars. Cloud, as usual, marched on without complaint.

At first Jack thought he had been daydreaming. Then he heard another 'pop', and he knew it was not a dream, but gunshot.

He made his way forward for several minutes. Then he brought Cloud to a halt. There was a soft breath of breeze. It faintly rustled the silvergreen leaves of the trees. Suddenly he heard a series of shots.

Jack urged Cloud forward until he could see from the cover of the trees out across the plain. He took in the scene at a glance.

From the tree line the plain gently sloped into a little valley. In the middle of the valley three hundred yards from Jack stood a log cabin. Thirty feet away from that was a barn. It was in flames.

A corral, well and hitching post were arranged near the barn. Several horses wheeled and galloped and reared in panic inside the corral.

Jack could make out two figures letting off constant gunfire. The fire was directed at a small war party of five Indians. They galloped around and around the small farmstead. Some were armed with bows and he could see arrows flying in the direction of the settlers. They also had firearms. Jack would occasionally see a puff of white smoke and shortly hear a pop, as the sound reached him. He could also hear the pounding of hoof beats. This seemed odd to him because the sound hit his ears just as the ponies legs lifted from the ground. He also heard the high pitched yipping of the attackers.

All this he absorbed in a second. The next moment he charged.

Cloud raced in at an angle so that only a part of her right side showed to the attackers.

Jack got off a quick shot and then slipped down over the left flank of Cloud hanging on only by his right arm and leg.

The shot drew the attention of the Indians. All they could see was a white pony racing in their direction. They paused in their attack, stupefied, not knowing where the shot had come from.

Suddenly, Jack swung up on Cloud and simultaneously discharged a volley of three shots. Two Indians fell instantly.

With a blood curdling yell, well rehearsed at bayonet drill, Jack charged the third Indian. Too late the Indian wheeled to meet his attacker, for a fourth shot from Jack's little revolver felled him.

Startled, the remaining two Indians hesitated, but only for a moment. Then they too, wheeled their ponies about, but to ride off in the opposite direction.

Jack took off after the fleeing Indians. He chased them for a mile discharging several more shots without result.

After assuring himself they were well gone, Jack reigned Cloud around and returned to the farmsite at a slow gallop.

"Howdy, stranger," said a man, as he only now straightened up from behind an overturned wagon.

"Howdy," said Jack.

"Much obliged," said the man.

"Is anybody hurt?" asked Jack.

"Are you okay Nance?" asked the old man.

"I'm fine," said a woman's voice.

Until that moment Jack had not taken in the other person. He turned and saw it was indeed a woman. She was small but robust. She set her rifle down then shook her hair back before walking over to Jack.

"I'm Nance Magee," she said. "This here's my father." She nodded to the old man.

"Howdy," the old man said again, this time sticking out his hand.

Jack took it by leaning over Cloud.

"Just call me Magee," said the old man as they shook. "All my friends do."

"You look tired and hungry," said Nance. "You get down off that horse. I had dinner on when them varmints struck. Can't do nothing about that barn. Might as well get some grub under our belts. Do you like roast turkey and mashed potatoes?"

She had looked attractive to Jack before. Now she looked beautiful.

"I hope you like apple pie. It's all I've got for dessert. Magee won't eat nothing

44

but apple pie."

Jack thought he might just be a little bit in love.

CHAPTER SIXTEEN

IT WAS several hours later. Jack had just finished the biggest meal he had ever eaten in his life.

First there was the turkey. A big golden roasted turkey. Nance cut two great slabs of white meat for him. To this she added one whole thigh. Then she scooped out the best dressing he had ever tasted. Jack thought she could pile no more on his plate. He kept saying thank you, that's enough, that's plenty, no more, thank you, but Nance went on as if she could not hear him. She poured zesty turkey gravy over the white meat then added a large scoop of fluffy mashed potatoes to his plate and poured gravy over that too.

He thought there could not possibly be more when she insisted he try some of her own cranberry preserves.

All of this he washed down with some tart chokecherry wine.

Jack was sure he could eat no more. Yet he astonished himself by eating not one, but two, slices of apple pie.

They took one more glass of wine at the table. Throughout dinner they all talked excitedly, sometimes in such a rush to speak that they spoke one over the other and then laughed.

But in two hours not only did they review the attack by the Indians but they also traded so much personal information that they already felt like old friends.

It was only then that they managed to pull themselves away from the table and move over to the cozy little living room.

From Jack's comfortable easy chair he could see the entire cabin. The kerosene lamps threw off a bright warm light. Over in the kitchen he could see the black metal woodburning stove with silver trim. It was just like his mother's. The oven door stood open and on it rested the remains of the turkey. On the stove top were the remains of the apple pie: two pieces, each three inches deep.

Magee sat on a kitchen chair with his arms folded across the back. He puffed contentedly at his pipe. He sported an enormous black and grey speckled beard. Jack could not place his age, but he still looked extremely powerful and vigorous.

Nance sat alone on a brown sofa with a brown chintz cover.

Jack looked at her again. She was much younger than he first imagined, perhaps seventeen, he thought. She also looked more beautiful. She smiled as she talked and Jack found he could pull his eyes away from her only with difficulty.

They talked on like this until nine o'clock, late for frontier people.

Then Nance said: "All right everybody. Time for bed."

She showed Jack into a bedroom in the south east corner of the cabin. She opened the window. Then she turned to Jack and said:

"Sleep well."

Then she was gone.

Jack slipped under the great white fluffy quilt. He felt warm and secure. It occurred to him that he had not felt quite this way since he had left home. Home, he thought, it seemed many years since he last saw home.

He turned his head so he could look directly out the window. The sky was dark. The stars winked. He gazed at them a long time as he thought about the Magees,

45

about Nance and the strange twists and turns of fate which brought them here.

Magee's mother and father, Sean and Nancy had been born in County Cork in Ireland. They had been married for some years when the potato blight struck in 1834. In the famine that followed they, like thousands of others, had been driven by poverty and hunger to seek a better life in the New World.

Magee was a young boy by that time. The three of them took passage in steerage on the packet Nantucket. The crossing had been stormy. Every one of the passengers had been violently seasick. Many prayed for death as a release. Only Magee had not been sick. He was all over the ship, full of curiosity and adventure. On one occasion he had found himself in the Captain's cabin. He looked in awe at all the books, the gimbal mounted lamp, the sextant, telescope and other nautical equipment.

He admired the rich teak cabin and imagined himself one day to be command of a ship like this.

He was caught by the steward, however, and rather unceremoniously dumped back into steerage.

Things grew more unpleasant for the passengers. His mother, who had never been strong, grew weaker by the day. She had eaten nothing for ten days. The face that Magee loved so much was pale and gaunt. Her eyes, surrounded by dark circles, grew bright with fright.

Watching his father and mother together, as his father held his mother's hand and wept, Magee knew even at this early age, that his mother could not long survive.

On their twenty-first day at sea she passed away quietly in his father's arms.

There were many who died on that voyage. The captain delivered only a few perfunctory words as his mother was buried at sea under leaden skies on a wet and windy day. All he could remember of the service later were the words, "We therefore commit her body to the deep in sure and certain hope of the resurrection to eternal life. Through our Lord Jesus Christ. Amen. May Providence have mercy on her soul." These words reverberated in his mind for many years afterward.

Magee grew to hate the sea thereafter and resolved to make his way in the world on land.

He and his father settled in Kingston. His father obtained work as a hostler in the local livery stable.

Magee did not like school. He spent all his extra hours around the stable. He loved to work with horses.

At seventeen he could see that his father would never prosper. They still lived in two rented rooms not far from the stable. He resolved to strike out on a new life in the West.

Then followed many years of wandering. He learned to hunt and trap. Starting first in northern Canada, he gradually moved on until he found himself in the North West Territories. He became a first class trapper in the far north and did a great deal of business with the Hudson's Bay Company.

Over the years he corresponded regularly with this father. As the years passed the correspondence grew more infrequent. One day he realized he had not heard from his father for nine months. He made enquiries through the company. After another month he received a letter from a kind woman, who had cared for his father during his last days. She wrote that his father had died. There was no apparent cause. She thought it may have been from loneliness.

Even though the funeral was over many months ago, he felt an urge to return. This he did in the spring.

Then his luck changed. Fortune began to smile on him. He met Molly Hogan.

She was a bright energetic and determined woman, many years his junior. He was completely taken with her.

He stayed the summer and in the fall they were married.

They remained in Kingston until early the following summer. They had to because two months after their wedding day, Molly announced she was pregnant.

They called their first son Hogan, which soon became "Hogie".

Magee couldn't wait to return to his trap line in the west. When mother and child were strong enough, they made their way back to the North West Territories.

Molly was soon pregnant again. This time there were no doctors present. Difficulties developed. Molly delivered herself of a baby girl but she herself died in child birth. Magee was grief stricken. For many months he did nothing. He was unable to work.

Then one day, his grief exhausted, he began to take an interest in life again. He took great interest in 'Nance', his baby daughter. He took such delight in his children, that he no longer wanted to be away from them the many months necessary to tend his trap line.

He decided to give up trapping and settle down to farm in the south.

That was sixteen years ago. He must know this country well, thought Jack, as he finally drifted off to sleep.

CHAPTER SEVENTEEN

JACK SLEPT till noon the first day. After a hearty breakfast of bangers and eggs, he and Nance went riding.

Magee had buried the bodies of the Indians. He ran their horses, which were indifferently grazing in the vicinity, into his corral. From one he removed a beautiful carved leather saddle. He insisted that Jack keep it.

"For services rendered," he said.

A horse blanket, bit and bridle and Jack was back in business.

Nance was a good horsewoman. She suggested they ride to the peak of Mulberry Mountain to see if they could catch any sign of Hogie who was due back from hunting that day.

Jack found that Mulberry was not really a mountain but a rise in the plain. On the other side looking north, however, you could see at least 20 miles across a valley. Jack estimated it to be at least 500 feet below the height of the mountain. You could have seen further, the land was so flat, but objects lost definition and eventually disappeared in a blue and violet haze.

Not a sign of Hogie was to be found. Nance and Jack returned home.

Magee was worried when they brought him the news.

I don't like it. Don't get me wrong. He's strong and he's smart. He can handle himself. He can shoot and hunt with the best. I still don't like it.

"He'll be all right," said Nance.

"You know I'm not worried 'cause he's late," replied Magee. "He's been late before. But things are not right out there. You heard what Jack said."

He was referring to the experiences that Jack had related the night before.

"And that's only the tip of the iceberg. Lots more has been happening on the plains. Some the Government doesn't know about."

They were silent then until Nance called them to dinner.

Jack had finished a second helping of bread pudding with thick cream and sugar.

He and Magee pushed themselves back from the table, and with many compliments to Nance, excused themselves.

Each took the position he had the night before. Magee puffed contentedly on his pipe.

Finally he said: "I've been thinking of that fellow that did the speech making. I think I know who that was."

Jack looked at him with a question in his expression.

"Poundmaker," he said. Then after a long pause he added, "Little far south for him though." "Nowadays he mostly stays put up around Cutknife. Think I know what he was doing though."

"Poundmaker?" queried Jack.

"Poundmaker, the great Cree Chief. Probably the greatest chief on the plains. Sure beats all hell out of the rest of 'em. Big Bear, Piapot, Black Bear, Beardy."

Jack could see Magee was in a mood to talk.

"I knew him, you know."

At this Jack could hear an audible sigh from Nance.

"I met him back around '80 or '81 on a wagon train from Battleford to Calgary. I was hired on as wagonmaster. The wagon train, was enormous, many wagons. It was the biggest wagon train I ever drove. Wagons loaded with everything imaginable; furniture, boxes, trunks and forage. I felt sorry for the horses.

"Many Indians travelled with us. It took me some time before I got to know them.

"One of them had a good deal of white in him. He had hired on as guide.

"Well, there ain't much trail between Battleford and Calgary. Anyway we left it frequently to gather firewood or replenish our water barrels along the way.

"Wasn't long before our guide became confused. He used to ride to the nearest ridge to survey the plains ahead. I can see him now sitting on his black pony and peering into the distance.

"Next thing you know this Indian fellow was riding out regular like to confer with him. You could see them talking and pointing. Then they both rode back to the camp, our 'guide' full of fresh directions.

"Didn't take much to know who was the real guide.

"Wasn't long before everyone knew his name. Course it was Poundmaker.

"Fine looking man he was. Solemn and dignified. And brave. Personal danger meant nothing to him.

"When he was a younger man, he led many a raiding party on the Blackfeet to the south, stealing their horses and killing their braves.

"But he grew wiser with the years and made peace with the Blackfoot. He was proud of this, as well he should be.

"He was quite a statesman. He scorned tribes that took no care of their women and children and their old but cared only for war.

"I can see him now, as we speak, Jack. He used to stretch himself out before the fire and talk in that low voice. We used to strain to hear him. On he would talk of his battles with the Blackfoot in the past and his hopes for peace with the white man in the future.

"All the while me feeding buffalo chips to the glowing embers of our fire.

He paused, then he went on.

"All the more reason I don't understand him making trouble up at Battleford in '83.

"I blame it all on that varmint Dewdney. The Crees were starving and he kept

48

promising this and promising that. Damn politicians. Never can believe 'em.

"Course Poundmaker could see that the northern Crees were getting no help, I guess he figured better to die like a man than starve like a slave.

"Now Riel's been stirring 'em up. You heard that o'course."

Jack nodded but Magee took no notice. He rambled on.

"He's telling 'em to join the cause. Fight for freedom and all that. I heard that he's telling 'em that the American Fenians and Metis have joined the cause and he's hinted strongly that he's got other help coming from the States. May have too. I've heard plenty of stories this last year about wagon loads of rifles and other war supplies making their way into Riel's hands. Some into Cree hands too, just enough to convince 'em."

Then he turned his attention to Poundmaker for a moment.

"He's a clever man, Poundmaker, trusting too. You'd think he's invested too much in peace to go on the warpath. But he's been pushed too far. I think he'll join the rebels. Still you never know, do you?"

Nance had joined by this time and though she tried to change the subject nothing would deter him. They talked well into the night, Magee doing most of the talking. Nance and Jack listened, Jack with special interest, to Magee's experiences with the Indians over a lifetime, his opinions of Riel, of the insurrection of '69 and the bill of rights, the rumours and stories from Battleford, Fort Pitt, Fish Creek, Duck Lake, Fort Carleton, Batoche and Prince Albert.

He spoke of the murders that had taken place recently on the prairies. He was especially vehement about two. Both were quite horrible. One victim had been a nearby rancher friend.

Then he got on to the politicians. Jack, being young and naive, had never heard politicians referred to in such derogatory terms. He was quite startled to hear John A. MacDonald referred to as "that Jackal, clinging to power." The worst he had ever heard him called was "old tomorrow."

Finally he got onto Black Bear. As much as he loved and admired Poundmaker, he damned Black Bear.

"He's a trouble maker," said Magee. "If Riel gets any of 'em to move it'll be Black Bear, mark my words."

"Is he a Cree too?" asked Jack.

"A southern Cree," said Magee. "But the government moved him north. They're moving as many north as they can. There has been too much trouble with Black Bear and others moving back and forth across the line and raising hell with the Indians to the south. Causing trouble with the Blackfoot in the southwest too."

"The Blackfoot again?" said Jack.

"That's right son. The Blackfoot nation. Crowfoot's crowd. Rather fight than farm. And if they ain't fighting they is huntin' buffalo. Well armed too. With Winchesters and plenty of ammunition. Run up from the south I reckon. Wouldn't take much to get them on the warpath. With their cousins and Bloods over by Fort McLeod and the Piegans just west of there, I figure there is about 5,000 of them."

"Five thousand," exclaimed Jack.

"More, if you count the Sarcees down by Calgary. They ain't really Blackfoot, but they is some fighters. Good horsemen too, and they have lots of fast ponies."

He went on at length about the four nations of the Blackfoot tribe. Crowfoot, their chief, was wise and level headed, he thought. He would have the good sense to stand aside if the Metis went to war.

"But he's getting old," said Magee. "He's having trouble controlling Yellow

Horse, his brother-in-law. Good lookin' young man, but no sense. Always stirring up the younger braves. Nothing he'd like better than to go to war."

"One Spot of the Bloods is rambunctious too. His fingers is itching."

"But they're pretty far from the action. General Middleton is more likely to have trouble with Black Bear and, I figure, with Chief Beardy over by Duck Lake. I bet he's already been scheming with Dumont. I guess I can't blame him much. They've been trying to scratch out a crop, but I hear it has been very poor. They eat a lot of muskrat but it's scarce. I hear they've been eating a lot of rabbit recently."

"Carleton agency ain't been much help. It's a wonder Big Child, that's Mis-ta-was-sis in Cree you know, and Ah-tah-ka-koop is so peaceful. They've been getting the same empty promises from the Carleton agency. But they is peace loving. I don't think they'll throw their lot in with Riel.

"Chief Piapot over by Indian Head may be trouble too…" He went on late into the evening to talk about the plains Indians. Jack was fascinated by his knowledge. He learned about the Sioux, the Chippewas, the Soto, the Stoneys and the Assiniboine, their ways, their habits, their present condition, their numbers and disposition. He found himself hoping that military intelligence had the information.

CHAPTER EIGHTEEN

THE DAYS lengthened into weeks. Jack was enjoying himself. Magee and Nance took delight in his company. Jack even found contentment in the pattern that emerged in their daily routine.

In the morning he worked around the small ranch with Magee. There was plenty to do. In addition to the usual chores, Jack helped clear the rubble from the fire. On the stone foundation which remained intact, he helped Magee make a good start on the new barn.

In the afternoon, after a hearty dinner, Nance and he went riding. They roamed the plains for miles around. Jack became familiar with the landscape. He learned to love the country just as Nance and Magee so obviously loved it.

In the evening Jack and Nance would sit in front of the fireplace. Magee would take his usual spot draped over the back of a kitchen chair and tell and retell his adventures on the plain.

Magee had travelled widely across the prairie. He worked as a guide, if he knew the country, or as wagonmaster. Most of the time he found himself working with the "buffalo folk" as he often called the Crees. Over the years he had learned the Cree language well, and in his conversations with Jack, began to intersperse Cree words with English words.

Always curious, Jack began to ask what a particular word meant. Magee was more than willing to oblige and soon the evening sessions, and daytime too, turned into lessons in the Cree language.

Nance, who, with Hogie, had often been left in the care of a Cree woman during Magee's absences on the trail, happily joined Magee in his efforts. Jack was soon learning Cree for the words useful in everyday life.

He found he had a facility for language. He learned fast. It became an obsession for all of them. Without anyone planning it they would try to spend the whole day without speaking English.

Jack's Cree flourished.

After some weeks had passed, Jack noticed that the enthusiasm for their little game had begun to ebb. Every day he and Nance had ridden out in a different direction. She always spent hours looking into the far distance.

He knew she was looking for Hogie. At night she spoke quietly to Magee. She told him of her search that day. Jack saw his spirits sag as the days passed. Magee knew the plains as well as any white man. He was now openly worried about his son.

Jack too was wrestling with his problems. He enjoyed his new friends very much. The time he spent alone with Nance were special to him. He could see she put aside anything she was doing if he asked her to go riding or for a walk. He felt Magee had come to rely on him as he would on his own son. Jack had come to love this place as he did his own home. They knew of his concern that he may be wanted by the army for desertion.

In little things they did and said, it was made plain to Jack that he was welcome to stay permanently.

Early one morning Jack was still in bed. He was between waking and sleeping. The sun had not yet appeared but its morning glow lit up the horizon. He pulled the quilt over his shoulders and snuggled down deeper into bed to escape the frosty morning air.

He turned his head slightly to the left and saw Nance above him. Her lips opened to speak, then suddenly her mouth was on his. Her eyes were closed. Her long brown lashes formed small crescents. For a lingering moment she held her lips to his. A warmth flooded Jack.

Then she pulled away. Again she tried to form words.

"I...I...," she said. Then she placed her head on his chest.

"It's cold," she finally said.

She wore only a flannel nightgown.

"Here," said Jack. He wrapped her body with the covers.

"I think I...I think I..." she began. She was so open, so vulnerable.

Jack took her in his arms and kissed her waiting lips.

That afternoon they went for a long ride back to Mulberry Mountain. The spring sun was warm. They reigned up at a spot where Nance could see far down the valley. They dismounted and spread themselves on the grassy verge.

Crocuses flourished everywhere. And blossoms of many kinds and colours engulfed them. Not twenty feet away hundreds of white and yellow butterflies fluttered for moments, then, as one, rushed off. The fragrance of wild roses drifted across the hillside in the gentle breeze.

Jack picked a handful of blossoms and offered them to Nance.

They laughed and talked and dreamed for hours. Nance said how nice it would be if he settled down nearby. Her father would help him build a cabin. There was lots of land for ranching. He could have a full life.

The sun drifted lower in the sky. It was at that point where it seems to pause as though reluctant to leave and end the day.

"Nance," said Jack. "I can't stay. You know that. I can't."

"Jack..." she said.

"Nance," he interrupted, "I've given this days and days of thought. I can't stay. I'm a soldier. I must return. No matter what the consequences. I must do my duty. For my country, for my comrades, for me.

"Yes, for me Nance, and for you."

Nance looked at Jack for a long time, her deep brown eyes brimming with tears.

CHAPTER NINETEEN

SOME DAYS had passed since that morning when Jack had finally left Magee and Nance. He had found it almost as hard to do as it was to leave his own home so many months before.

After riding north for about half a mile he had turned to take a last look. They still stood rooted to the spot where he had left them. He felt their loneliness and anxiety across the expanse of prairie turf.

Magee knew Jack was headed north to re-establish contact with the North West Field Force. Jack had promised to keep eye for any evidence of Hogie and to send any word he may have about him back to the ranch. He could see Nance and Magee had difficulty maintaining a stoic front in the face of all the turbulence on the plains. He had learned so much about Hogie he felt he knew him. He shared their sorrow.

Now Cloud moved on vigorously. She had recouped her strength and fattened up. Her powerful legs moved confidently. Jack put his hands to his sides and felt the Winchester shooters at either hip. Magee insisted that Jack have them. Jack had resisted, knowing them to be Magee's favourites. Magee would have none of it, insisting that Jack would have more need of them than he. Finally Jack relented.

He whipped them out and hefted them. Giving them a twirl he popped them back into their matching holsters. He had no need to test them since he had used them often back at the ranch.

At about eleven in the morning, Cloud crested a ridge. Down across the valley and off to his right, moving west at what seemed a snail's pace, was a red coach drawn by a single horse. He moved on down the hill and across the valley floor. He watched the progress of the wagon from time to time. Just before noon they met on the trail.

Behind the driver's seat a door led into the coach. At the back were two steps and a second door. Both were closed. The words "Hartley's Products" was printed in gold lettering across each side. Beneath this on the right ran a list in black letters:
"Nostrums for every malady"
"Specifics prepared upon request"
"Snake oil for your man"
"Refreshments of all kinds"
Beneath this list were printed the words, "Doc H. Hartley, M.D. prop."
On the left the list read:
"Wills (Holograph 1/2 price)"
"Probate"
"Deeds and conveyances"
"Criminal lawyer par excellence"
And beneath that list the words:
"Judge H. Hartley, L.L.B.
Barrister, Solicitor,
Attorney-at-Law."
The wagon halted.
A tall man dressed in a three piece frock coat unwound himself in the driver's seat. He stretched and then addressed Jack.
"Howdy cowboy, Reverend Hartley at your service."
"Howdy," said Jack, and then "Reverend?"
"Yes sir, Doctor of Divinity. Funerals, marriages or regular Sunday services.

Minimum charge five dollars."

"But your sign…" began Jack.

"Yes, the sign," Reverend Hartley broke in. He gave Jack a big smile revealing only two long yellow teeth one up and one down, but on opposite sides of his jaw.

He jumped down from the wagon and flexed his knees twice.

"I provide every service. Frontier, you know. Much in demand," he explained.

Jack stared at him in disbelief.

"Well qualified too, you know. I have the sheepskin if you care to look. C.V.C.S.," he added as though to conclude his explanation.

"C.V.C.S.?" Jack asked.

"Chicago Vocational Correspondence School. Top marks too you know."

Jack had dismounted too during the conversation. Cloud could do with a rest. They talked for a while. Reverend Hartley offered him a drink of whiskey, which he refused.

Then Reverend Hartley, having noticed Jack's shooters, offered to sell him ammunition. Jack declined.

Jack noticed that the Reverend had begun to look at him oddly. He tried not to take notice, but when the Reverend persisted, Jack stopped talking and stared back.

"Sorry my boy," said the Reverend. "Not polite to stare, I know." Then suddenly he blurted:

"You ain't Canada Jack, is you?"

Jack was stunned. He could scarcely believe his ears.

"Canada Jack?" he said guardedly.

"Yeh, Canada Jack. That's his nickname. His real moniker is…just a minute." He broke off conversation to rummage in a carpet bag on the seat of his wagon. He came up with a piece of paper in his hands and a triumphant look in his eyes.

"Lookee," he said. He handed the paper to Jack. Jack took it from his hand. When he spread it out, he nearly collapsed with shock. He felt his face redden with embarrassment as he read the document.

WANTED ALIVE

"Canada Jack" Holden

TROOPER CAN. MILITIA

Fair hair and complexion, above average height, strong build.

$25.00 reward paid for information leading to the arrest of this man.

WANTED FOR DESERTION.

Signed:

Colonel Wilbert Trubshaw

C.O. CAN. MILITARY RANGERS

There was more small print giving particulars as to how a claim could be lodged. Jack struggled for composure before he looked up. When he did so, the Reverend was eyeing him suspiciously.

The words refused to come at first and Jack shook his head in the negative. Finally he spoke:

"Don't know him," said Jack, not giving a direct reply. "Nice sum of money though. I could use twenty-five dollars myself." Jack handed the wanted poster back.

There was more conversation. Reverend Hartley was headed for Calgary. When he heard Jack was headed north he began to caution him. But all the while he refused to take his eyes off Jack.

At that moment, Jack heard a 'thump' from the wagon. Reverend Hartley stopped speaking for a moment, then grinned his toothless grin and went on talking about the rebellious condition of the prairies and how it was best to leave, as though they had heard nothing. Then Jack heard two thumps. It sounded like someone was pounding inside.

Hartley continued to talk as though none of this were happening. Then over Hartley's monologue, Jack thought he heard a woman's muffled voice say:

"Nistikwan."

Finally Hartley paused. He grinned obsequiously and said.

"My woman."

"Nistikwan?" Jack looked at Hartley questioningly.

"My squaw, she calls me Nistikwan. It means "generous one" in Cree."

Jack had learned enough Cree to know that someone inside was moaning and complaining about her head. Finally he said to Hartley: "Open it."

"Like hell I will. This ain't none of your business. This is family."

"All right. If you won't, I will." With that Jack swiftly moved around to the rear of the wagon, threw the bolt and ripped open the door.

A young Indian woman tumbled out on to the ground.

Suddenly Hartley threw himself at Jack's throat. He had enormous strength. Jack fell back gagging. Hartley was on top of him now forcing his thumbs into Jack's throat.

Jack could smell the garlic on Hartley's breath. A single rivulet of sweat made its way over the ridge of Hartley's nose down to its tip. It glistened there and grew. It was about to drop into Jack's teeth when he brought his right fist up and whacked Hartley with a sickening blow to the left temple.

Hartley rolled off, slightly stunned.

Jack picked himself up and staggered backward, still somewhat shaken. Then he heard a vicious scream. He saw the flash of a knife as Hartley lunged again.

In a flash Jack's shooter blasted Hartley even as he flew toward Jack. His body did a slow clockwise roll and he came down with a dull thump next to the wagon.

His sightless eyes stared up at the sky.

"Have you been hurt?" Jack said haltingly in Cree.

"My head," she repeated. "My head hurts. He beat me."

He looked at her. He could see bruises on her cheek and on her arms.

Jack took a step toward her, putting out his hand. She started, shrinking back.

He could see now that she was trembling. Her eyes were bright and wide with fright.

In a low soft voice, Jack said to her: "It's all right now. Nobody's going to hurt you now."

He took great care not to make any move in her direction. He could see her shake. Her chin trembled. It's high noon, the sun is beating down, Jack thought, she's in shock.

Jack went into the back of the wagon. He came holding a red mackintosh blanket.

"Here," he said quietly, "Put this around your shoulders."

He maintained his distance, but held the blanket toward her.

For a long time she lay there, propped upon one elbow. She did not move. Jack merely squatted, his hand still extending the blanket.

Finally her hand reached out tentatively. Without moving from his spot, Jack shifted forward putting one knee to the ground and reached over with the blanket.

She took it and sitting up drew it about her shoulders.

Jack said nothing. He simply watched her. For a long while she continued to tremble. She said nothing. She looked small and vulnerable.

When she appeared to have settled down some, Jack spoke again.

"Can I get you something? Would you like a drink of water?"

After a moment she nodded her head.

Jack returned with a water canteen after once again briefly rummaging inside the wagon. He gave it to her and this time she did not draw back in fright.

He looked around. They were very exposed. They sat in the middle of the large open plain. He felt uneasy. Should any stranger passing by stop to visit, there was Reverend Hartley staring up, his lifeless eyes demanding an explanation.

Jack looked away from the body quickly. They must move and move quickly. He would feel more comfortable away from there. He was sure they could be seen by anyone within twenty miles. He felt as though he would be spotted at any time by hostile Indians.

He turned again to the girl.

"Can you walk?" he asked.

She stood and took a few tentative steps forward. She limped.

Jack made a quick decision.

"Up here," he said, patting the driver's seat at the front of the wagon.

He gently helped her up. Then he removed saddle and bridle from Cloud and threw them behind the seat, swung up himself, and with a flick of the reigns, the wagon lurched forward.

They had travelled for three hours in total silence. Cloud followed along, occasionally galloping off to right or left to exercise her high spirits. Jack had suggested that the girl make a bed and lie down inside the wagon. She made no reply. Neither did she move.

Small wonder, thought Jack. She had been locked in there. It was unlikely she would voluntarily return for a while.

He reached the edge of a bush of grey willows. As he drove the wagon along the perimeter he found he was entering a natural passageway formed by a second stand of willows on the left. In a moment he was driving the wagon into a sparse tall stand of birch trees. The land sloped gently downward. He moved forward until, through the trees, he could see water.

He brought the wagon around in a clearing at the water's edge and stopped.

A perfect spot. A brook fifteen feet way gurgled and spilled its way into the lake.

He jumped down. Then he turned and held up both arms to help the girl down.

After a moment's hesitation, she stepped forward and he gently lifted her to the ground. She stood in front of Jack for a minute and looked up into his eyes. The top of her head came level with his chin. Finally Jack removed his hands from her sides.

The sun was setting now and Jack quickly went about the job of setting up camp. The girl was obviously hurting. He put down several blankets that he had retrieved from the wagon. He spread them carefully on a flat grassy area about six feet from the brook. A log lay on the ground perpendicular to the brook and Jack threw his saddle and more bedding over it to provide a comfortable rest for their arms or backs.

Then he led the girl over to the blankets and insisted that she rest there. She was stiff and had difficulties walking. She had obviously been badly beaten.

Between the blanket and the lake he quickly built a small fire. He put some water on to boil.

As he foraged in the wagon, he found more and more. Canned goods of every kind, tea and bread and flour.

He even found lamps and a tent. The latter he quickly pitched next to the blanket for night was falling quickly now.

When he had finished erecting the tent the water on the fire was boiling vigorously. He first made some hot tea and gave it to the girl. Then he made some hot compresses. After some explanation and demonstration, she let him apply these to her exposed bruises.

He managed to find a canned ham. He opened and removed it and drove two willows through the centre. He placed this over two Y-shaped willows erected on either side of the fire and it was not long before he had barbecued the ham.

They both ate hungrily. Afterward they sat for a long time in silence and watched the red glowing sun sink into the lake. The night quickly grew chill and they huddled closer to the fire. Its embers glowed white in the darkness.

"I've made a bed for you in the tent," said Jack in his shaky Cree. "You must get some rest."

She said nothing to this. Jack looked at her in the firelight. Her shiny black hair fell about her shoulders and over her breasts. She wore a doeskin dress. It had no sleeves but came down to her ankles. It was covered here and there with fine quill work. Her black hair framed an oval face of tawny brown skin. Her lips were full but delicate, as finely carved as a Dresden doll. It was her eyes, however, that had first captured Jack's attention. They were so brown they looked black. As Jack had worked, she followed him with her eyes. When she looked sideways, he saw them almost disappear behind enormous black eyelashes. Arched above her eyes were lovely black eyebrows.

Jack thought she had quite the most beautiful eyes he had ever seen.

"What is your name?" he asked.

She did not understand.

"What is your name?" he repeated. Still she did not respond. She merely watched him from beneath her long eyelashes. The fire sparkled in her dark eyes.

Jack tapped his chest with both hands.

"My name is Jack," he said. "I'm from Canada."

She looked at him.

"Canada," he repeated again. "Jack" he said, tapping his chest again.

"Kanata Jack," she said, still watching him.

"No, no," said Jack. "Well, yes, in a way," he said and chuckled. "My chums call me 'Canada Jack'."

After a pause, he said: "Canada Jack," tapping himself on the chest again. Then he pointed at her with both hands and said again:

"What is your name?"

She touched her chest with both of her hands.

"One Feather," she said.

CHAPTER TWENTY

THAT NIGHT she began to shake once more. This time, however, it was not from either shock or fright. First she was chilled to the bone. Then she developed a fever.

All night long and into the following day she drifted in and out of delirium. She

56

muttered Cree in a soft anguished voice. Jack was able to understand little of it.

The moisture poured from her skin, drenching her lovely doeskin dress. Gently he removed it. She tossed from side to side and moaned from time to time. He managed to slowly work it up, carefully raising her body to slip the dress from beneath. Then he softly swabbed her body from head to foot with towels he had scavenged from the wagon.

The perspiration continued and he found he had to wipe her head constantly. Every four hours he patiently towelled her neck and her arms. Then, putting his left arm behind her shoulders and raising her, he thoroughly wiped her entire back down to her buttocks. He gently lowered her again and blotted the moisture between and beneath her breasts.

He watched her chest heaving as she drew rapid shallow breaths.

He continued towelling across her pale golden tummy and down each leg.

He found that despite his constant efforts to keep her dry the bedclothes became soaked. He found extra bedclothes in the wagon and exchanged them. Then he rinsed and dried the old.

As he sat and watched her heaving chest in the flicker of the lamplight he began to worry whether she would survive. He felt her forehead. She was burning up.

During each moment of coherence, he practically forced her to take something to drink; either tea or water. At these moments she seemed indifferent to her fate.

Desperately Jack searched the wagon throughout for some specific that could help One Feather. He found white bottles, blue bottles, opaque bottles, bottles of camphor, paregoric and other tinctures. He found laudanum, alcohol, belladonna and pills of every description, but nothing that held any promise of help.

He spotted an almanac in the drawer of a desk. While One Feather slept Jack poured through the book from cover to cover. He found nothing that could help.

He pulled the drawer open to replace the book and his eye fell on a white box at the back. He reached down and scooped it up. The label read: "Salicylic acid powder. The miracle drug. Good for fever, grippe, reumatiz and a host of other ailments."

The box was sealed. Quickly Jack ripped it open at one end. He put his finger into the fine white powder and placed a few crystals on the end of his tongue. It had a bitter unpleasant taste. It was so pronounced that he screwed up his face in reaction.

There were no directions on the box. How much should be administered? How could he get her to swallow without choking? It never entered his mind not to try it. Such was his concern for the survival of One Feather.

He hurried down to the brook. He filled a glass to the brim with the cold clear spring water.

When he returned to the tent One Feather was experiencing one of her lucid moments.

Quickly Jack took a spoonful of the white powder. With gestures and in broken Cree he explained to One Feather she must place the white powder on her tongue and immediately wash it back taking all of the water.

Meekly she did as she was told. At first she nearly gagged, but she did as he asked. She managed to wash it all back, drinking the water down to the last drop. Then she fell back and soon was off into delirium again.

Now Jack could only wait. Though he was not sure he figured this to be her third night of fever. He maintained his vigil scarcely leaving her side even for a moment.

Then, at dawn something drew his attention to One Feather. It was her breathing. The once quick stertorous breathing was gone. Now her breathing was gentle, prolonged and relaxed. The sweating too had stopped.

A wave of relief engulfed Jack. He fell back into a deep sleep.

CHAPTER TWENTY ONE

LATER THAT morning One Feather awakened. It took a moment for her to realize that her headache was gone. Her body no longer ached. Neither did her skin feel sensitive and she had stopped perspiring. Her bedclothes felt warm and dry. She wiggled her toes.

She looked around the tent. Jack was sprawled back fully clothed and sound asleep.

She moved to get up, but immediately fell back weak and exhausted.

She saw her favourite dress hanging near the entrance. Vaguely she remembered Jack caring for her. As she ran her hands down her naked sides beneath the blankets, she experienced a moment of embarrassment. Then she looked over at Jack and the thought vanished.

She watched him for an hour as he lay there breathing deeply and regularly.

All that day Jack fussed about feeding her and fetching cooling water from the spring. He could see her strength improve by the hour. She smiled at him as he passed her yet another glass of water. She dropped her eyelids as she began to drink in great long draughts.

At that moment Jack felt that her smile of gratitude was all the reward he could ever want.

The following morning Jack woke at about eleven o'clock. He felt refreshed. He lay still for a moment as his ears took in the silent sounds of spring. Then sparrows began to sing. He was jolted into the present.

He looked over to One Feather. She was gone!

A moment of panic seized him. He leaped from his bed and, not waiting to draw his breeches on over his shorts, he ran outside. He immediately felt the hot morning sun on his bare back.

He darted his eyes about the campsite. He saw no sign of her.

He could see easterly along the lakeshore. Only the two horses grazed nearby. Betsy (as he had mentally named the other horse), enjoying her freedom from harness, ate continuously.

To the west stood a thicket of willows. He pushed his way through. It was twelve feet deep. Emerging on the other side he cast his eyes westerly. He saw no one. Then he looked over to the lake.

She stood there, ankle deep in water, clad only in a doeskin breechcloth.

For some time she did not move. Her damp tawny brown skin shone. Rivulets of water erratically coursed down her chest. At the end they paused and grew. For a second, they sparkled, refracting color, before falling or quickly running on.

Slowly she resumed her bath, oblivious of his gaze. He did not know how long he stood there watching, but gradually he grew self conscious. He felt as though he were eavesdropping.

He turned slightly to retrace his steps. A twig snapped. Like a deer sensing danger, her head shot up. She looked around. Seeing nothing, she was about to continue when her eyes found him, frozen still, amongst the birch trees.

Her hands quickly covered herself. Their eyes remained locked. Then slowly her hands fell to her sides.

58

She took three steps to the sandy beach. Looking at him still, she slowly raised her right hand and stretched it out to him, palm up, breast high.

As though hypnotized, Jack moved out of the trees and down to the sand.

They stood facing each other. He looked down at her face, only inches away. Her dark eyes looked up into his. Then with a slight movement she raised herself and lightly brushed his lips with her own.

"Thank you," she whispered, breathlessly.

Suddenly his lips were crushing hers. He drew her body into his. Only for a moment did she hesitate. Then she wound her arms around his back. He could feel her hand move through the hair at the back of his head. She pulled his head down to her lips hard and kissed him fervently.

Jack suddenly felt something ignite in his body.

He held her closer. Her body lifted and her feet rose out of the sand.

For many moments they clung together.

He relaxed his hold. Her feet were once more resting in the sand.

"One Feather…," he began. But she had turned and had fled before he could finish his words.

Startled, Jack stood there for a moment. Then he bolted after her.

He cleared the thicket just in time to see her grab Betsy's mane and swing up onto her back.

With a kick of her heels the horse jumped forward and was off at a gallop. Cloud, standing closer to Jack watched the departing horse and rider.

With a single bound over her hind quarters, Jack was astride Cloud bareback. Cloud started off at a gallop after One Feather.

Confused and distracted, One Feather fled the campsite. She could still feel the muscles of his chest and arms as he had held her. She let the horse carry her, not caring where it went, but wanting only to escape the overpowering emotion that had seized her body.

She galloped on. She could sense rather than see Jack and Cloud in pursuit. The birch trees were becoming sparse. Then suddenly she was out of the forest. Betsy increased her pace. One Feather's lustrous black hair flew out behind her. Now she could feel the sun on her back. The coarse hair of her horse pricked the tender inside of her thighs. She felt the warmth of her mount increase as she rode.

She found she was riding up a draw. Low hills on either side of her seemed to envelope her, protect her. On she went. She heard the soft thud of hoofs in the yellow grassy turf. Then suddenly the hills swept around the front of her cutting off her path.

Betsy reared and neighed loudly. Then down she came and stepped around on the spot for several seconds.

One Feather slid from the back of her horse just as Jack came riding up.

He too slid from the bare back of Cloud and in seconds had swept her up into his arms again.

He could feel her respond. She clung to him desperately. He felt her body, warmed by the sun, pressing into his chest. He kissed her long and deeply. She responded eagerly.

Their bodies were like one as they stood there under the blazing sun in this private world with only their two ponies as witness.

Like two thirsty people who had now drunk their fill they released each other.

Jack held both her hands in his. Still unable to speak they continued to look at each other. They feasted their eyes.

It started as a slight tremble in the earth, almost imperceptible. But it was definitely there. Then a low rumble could be heard. Slowly, ever so slowly, it grew into a great roll, until it sounded like thunder.

Jack released One Feather's hands as she looked questioningly into his eyes. He ran for the steep slope of the hills. With staggering strides he made it quickly to the top. What he saw astonished him.

There below, spread out over many miles of yellow grass prairie rode hundreds of armed Indians. For many minutes Jack watched in stupefaction. They seemed to be riding north westerly. He saw every kind of pony: many chestnut, some white, others black, a sprinkling of pinto and many grey.

Their riders rode with purpose. All were armed, many, Jack could see, with the latest Remington breach loading rifles. Many others had the old muzzle loaders. Still others rode only with bows or spears and shields.

He could make out several riders galloping at the front of the war party. They wore elaborate head dress. He estimated the number of Indians at about two hundred and fifty. Many of them wore a single feather at the back of their heads, held there by a headband. The party raised great clouds of dust.

Their moves thundered on deafeningly.

Suddenly Jack felt a hand on his bare arm. He turned to find One Feather crouched by his side. Instinctively he put a hand on her back. As he did so he realized that he was trying to ensure she would stay down, out of sight.

Before he could sort out his thoughts he heard her say one word:

"Beardy!"

As Jack and One Feather made their way back to camp, he said little. He was lost in thought.

CHAPTER TWENTY-TWO

AS ONE day followed another, Jack and One Feather got to know each other. He learned that her best girl friend was Beavereye. One Feather loved her dearly because she was always laughing. She had a happy spirit.

Jack also learned how One Feather came to be a prisoner of Reverend Hartley. Beavereye's older brother, King Bird, wanted One Feather for his teepee. He had bothered One Feather for about a year now. However, she did not love him. As a matter of fact, she did not even like him. He was tall and strong and much respected. He was a good buffalo hunter. He had his own teepee and two horses. He was quite rich. But try as he might he could not persuade One Feather to become his wife. She refused to go into his teepee.

It was not so much that she had known only seventeen summers and he twenty-five. That did not help, it is true, but that was not the real problem with King Bird.

His problem was that he had become too boastful. If he came back from a hunt having killed one buffalo it suddenly became two. If he owned two horses, why, in two weeks, he would own four. If someone else killed a buffalo, well, King Bird was right there to describe how he had helped. And if he had not acted as quickly as he did, no buffalo would have been killed.

She disliked his strutting and chest pounding. She disliked as well his boastful confidence that soon he would kill a white man. One Feather looked apprehensively at Jack as she told him this. King Bird was given to making long speeches about the evil white man, how he had stolen Indian land and how his promises were never kept.

He was constantly encouraging other young braves to train for that day that would come "before many moons" when they would go to war against the white man.

He had now convinced others that to strengthen resolve and show commitment, the young braves, each in his turn, should perform a Sundance.

"What," Jack asked, "is a Sundance?"

One Feather described the ceremony. Jack was puzzled as to why she spoke of it with such distaste until she described the emotional climax. A thong was passed beneath the skin of a young brave's back. One below his left shoulder and the other below his right. These thongs were then tied to a strong but resilient birch tree that had been bent over for the purpose. After ensuring the thongs had been made fast the tree was then released and the body of the young brave was lifted from the ground.

Jack flinched at her description, but his reaction did not equal hers.

"That's for Sarcees," she spat, "not for real Crees."

Jack had never seen her like this before. She was quite evidently disgusted that people of her tribe should be persuaded to perform such a rite.

Revolted as she was she tried to persuade Beavereye to run away with her. The two of them had left the camp before for days at a time. They had a secret place on this very lake. Then she pointed down the lakeshore to the east.

"One day's walk that way," she said.

Beavereye would not leave, however. So One Feather had gone on her own.

She began to describe how she had walked, she had no other means, and as she spoke Jack could see she was reliving the experience.

After slipping out of the Indian encampment she had walked for perhaps one quarter of a day. The sun stood two hands off the horizon. She was tired and the day grew hotter. She had brought nothing to drink. She knew there was always plenty of water at the secret place. Beavereye and she had never gone thirsty. This morning, however, she was plenty thirsty as she walked briskly along. Then she became aware of the jangle of harness and the creaking of wheels. She turned and, to her surprise, found a horse and wagon moving slowly along behind her some short distance away.

Gradually the wagon drew abreast of her. The driver was a man. He spoke to her, but speaking only Cree, she did not understand him.

Then he patted the bench next to where he sat. She shook her head no.

He smiled and jumped down from the wagon.

"He had only two teeth," she said, pointing to her own mouth to show just which. She laughed. Then she shook her head in revulsion, and said, "He smelled bad. King Bird told me all white men smell bad. You don't smell bad."

She put her small hands on Jack's hands. She opened her large eyes wider as she looked at him.

"You smell sweet like sap from the poplar."

She paused, then resumed her narrative.

"He offered me a drink. I was so thirsty, my mouth and throat were dry. I needed a large drink of cool spring water. I love that," she added.

"He handed a silver flask to me. I turned it back and drank with a great thirst.

"It scorched my throat," she said, shaking her head from side to side once again. She twisted her lips to make a sour expression and moved her head and shoulders backward.

Finally she said: "It tasted awful. It did not quench my thirst at all. It hurt my throat and then made my body feel funny."

Again she paused. Then she looked up at Jack and said, "Do you think it was firewater? It sure tasted like fire!"

Jack nodded.

She went on.

"Then he grabbed me by the arm and pushed me toward the wagon. I resisted and he pushed some more.

"He said something to me. I think he was trying to persuade me to go with him, to get up on the wagon seat.

"I said to him I did not want to do that, to let me go.

"Then he grabbed me very hard around the waist. It hurt me. He tried to force me up. I pushed back very hard. He did not free me – I hit his chest and tried to scratch his face. Suddenly he released me and began to pound me with his fists.

"He screamed. I think he was cursing me. He hit my face. You saw how he hurt me there. He hit me here and here." She pointed to several other spots on her body.

She looked at Jack and said softly, "You saw how he hurt me there."

"Next I was down on my knees. He continued to beat on me.

"I passed out. The next thing I remember is waking up in the wagon. I hurt very much. Especially my head."

As she said this she touched her head, remembering.

"Then I heard voices." She turned to Jack. "One was your voice, Kanata Jack. You saved my life. I do not think I would have long to live with that man. He beat me too much."

She paused again. Then she concluded:

"You saved my life twice."

Jack never tired of hearing her voice. It had a hesitant breathless quality. He found her soft, gentle and kind. To everything she did she brought enthusiasm. And she did everything with a certain dignified natural grace.

As the days unfolded Jack found in her many surprising qualities.

One day she taught him how to snare muskrat. With a sharp knife he found for her in the wagon, she skinned and eviscerated the animal in only a few moments.

In the evening she rubbed the muskrat inside and out with herbs she found around the campsite. Then she stuffed it with more herbs, wrapped the whole in some large leaves and placed it in the glowing white embers of their campfire.

That night Jack enjoyed a very delicious and exotic meal.

She fashioned a crude spear with a knife and taught him to spear fish in the brook and in the shallows of the lake.

When she succeeded in spearing a fish she laughed in glee. Her laughter echoed along the forest edge. Two strutting white gulls suddenly scrambled into the sky.

At this they both laughed heartily, raising a great squawking and fluttering amongst the magpies, crows and sparrows in the surrounding trees. Even the squirrels and gophers ran for cover.

One Feather laughed so loud she put one hand over her mouth in embarrassment.

Jack did not know when he had ever been so happy.

CHAPTER TWENTY-THREE

JACK KNEW that this could not go on forever. Whatever the future might hold, for the present he had his duty to do.

He knew that he could delay no longer.

He had asked One Feather to put aside her morning chores. Taking her by the hand he led her over to the log near the campfire and sat her down.

He hesitated. He did not know how to tell her that he must soon be leaving. He did not know even how to begin. How could he explain it to her?

He did not have to, for at that moment a wailing, moaning scream pierced the air.

His head snapped around. Just in time he saw a war club rocket toward his temple.

He ducked. The club flew by. He was dimly aware of a thump as it hit the earth. The club had missed him but the body flying toward him did not.

He was hit with a terrific blow to his midriff. He catapulted backward, head over heels.

He lay gasping on the ground.

Before he could move he was hit again, his attacker this time letting out an angry howl.

As he struggled to save his life, Jack realized he was fighting with an enormously strong Indian warrior, stripped to the waist and bent on annihilation.

Jack was now on his back. He felt a forearm against his neck. It was crushing, crushing, crushing. He felt he would suffocate. His lungs seemed about to explode. His eyes grew dim and then he saw stars.

With super human effort he pushed at his tormentor's body. It lifted just enough for Jack to bring his knees between them.

He felt faint. He might lose consciousness at any moment. In a last desperate effort he thrust his legs rapidly out. His assailant shot backwards as Jack grasped for air.

Almost too late he saw a flash of light. The Indian now had a grip on a log, the end of which was burning. He struck at Jack's head with terrific force.

Jack rolled. The burning wood missed his head by inches.

Jack continued his roll right on to his hands and knees and as he did so he sprang to his feet.

The Indian now pressed his attack, swinging the burning log at Jack with powerful slashes. Jack nimbly sidestepped and ducked. In a rage of frustration the Indian took a giant swing at Jack's head. Again Jack ducked. The log flew out of the Indian's hands and crashed into the front of the wagon.

In a moment the wagon was ablaze.

Now the two were slugging at each other with great whacking blows. Bare knuckled, each blow landed with a sickening crack.

Jack advanced on his adversary. Warding off all counter punches, Jack threw punch after punch of deadly blows. With each one his enemy staggered back. Suddenly the Indian let out a high pitched scream. He had stepped on hot coals at the perimeter of the fire.

In an access of rage, he threw his body at Jack, propelling both to the ground once more. When the rolling stopped Jack found his attacker once more on top raining blows on his head and neck.

This time his strength could not save him. His arms flailed, his hands grasping at thin air. He found he was no longer able to defend himself. His strength was ebbing. Again he was losing consciousness.

Then suddenly the punching stopped.

Gradually as if in slow motion, his attacker toppled off his chest.

Behind him stood One Feather. In her hand she held the war club.

Relief and love flooded Jack.

Slowly Jack regained his feet. Mechanically he brushed at the stains on his breeches, while stonily he looked about the campsite.

Simultaneously One Feather and Jack became aware of a low chuckle just beyond the edge of the clearing.

They looked over in that direction.

What Jack saw stunned him: five mounted Indians.

They were lined up and except for the nearest one who chuckled still, not a sound was uttered. A riderless pony grazed indifferently next to the farthest Indian.

Jack was too stupefied and fatigued to do or say anything. He just stared at the Indian in the centre. He was taller than the others and the horse on which he sat was larger than the other horses. He had a high noble forehead, dark eyes, a narrow nose flaring at the bottom and high cheek bones. His cheeks were concave accentuating his wide full mouth which was turned down at the ends.

His dark hair was piled up on top of his head and fell down on either side of his face to his shoulders, where it ended in braids.

He was adorned with two feathers, one on either side of his head, and a beaded necklace. More beads and two medallions decorated his braids. He wore a buckskin shirt and leggings.

His eyes peered out at Jack from beneath heavy brows.

All of this Jack's eyes absorbed in a second.

One Feather jarred his trance:

"Father," she said.

"Father?" repeated Jack incredulously.

"Yes, this is my father," repeated One Feather. She turned to look at Jack. Then she added: "Black Bear!"

CHAPTER TWENTY-FOUR

THE EIGHT riders had moved at a continuous gallop for several hours. Their ponies threw up a small trail of dust from the pale yellow grass.

In the lead rode Black Bear. He was flanked by two Indians. Jack followed on Cloud, and two more Indians brought up the rear. One Feather for the most part rode behind these two, but from time to time angled Betsy forward to sidle up to Black Bear. She would engage in earnest conversation. He would say not a word, maintaining his visage firmly forward during her entire supplication.

Bringing up the tail end of the party was King Bird. He rode in disgrace.

Jack soon learned that the rider to his rear on the right was called Miserable Man. He was the Indian who was chuckling at their first encounter.

Now he kept a strong running commentary about King Bird, in a voice loud enough to ensure every word could be heard by King Bird and anyone else nearby.

"King Bird is in love," he said.

After awhile:

"The great warrior will flex his fine muscles, he will show all, he will show all what a fine brave he is."

Another pause, and then:

"The great warrior will win his woman. She will see what a fine warrior he is."

After a time:

"After all, is he not the finest warrior in the tribe?"

"He is the greatest hunter."

He rode some, and then:

"He kills the most buffalo."

A pause, then:

"He kills the biggest Buffalo."

"He has the best horses."

"He has the finest teepee."

"Shut up," snarled King Bird. For a moment his morale had revived.

"Oh yes," said Miserable Man, "the finest teepee. And he will have the finest woman too. He will have the daughter of Chief Black Bear in his teepee. Such a fine great warrior."

A pause for timing and then:

"The only problem is that she is a mightier warrior than he."

At this he broke into a prolonged bout of laughter. The Indian to his left laughed too, and even Jack suppressed a smile.

At first Jack was puzzled as to how Miserable Man got his name, he was always so jolly. Now Jack was beginning to understand.

For the second time, he thought, I am a prisoner. His hands were bound together and loosely tethered to his saddlehorn. For the first time he began to despair of ever returning to his unit.

After the initial shock had evaporated and Jack had regained his breath, things had moved swiftly.

One Feather had tried to explain to her father. He had silenced her with one command:

"Shut up, woman!"

Then he turned his attention to Jack. He ordered his hands bound. Cloud and Betsy were saddled up.

Miserable Man and a second Indian were ordered to search the campsite for anything of value. A few items were found and quickly packed.

The wagon was a mass of charred smoking ruins. Nothing of value would be found there. The Indians poked through it anyway, occasionally unbending to hold up an object and exclaim in awe. Various articles were tucked away here and there in their clothes or on their ponies. None of it appeared to Jack to have any value.

After scavenging an hour, upon a muttered command from Black Bear, they all mounted up and rode off.

Jack cast a fond glance back at his home of many days. He remembered the many things he had learned and experienced there. As he turned forward he noticed One Feather looking back too. Then she turned and saw him watching her. For a long time they gazed at each other.

The party continued its progress. It appeared to Jack that they were skirting the east end of the lake. He noticed the leader took great care to remain within a quick ride of the sheltering trees. Jack knew why he maintained this habit while travelling. Did all plains people keep close to shelter? Or did this band have any more reason to be worried now than it usually did. For a moment Jack thought they were being careful because military forces may be near. I am allowing my fantasies to affect my judgement, he thought, and promptly dismissed the idea from his mind.

To occupy his mind he studied his captors and their horses. Black Bear rode a very powerful stallion. It moved with grace and ease over the prairie. Miserable Man was riding a leggy roan. She too moved along easily.

He turned his attention to the rider on his left rear. He was quite young, but bore himself with great dignity. He rode a pinto. Jack noticed how very dutiful and obedient he was to the slightest suggestion made to him. He was especially respectful of Black Bear. Later Jack learned why. He was Travelling Spirit, a son of

65

Black Bear.

Flanking Black Bear and to his left rode an Indian of mean countenance. He never simply looked at Jack but glared at him. He also put on airs. He obviously took enormous pride in his riding position, deriving there-from much status (in his mind) over the others. This man Jack later learned was Bad Child.

To the right of Black Bear rode Yellow Bear. Jack noticed Yellow Bear had very little to say, yet Black Bear consulted him most often. When Yellow Bear had something to say evidently it was worthwhile. Several times after Yellow Bear was consulted, Black Bear gave orders for an abrupt change of direction.

Yellow Bear often left the little party making forays on his own. He would gallop off without notice. Jack's eyes would follow him riding away over the small rolling hills on his chestnut cayuse. Soon he would appear in silhouette on the crest of some distant hill: rider and horse. For many minutes he could be seen scanning the distance horizon. Soon Jack could see him returning at a gallop over the ever-changing scene to make his report to Black Bear.

The party now moved at a steady pace, the ponies alternately trotting, then quickening to a slow gallop. After a while Yellow Bear rode off to the east and the party slowed to a walk. It was clear they were all tired, even the ponies strained to make every painful step.

They were also bored and suddenly Miserable Man broke into a chant:

"Hi Yi Hi Yi Hi Yi," He started in quiet falsetto voice. He placed emphasis on every second syllable. He went on for some time like this. He appeared to be setting a rhythm. Then he broke into song.

Soon several others joined in. Jack, his understanding of Cree limited, perceived little of what they sang. He made out the word "Buffalo". It came up repeatedly. He also understood the words "hunt" and "feast".

They sang in low intimate voices, as though wanting only their own riding party to hear. Some of their voices were quite rich. They all held the tune and the rhythm without difficulty.

Their spirits soon improved with the singing.

Perhaps they imagined a successful buffalo hunt and the marvellous feast that would follow.

Even the horses' steps picked up.

Eventually Yellow Bear could again be seen. He appeared to be quite excited for he constantly spurred his pony into a faster gallop.

Shortly he rode up the last few steps and reigned in before Black Bear, his pony stepping in place with excitement.

Jack heard Yellow Bear say:

"Mēyo āchimowin."

Good news, he had said. Jack strained forward to catch the conversation. Yellow Bear spoke excitedly but in deep low tones to Black Bear, who spoke almost not at all. Black Bear seemed to speak only to ask for clarification.

At first Jack was confident of news of the militia. Then once again he heard the word "buffalo". He saw Yellow Bear point repeatedly. Evidently he was trying to explain where he had seen a buffalo.

By this time it was clear to the entire party that he had spotted a buffalo. Jack could sense the entire party was infected by the excitement. Buffalo seldom roamed alone. If one buffalo had been spotted, surely others would be found nearby.

It was late in the afternoon. Dusk was approaching. The sunlight from the horizon filtered across the dusty prairie sky to cast a copper mantle over the riding party and reflect ochre in the tawny brown faces of the Indians.

Jack thought he had never before seen a more handsome people.

Abruptly Black Bear turned and beckoned to Travelling Spirit to come over.

Again Yellow Bear lapsed into a lengthy discourse. This time he added elaborate gestures to his pointing.

Travelling Spirit nodded from time to time to show he understood.

When Yellow Bear had finished speaking they both turned to look at Black Bear. Now Jack could hear Black Bear clearly.

"Can you find this place?" he asked of Travelling Spirit.

"Yes," nodded Travelling Spirit.

"For many months we have had no buffalo. For many months we have lived on 'wachusk'.

Jack knew he was referring to muskrat.

"Can you track this buffalo?" he asked again.

Travelling Spirit nodded once again.

"Find the buffalo herd. Track it. Learn its direction. Before the new moon rises bring us the news."

Jack watched the three Indians as they spoke. Once more the image overwhelmed him. They and their buckskin clothes were bathed in the golden glow of the setting sun.

The conversation continued for a moment, then Travelling Spirit reigned his pony around and started off at a gallop toward the east.

"Good hunting," Black Bear called after him.

The sun turned from gold to crimson now as it moved toward the horizon. For several moments their eyes followed the departing horseman. Then Black Bear kicked his heels into his pony and she started with a bolt in a northerly direction. The entire party moved off at a fast gallop.

Evidently they would try to cover the remaining miles before darkness.

Soon the party approached low rolling hills.

They were covered here and there with trees.

In the setting sun, with the trunks of birch and poplar trees taking on a pink and sometimes yellow hue, the riders slowed, to a walk. They made a gradual descent now, through the sparse forest.

Below, Jack caught sight of the campsite. A number of teepees perhaps as many as twenty-five, stood in a large circle. They too reflected the color of the dying sun. A short distance beyond was a small lake. Its surrounding shores were dark in the evening light.

As the party rode forward several dogs met them, turned, and followed barking as they rode into the centre of camp.

Young children ran up shouting and laughing. Several women emerged from the dark interior of tents and, talking volubly, approached the horsemen.

Jack could not hear the instructions of Black Bear over the tumult, but Miserable Man materialized at his side and motioned for him to dismount.

An Indian appeared and began to lead Cloud away. Jack started to object but immediately thought better of it. Indians loved horses. It was not likely that Cloud would come to harm.

As Miserable Man led Jack away he heard excited questions and commentary from the small gathering.

"Where is Travelling Spirit?"

"Who is the White Man?"

"Buffalo, you have seen Buffalo? Where, how many?"

"Travelling Spirit will not find the buffalo herd."

"Did the white man steal One Feather?"

"Where did you find One Feather."

"Her mother has been worried sick."

"Did the white man hurt One Feather?"

They were still asking questions and chattering as Miserable Man led Jack to a small makeshift stockade.

It had been constructed of birch logs crudely lashed together by leather thongs. It was no more than eight feet by five feet in dimension. Its walls were about ten feet high.

The last thing Jack saw before he was shoved inside was Cloud being led into a corral, holding many other horses, far on the other side of the camp. Several Indians guarded the entrance to the stockade. The gate slammed shut. Jack turned to survey the gloomy interior. Huddled in the corner was another man. Jack peered at him closely. The man looked up. He was a white man.

"Howdy," the man said, rising.

"Howdy," said Jack.

"Glad to have company. Mighty lonely in here. The food ain't so hot either."

Something about the timbre of the man's voice struck a chord in Jack.

What's your name stranger? the friendly man went on.

"Jack," he said. "They call me 'Canada Jack'." He put out his hand as he said this. Then he asked, "What's yours?" already anticipating the answer.

"Hogie," the man replied. "Hogie Magee!"

CHAPTER TWENTY-FIVE

ONE FEATHER did not rest. She told Beavereye everything that had taken place. She also told her mother everything that had taken place. Everything that is except the private experiences. These she shared only with Beavereye.

Soon her mother spoke to Black Bear. He was skeptical. He had reason to be skeptical. Canada Jack was a white man, after all. And all the Indians of his tribe knew from experience that there was little reason to trust a white man.

Very shortly the whole encampment knew what had happened to One Feather. They knew also that 'Kanata Jack' had saved her life, not once, but twice.

"There is no reason to lock him up," pleaded One Feather. "He will not run away. Anyway, what did he do but save my life. I would not be here if it were not for Kanata Jack. What reason is there to lock him up?"

Black Bear sat in his tent and listened to One Feather. He had listened to her and her mother for hours.

He had suffered jibes and other comments all morning long from others around camp, especially Beavereye.

"Why do you lock him up?" they kept asking him. "What has he done but be kind to her. What has he done wrong?"

The more Black Bear heard these entreaties the more he wavered. His distrust of white men ran deep.

Then One Feather hit upon one irrefutable argument.

"Anyway how can he leave without his pony? It is locked up with the others. They are always guarded. Do you think he will run away on foot?"

She laughed at this idea.

As Black Bear heard the laughter of his daughter, whom he loved very much, his resolution began to crumble.

Then she added:

"Anyway he will not leave without his pony. I have seen him with her. He loves her. He will not leave without his pony." she repeated.

With this argument Black Bear finally relented. He too loved his horse. He realized that Kanata Jack would not leave without his horse.

"All right," he said to One Feather. "I will free him. But he is your responsibility. Do not let him out of your sight."

It was, perhaps, the most welcome command her father had ever given her; it was also the most superfluous.

"Yes father," she said, trying not to let her happiness show on her face.

When Hogie had learned that Jack knew his sister and his father he was elated. The questions tumbled from his mouth one after the other. He continued with his questions until long after dark, the two of them conversing in low voices.

Jack had been given a single blanket. The ground in the stockade was chilly, damp and rough. He did not seem to notice. So fatigued was he that he rolled up in the blanket on the dirt floor and soon fell asleep.

Hogie was still talking and asking questions. It was some time before he realized Jack was no longer awake.

The next morning was different. After a sound sleep Jack had thrown off his fatigue. He was awake with the singing of the first sparrow. It was then that he learned what had befallen Hogie that he should now find himself a prisoner.

Many days ago, so many that he had lost count, Hogie had drifted north seeking some good buffalo hunting. For days he had seen nothing. Not like the old days. His father used to entertain Nance and Hogie with tales of his buffalo hunting days. Enormous herds wandered the great plains. No one, white or Indian, ever had to go hungry or without warm clothing. For the buffalo provided both in abundance.

Magee had described enormous roving herds he had seen that resembled nothing so much as a giant cloud shadow slipping across the face of the prairie.

"Listening to it was like hearing a never ending roll of thunder," he had told Hogie. "Incredible it was."

But buffalo hunting had fallen on mean times, particularly south of the border.

Magee had seen it. Great hordes of easterners came west for sport. Thousands of buffalo were slaughtered. Other white men organized in order to efficiently harvest buffalo. Not for food. Merely to take the hide. He had seen buffalo hides piled twenty feet deep, forty feet long and twenty feet in width.

Hogie still carried this picture, just as described by his father, in his mind's eye. For some reason he saw a man reclining atop the pile of hides. The man wore a bowler. He looked so small on that mountain of buffalo skins.

These commercial hunters shipped the skins east. The carcasses were left to rot.

Magee had hunted buffalo south of the border. Yes, and some on the great plains of the north west. The great slaughter reached its peak in the mid seventies.

Magee had sickened of it. The protests of the Indians went unheeded. Their staple food was fast disappearing. Magee had great sympathy for them.

Hogie had learned well how to hunt. He learned even better never to hunt except for need.

Every year it became more difficult to kill buffalo. Every year they became more difficult to find. When Hogie did find buffalo they did not resemble the great herds described by his father.

In recent years, as the hunting had been left more and more to Hogie, he had found he had to travel ever farther to find a buffalo and make a kill.

This year he travelled further than he ever did before. Late one afternoon he spotted a single buffalo. It was many miles away. He tracked it, but because of the many folds in the land and the many shrubs and forest patches, he repeatedly lost it.

He became fatigued and careless. The next thing he knew he was looking down the barrel of a Winchester rifle. Indians. Three of them. And they were very angry.

"Why were they so angry?" asked Jack.

"I was trespassing on their hunting ground," replied Hogie gloomily.

An hour after sunup, after his second night in the lockup, Jack heard the wooden bolt of the gate thrown. It opened. There stood One Feather.

Jack was invited out. An Indian guard stepped aside for Jack but pushed Hogie back when he tried to follow Jack out.

"Am I free?" was Jack's first question to One Feather.

"You are not free as the crow is free," said One Feather, "but you are free."

She led Jack through the camp. She stopped in front of a teepee. An old woman was seated there. Her hair was grey and she had no teeth. She had alert dark eyes.

"This is my grandmother," said One Feather. "She will give us something to eat."

"How do you do," said Jack formally.

The old woman chuckled.

"She is called 'Ah-Pay'." said One Feather.

At this the old lady smiled and nodded her head vigorously.

She put out large amounts of berries. Then some smoked fish. Jack was starved. The fish was delicious and he wolfed it down. This seemed to please Ah-Pay for she said:

"Kinosew."

Jack knew this meant fish. He said to her:

"Good fish. Very good fish. I have had enough. I cannot eat more." He rubbed his stomach as he said this in the best Cree he could muster.

This pleased the old woman enormously. She smiled her toothless smile at Jack and said:

"Good boy."

Then she turned to One Feather and repeated:

"Good boy." This time she patted Jack's arm as she spoke. Then she muttered something to One Feather so quietly that Jack could not understand what it was she said. But One Feather blushed and was very embarrassed.

After eating, One Feather took Jack through her camp for a walk. She made an elaborate show of pointing out things of interest and introducing him. But she was very proud, and quite possessive. She let no one become too familiar with Jack. This was especially the case with the other young women in the camp. If they smiled at Jack he was not allowed to linger long. She took him by the arm and walked to the next point of interest.

One girl took to following the pair from site to site. She was shorter than One Feather. She was plump but not unpleasantly so. She had round cheeks and when Jack turned to look at her she broke into a broad smile showing fine white teeth. She wore her black hair in braids. Over each braid she had drawn a bright yellow clasp resembling a large bead.

She was the same age as One Feather.

70

Finally One Feather was forced to introduce her. It was Beavereye. Henceforth her friend was allowed to follow them at a discreet distance.

Jack particularly admired the teepees. These were constructed of trees that had been stripped, and buffalo hide.

Some teepees were beautifully decorated. Colorful paint was applied. Some bore the figures of buffalo, others the shapes of birds. One was decorated around its entire circumference with the different phases of the moon. The different decorations were imaginative and artistically done.

Each tent had a fireplace and fur pallets for beds. In addition Jack saw bags, pots, pans, clothing for every description and woven willow furniture.

Many of the people wore clothing that had been purchased from the white man, but Jack saw much that was not. Like One Feather, Beavereye wore a dress made of doeskin. She also wore moccasins. Both dress and moccasins were colorfully decorated with beads and quills. During the cold weather and in the winter, One Feather told Jack, they also wore leggings. The women wore leggings up to their knees; the men to their hips. These too were decorated.

They passed several racks where hides were stretched for curing and others where meat was curing and drying.

As they passed by one teepee a woman was busy cleaning fish. Next to her was a small tripod, about four or five feet high. Several brackets rested horizontally across the tripod and fish fillets were draped over the brackets. Beneath burned a low fire sending up smoke.

One Feather said that they liked this campsite because this lake provided plenty of fish for smoking.

She said they used to eat a lot of buffalo. It was scarce now so they ate more muskrat, deer, wild birds, and a lot of rabbit. They also ate roots and berries.

One Feather loved pemmican, but she had not eaten it for a long time. She explained to Jack how it was made with dried meat and berries.

"Perhaps Travelling Spirit will find the buffalo," she sighed, "Then we will all have pemmican again."

Everybody in camp knew that Travelling Spirit was tracking buffalo. They all anticipated his return.

That afternoon Jack decided to check on Cloud. In order to do so he had to walk through the centre of the little encampment.

He started out alone but soon a number of children followed him. They were laughing and chattering as they hopped and danced along behind him. Then they were joined by the dogs of the village and his trip to the corral became a parade.

Just as Jack approached the compound with the horses, One Feather caught up with him. She pulled at his sleeve. With several more steps, however, Jack reached the gate. Two Indians stepped forward from a group loitering nearby, to bar his way.

Both were armed with hunting knives. They stood in his path with their arms folded, but they said nothing.

Over their shoulders Jack could see the horses. Some were standing idle switching their tails. Others were grazing. A few walked slowly around searching for shade or grass or a change of scene.

Jack spotted Cloud. He called out her name and her head came up at the sound of his voice. She immediately walked over to the gate.

Jack tried to work his way by the guards but there was no way they were going to let him pass without force.

One Feather pulled again at his sleeve. Jack hesitated but when she persisted he turned to leave with her.

As he did so he noticed King Bird squatting by the paddock with five or six other braves.

He glared at Jack. Then he broke into a malicious grin.

Jack could feel King Bird's eyes on his back as he left with One Feather.

Later, when Jack reflected on the incident at the corral he understood why he had been released from custody so readily.

Over the following days Jack came to know the camp quite well. One Feather was very friendly with everyone. In return she was welcome everywhere.

At first the adults kept their distance from Jack. They knew his ambivalent position in the campsite. But under the guidance of One Feather their suspicions soon cleared. They became less hesitant to meet the stranger. Once they spoke to him and found that he could understand them and even speak a few words of Cree, enough to communicate with them, all the barriers fell and they became very friendly.

They laughed and called out to him when they saw him. The women especially seemed to like him. They repeatedly invited him to sit and talk. He was continually offered food. So much did he eat that he began to fear getting fat. But he was hesitant to turn down any hospitality. He did not wish to offend anyone.

He met warriors, weavers and medicine men.

He met people with many different names: Horsefall, Asapase, Queweyance, Wuttunee, Napope, Awasis, Toutsaint, Blue Cloud, Tootoosis, Thivierge, Mosquito, Peekeekoot, Bird, Dustyhorn, Eh-ah-paise, Whitehawke, Baldhead, Bigsky, Moosewaypayo, Greyeyes, One Who Talks, One Who Walks, Wandering Man, One Who Laughs, Many Horses, Little Crow, Little Pine, Horse, Kote, Cuthand, Redwing, Swiftwolf, and Cardinal. There were many with the name Bear.

They were names that he found different from those he was used to hearing. But he liked them. He was able to remember them quite well and soon was greeting many around the campsite by calling out their names.

While most of the villagers were friendly, one was not. Black Bear kept himself aloof. While great respect was shown to him and he was well liked, he kept his distance from everyone except a small group of older Indians with whom he conferred often and with whom he did most of his socializing.

There was one small group who did not associate with Jack. This was the group surrounding King Bird.

There were about eight or nine in his retinue. They were always strutting about, often wearing war paint. They engaged in wrestling matches with each other. Stripped to the waist they would struggle and grunt fiercely as they tried to best one another.

They often left on horseback as a group to practise their war skills with spears and shields, bows and arrows and also with guns.

One Feather said that they used to practise at the edge of the village. They had fallen into the habit of riding furiously up and down near the campsite, hoping to impress the others. They kicked up so much dust, however, that the women of the village chased them away. She laughed as she remembered this.

The thought of his duty never left Jack's mind for long. As much as he had come to like the villagers he realized he was still their prisoner. There was a battle to be fought and, however mixed his feelings might be, he knew where that duty lay.

There was also Hogie. He had made a solemn promise to Nance and Magee to assist Hogie to return if such an opportunity should come his way. Even without such a promise, he would have done no less.

He was constantly surveying the camp to memorize the layout. So important was this that he had committed to memory every teepee, every travois, every fire pit and smoking rack.

He was not allowed anywhere near the lockup, but he studied it at a distance. It was crude, but it was sturdy. What was worse it was guarded. He found that no matter whether it was night or day at least one Indian was to be found loitering nearby. The guard was always a man and almost invariably someone from King Bird's little group.

One particularly hot afternoon One Feather suggested to Jack that they walk down by the lake. Jack seized the opportunity to be alone with her. They had not been alone since their arrival at the village. They had spent the afternoon with Beavereye in the forest and scrub brush nearby to check her rabbit snares. But she had been nearby constantly. They had had no time to themselves. Now Jack welcomed the opportunity to be alone with One Feather.

One Feather led Jack down the lakeshore. She walked along the shoreline until coming to a willow bush. He was surprised when she disappeared into the bush. But he followed her. He found himself on a narrow foot path. They followed the foot path for about forty feet and then emerged once again on the lakeshore.

Jack saw three boats. They were well up out of the lake. All were turned over to keep them dry inside.

Two of them were bark canoes.

The third boat was new to Jack. It was round and quite deep, perhaps three feet deep. It was covered not with bark but buffalo skins.

Jack turned over the canoe chosen by One Feather and pushed it into the water.

Before he could help her, One Feather had hopped in.

Jack climbed in himself. Each picked up a paddle and they pushed away from the shore.

The sun beat down on their shoulders. The water glittered, cool and inviting.

At the stern Jack dipped his paddle in and pulled it back firmly. The light canoe shot ahead. Occasionally the two changed sides. They paddled on without interruption until they were two or three miles down the shoreline.

They eased up on their pace now. Jack found that he could paddle alone and move the canoe along at a leisurely speed. With each stroke he turned the blade at the stern, steering the boat parallel to the shore.

They both drank in the silent beauty of the countryside. As the shoreline slipped by Jack noticed the occasional pine tree. Most of the trees were not evergreen.

Neither spoke. The only sounds herd were the gurgle of water passing the hull of the canoe and the occasional call of a bird floating out across the silent lake.

One Feather broke their reverie. She pointed to a strip of sandy beach that lay one quarter of a mile off their starboard bow. Slowly Jack paddled over in that direction.

As soon as they were within sixty feet of it he could see that it was long and wide. The sand was clean and bright.

The canoe easily slipped up on the sandy beach. One Feather stepped out. Jack stepped forward in the canoe, then he too jumped out on to the sand.

He had doffed his shirt and boots shortly after starting out. Now the warm sand felt good on his feet. The sun felt hot and good on his back.

Without waiting for One Feather to spread a blanket Jack spread himself out on the sand and, closing his eyes, turned his face to the sun. One Feather did the same. They had come five miles or more and now the relaxation of his muscles spread through his body like balm and he felt good.

CHAPTER TWENTY-SIX

OVER THE many days, as One Feather had shown Jack everything in her village and made him acquainted with its people, he had never stopped expressing his admiration. And he was sincere. He found the village appealing, even beautiful and he told her so. He enjoyed the people. She could see this, but still he never failed to tell her.

He even took delight in their names. He found them so expressive. All the while he could not help but see the satisfaction in One Feather's face. She was proud of her village, her people and her tribe. As she saw how genuine his reaction was, her confidence in their relationship grew. That only made her more beautiful in his eyes.

One Feather was a quiet person. She seldom spoke. Now, suddenly, she spoke and almost startled Jack who was on the verge of dozing off.

"You like my village?" she enquired.

She knows I do thought Jack, she merely likes to hear it again and again.

"You know I do One Feather. It is unlike anything I have ever seen. It is beautiful."

He raised himself on his left elbow and looked down at her. Her chest was moving gently with her breathing. Her eyes were closed, her face turned to the sun.

Then he added, "There is a sort of harmony to the life of your village."

She smiled at the compliment.

"King Bird and his friends are not harmonious, though," said Jack. "I think they want trouble."

"They want to fight the white man," she said. "They think the white man will steal our land. King Bird says the white man has killed the buffalo. The buffalo gives us food, and shelter too. He says the white man has taken these and he will take our land too."

She was in a mood to speak. Jack let her go on.

"He tried to take the land of our cousins, the Metis. My father, Black Bear, met Dumont. The Metis will fight the white man soon. King Bird has said that Black Bear will help. He says he has heard that the council has agreed to help the Metis fight the white man.

"You are not like other white men. I have heard my father speak of them. They cannot be trusted."

She raised herself on her right elbow and looked into Jack's eyes.

Then she said:

"You can be trusted. You like the Indian." She paused for a long time, then she said again:

"You are not like the other white men."

Jack looked at her steadily. Then he said:

"But I am a white man. I am with the white man's army. You know that One Feather."

"Yes," she said. "But you are not fighting. You are not with the soldiers, fighting. You are here, with me, in my village. You like my people. You like my village."

Then she said:

"You could stay with my village."

She looked at him for a moment when she said this and then quickly looked away.

"I cannot stay in your village now," said Jack, unsure himself of exactly what he meant, but quite surprised he said it.

His conscience immediately assailed him. He added:

"My duty now is to return to my unit. I can think of myself only when my duty is done."

Jack was not sure if she understood what he had said. He was not sure if he had found the right words to say it.

One Feather put her head back on the sand and closed her eyes again.

"You are kind and gentle, One Feather. You have made my heart full. Each morning I look first to see you. I wait for you to leave your teepee. My eyes follow you everywhere, One Feather, do you know that?"

"Yes," she said in a voice so small that Jack had nearly to strain to hear it.

After a while Jack continued:

"I trust you too One Feather."

"I told you that I know the sister of the white prisoner. I know his father. They are my friends. They miss him. They are sick over his loss. They want him back."

He stopped and watched her. There was no reaction so he plunged on.

"I promised to help him return to his home."

He waited. Still no reaction. He continued.

"I want to set him free, One Feather, will you help me?"

"But he is our prisoner," said One Feather. "He hunts our buffalo. It is against my people."

She had spoken quite firmly and that seemed to end the conversation. After he watched her for some minutes and nothing more was said, Jack laid his head back and soon was dozing in the sun.

The next thing he heard was a splash. Distantly he thought he heard his name called. He was immediately awake.

He looked around. One Feather was not at his side. His heart gave a leap. Something had happened to her, he thought.

His eyes quickly searched the surrounding area. Then they followed the beach into the distance on either side. He traced the rim of the forest which crowded the beach along the shore. Not a sign of One Feather.

As he turned back his eyes fell on the canoe.

There, casually thrown over a strut, lay her dress. Simultaneously he heard a splash. He looked out over the water. It glittered in the late afternoon sun. Then his eyes found her and a wave of relief washed through him.

He doffed his breeches, throwing them into the canoe over One Feather's clothing, and clad in his shorts ran into the water.

After the heat of the sun it felt chilly. When he was waist high he plunged in over his head. The cool water jolted his body. He felt fully awake. The water was exhilarating. In powerful strokes he moved through the water to One Feather.

Just as he was about to meet her she dived. Another two strokes and he too plunged down.

He opened his eyes. He could not see her. The water was a pellucid green. His white arms reached forward and down. He brought them back smartly and his body drifted deeper. The color of the water grew darker not but shafts of light still lit his way. Another stroke or two and he found himself in deep blue water.

His lungs were beginning to protest. He would have to surface shortly.

He turned his body. He was vertical now. He moved his hands, pushing water to the surface. It was all he could do to keep his body down.

He was about to give up when he caught a glimpse of movement about six feet away.

Once again he reached forward with his powerful arms. He drew his body forward with each stroke. His body planing in the deep, he kicked vigorously.

Now he saw One Feather. She drifted vertically. Her arms worked constantly to keep herself down at this depth.

Too late she caught sight of Jack. As his arms circled her waist she reached for the surface. Their bodies were together now and Jack with one arm assisted One Feather to bring them up.

As they broke the surface both of them gasped for air, drinking it in greedily.

Jack then put both of his arms around One Feather and brought her firmly against him. With only his legs treading water he was easily able to keep them both afloat.

He could feel her heaving chest settle down. He felt fully alive enjoying the sun and the water.

One Feather put her arms around his neck. She kissed him quickly, only brushing his lips. Then, after both had again replenished their lungs, she kissed him again full and hard on the lips. She clung to him firmly now, winding her legs around his waist and locking them. For long minutes, pausing only to gasp for more air she kissed him on his lips, his eyes, his cheeks, his forehead and then hard and long on his lips again.

Then she drew back her head. Jack saw droplets of water speckle her face, especially her eyelashes, where a single droplet seemed to be captured at the end of every lash. Refracting the rays of the hot sun, they sparkled in every color of the rainbow.

"Kanata Jack," she said, "You will hunt buffalo for me."

"Me?" said Jack. It was an amused question.

"Yes, you," she replied.

"But, but…" began Jack.

She cut him off:

"King Bird wants to hunt buffalo for me. But I do not want him to hunt for me. He will want me to live in his teepee. If he kills many buffalo he thinks I will marry him and live in his teepee."

"He would be rich if he killed many buffalo," said Jack.

"I do not care if he kills one buffalo or one hundred buffalo. I will not marry King Bird. I will not move into his teepee."

"I would hunt buffalo for you, One Feather," said Jack, "but they won't even let me see my pony let alone ride her."

"Yes, you can," she said.

"They will not let me go on the buffalo hunt, One Feather. I am a prisoner. They will not trust me."

"They will let you go on the buffalo hunt."

"But Black Bear…" he said.

"I will speak to Black Bear. My father will do this for me. He will let you go on the buffalo hunt."

She paused. Then she said:

"I want you to hunt buffalo for me. Will you hunt buffalo for me?" Again she moved her head back and looked directly into his eyes.

At that moment Jack knew he could deny her nothing.

"I will hunt buffalo for you, One Feather.

It would be an honour for me to hunt buffalo for you."

With that she kissed him firmly on the lips and once again winding her arms and legs hard around him, crushed her body against his.

When she paused for breath he said:

"How do you know there will be buffalo to hunt. Travelling Spirit has not returned. So far we have spotted only a single buffalo. Not enough for a buffalo hunt."

"I know it," she said simply. "There will be a buffalo hunt."

CHAPTER TWENTY-SEVEN

THEY HAD forgotten time. The sun was setting when they started back. Both One Feather and Jack paddled with a will. They took no notice of the sunset.

Soon the sun was sitting like a huge crimson ball far across the lake. A few threads of forgotten cloud filtered across its face. The cloud looked dark but in turn glittered gold and orange at its edges. Then, as it spun off the surface of the sun it turned first white and then black.

The next moment the sun was merely peeking over the surface of the water. Two pelicans, just shadows in the sky, flew down the horizon.

Suddenly the sun was gone. The two paddlers heard the call of a lonely loon echo across the water.

They paid it no heed, but paddled on.

It seemed only the next moment that the lake, the shore and even the sky had been plunged into blue darkness. A shiny path led from the canoe, out over the cool dark water, to a point on the lake over which stood a crescent moon.

They paddled on. One Feather was flagging.

Jack knew because his own strokes had become harder. But the canoe continued on with undiminished speed.

"Rest One Feather," he whispered, unnecessarily. "We're not far away. I can do it from here."

After a few more strokes she put her paddle across the gunwales of the canoe. Only occasionally now did she add a helpful stroke.

Once Jack sensed something off to his right in the darkness. He heard nothing that he could identify. When he peered out over the dark water he could see nothing. It is ridiculous he said to himself. The only thing out there is water.

As he leaned into the next stroke, however, he heard a swish sound behind his ears.

He stopped and sat quietly for a moment, trying to figure out the sound.

Then suddenly he heard "Thunk!" He looked down in the direction of the sound.

Imbedded right into the starboard hull, not six inches below the gunwales was an arrow. Were it not for the side of the canoe, it would have pierced his thigh.

One Feather had turned around at the last sound. For a moment they both stared at the arrow in silence.

Then Jack quietly commanded: "Lie flat, One Feather. Lie flat on the bottom of the canoe. Someone's shooting at us.

"Someone is trying to kill me!"

The sound of yet another arrow whizzing through the black night air between them was all the urging she needed. In a moment she could not be seen over the sides of the canoe.

In a flash Jack had slipped into the black forbidding waters. He had gone over the port side. He moved carefully to the stern.

In vain he looked into the darkness. Our canoe must have been lit by the moon, else he could not have been so accurate, thought Jack.

Slowly Jack dog-paddled from the protection of the hull in the direction from which came the arrow shots. He moved carefully, to ensure he did not raise any white phosphorescence in the water.

Within moments the moon lit up another canoe. A single person occupied the stern. It was too dark to discern features, but it was a man. He wore two feathers in his headband.

Making a mental note of the location and drift of his own canoe he submerged and made his way around the far side of his assailant's boat.

He surfaced slowly. Silently he drew his breath.

There, four feet away, he saw the back of his enemy. He was peering over the lake. His bow rested across the canoe in front of him.

Jack looked up at the moon. A few shreds of clouds moved across its face.

Any moment now the moon will light up my canoe, thought Jack. It's now or never.

With silent underwater strokes of his arms he was at the side of the canoe.

Something must have warned the Indian for he began to turn just as Jack's strong arm shot out of the water and grabbed him by the neck. With a mighty heave, a bang and a splash the Indian was in the water.

Hands groped and clutched at Jack. He managed to shrug them off. For a moment the two struggling men submerged. The Indian, in a moment of luck, caught the front of Jack's shirt. Next his hands were on Jack's throat. His grip was vice-like.

They surfaced. Jack could not get air. He brought his knee up sharply into the abdomen of the Indian. His grip loosened only slightly. Then Jack threw a terrific punch across the surface of the water. It landed with a wet splat behind the left ear of the Indian and suddenly his grip released and Jack was breathing once more.

But the Indian was gone too. Jack looked around a full three hundred and sixty degrees. No one.

He could be anywhere below thought Jack. He could, in a moment be back in his canoe.

Or mine, thought Jack in a flash. How could I have left One Feather.

With that one thought still running through his mind he lit out for his boat as fast as he could swim, still trying not to raise a telltale wake of white water.

He gained his boat in a trice. Again he moved to the farther side.

"Are you OK?" he whispered to One Feather.

"Yes, are you?"

"I am. I got him, but lost him again in the darkness. Stay down. He could shoot again. I'll push the canoe in the water. It can't be far now. We'll make it."

There were no more arrows that night. No more attacks. Jack moved watchfully, carefully and ever so slowly. They made it back but it took them several hours.

Jack was thoroughly chilled when they arrived. One Feather insisted that he come to her teepee. A fire would be on. It would be warm.

Jack hesitated thinking Black Bear might be there, but as he soon found, he was not.

One Feather handed him a blanket. She ordered him to strip right down. He folded the blanket around himself and sat up against the willow back rest she pushed up near the glowing embers in the centre of the teepee.

As he warmed himself she made herself busy hanging his wet clothing up to dry.

Then she rubbed his back and sides for a while. It felt good. His tense muscles relaxed and the warmth of the fire seemed to penetrate his body.

He felt himself beginning to dry.

One Feather was off again rummaging around amongst some buffalo hides in the dark recesses of the teepee.

In a moment she came up triumphantly holding some garments in her hands.

"I've found them. I made them for Travelling Spirit, but they will fit you."

She moved them back and forth in front of Jack, showing him her handiwork. Then she commanded, "Put them on."

Jack took the clothing. One Feather turned her back and busied herself again. This time she made something hot for him to drink.

He dropped the blanket and quickly put on the breech cloth. The finely finished doeskin was soft and smooth.

Then he picked up two similar brightly and artistically beaded leggings. He first slipped on the left one. It came right up to the top of this thigh. Then he slipped on the right one. He was fully covered now from his ankles to his waist.

"One Feather," he said quietly.

She turned. Her dark eyes sparkled and glowed in the firelight. They glowed with admiration.

She took two steps forward. She looked up at him and said:

"You are my brave."

Once again she was in his arms.

After a while she found a new lovely beaded shirt. This also was made for Travelling Spirit and it too fit him perfectly. Then she produced some moccasins that he slipped on and his dress was complete.

She was about to speak when they heard a disturbance. They both stepped outside and there by the large campfire in the centre of the camp, still mounted on his pony, was Travelling Spirit.

And around him stood Black Bear and almost every adult in the village. All were talking excitedly. Travelling Spirit gestured and talked and pointed.

He had found the buffalo herd!

CHAPTER TWENTY-EIGHT

THE HUNTING party had been riding all morning. The sun was approaching its zenith.

They had started in the chill of dawn. Both man and horse had expelled small clouds of white vapour into the air. As the morning wore on it became warmer, just comfortable to ride. Now it was beginning to get hot.

One Feather had been as good as her word. Not only had Jack joined the hunting party, but he had been given his shooters and Cloud for the duration of the hunt.

It was still dark when a figure had entered the teepee where Jack was sleeping. It was One Feather.

She watched him for just a moment. Outside could be heard muttered conversation as the hunting party made ready to leave. She could hear the ponies snorting and neighing in complaint at being so early disturbed. She also heard the irregular stomping of hooves as they pranced in an effort to avoid the hostlers.

She planted a big kiss on his cheek. He turned and looked into her eyes. She was only inches from his face. He put his arms about her and drew her down.

They kissed for a long lingering moment. Then she pulled back.

"They're waiting for you," she said.

For a moment Jack did not understand.

Then she said:

"Here," and passed him his two holstered shooters. "Black Bear has ordered that you may use Cloud. Bring me some buffalo."

Jack had not waited for further explanation. He and One Feather emerged from the teepee into the dim scattered morning light. Over by the corral the shadows of men and horses moved. Some riders were already mounted and waiting.

There was no time to lose. One Feather pressed a package into his hands as they parted, he for the corral; she for the communal fire.

There had been no time to change. He still wore the clothing given to him the night before by One Feather.

Cloud nuzzled Jack, happy to see him. Jack stroked the side of her head for several seconds and then in a single swift motion mounted her.

The riders had left then without any further delay.

Jack rode in the centre of the party, whether by accident or design, he could not say.

He figured the hunting party to be about eighteen strong. Black Bear, mounted on his big stallion rode in front with his two companions. Bad Child as usual rode to his left. On his right rode Yellow Bear.

As dawn broke Jack noticed that Travelling Spirit had been permitted to ride up front for long periods of time. He also respectfully fell back from time to time, resuming his position with the rest of the party.

Jack was anxious to learn if King Bird was with the party. Finally, as dawn broke he could see King Bird, a petulant look on his face, riding with the pack. Jack studied King Bird to find whether he had any cuts or bruising on his head behind the left ear, but he was unable to see.

He saw Miserable Man. He was muttering and talking as usual.

As the daylight grew and the riders traded places he saw others who had come for the hunt.

Man-Who-Wins was there riding his black mangey cayuse. He had the reputation for great cunning as a trader. The others were always warning one another to take care when doing business with him. When trading was to be done with the Indian Agent, they always tried to enlist him to do it for them. It was said that even Black Bear had occasionally pushed him forward when dealing with the Government.

Riding with Man-Who-Wins was Love-Man. Jack knew little about Love-Man but thought him to be a particularly handsome Indian. He rode a fine small roan.

Almost immediately behind Jack rode Man-Talking-to-Another. He was perhaps the most widely travelled of the whole village. He had spent a great deal of time south of the border. He had hunted buffalo in Dakota and Montana Territory. He knew a great number of Chiefs, many of whom he claimed as friends. He had also hunted with the Black-Foot and knew Crowfoot.

He was also an experienced warrior. He was often consulted by Black Bear, the last time only a month before. At that time Black Bear with a small party including Man-Talking-to-Another, had travelled many miles to meet a party from Batoche. It was rumoured that Metis leader Dumont was present and some believed that Riel himself had been present.

80

However, Man-Talking-to-Another was most admired and sought after for something he had done nine years before. He had fought at the Battle of the Little Bighorn in 1876. Many believed that he had personally killed the boy general, the famous General Custer.

Man-Talking-to-Another never personally made that claim. Neither did he deny the story.

Man-Who-Walks was there as were many others whom Jack recognized from the village. All were armed. There were no war clubs to be seen. But there was plenty of other armament: old muzzle loaders, new Winchester breech loading rifles, several revolvers, bows and even an assortment of spears. Jack also saw many knives.

Bringing up the rear of the party were a number of younger braves, some no older than thirteen or fourteen. They rode ponies that had seen better days behind which they dragged a number of travois.

If the hunt was successful, the hunting party wanted to be sure they could transport the hides and meat back to the village.

Judging by the size of the hunting party, that might take several trips, thought Jack.

The party moved along at a trot. Just as before, Yellow Bear rode off to left and right to scout the country side. This time, however, he was joined by Travelling Spirit. A second scouting team made lengthy forays, always on the opposite flank to Yellow Bear.

As the sun moved overhead it became apparent to Jack that Black Bear was not prepared to stop for a noon break. He noticed several others around him eating from little hide bags that hung from their ponies.

Then Jack remembered the small parcel that One Feather had thrust into his hands. He opened it and found she had packed him some pemmican.

He was starved and he quickly stuffed it down. It was delicious, but gone too soon. He felt good now and was grateful to One Feather for her thoughtfulness.

He silently thanked One Feather a second time when he noticed Yellow Bear returning from the right flank at a terrific gallop. There would be no time to stop now for any reason. It could mean only one thing: he and Travelling Spirit had again spotted the buffalo herd.

Jack looked at the sky. He figured the time to be about two-thirty.

Immediately Black Bear reigned his horse about. Yellow Bear reigned in his horse coming to a dead halt from a fast gallop. His horse snorted and stomped, then shook its foaming mouth with a shudder.

Miserable Man, Man-Who-Wins, Travelling Spirit and Man-Talking-to-Another joined Bad Child and Yellow Bear in the pow-wow with Black Bear.

Jack could see Yellow Bear gracefully moving his arms about as he spoke. Several times he raised himself on his horse to point to distant rises in the plain.

Abruptly the conference ended, the leaders broke away to motion over other riders assigned to their group.

Miserable Man nodded to Jack who cantered his horses over to find Travelling Spirit and several others in the same party.

He was relieved to note that King Bird had been assigned to Yellow Bear. Quite unconsciously King Bird had gingerly covered the left side of his head on several occasions.

CHAPTER TWENTY-NINE

OF COURSE Jack had never experienced a buffalo hunt before. However he had been hunting back east. It was no surprise therefore that the party did not gallop off with great eclat into the hunt. He knew, without the necessity of being told, that that way they would alert and perhaps stampede the herd.

The wind blew very gently from the north west. Great care was exercised to ensure none of the hunters found himself to windward of the buffalo.

Miserable Man, Jack, Travelling Spirit and two others moved off to take up a flanking position far to the east of the central body of the hunting party. Before he rode off, Jack noticed two men in his party scoop up a number of large buffalo robes from the travois.

The five riders skirted the foot of a long ridge to their left. They moved at a canter, occasionally they slowed to a walk. A sparse scattering of trees covered the most northerly reaches of the ridge. They picked their way through.

Gradually they crested the ridge and Miserable Man immediately stopped the party to survey the land ahead.

At first Jack's view was obstructed by trees. He moved Cloud several feet and looked down the ridge, and slightly to the west.

Before them on a treeless plain stood an enormous herd of buffalo. Jack did not count them, but guessed there must be more than eighty, perhaps as many as a hundred. Some were grazing, others simply stood idle. Still others walked slowly about, occasionally raising their great heads as though to sniff the winds. Some were completely indifferent and lay on the ground. Several rolled on their backs vigorously as though to drive away an aggravating itch.

Jack watched, transfixed at the mammoth herd below. He had never seen so many wild animals run free in nature.

Then Miserable Man spoke:

"We will take as many as possible without guns. Black Bear has decided it will be impossible to use the jumping pound."

"Jumping pound?" said Jack. He was immediately sorry that he spoke. Miserable Man glowered at this ignorant remark and the others quietly chuckled. Travelling Spirit pulled at the sleeve of Jack's shirt. He moved his head sideways to the left.

Miserable Man continued:

"You and you," he said, pointing at Travelling Spirit and Jack, "take buffalo robes. Ride carefully down there." He pointed far to the north east, the far easterly end of the herd near the tree line.

"Leave your ponies well back in the trees. They must not hear you." He was referring to the buffalo.

"Travelling Spirit will show you what to do."

He turned to the others:

"We will be down there." He pointed straight down to the centre of the eastern flank of the herd.

"You two," again he pointed, "Bring buffalo robes."

The robes were divided and before Jack could say anything the party dispersed. He wanted to ask questions. What was a jumping pound? Why could they not use it? What was he expected to do? Why did he need a buffalo robe?

He followed Travelling Spirit. He hoped that soon Travelling Spirit would explain what was about to happen, what was expected of him.

They made their way down the hillside. Brownish black rotten leaves covered the floor of the forest. Jack found they muffled the sound of the ponies' hooves.

When the two of them were one hundred and fifty feet from the forest edge Travelling Spirit stopped and dismounted. Jack did the same.

Travelling Spirit squatted there in front of his horse and when Jack did too, Travelling Spirit began to speak in a voice so low that Jack found he had to strain to hear his words.

"The jumping pound is over there," he pointed east, "Many miles from here."

"What is a jumping pound?" asked Jack.

Travelling Spirit cleared away the dead leaves, twigs and debris from a small patch of earth.

"We can kill many buffalo when we use the jumping pound," he said.

He began to draw quickly on the earth. He drew a "V" shape that ended against two parallel lines.

"That is a cliff or steep river bank," he said. "Up there," he pointed east in a steep cut, on a ravine. It is very deep. We have planted many sharp stakes in that ravine.

"This and this," he pointed to the "V", "is a barrier of stumps and tree trunks. Gradually they come close together here," he pointed to the bottom of the "V", "where the cliff is."

Jack began to understand.

Travelling Spirit went on. "We drive the herd east toward the wide end of the V. The buffalo are guided into the jumping pound."

"But why do you not use it now?" asked Jack.

"To drive the herd that way we must surround the herd to the north. We cannot do that for the wind would carry our scent to the buffalo. They would stampede long before we got into position.

"Anyway," he said, "We do not have enough men to guide the herd. The pound is many miles away."

"But, but…" Jack started.

"Hold!" Travelling Spirit said. He held up his hand, palm out facing Jack. "You talk too much, we have no time now."

His face was stern. For the second time that day Jack felt foolish.

Then suddenly Travelling Spirit's face broke into a smile. "You like my sister One Feather?" he said.

Jack blushed, embarrassed.

"Come," he said, "Let us kill buffalo for One Feather!"

With quick movements he took the two buffalo robes and passed one to Jack. Then he handed Jack a bow and some arrows.

"Do not use your shooters," he said.

Jack tucked the arrows into the waist band of his breech cloth. He then imitated Travelling Spirit, pulled the buffalo robe over his back and head, securing it loosely around his arms, his chest and his neck.

Travelling Spirit crouched. He was completely hidden from view. Even his head was covered.

Jack found that though the fur and hide came under his chin and about his face, he could still see very well. The hide smelled musty, but Jack did not find it unpleasant.

He crouched beside Travelling Spirit on hands and knees.

"Do not shoot unless you are certain to kill," said Travelling Spirit. "You will kill if your arrow is true, here, here and here," he said, pointing to eyes, then sweeping his hand back to ears and neck in turn.

"It is no use shooting to wound. That will only cause much agony to the buffalo. It will alarm the other buffalo. We must kill as many buffalo like this as we can."

Then he added, "If your bow is strong and your draw is powerful you may kill here," he pointed to his upper ribs. "But that is dangerous and unreliable."

"We will be very close to the buffalo. You will see. Do nothing to alarm them. A stampede could kill many braves."

He gave Jack no time for questions or second thoughts: "Come," he said and crawled quietly and slowly toward the edge of the trees.

Jack followed. The floor of the forest was dank. The sun, shining through the leaves and branches as they shifted in the wind, speckled the ground with sunlight.

Jack moved alongside Travelling Spirit until they were about to emerge from the tree line. Then Travelling Spirit signalled Jack to move off and keep some distance.

Jack now crawled slowly across the plain. The grass was quite tall and green. As the wind blew, the grass moved in graceful wavelike motion.

He could smell the herd. It reminded him faintly of the livestock smell of the livery stable back in Cobourg.

For a moment then, his present situation struck him as odd. What am I doing here stalking buffalo, he asked himself. I am supposed to be fighting for my country. I must report for duty, I must report on bluecoat.

But he found in that brief moment of distraction he was moving too fast. He thrust every thought out of his mind except the business at hand. But he moved on very slowly and carefully.

With a glance to his right he saw Travelling Spirit within thirty-five feet of the herd.

Jack stopped and looked left. For over to the west he saw several others stalking buffalo.

Then he heard a 'thunk' sound followed by a slight grunt. He looked again to his right just in time to see a buffalo slump to the ground, an arrow behind its eye.

It moved not a muscle. It was dead before it hit the ground, thought Jack.

Jack moved forward again.

When he first saw the buffalo from above, the animals resembled nothing so much as dark beetles scattered across the plain. Now, as he moved to within thirty feet of one large buffalo, it was quite different.

It was a male and it was huge. Jack remained stock still. He saw the brown hooded eyes look at him. Was it with curiosity wondered Jack, or was it with indifference. Its head went down for a moment as if to graze, then came right back up. It's looking at me, thought Jack. He dared not even breathe.

Its head, neck, upper torso and front legs were all covered with a gorgeous rich cinnamon colored fur. Jack could even see it ruffle occasionally in the wind. The fur on the lower part of its body was much shorter and of a slightly darker brown. The buffalo switched its tail now and then to disturb the odd fly.

Jack turned his attention once again to the head of the buffalo. It had a yellowish white horn about eight inches behind and slightly above its ever watchful eye.

Just between these two and slightly below thought Jack.

At that very moment the animal shuddered, shook its head up and down twice and stomped the sod with its left hind hoof.

Stop dreaming said Jack to himself. You don't have time to admire the beast. Kill, when you have opportunity. He mentally shook himself as if trying to wake from a dream.

The animal dropped its head once again to graze. Then it came up chewing. Otherwise it was motionless.

Jack slowly brought up his right foot and planted it on the ground. He raised the bow and with his left hand slotted an arrow to the bowstring. The arrow now rested on his right hand at the bow.

Slowly he drew back on the arrow with his left hand. The bow was flexible but very strong. Up a little he said to himself, and took aim for a spot below and to the right of the point at which the horn met the head.

The head of the bull buffalo was perfectly motionless now. Jack drew a breath, held it, and then released the arrow.

He did not see it in flight. But he heard the "thunk" as it struck.

He could see it, sunk about seven inches into the head of the buffalo.

Then the buffalo simply collapsed.

Jack suppressed a primitive urge to shout. He looked to his left, then to his right. It was as though this moment had not happened. Nothing moved. Everything remained the same.

Even the buffalo went on as before. They took no notice of their fallen member.

He could see Travelling Spirit now stalking another buffalo. This one was at least seventy yards northerly of Jack.

Jack turned his attention back to the nearest animal. There was another buffalo grazing about fifty yards west of him and he began to make his way in that direction.

This buffalo had strayed some distance from the herd. Out of the corner of his eye Jack could see the main herd, somnolent under the Spring sun, some distance to the north, and west. He was amazed at how quiet it was. All these animals, and apart from an occasional grunt, all he heard was a cricket chirping nearby.

He wondered how the rest of the party was faring. It had appeared to him that the hunters were positioned along the south and slightly to the west of the herd with King Bird and several others detailed to the far north west flanking position.

King Bird had been well armed with the latest Winchester in addition to the bow and arrows.

Jack felt secure, knowing King Bird was so far away. His mind dwelt for a moment on how well armed the hunting party was; all the latest in firearms.

Once again he turned his attention back to the matter at hand.

He could only move a few feet at a time. Any more may startle or arouse the herd. It took a long time to place himself in position, though it seemed only minutes to Jack.

Now he was within shooting distance, only thirty feet away. But the buffalo was facing him, its head down tearing grass. The buffalo brought its head up chewing. It looked directly at Jack. It seemed to stare at Jack for an age. Then it stopped chewing but continued to watch Jack.

Abruptly it turned right and took two ponderous steps. It now presented a perfect target.

Jack took aim and released a powerful shot. The arrow struck with such force the animal seemed to stagger for a moment. The arrow had completely pierced the neck of the buffalo. It took several more steps as it shook its head violently from side to side, as though to shed the arrow. Its mouth opened as if to roar but no sound emerged. Then the beast crumpled. After a moment its hind leg twitched several times.

Jack watched it for several more minutes. It no longer moved.

He turned to survey the herd. He estimated the nearest buffalo to be at least three hundred feet distant. Far to his right crouched Travelling Spirit. He had just made another kill and he too was far removed from the herd.

Jack contemplated the scene, trying to decide on which direction to move. The sun was intense up above and it was hot under the robe. The must smell began to bother him. He wondered how much longer the hunt would continue.

Then just as he was about to move he sensed a stirring in the herd. Their heads were up and not an animal was chewing.

As if by magic the entire herd began to move. They walked and then they trotted. Some turned to move in closer to others.

For a moment it was difficult to discern in just which direction they were moving.

Then suddenly it was clear. The entire herd was moving off to the north west.

The minutes seemed like seconds. Jack sensed real danger to Travelling Spirit and himself.

A shot rang out far across the plain to the north west. As one, the herd seemed to falter.

Jack stood. He threw off his robe and with all the power his lungs could command sent a high pitched piercing whistle in the direction of Cloud.

A second shot rang out. It too seemed to come from the north west. Simultaneously the entire herd wheeled in a clockwise motion. They moved together, as if with a single mind.

A thought flashed through Jack's mind. Just like a swarm of wasps. Then he saw Cloud galloping toward him across the grass.

CHAPTER THIRTY

THE HERD'S momentum had increased. From a low rumble the pounding of hooves had became a roar. The herd had done a complete reversal in direction and now headed south east.

It was difficult to see if they would come around as far as Jack, but Travelling Spirit was directly in their path.

The panic of the herd was palpable. They shifted from a canter to a gallop and then to a furious gallop.

Travelling Spirit too saw he was in imminent danger. He stood. He threw off his robe. He ran a few steps, stumbled, regained his footing and then throwing aside his bow began to run in earnest.

The speed of the herd at full gallop was awesome. Travelling Spirit lost ground at every step.

Cloud bore down upon Jack at full gallop. She and Jack had practised this many times in the past. With only slightly diminished speed she breasted Jack who scooped his left hand under and around her neck near the withers. In a continuous graceful movement Jack levered himself up onto the back of Cloud. The two now raced off after Travelling Spirit. He was running easterly as though he were trying to outrun the stampeding herd. Jack could see he was hoping to make it to the safety of the trees.

The herd was pounding along to Jack's left now. It was also moving easterly. Nothing could be heard above the roar of hoofbeats. Clouds of dust rose from the prairie over the shifting crashing relentless herd of animals.

Ahead, Travelling Spirit ran for his very life. The herd was now within thirty feet of him. He stole a glance back to see the animals spread out behind him on either side.

He also saw Jack astride his white pony riding to the right of the herd.

Jack reigned her over to the left in the ten feet remaining between the stampeding buffalo and Travelling Spirit.

"Ha, Ha," shouted Jack. Travelling Spirit turned. Cloud appeared to be running at the head of the herd.

He saw Jack. He stumbled. But as he did so his left arm came up, reaching to Jack.

Jack bent across Cloud, his head and body flat along the right side of her neck. His right hand slipped under Travelling Spirit's upraised arm. His vice-like grip seized Travelling Spirit above the elbow and, as if they had practised this all their lives, Jack swung Travelling Spirit up behind him.

The herd was pounding on the heels of Cloud. The second passenger seemed to make no difference to her. Travelling Spirit threw his arms around Jack's waist as Cloud surged ahead of the herd.

Suddenly the roar of the stampeding beasts which had been all around them fell away. Cloud galloped in a great arc to the right. After clearing to the right running edge of the stampede, Jack drove Cloud back along the tree line. The buffalo galloped not thirty feet away.

"Here," shouted Jack, reigning in his pony. Cloud came to a sudden halt and Travelling Spirit leaped off at a run.

Within moments he had returned astride his own pony, Winchester in hand.

What now, thought Jack. But he soon found out.

With a wave of his rifle, Travelling Spirit started off at a gallop after the buffalo.

For a moment Jack hesitated. Then with a light prod of his heels Cloud bolted after him.

CHAPTER THIRTY-ONE

THE HERD was already more than a quarter of a mile ahead of them. Travelling Spirit and Jack bore down on their ponies to catch up.

To his left through the dust Jack could see a few other Indians in hot pursuit. He could not make out who they were. Now and then he heard the popping of shots far away. Some must be close enough to fire he thought, and he urged Cloud into greater speed.

Travelling Spirit had gradually moved to the left. That put the buffalo dead ahead of him but still too far ahead. In order to avoid clouds of dust Jack kept to the right flank of the herd, riding along the tree line.

Soon Jack and Travelling Spirit were within two hundred and fifty yards of the buffalo. The herd pounded on with unflagging speed.

He heard the sharp report of a nearby gun. It was Travelling Spirit firing.

No buffalo fell. He must have missed, thought Jack.

Driving on with determination Jack soon put himself within reasonable distance for a shot with hand guns. Cloud reduced her gallop and maintained a constant distance. They continued this way for a few hundred yards. Then Jack drew his right shooter.

Holding the reigns in his left hand he slowly moved Cloud left to allow a good view to the right of her mane, of the rear right flank of the buffalo herd.

Relaxed now and riding easy he let off his first shot.

Nothing.

He was sure he had taken good aim. But he had missed.

A second shot brought the same result. Meanwhile he had heard several more shots from Travelling Spirit and on the second a single buffalo stumbled and fell. Jack saw it rise on its front legs and strain to get up. It was no use. It collapsed again. This time to stay down.

This time I will not miss, he thought. He and Cloud shot forward until he was within thirty feet of the trailing animal.

This time when he fired there were immediate results. The animal caved in front, its forelegs collapsing. Then the enormous body of the animal somersaulted forward only ten feet ahead of Cloud.

"Stay down," Jack shouted at the animal, fearful of a collision. He saw the animal, as if in slow motion, slowly fall beneath Cloud's powerful front legs. Simultaneously Jack felt the sensation of lift and forward thrust. First her mane rose, then Jack. His hips were thrust forward in the saddle, then his body followed.

Cloud's hoof beats ceased for a moment. Then it was down and on again at a relentless gallop.

He fired again and he heard another shot from Travelling Spirit. Another two buffalo fell, this time well out of his path.

Through the dust he saw the great stampeding herd begin to split. Over the thunderous pounding of a hundred hooves, he heard falsetto cries:

"Hi, Hi, Hi,"

He heard a volley of shooting, this time at the sky.

What caused the great herd to split he did not know but he saw two thirds of the herd stampede to the left.

He heard more shouts far to the left and more shooting. He made a move to follow the main herd. As he moved left Travelling Spirit galloped within fifteen feet of him and began to shout:

"No, No!"

Jack looked over, puzzled.

In the din he heard Travelling Spirit shout:

"Pound, pound!"

"What?" shouted Jack.

"The pound, the jumping pound."

The words began to sink in. He wanted to use the jumping pound.

"That way," he shouted. He raised his right arm straight forward in the direction of the much reduced heard.

"How far?" shouted Jack.

Travelling Spirit did not hear him.

"How far?" Jack shouted again.

"Not far. Not far." he shouted back.

Then he shouted:

"Take the right flank. I'll take the left. Keep them going."

With that last instruction Travelling Spirit rode off to cover the left flank.

The tree line and ridge formed a natural barrier to the right. Jack's only problem was to keep the stampede going. He took up shouting and firing like he had heard the others do. Whenever the herd showed any sign of flagging he let off another round of shooting and shouting.

Far to his left he saw Travelling Spirit work the entire side of the herd. Sometimes forward and sometimes back, he rode and shouted and screamed to keep the herd on track.

To cover the left rear Jack found he had to ride back and forth across the entire stern of the herd.

Now and then he let off a shot directly at a buffalo, but moving so much he had difficulty getting a good aim. Once however, a large bull dropped out of the pack and fell. He noticed the surrounding animals balk for just a moment. He decided to try no more kills until he reached the jumping pound.

Then he heard more screaming. He looked over to see Travelling Spirit waving at him frantically. He saw him point ahead.

Jack looked. Ahead to the left a long arm of stumps and fallen trees reached out to embrace the stampeding herd. The ridge on his right dropped abruptly giving way to a similar arm to the right. They converged over a distance of three hundred yards to within fifty feet of each other, and after that, was nothing.

The land just seemed to end. Beyond, Jack saw only the far bank of a Coulee.

The buffalo galloped into the waiting arms of the jumping pound and off the abyss waiting for them.

Jack reigned up to watch. A few stragglers at the rear slowed to a trot. It was almost as though they knew what awaited them.

Then Jack heard the report of a rifle and one dropped to the ground. The two remaining buffalo had stopped. They did not move. It was as though they knew their time had come. Either way lay death, and they waited, resigned. Another shot and then another. The last two remaining buffalo had dropped dead at the lip of the cliff.

The sudden silence was awesome. The thundering hooves had ceased.

At first Jack felt elated. Then slightly embarrassed and finally, vaguely ashamed.

A few buffalo had not been killed by the fall. Their cries of pain and terror could be heard faintly from below.

Travelling Spirit climbed down the face of the ravine to administer the coup de grâce. Jack declined to help. He lent a shooter to Travelling Spirit instead.

CHAPTER THIRTY-TWO

THE TRIP back seemed much shorter than the trip out.

Jack looked again at the sky. The sun had not moved much. Only several hours had passed since the hunt began.

The party was smaller now. The younger braves had been left to guard the kill and begin the process of skinning. They would be joined later by others from the camp. The travois would be well used over the next few days.

Miraculously no one had been killed or injured in the stampede. Miserable Man had ridden ahead with Black Bear for many miles on the return trip. Then he had fallen back and had taken up a position to the left of Jack.

It was from Miserable Man that Jack learned what had happened.

Against instructions, King Bird had taken his rifle into the field. He had panicked when the disturbance shook the tranquillity of the herd. He had fired a shot to turn the herd away from him, then a second shot for good measure.

Miserable Man suspected that King Bird had moved too far north. The buffalo had sensed his presence from the wind and had begun to panic.

No one knew what had caused the herd to divide. Some in the hunting party had managed to follow the main herd but most had not. It had soon dispersed and no more buffalo had been killed.

Strangely, no one was resentful toward King Bird. The hunt had ended in a great, if unexpected, success. Everyone was in a good mood.

King Bird was hinting that he had deliberately stampeded the herd knowing there would be a greater kill at the jumping pound. As far as Jack could tell, no one believed him. But then, no one seemed to care. No one took the trouble to dispute him.

The hunt had been rewarded by success. That was all that mattered.

It was from Miserable Man that Jack learned Black Bear was grateful to him. Travelling Spirit had told how Jack had saved his life. Everyone knew about it.

As they rode in the late afternoon sun, brave after brave sidled up to Jack to ride alongside for a few minutes. Some said nothing, that action alone being sufficient to show respect. Others complimented him on his fine pony and his horsemanship. Still others were open in their admiration, paying him lavish compliments. King Bird remained aloof; his resentment only growing.

Fatigue began to set in. As dusk approached, Jack's mind was not on compliments. He felt good in the company of such fine horsemen and hunters. But his mind was on the Rangers, his military comrades.

Jack knew that by now the entire company of Rangers would have arrived in the West with the North West Field Force. His duty was there, with them.

As painful as it would be to leave One Feather and as difficult to leave the comradeship he had known that day, he had to go. He had to return to his unit. And it must be soon. He prayed that it was not already too late, that battle had not already been joined, that bluecoat had not already struck.

Perhaps Black Bear would demonstrate his gratitude. Perhaps he would now release Jack and Hogie.

At twilight they rode into camp. He dismounted and a brave took the reigns of his pony and led her off to the paddock. Another brave sheepishly put out his hands for the shooters.

He now knew his hopes were in vain. It was not to be. He walked back to his teepee in despair.

That night the mood in the camp was jubilant. There was great celebration.

Jack remained in his teepee. He was dejected. Whatever the future might hold, he knew his present duty was to return to his unit. Although he had resolved to see Hogie free he knew that nothing must stand in his way. He must make an effort to escape.

He heard voices drifting up from the communal fire. He thought he heard Travelling Spirit speak. Then he heard King Bird. He could make out nothing of what was said, but he heard laughter and at one point a loud cheer.

He was curious but not curious enough to go down to the fire and learn what was happening. Anyway, he knew there would be much bragging from King Bird and not a few lies. And there would be much exaggeration from the others. Like all hunters, the exaggeration over many re-tellings would ferment and one day mature into fact.

He was lying on a buffalo robe. A small fire flickered in the centre of the tent. He could see a narrow corner of night sky through the chimney. As he pondered his predicament he heard a faint brush against the teepee. Then the flap was thrown back and One Feather entered.

She held her finger to her lips to ensure silence.

"I cannot stay," she said. "But I had to see you. I have heard what you did. All of my people admire what you have done. Travelling Spirit says that you have earned your freedom."

Jack's heart gave a leap. Just as quickly his hopes were dashed.

"King Bird argued against this. He claims he has credit for many buffalo. Even your jumping pound buffalo. He is strutting and boasting. They are quite amused by his stories."

"What about my freedom?" interrupted Jack. "What does Black Bear say?"

"Travelling Spirit has asked my father to release you. But King Bird and his braves say you have not proved you are a great hunter, you have not proved that you are as brave as Black Bear's hunters. He says anyone could have done what you did. He speaks with great conviction. Many now have doubts."

"What can I do One Feather?" he asked. "I must go and Hogie must go with me."

"Tomorrow night there will be a Sundance. That is not our custom, but King Bird has persuaded Black Bear and the others."

"King Bird will do the Sundance. He says he is not afraid. He will prove how brave he is, that he is not afraid of pain. He says that you are not brave. You are a coward. You will not do the Sundance."

"Why should I do the Sundance, One Feather? Why should I prove anything?"

"I know you are not a coward. I know you are brave," she said.

"Why would I do the Sundance then, for King Bird?"

"No," she said. "Not for King Bird but for Black Bear."

"I don't understand. For Black Bear? Why for Black Bear?"

"Black Bear has said if you and Hogie do the Sundance tomorrow, he will set you free!"

Freedom! thought Jack. But at such a price.

"I must go," she continued. "Early tomorrow I will ride to the jumping pound. I must help with the buffalo. I will be back by dusk."

She paused and for a long time they looked at one another.

Then she said, "Do not do the Sundance."

"One Feather," he said, "Tomorrow night when you return, will you leave your pony at lonesome pine. Do not bring your pony to the paddock. Leave it by the tree. Will you do that for me?"

She did not answer the question. She thought for a time as she looked at him. Her large brown eyes were brimming with tears.

He tried to speak but could not.

Then she said simply, "You will come back."

She brushed his lips with her own and then she was gone.

CHAPTER THIRTY-THREE

JACK DID not sleep that night. He was restless and he was thinking. As the first scattering of light from the dawn filtered down the chimney of the teepee he heard the party leave on horseback for the jumping pound. One Feather was gone. A great feeling of loneliness welled up inside Jack.

That day he did little. He slept some and about noon wandered over to Ah-Pay's teepee.

She had heard about the hunt. Her affection and admiration for Jack was obvious.

They sat and chatted by the fire for an hour, as she plied him with one culinary delight after another.

As he was about to leave Miserable Man walked by on his way to the paddock. Jack excused himself and caught up to him. They exchanged a few pleasantries and then Jack asked Miserable Man if he could arrange a visit for him with the prisoner, Hogie.

Miserable Man was agreeable. He said he would see what he could do.

He was as good as his word. About three o'clock Man-Who-Walks came by to take him over to the lockup.

The latch was thrown and Jack walked in. Hogie was surprised. At first he did not recognize Jack who still wore his Indian clothes. After the initial shock, when he did recognize Jack, he clamoured with questions.

Locked up as he had been he knew nothing of what had been going on since Jack's release. It took some time for Jack to bring him up to date.

When Jack told him about the hunt he leaned forward with interest. He exclaimed about the number of buffalo. Such a herd had not been seen for years on the northern plains.

Then Jack told him of the narrow escape of Travelling Spirit and Hogie whistled under his breath.

Finally Jack told Hogie about King Bird and the offer that had been made by Black Bear: if they took part in the Sundance they would be given their freedom.

"I don't mind dancing," Hogie said eagerly, "as long as they set me free!"

"I don't think you quite understand," said Jack.

He then went on to explain to Hogie what a Sundance was and what took place at a Sundance.

Hogie winced when he heard the part Jack and he were destined to play.

"We're not going to wait for the Sundance," Jack went on. "It's at midnight tonight. We're going to escape before that.

"Be ready. Somehow I'll get you out of here. And before midnight too."

CHAPTER THIRTY-FOUR

AS THE afternoon wore on, Jack noticed a great deal of activity in the camp. Black Bear was deep in conversation with the elders and some strangers. Several of the strangers were not Indians. People moved to and fro. Many braves were cleaning weapons and checking and distributing ammunition. Jack knew these were not preparations for another buffalo hunt. That would not be necessary for some time to come.

Hogie's reaction to his appearance had given Jack an idea. After retrieving several pieces of charcoal from the communal fire he retreated to his teepee where he remained the rest of the day.

Toward dusk he had an unexpected visitor. Miserable Man came up to his teepee. After exchanging several words of greeting Jack fully expected him to leave. But he did not. He took up a position directly in front of the entrance, sat down, and crossed his legs. He was going nowhere.

And neither was Jack. He was not sure of the nature of Miserable Man's visit. Was it to keep him company before the Sundance, to ensure his courage did not flag? Was it to distract him from unpleasant thoughts about the coming ceremony? Or was Miserable Man just plain guard?

Jack concluded he was a little bit of all of these.

For a while Miserable Man muttered to himself, then, for a while, he sang quietly.

Jack brought him a willow back rest. He squatted beside him for a while.

Miserable Man chuckled softly. Then, without looking at Jack, he said:

"You have great courage."

"No," said Jack. "But I must leave. I must go back to my chief. I have been too long away."

"Yes, you have great courage."

"If I take part in the ceremony Black Bear will let me go back. Return to my chief."

"When you finish the ceremony you will be a brave. You can stay here with us."

"No," said Jack. "I will leave."

"King Bird would like you to leave."

"Yes," said Jack.

"So," said Miserable Man, "stay here in our village." He laughed quietly to himself.

"King Bird would not like that." His shoulders shook with silent mirth.

"King Bird is without courage."

"King Bird?" said Jack surprised.

"King Bird," he said and nodded. "He will find an excuse not to do the Sundance, I think."

He nodded again in confirmation of his speculation. Then he said:

"Standing Ready will be first."

"Not me?" enquired Jack.

"No, not you. Standing Ready. He is a slave to King Bird. He thinks King Bird will be chief one day. That will never happen. King Bird told him to be first. He will be first. He will do what King Bird orders him to do."

"Who's to be second." asked Jack.

"The prisoner," said Miserable Man.

"You mean Hogie, the White Man?" said Jack.

Miserable Man pointed in the direction of the lockup.

"Yes the White Man. The trespasser."

"Then who? Who's next?"

"You," he turned to look at Jack and smiled his toothless smile.

"And King Bird last?" asked Jack.

"Yes. But maybe no," he answered. "I think he will find reasons not to do it. This is not for us. He talked Black Bear into this. It is not true Cree. It is not our way. He wants to show off. Maybe he will find an excuse. Change his mind. We will see."

Darkness had fallen. Jack could not see the face of Miserable Man, only his dark shape. The conversation seemed to have ended so Jack got up and re-entered the teepee.

There was no longer any reason to wait. Miserable Man was not going to move until it was time to take Jack down for the ceremony.

Jack took the charcoal and busied himself blackening his hair. His hair had grown very long. It took more time and more charcoal then expected.

As he worked he heard the drums begin. They sounded a slow rhythm. After a while the men gathered around the communal fire and began to chant.

Jack quickened his work. He did not know how long the ceremony would proceed before the first "brave" would be brought forth.

After completely blackening his hair he began to work on his face. He heard the tempo of the drumbeat accelerate just a notch. He had a lot of skin yet to cover. But he was soon finished, thanks to the shirt and leggings.

Jack heard the rhythmic crying of the celebrants.

Suddenly he was startled. Miserable Man had joined in. He sounded loud and discordant right outside the teepee. Jack had not lit a fire inside the teepee. Neither had he lit any candles. In the darkness he rummaged deep in the pile of buffalo robes until he found what he was looking for. A war club.

Without waiting a moment he moved softly over to the teepee entrance.

All that could be seen was a hand arcing over the head of Miserable Man. With a soft "thunk" the chanting stopped and Miserable Man's head slumped forward.

The willow back rest was solid. It held Miserable Man's body in place. He appeared merely to be resting.

CHAPTER THIRTY-FIVE

JACK STEPPED from the teepee in the darkness. The chorus of chanting that came from the camp centre and the tempo of drums again increased. It gave Jack the urge to hurry.

I must not, thought Jack. Take your time, he told himself. Be careful not to draw attention.

Staying well back, on the edge of the camp, he made his way from tree to tree.

He could see the fire about a hundred and seventy feet away. It lit the circle of brown faces surrounding it.

Their attention is firmly fixed on the ceremony, thought Jack. They will not take notice of me.

Suddenly a pan banged and a sharp voice spoke.

Jack froze. Slowly he turned his head. He looked down from the trees toward the camp. Twenty feet away a woman scolded a child. The child began to cry.

Jack breathed a silent prayer of relief.

He had about a hundred yards to go to the paddock entrance. Perhaps there will be no guard tonight, with the ceremony, and Miserable Man to guard me, he thought.

Just then the chanting took a loud leap in volume, shaking Jack visibly. He stopped for a moment to gather his determination. It was two against several hundred people, he thought. Then he tried to dismiss this from his mind.

The ceremony was quite obviously reaching a new stage. He looked over at the fire. A brave was suspended fifteen feet over the celebrants. His body still moved slowly up and down as the tree suspending him settled down.

Hogie's next, thought Jack. He forced his eyes away from the scene.

He grew more careful as he approached the gate of the paddock. He stopped. For a moment he saw no one. Then he saw movement in the darkness.

"A guard!" he exclaimed under his breath.

He took a few more steps toward the gate. The Indian guard turned. What he saw took his breath away.

King Bird!

King Bird paced slowly back and forth. In his waistband glinted steel. He was armed with a knife.

For some time Jack remained in the shadows. He surveyed the scene. He measured the distance to King Bird, with his eyes. To approach in a rush would provide too much warning.

Then he realized how foolish that would be. He had forgotten his attire. Why else had he so painstakingly charcoaled up his body?

He thought about Miserable Man, about their conversation. Jack had experience of King Bird. Miserable Man could say what he liked. Jack knew differently. From his own experience he knew King Bird was not a coward. King Bird is a braggart and he likes to strut. His deed never measures up to his word. How could it? Miserable Man simply disliked King Bird, so he misjudged him. King Bird was no coward.

And Jack knew from personal experience he was powerful, treacherous and crafty.

Another change in pitch and tempo down by the fire drew Jack's attention. Standing Ready was still swaying over the heads of the gathering. Why the change, thought Jack.

Then he saw the reason. Hogie was being escorted through the crowd toward the centre of the gathering. Pushed would more accurately describe the process; two Indians maintained steady pressure on his back. His steps were taken only to avoid falling forward on his face.

There is no more time to lose, thought Jack.

He walked on. He tried to appear normal. As he came to within twenty feet of the corral King Bird turned. He saw Jack but before he could speak Jack spoke:

"I came to relieve you."

"So soon?" replied King Bird.

"Yellow Bear asked me to."

"Why?"

"He said you may enjoy yourself down there. The White Man is next."

"That quickly?" said King Bird, and for the first time Jack sensed a nervous note in King Bird's voice. He has wanted this for so long, thought Jack. He has pushed for it. Now it's here. Is it possible he believed it would never happen? The time would never arrive?

"Hurry down," Jack continued. "See the trespasser shake. He's not so brave as you."

King Bird remained rooted to the spot. His eyes rivetted on the happening down by the fire.

Now Jack was almost at his side.

Slowly King Bird tore his eyes away from the Sundance, to look at Jack.

"You!" he shouted, and lunged for Jack.

Jack neatly sidestepped leaving his left leg for King Bird. Over flew the Indian. He landed on his side but in a second had rolled to a crouch on his feet. The knife was in his hand.

"Now I'm going to kill you," he said. His voice was even and deadly.

Jack faced him, legs apart, arms out and forward. Ready for any move by King Bird.

King Bird flipped the knife from left hand to right. The blade flashed menacingly. Jack shifted slightly on his feet.

King Bird now held the knife blade up. Slowly he rose. He stood on the balls of his feet facing Jack. He looked light and quick.

He moved right and Jack, facing him, slowly shifted to his right maintaining relative position.

"Corrupt white devil," snarled King Bird.

Jack said nothing. He only watched warily. He wished he had brought the war club.

Suddenly King Bird rushed Jack. He slashed left and right with the knife. The tip flicked the sleeve of Jack's shirt. Each time Jack managed to shift and jump in retreat.

"You have the knife, King Bird," he said, "not I." He cupped his hand and beckoned King Bird forward with his fingers. "Come on. Come on."

King Bird continued to circle. He glared his hatred at Jack.

"You are not worthy of One Feather," he hissed. He slashed again as he finished this statement.

Again Jack dodged successfully.

I'm distracting him, thought Jack.

"King Bird is only a coward!" he said. "Come on, come on 'Coward Bird'."

With that King Bird's fury grew. He slashed wildly toward Jack's outstretched arm.

Jack snapped his hand back quickly. Each time King Bird missed.

"Come on Coward Bird. Slave Bird. You are not a King Bird, you are a weasel. One Feather is too good for you. Never would she go to your teepee. She laughs at you."

That was too much for King Bird. Throwing aside all caution he rushed Jack, slashing.

Jack dodged several times, then ducked and came inside the slashing arms. He hit King Bird a blow with his fist striking him squarely on the jaw. King Bird staggered back, stunned.

Jack pressed his advantage. He pounded King Bird with left and right. King Bird fell back dazed, then he stumbled.

Jack leaped on him. He grabbed his right wrist, King Bird strained to throw Jack off, to release his knife hand. His left hand beat at Jack's face and ear. Jack struggled to capture this hand too.

Suddenly King Bird had a rock in his left hand. It rocketed up.

Jack felt the blow to his neck. He rolled away. For a moment he was stunned and totally disoriented. The pain was intense.

Too late he saw King Bird leaping for him. The Indian landed with a force that knocked the wind from Jack's lungs. Just in time, however, he grabbed King Bird's right hand as the knife flashed toward his neck.

Jack found he had little strength to hold the knife hand from moving upward toward his chin.

Applying all his strength now, King Bird forced his advantage. The knife inched forward. Jack could feel its cold sharp tip scrape across his throat.

While his left hand tried to hold off the knife, his right flailed around trying to find a vulnerable spot.

King Bird's face was pressed up against Jack's. Jack felt the sweat pour from his skin. He heard the fast heavy breathing of King Bird. The right temple of King Bird's head pressed hard against the right side of Jack's head.

Suddenly Jack brought his right hand across in a powerful blow to King Bird's left ear. Simultaneously he moved his own head violently to the left and released his grip on King Bird's hand. The pressure suddenly gone, King Bird's head and neck suddenly shifted four deadly inches to the right as his hand shot forward plunging the knife into his own throat.

Jack pushed. King Bird rolled off Jack. The only breathing Jack heard was his own. The knife was buried to the hilt where King Bird's neck met his chin.

Jack watched hypnotized. King Bird was on his back, his right hand stretched out. The fingers were contorted and rigid. His body arched, only his shoulders and his feet touched the earth. His legs slowly, mindlessly, walked his body to the left. Then with a rattle and a swift expulsion of breath, the arch collapsed. The body was still.

King Bird was dead.

CHAPTER THIRTY-SIX

JACK SAT there dazed. He stared at the body.

Gradually the sound of drums and chanting penetrated his consciousness.

"Hogie!" he exclaimed in a whisper.

He jumped to his feet. Without a glance back he threw open the gate and rushed inside.

As he ran toward Cloud the other ponies shifted and trotted. He leaped onto the back of his horse and with a shout started for the gate.

A number of horses, startled, poured through the gate before Jack. Jack continued his shouting. He flailed his arms. The frightened ponies galloped around. The gate remained ajar as Cloud galloped through followed by dozens of horses.

In a stampede they followed Jack toward the centre of camp.

Jack felt the confident stride of Cloud. Trees flashed by. Dead ahead he saw the crowd. Their faces all turned in his direction.

In a tableau frozen from an instant in time he saw the frightened faces, then the fire. To the right he saw Hogie. He was naked to the waist, his back turned to an Indian man. In the right hand of the man was a bone needle seven inches long. Threaded in the needle was a leather thong which hung and ended out of view.

Suddenly the stop action ended. The first bodies in the path of Cloud melted back. Others did not.

In one giant leap Cloud sailed over the remaining six feet of crowd, some sitting, others kneeling. She glided gracefully down between the fire and Hogie. Another pace forward. Jack swept Hogie up behind him and suddenly the fire and crowd had been left behind.

Jack heard shouting and cursing and screaming. In his mind he could see the confused crowd milling beneath the helpless figure of Standing Ready.

They won't be confused for long, he thought, as he pressed Cloud to gallop even faster. But it will take them some time to round up their ponies.

Darkness wrapped itself around the two as Cloud raced into the depths of the forest.

A gentle nudge with his left knee and she gently eased to the right, in the direction of lonesome pine.

The white birch trees seemed to flash by. How can Cloud find a path so swiftly through these trees, he thought.

Hogie clung to his waist.

"Thanks, Jack. Thanks. Thanks. Oh God. Thanks Jack." He kept repeating this litany in a breathless whisper in Jack's ear.

Cloud plunged on. The minutes seemed like hours.

Another gentle nudge to the right. Jack sensed rather than knew the direction of lonesome pine.

Then the moon broke through, only briefly, but long enough for Jack to confirm he was on the right path.

"Hang on," Jack said. "We'll be there in jig time."

Hogie did not know what Jack was talking about, but he wrapped his arms around Jack even tighter.

Five minutes later Jack said:

"We're almost there."

He eased Cloud back. Then he slowed her from a gallop to a trot. The birch trees became ever more sparse then discontinued entirely.

In the middle of a small meadow stood a single pine. Standing quietly by the pine, watching Jack carefully, stood a horse.

"God bless you, One Feather," Jack prayed quietly.

He eased Cloud to a walk. Then he stopped her next to the pony.

Without touching foot to earth, Hogie leaped onto the back of the waiting pony and the two horsemen were off at a gallop.

They did not see a small slip of a figure in the shadows of the nearby birch trees.

One Feather stepped forward into the moonlight. Once again her dark eyes brimmed with tears. They sparkled now in the light of the moon.

She raised an arm in the direction of the disappearing riders.

Then she said quietly: "Come back to me Kanata Jack." And after a moment she dropped her arms to her side.

CHAPTER THIRTY-SEVEN

AHEAD LAY darkness. To their backs the first signs of approaching day appeared. Slowly a crimson band filtered across the horizon. Above that rested a large swath of pearl grey sky.

They had been riding without letup for four and a half hours. At no time had any sign of pursuit been seen.

They are looking west, into darkness, thought Jack, we are quite safe. But still they rode on.

They found themselves in gently rolling hills. Jack judged the time to be about ten in the morning. Alternatively they galloped then cantered their ponies.

Finally Jack said: "It is time to rest the ponies. Let's pull up."

They stopped, dismounted, and after hobbling Hogie's horse, stretched out in the warm noon sun for a rest. Sleep was quite impossible, they were so excited.

The sun grew hotter as the afternoon wore on. Finally Jack roused Hogie and they rode on.

Jack knew that the army would have arrived in the west weeks before. It was likely they were already deployed, ready for battle. He knew also that the probable location of his unit would be west of his present position, along the South Saskatchewan River. Hogie and he were free. They may have been followed, but if so, the Indians had lost the trail hours before.

His duty to Hogie was done. His duty to self and country had yet to be discharged.

Abruptly he reigned in. Surprised, Hogie too came to a halt.

"It's time to say goodbye," said Jack.

Hogie walked his horse closer to Cloud.

"I must go," said Jack.

"Don't," said Hogie.

"I must," replied Jack.

"Come with me, Jack," said Hogie.

"You know I can not do that."

"There's room for you back home."

"Thanks Hogie, but I must get back to my unit. I have important information. Much of it thanks to your Dad. I must get that information back. You know I'd have to return to the Rangers, even if I didn't have intelligence information."

Hogie looked at Jack. He knew Jack was determined. He knew Jack was right.

"I...I..." he said.

He was interrupted by Jack: "No Hogie, don't say anything."

"But...But...I owe my life to you."

"No more Hogie. I did it for you; but I also did it for Nance and Magee."

There was a long silent pause. Hogie began to speak again, but his emotions choked off any words.

"No long goodbye, Hogie."

Jack reached out to shake his hand. Hogie grasped Jack's hand with both of his and shook vigorously. He smiled at Jack through his tears.

"Good riding," said Jack.

"Yes," said Hogie, blinking back the tears. He could say no more.

Then Jack said, "I will see you again you know."

Then he reigned Cloud around and galloped off.

Hogie watched his friend for a long time. Jack was only a speck on the horizon when Hogie turned away and started again for home.

CHAPTER THIRTY-EIGHT

JACK RODE for many hours before pausing for any rest. He now rode north west. A sixth sense told him to ride in this direction. He felt now, that he had no more time to lose.

It was only with great reluctance that he stopped for the night. And with great fatigue. Of the last forty-eight hours he had slept only two.

At twilight he was blessed with luck. He had been watching a bush for many hours as he rode. He continued to ride toward the bush which soon became a small grove of trees. He reconnoitred the area and found the grove to be U-shaped.

And cupped in the bottom of the U was a small slough.

Water for Cloud and for himself.

It was dark by the time he found this spot. He felt faint with exhaustion and fatigue. He neither washed nor ate, but found a lush growth of grass and laid himself out for a welcome sleep.

And sleep he did. The sun was high in the morning sky and still he slept.

What really awakened Jack was snorting and then neighing from Cloud.

He opened his eyes to find them blinded by the glare of the sun. He was staring straight into it.

He had a funny feeling. A feeling that he was not alone.

He had still not moved when a shadow crossed over the sun. He heard other horses stepping. Then he heard voices and his heart fell.

They were Cree voices!

Jack sat bolt upright. Before him, mounted, was Black Bear. On his head he wore a war bonnet. He was armed.

Strung out on either side were many others, all mounted, all armed, ready for battle.

PART FIVE

BATTLE

CHAPTER THIRTY-NINE

THE WAR party rode westerly. They rode all day long. Once again a prisoner, Jack rode in the centre. Jack recognized almost all of the armed raiding party.

Next to Jack rode Travelling Spirit. He alone amongst the men spoke to Jack. He gave no information, merely directions. It soon became apparent to Jack that Travelling Spirit had been detailed to guard Jack.

From the others the most Jack received was stares and glares. No one was friendly any more. Jack did not have to wonder why. King Bird was not amongst them. Jack did not have to be told that nothing else that happened that night pleased them either.

Prisoner again! Jack chastised himself mentally. How negligent. How could I have slept. How could I have even rested without hiding first.

How could I have stopped at a watering hole! I should have known that experienced riders of the plains would know every watering hole in their path or within thirty miles of it.

He cursed himself and blamed himself. A wave of despair washed over him. He resigned himself to his fate. He would never recover his unit. It was simply not meant to be. He was finished.

At the front rode Black Bear, the Chief, as usual. And as usual he was flanked to left and right by Bad Child and Yellow Bear.

Miserable Man, as he so often did, took up a position at the rear. And as usual he chattered and sang quietly to himself. He saw Love Man and Man-Who-Wins, and Man-Who-Walks. Everyone who took part in the buffalo hunt was present and then some.

And all armed to the teeth.

Jack felt truly sorry for himself. He was dejected. He sagged low in the saddle.

To add to the feelings of dejection, the day became blustery. Clouds covered the sun. They blocked out the warmth and sunshine which always gave his spirits a lift.

Soon the clouds covered the entire sky leaving the landscape without color. The wind scudded the low flying clouds above and shook the lifeless prairie grass below. The weather seemed now to have penetrated his very spirit. Jack rode on like an automation. His mind no longer functioned. He was a robot.

Many miles he rode in this frame of mind. It was with surprise then, that he heard Travelling Spirit speak his name. It jarred him from his reverie of self pity.

"Kanata Jack."

Jack looked over to Travelling Spirit. Travelling Spirit returned his glance and smiled.

"That is your name."

Jack did not reply. Neither did he return the smile.

"That is what we of the plains call you."

There was still no sign of response from Jack.

Then he said: "Is that your true name?"

He waited. Then he went on: "That is the name we learned from One Feather."

Finally Jack answered. Her name shook him to his senses.

"How is One Feather?" he asked.

"She is fine, but I think she misses you. She kept to her teepee all day yesterday."

"Did you speak to her?"

"Yes, I did. But no one else is speaking to her."

"Why not, she did nothing."

"You know that is not true."

"That is true."

"Kanata Jack knows that he speaks with a tongue that is false. Do not do that." He made this last comment after looking directly into Jack's eyes.

"Why do they not speak to her."

"You know, but I will tell you anyway."

"Yes, please tell me," Jack said sarcastically.

Travelling Spirit took no notice of his tone, but went on: "She was there by lonesome pine. She lied to us. Lied."

"What do you mean? Why do you say she lied? Lied about what?"

"She was asked which way you went. She pointed south. You travelled west. Didn't you?"

Jack made no reply.

"You went west. She pointed south. That is why you were not recaptured."

"She did not see me."

"Yes she did. Do not lie to me."

Again Jack had no reply. After some time he said: "What will happen to her?"

"Who, what?" said Travelling Spirit. For a moment he had forgotten the conversation. Then he said:

"I think nothing. Yes, nothing. They are not sure. They think this but they are not sure. Anyway, I will not tell them."

"You," said Jack. "What would you tell them?"

"What you told me. I will not tell them what you told me."

Jack had told him nothing. With his lips at least. By his manner he had told Travelling Spirit much. I think she is safe in his hands, Jack mused, as they rode on.

"Why did you kill King Bird?" said Travelling Spirit after a while.

This guy should be a lawyer, thought Jack. Then he said: "He tried to kill me." Why not admit what he knows anyway, Jack thought. He had nothing more to lose.

"That was a bad thing to do," said Travelling Spirit.

"No it was not. It was not a bad thing to do. It was a good thing. He was mean, vicious and a liar. And not a real Cree. Not a good one anyway."

"He was Cree," said Travelling Spirit mildly.

"The Sundance!" Jack spat out angrily. "That is Cree?"

To this Travelling Spirit made no reply.

Finally Jack spoke again: "He had my pony. He would not let me take my pony. He tried to kill me. I killed him to defend myself and take my pony."

"We would have given you your pony."

"That is not true."

"Yes, it is," he said slowly. "You were told you would be given your pony."

"Yes, after the Sundance. After the Sundance. After Hogie and I had done the Sundance.

"I am not Cree. Hogie is not Cree. Why should we do the Sundance?

"That is not 'giving my pony back', as you say."

"Now Travelling Spirit speaks with a false tongue. That is not like Travelling Spirit.

"I think the spirit of King Bird did not join the Great Spirit. I think the spirit of King Bird has taken roost in the breast of Travelling Spirit. And that is too bad."

Travelling Spirit was stung by this last remark. He was deeply offended.

Perhaps I have gone too far, thought Jack. He softened his remarks. He said:

"I loved the heart of Travelling Spirit. It was honest and noble and always to be trusted. By everyone. Even by me, a White Man. When Travelling Spirit spoke I knew it was from the heart and was true.

"I do not like to hear another Travelling Spirit." Jack said this last sentence firmly.

Travelling Spirit seemed somewhat mollified. He eased back into his natural self.

Jack wondered at the many facets to the character of his friend. He wondered too about his future at the hands of Black Bear and the others. They were certainly less well disposed to him than Travelling Spirit. In their eyes he was a murderer.

He did not have to wonder at the fate of murderers!

He did not have long to ponder this question.

It was late afternoon. They sky remained overcast and it was quite cool. Yellow Bear had made frequent forays to scout the territory ahead in the path of the party, and also to its right and left.

Jack had seen him return at a high gallop from the south west a few minutes before. A conference was held with Black Bear. There was excited chatter, none of which Jack understood. Then the party started at a fast gallop to the south west.

Travelling Spirit was still at his side. Finally Jack could wait no longer.

"Where are we headed," he shouted to Travelling Spirit.

The reply was a long time coming, but when it did it stunned Jack.

"We are going to join Dumont. We are going to fight the Army."

Once again Travelling Spirit turned to Jack and gave him a broad grin.

CHAPTER FORTY

THE TERRAIN changed gradually as the party approached the west band of the great South Saskatchewan River. The grass remained a lifeless yellow under the grey clouds. But the level plain gave way to gentle rolling and pitching. Here and there stood large bush obstructions. The riders skirted these. The brush was too thick to permit easy penetration. The forest too spilled over the high river bands sending little searching fingerlets across the fields.

Jack rode along, still hemmed in by his fellow riders.

As they crested a small rise Jack heard popping sounds. At first it was difficult to tell their origin. Sometimes they seemed to come from the north or north west. Other times from the south.

As they rode further south, however, it became clear the shooting was from the south.

Then Jack heard a particularly loud but muffled thump. Nine pounders thought Jack. Artillery! He had last seen nine pounders at the training depot back home.

The North West Field Force was here!

His spirits soared. He found his confidence, at a low ebb for many hours, return with a rush. So near and yet so far.

It was not long before he saw a rider approach from the south. He rode a spotted grey and white stallion. As he drew near Jack noticed that he was not an Indian.

He was swarthy, however, with an already dark complexion, deeply tanned from many years on the open plain.

He rode right up to Black Bear and brought his horse to a halt. He had quick dark eyes. They took in the war party at a glance.

He spoke in an authoritative voice. Jack had no trouble hearing it. Although he spoke Cree, it was with a strange accent.

An animated discussion followed. The newcomer was apparently disappointed at the small size of the reinforcements. He complained, but Black Bear shrugged off the complaints with a lofty wave of his hand.

"Where are we?" whispered Jack to Travelling Spirit. "Who is this?"

For several minutes Travelling Spirit did not reply. He continued to listen to the leaders' conversation up front. Then he turned to Jack.

"This is called Fish Creek by the White Man. It is not far from the home of that one." He nodded in the direction of the stranger who had greeted them.

"Well, who is he?" repeated Jack.

"That man is the White General. He is Gabriel Dumont," replied Travelling Spirit.

So often had Jack heard of the great Gabriel Dumont that he turned his attention back with renewed interest. As far as Jack could see, with the man seated astride his horse, he was not tall. Rather he was stocky. He looked powerful and in the full vigour of manhood. He had a commanding presence. Jack noticed that Black Bear, who did this for no one else, tended to defer to him.

The two spoke for several more minutes. Jack continued to have difficulty understanding him because of the strange accent.

Gabriel Dumont waved his large weatherbeaten hands slowly to the west several times. The fringes of his buckskin jacket shivered in the wind. Then he drew his hand back in a line to the east and pushed back the wide brim of his hat.

Black Bear nodded several more times. Then he beckoned to Bad Child and Yellow Bear to come closer and he began to give them instructions. They listened intently while Gabriel Dumont peered from behind a large full black beard at the three of them. He looked idly over the remainder of the party. His watchful eyes had passed over Jack. When he had finished Jack noticed that he stole a second glance. Clearly he was curious.

But he did not ask any questions. A moment later the pow wow ended. The orders were clear apparently, for Black Bear now gave brief instructions, inaudible to all except the leaders. Then, abruptly, the party dispersed.

Black Bear and several others followed Gabriel Dumont in a south westerly direction. The rest of the party fanned out. Some rode more westerly, in the direction of the river. Others rode more directly south. Amongst the latter were Travelling Spirit and his charge, Jack.

CHAPTER FORTY-ONE

THE SOUND of gunfire was much more audible now. It was punctuated now and then with a blast from the nine pounders. Jack was barely conscious of the sound of shots or bullets, but he could easily hear the blast of artillery as it discharged. He noticed that the Indian ponies startled at this sound. They were evidently not accustomed to the heavy reverberating report of artillery fire.

They soon will be, thought Jack.

It was not long before Travelling Spirit and Jack were detailed to the extreme left flank. Dutifully, they rode off alone.

Again Jack was curious and pressed Travelling Spirit for answers.

"What happened? What's going on?" he asked.

"You're to stick to me," said Travelling Spirit laconically.

"I know that," said Jack. "What happened back there?"

Travelling Spirit did not answer right away, but when he did Jack was quite pleased.

"We are late. Thanks to you. They have been in action all day."

"Where are they?" asked Jack.

"Gabriel told Black Bear that a deep ravine runs from the river directly east to a point south of us. His scouts have been watching the approach of the army for several days. They know every step the Army General takes.

"He split his forces to two. He sent half his Army to the west bank of the river.

"Gabriel decided to dig in here on the east side and take on the enemy while they're divided. He thinks the enemy general was quite foolish to do this. Gabriel has had to fight only half his enemy.

"Where are we headed?" asked Jack.

"Gabriel has his men well dug in on the face of the north slope of the ravine. They have been there for a day now. The enemy cannot see them at all, so well covered by bush and grass are his positions. They are scattered along from the west bank of the river to a point directly ahead of us. You and I will take up a position opposite the right flank of the White Army."

They rode several hundred yards more. A sparse grove of poplar trees stood in front of them. They slowly walked their ponies through the trees.

Travelling Spirit chuckled several times. Finally he could contain himself no longer.

"Gabriel said he has had only a few casualties, the enemy many. They have almost no protection. Their General marched them straight into his ambush. He said it is easier than shooting buffalo." Again Travelling Spirit could not suppress a chuckle.

About twenty feet ahead, the trees ended. The two horsemen stopped and peered ahead. They were well covered by the trees and thick shrubs growing as high as Clouds withers. Some grew even higher. Jack was astonished at the length of the grass too. Some of it along the edge of the forest looked fifty inches high.

How well concealed the enemy must be, he thought. It is no wonder Dumont has so few casualties.

Beyond the forest and grass was a broad meadow. A depression really. The easterly end of the ravine, thought Jack.

The shooting was sporadic. Jack kept an alert vigil to the south as Travelling Spirit studied the terrain for a possible site with sufficient cover. By now it was early in the afternoon.

Travelling Spirit said: "I don't think we'll be here long. Gabriel will break off the engagement before dusk. He said he has done as much damage as he can today.

"Apparently the enemy has grown wise. He is bringing the rest of his army across the river to the east bank. No use fighting the whole army here.

"We will not be here long," he repeated. Then he interrupted his musings. "Over there," he said.

He pointed off to the right and ahead.

At first Jack thought he was pointing off across no man's land. His eyes scanned the far side of the meadow. He thought he saw movement there.

Khaki? Surely not khaki! That would be his own unit. The Rangers wore khaki uniforms. His eyes searched the bush line again for the same spot.

This time he was sure. A soldier in military khaki. He could even make out the pith helmet.

"Not there," said Travelling Spirit interrupting Jack's thoughts, "down there."

He pointed again. This time Jack's eyes followed. Nestled just beyond the tree line and behind a stand of long grass he saw a natural little trench. A fold in the earth to the south provided natural cover.

"We'll leave the ponies here," said Travelling Spirit. He began to dismount.

"Not me," said Jack.

Travelling Spirit turned to look at him.

"What," he said.

"Not me," said Jack again. "I'm not fighting my own men, my own comrades."

"What did you say?" repeated Travelling Spirit. This time he did not sound friendly. His voice sounded cold and distant.

"I'm not..." Jack began.

Travelling Spirit brought his Remington rifle out of its saddle holster and pointed it across his pony at Jack on his left.

"I..." began Jack again.

Travelling Spirit interrupted Jack by cocking the rifle.

The two men looked at each other. Neither so much as blinked. Finally Jack broke the silence.

"I'm on my way Travelling Spirit. I'm going back to my people. It's time to say goodbye."

Travelling Spirit said nothing. He merely raised the rifle and aimed it at Jack.

Jack gave Cloud an authoritative kick of his heels. She bolted forward. Another kick and she broke into a gallop.

Out of the forest they went. She plunged through the tall grass and raced into no man's land. Jack leaned into the wind. Cloud's white mane flew out behind brushing his face.

They fairly flew toward army lines. Jack tensed. Any moment he expected the crack of a rifle shot, the sting of a bullet in the back.

It did not come.

Another thirty yards to go. Cloud galloped as she never had before. He's not going to do it. He can't bring himself to do it, thought Jack.

The shot never came.

"God bless that fine man," Jack said aloud to the whole world.

Lieutenant Richards settled down in his trench once more. He had been there most of the day, at the extreme right flank of the line. The rest of the Rangers were spread out at intervals to the west.

It was cold. He had seen little action that day, though he heard plenty. All day long there had been the popping and banging of rifles. Occasionally he heard the crash of nine pounder rounds as they were lobbed across the ravine to the west. Not a few times did he hear the terrified whinny of horses in the rear echelon.

He wished somebody had ordered them removed far to the rear. Quietly he cursed the incompetence of Middleton and Trubshaw, and wished once more that a man like Colonel Williams were in command of the Rangers.

He dismissed these unmilitary thoughts from his mind. Again he peered across no man's land. In the grey overcast day it was almost impossible to penetrate the forest without a glass. It grew darker only a few feet into the tree line. He felt sure he had seen something move.

On your toes, Lieutenant, he told himself. Keep a sharp eye out.

He shook his head to clear it. Then he concentrated. He shifted his rifle and raised his head just a bit to get a better view over the tall grass and across the meadow.

Again it moved. Now he was definite. The enemy was not two hundred and fifty yards away.

Suddenly an Indian broke through the tree line. He went immediately into a gallop. His white horse streaked directly toward Lieutenant Richard's trench.

The Lieutenant, was so busy preparing to defend himself that he did not see another Indian emerge from the trees mounted on a pony. Neither did he see the Indian raise a rifle and aim it at the rider.

Of course he heard no shot, for no shot was fired.

Lieutenant Richards snapped up his rifle and took aim at his attacker.

Hold your fire he told himself. Wait until he's well within range. Wait until he's a sure target. The Indian rode as if his life depended on it. Why is he charging alone? This thought passed through the Lieutenant's mind but then disappeared like the mists of morning.

Now the rider loomed large. The Lieutenant said, now. He tightened his finger on the trigger. He squeezed.

The Indian was yelling.

Curse him, thought the Lieutenant. He can't scare me with a blood curdling yell.

All this occurred in a wink of time.

Again he squeezed back on the trigger.

"No, no," shouted the Indian.

English, thought Lieutenant Richards, he speaks English.

Then the Indian was within twenty feet of him. It's now or never, thought the Lieutenant and suddenly he was hearing his name called.

"Lieutenant Richards, Lieutenant Richards, it's me. Don't shoot. It's me. It's me. "Don't shoot."

He had hesitated too long.

The Indian pony came to a rearing halt right in his trench.

The Indian vaulted from his pony down toward the Lieutenant. And then stopped. There was no tomahawk, no war club, no knife.

The Indian just stood there looking at him and grinning from ear to ear.

"It's me," said the Indian. "Jack."

The Lieutenant blinked his eyes in disbelief.

"Yes," shouted the Indian. "It's me Lieutenant, Canada Jack. Reporting for duty." And then the Indian saluted!

Several moments passed before Lieutenant Richards fully comprehended that the Indian who stood before him was not an Indian at all. He was Private Jack Holden of the Canadian Military Rangers.

And then he was so astonished that he did something that was quite unmilitary. He threw his arms around Jack and gave him a big hug.

"Jack," he exclaimed, "Jack. Jack Holden."

His incredulity mingled with delight to see his old friend back.

"I thought you were dead. Sure as we're standing here, I thought you were dead."

"I'm not, Lieutenant. I'm here, alive and kicking."

The Lieutenant grasped Jack's arms in his hands and shook him several times as though to drive away a ghostly image. "Jack, Jack, Jack," he repeated over and over again.

"I think we'd better get down Lieutenant. The enemy is just across there, and he might start shooting."

Jack's words brought both men back to reality. They dropped down and took cover in Lieutenant Richard's trench. Lieutenant Richards felt odd lying there. Even knowing it was Jack and not an Indian, he still felt uneasy. For an hour his subconscious refused to allow him to turn his back on Jack. He repeatedly turned his head to look at him and he asked him unnecessary questions just to be able to hear him speak again. This seemed to reassure the Lieutenant. Finally he began to relax.

Jack surveyed the trees on the far side of no man's land. From the moment he took cover he watched for signs of Travelling Spirit. He was nowhere to be seen. Not then, not ever.

Jack offered a silent prayer for Travelling Spirit. Jack had done no more for him that he would have done for any man, when he yanked him from certain death beneath the sharp pounding hooves of the buffalo. Travelling Spirit had rebelled against tribal solidarity when he refused to shoot Jack. A good and faithful member of the tribe, his strength of character transcended lesser obligations.

Travelling Spirit had proved himself to be more than simply a friend, but Jack was unable to identify the full stature of the man.

CHAPTER FORTY-TWO

DESULTORY FIRING continued for several hours after Jack's escape.

There was little action on the east end of the front and they carried on a watchful conversation. The Lieutenant could hardly restrain his curiosity. Jack tried to begin at the beginning, but he was constantly interrupted. Lieutenant Richards wanted to know how it came to pass that Jack dressed like an Indian, and looking and riding like an Indian had landed on his old unit just like that.

Patiently, Jack told the whole story, frequently having to back track to pick up the threads and put it all in some semblance of chronological order. But he did, finally, get the whole adventure told.

The Lieutenant, of course, gave his rapt attention, probing for details again and again.

Several times he reached over to examine Jack's leggings or shirt.

He nodded his head when Jack described the escape. Then he stopped Jack to question him in detail about "bluecoat" and his probable identity.

"I've given that a lot of thought, Sir, but I haven't come up with any answer."

"'Bluecoat' sounds like he may be American. Don't the American military wear blue uniforms?"

"They do, Jack, but I don't imagine he would arrive here in uniform if he were going to sabotage our campaign or to spy on military movements for Riel."

"Anyway we have one American serving with us. Captain Howard. You don't think he's the one do you?"

"I don't know, Sir. I don't think so. I think you're right. They wouldn't send a spy here in uniform."

They both pondered this for a moment. Then Lieutenant Richards said:

"I'm sure he's not the one. I know the man a little. Square shooter. What you see is what you get. He's here to demonstrate his gatling gun. Very proud of it. Wants to sell it to the Canadian Government. He showed it to me. Damnable instrument of war," he said as an aside.

"We have had some strange happenings in the last few weeks though."

"Like what?" Jack asked.

"Several days ago General Middleton ordered a hospital wagon should be floated across to the Grenadiers on the west bank of the river."

"The east bank of the river is steep. More like a cliff than a river bank. Anyway some of our boys tied a line to it and eased it down the bluff. The wagon broke free and careened down, right into the river. Broke the leg of one of Houghton's boys. Somebody in the 90th Battalion. Private, I think."

"What happened?"

"The line was examined later. It had been cut near through."

"But who did it?" asked Jack.

"Don't know. Not even sure it was deliberate. And our boys are the ones who handled the line."

"You said 'happenings'," Jack reminded him. "Did something else happen?"

"As a matter of fact yes. And this time there was no question. Foul play was suspected by Colonel Trubshaw immediately."

"Colonel Trubshaw?"

"Yes. Colonel Trubshaw. We bivouacked a few miles south of here one night. A nice spot. Commanding view of the river and over to the west bank."

"The next morning one of our ammunition wagons could not be accounted for."

"How do you mean?"

"Disappeared!"

"Disappeared!"

"Disappeared, how do you mean disappeared? How can a wagon disappear, just like that, into thin air?"

"We don't know Jack. All we do know is that it was gone the next morning when the Quartermaster checked off stores before we resumed our march."

Jack shook his head.

"I feel a bit guilty there," he added after a time.

"I don't understand," said Jack.

"Well, we were in charge."

"You mean the Rangers?"

"The Rangers, yes, Jack. As a matter of fact my troop. We were guarding the military stores."

"Phew," was the only comment Jack made.

"The boys took turns at watch that night. None of them saw it happen. They're good men, too. I just don't see any explanation."

"Colonel Trubshaw was apoplectic. He was huffing with rage. Very embarrassed. The General was quite annoyed. Understandably so. It's a long haul to get ammunition out here. Rifle ammunition too."

"What's going to happen," asked Jack.

"Well, the General says there's no time to investigate now. We're on the march. It will have to wait until we settle down some. Maybe after we deal with this bunch." He nodded toward the far tree line and the enemy.

Jack had described how he came to meet Magee. How he related the intelligence information that Magee had given to him. The Lieutenant listened eagerly. When Jack gave him intelligence on the probable movement and commitment of Indians in the event of hostility, Lieutenant Richards said:

"This information's got to go to the General."

"I thought it might be important." said Jack.

"You bet it is."

"Believe me, Lieutenant, I have done my best to get back. To report any intelligence that might be useful. Magee thought Black Bear would be trouble, and where is he? Over there," he pointed, answering his own question.

"And Beardy. He'll be with them. I'll bet some of his men are with Dumont today too.

"Apart from these two, he seemed to think we had most to fear from Big Bear. He says…"

"Big Bear," interrupted the Lieutenant. "There's already been trouble from him."

"What's happened?" asked Jack.

"Massacre, that's what."

"Massacre!"

"Yeh, a massacre up at Frog Lake. Several weeks back."

"What do you mean a massacre?"

"Just like that. He and his braves rode into the Frog Lake settlement and murdered settlers."

"Wasn't there anyone there to defend them?" asked Jack.

"They were far beyond the reach of any help from us or the North West Mounted Police. They had to fend for themselves."

"What happened?"

"We don't know much at this stage. There are quite a number of Indians.

"One settler was ordered to march to the Indian camp. He refused and they shot him on the spot.

"Then all hell broke loose. They just began shooting. They shot the wounded. They even shot several priests.

"Some ran, but it didn't do them any good. The Indians went after them and cut'em down like buffalo."

Jack shook his head. To Lieutenant Richards it seemed all quite absurd. Here was this man who, for all the world, looked like an Indian, shaking his head in disgust.

"They had quite a party. They took prisoners, mutilated some of the bodies and celebrated and carried on…"

"What happened to the prisoners?" asked Jack.

"Don't know yet. Still alive, I think. I suppose there's still hope. But they'd have a better chance if Big Bear settled down."

"He hasn't?" asked Jack.

"Not the last we heard."

"What else?" asked Jack, scarcely believing there could be more.

"Well, about ten or twelve days later he was over to Fort Pitt, not far away, and raising hell. But we had a good man there."

"Yeh? Who was that?"

"Frank Dickens. Ever hear of him?"

"No, should I?"

"Well no, but I'll bet you heard of his father, the writer."

"Charles Dickens?" said Jack.

"None other," replied Lieutenant Richards.

"What's he doing out here. I mean Frank Dickens. What's he got to do with this."

"Plenty. He's an Inspector with the North West Mounted Police. Has been for years. I hear he likes a drop, but he's a good man. Seen action in India, Montana. He's been all over the plains this side of the border.

"Bet he's seen more of the world and its ways than his famous father!

"Anyway, he and a small force of twenty odd were guarding the Fort. Big Bear and about three hundred braves surrounded them and threatened to attack if they didn't surrender.

"Apparently the Fort's in bad shape, pretty well unprotected."

"My God! Did they?" asked Jack.

"Sure they did. The civilians that is. Damn fools. Now they're prisoners of Big Bear.

"Then he offered the Mounties a chance to surrender.

"They refused.

"Finally he offered them safe passage in exchange for the Fort.

"What did they do?"

"Well, Dickens just sent them back a note. It said: 'Big Bear, go to hell'."

At this point Lieutenant Richards stopped his story. Chuckling to himself he warily raised himself up to survey the enemy lines.

"The men got a good laugh out of that, let me tell you."

"What did Big Bear do?"

"What else could he do? What would he do? He attacked."

"My God," said Jack. "Three hundred to twenty? What happened?"

"Well, you know, those few Mounties beat off the whole lot. But I guess it was pretty hairy for a while.

"Amazing, isn't it?" he said, after a thoughtful pause.

Jack had been totally absorbed by the story the Lieutenant had been telling. He did not notice that battlefield had been silent for some time until the Lieutenant said:

"It's quiet Jack. No shooting for some time. What do you think's happening?"

"They're leaving," said Jack.

"What makes you say that," asked the Lieutenant.

"Travelling Spirit…" he started to say, then corrected himself. "They told me they were going to break off action soon."

"How do you know we can trust them," said Lieutenant Richards.

For a reply Jack merely turned and looked into the Lieutenant's face.

Occasional shots were heard. Not from the enemy but from a nervous private.

Suddenly Jack nudged the Lieutenant.

"Over there," he said, pointing. Off to the north east the Lieutenant saw about a hundred and twenty-five riders galloping away. They stopped and reigned their ponies around for a moment. Then they broke into loud jeering and cheering, waving rifles in the air. Then they turned and rode off.

"That's all?" he exclaimed. "Fewer than two hundred men."

"I think so," said Jack.

They watched the departing riders for several minutes. Then Jack said:

"That's Gabriel Dumont on the grey spotted pony in the front."

"You don't say," said the Lieutenant.

"That's him," confirmed Jack. "A great general."

This time it was Lieutenant Richards' turn to give Jack a look.

"I mean…aah…they think he's a good leader." corrected Jack. "Even the Indians. Lots of respect."

After a few minutes the Lieutenant said:

"You think that's the end of them?"

"For now," said Jack. "There'll be no more fighting here. They'll wait to fight another day, another place."

"I think we'd better report to Colonel Trubshaw," said Lieutenant Richards as he moved to rise.

"Lieutenant, Sir," said Jack. He touched the Lieutenant on the sleeve. Lieutenant Richards moved back down beside Jack.

"Yes, Jack?"

"Well, Sir, what about me?"

"What do you mean, Jack?"

"What's my status, Sir?" Jack could feel the formality seep back into their relationship. "Am I okay, Sir? I've heard that the army…they think I deserted. I didn't Sir."

"I'm afraid, Jack, that there's a bit of trouble there. I had to report what happened.

"After the explosion the gun battle went on for hours. They just wouldn't let go. I think they may have been after our ponies. The ammunition was all gone.

"They withdrew into the woods, but if we made so much as a move to scratch, they started up with the firing again. They pinned us down for a long time, taking pot shots at us.

"We had one killed and two wounded.

"Thank God they finally just gave up and left.

"I had to report to Colonel Trubshaw when he arrived with the rest of the Rangers.

"He demanded that we check with the North West Mounted Police detachment down the line.

"I hold him we already had. Of course, they never saw you.

"We waited. You didn't return. I had to tell him Jack. Those were the facts.

"You know Colonel Trubshaw. Of course he was furious. I tired to calm him down. I told him anything could have happened.

"He wouldn't hear any of it. 'What could have happened?' he asked sarcastically. 'Hit by a buggy perhaps? Or a runaway dray?' He just scoffed at my suggestions.

"He finally began to question my loyalty.

"I did my best for you Jack. It was no use."

"Then it's true…I'm, I'm…"

"Afraid so, Jack. You're going to be on charge."

"For…for…" Jack could not bring himself to say it.

Lieutenant Richards said it for him:

"For desertion. Desertion under fire."

"Lieutenant, I've got to know one thing."

"What's that Jack?"

"Do you believe it? I don't know what I'd do if you didn't believe in me. Do you believe it?"

"No Jack. You know I don't. I know I've heard the truth from you out here. I know you, Jack."

"Thanks Lieutenant."

"Jack you know I'll do all that I can for you."

"Let's go in."

CHAPTER FORTY-THREE

THE FRONT was spread out over several miles.

Cloud, propelled onward by a light slap on the hind quarters when Jack had dismounted, had taken refuge well back of the lines. The two first walked over to retrieve her before turning west for the walk back.

Cloud seemed to recognize Lieutenant Richards. She whinnied and nodded her head when he stroked her.

The three then began a slow walk back along the rear lines of the troops.

Many of the troops remained in their positions but most had been relieved of duty. Soldiers milled about everywhere. Jack saw scarlet, black and green tunics everywhere as well as the khaki uniforms of the Rangers.

He saw men from the 90th Battalion of Winnipeg. They were the most numerous and they seemed to be all over the scene. Some returning from the line. Others running to and fro with errands. Officers shouted commands, soldiers scurried. One officer in a black tunic became extremely angry. His command had not been executed promptly and, his red cheeks puffed out, he complained huffily to a subordinate.

Jack saw men of C Infantry and Boulton's Mounted Corps. Some were busy cleaning rifles, others seemed to mill about on errands for officers.

He also saw men of the Royal Grenadiers. They too were numerous and could be seen going about their business everywhere.

French's Scouts were there and Jack noticed a few men from the Winnipeg Battery. They were busy moving their artillery pieces.

As he and the Lieutenant made their way further back in the lines they had to circle dense patches of bush. Jack could smell the acrid air. The wind had died earlier that day and the smoke and fumes of shots and cannon still clung in the atmosphere.

Several times Jack saw someone he knew and waved at him. Each time he got an astonished look in return. Obviously they did not recognize him.

One time a soldier from the 90th called out:

"Hey, the Lieutenant's got himself a prisoner."

Another, a private with the Grenadiers shouted:

"Hey, Lieutenant, what're you doing, consorting with the enemy?"

His Sergeant said, "Shut it down private. I've heard from you once too often today."

Two stretcher bearers walked swiftly by on their right. They carried a litter on which rested a private. The private raised himself up on one elbow and started to shout obscenities at Jack. The orderly at the rear of the litter said: "Settle down Kemp. He ain't gonna do you no more harm."

Jack and the Lieutenant were just rounding the western edge of a grove of trees when a pair of teamsters came careening by with an ammunition wagon. They were headed belatedly for the front.

On a ridge to their right behind a low russet strip of brush, Jack could see artillery pieces deployed.

There appeared to be five guns, all from A Battery. None of them was being fired. The men worked and fussed about. They were lovingly cleaning their weapons.

Everywhere, it appeared, confusion reigned; boxes littered about; horses and drivers on the move; sergeants shouting; privates saluting.

A few tents appeared now and then. Men were carried in; others hobbled out. Here too men scrambled about in what appeared to Jack to be confusion.

A short distance from one tent lay five soldiers. Though they were on stretchers, they moved not at all. Jack looked more closely. They were dead. Most of them were young. Jack's age. Most appeared to be from the 90th. Except one. He looked vaguely familiar. Suddenly, Jack realized he was looking at Gunner Cook. Back east at training depot Jack had known him slightly. He was shy, but very friendly to Jack. He always had a ready laugh. Jack remembered him well now. He had been with A Battery.

Suddenly they heard a man shout. Jack and the Lieutenant turned from the dead and looked at the tent.

A scream rent the air.

"Hold the leg," said a loud voice in the tent. "Hold that man."

Groans and whimpers began in the tent.

Jack and the Lieutenant left the area quickly.

Lieutenant Richards indicated they would turn right where a line of white canvas tents had been erected.

In front of the largest flew the Union Jack. Below it flew the standard of the North West Field Force. Several sentries stood rigidly to attention in front of the tent. Officers came and went, some carrying map cases. They were not far away. Jack could make out the murmur of voices from inside the tent.

"Headquarters," said Lieutenant Richards. General Middleton's tent. We stop here."

He stopped in front of a smaller tent several places before the General's tent.

"Wait here, Jack. I think it would be best if I saw him first."

Jack stopped several yards from the entrance to Colonel Trubshaw's tent.

"Colonel, it's me. Lieutenant Richards. Could I see you for a few minutes, Sir?"

Jack could hear the reply though he could not make out the words. But Lieutenant Richards threw back the tent flap and entered.

Jack remained where the Lieutenant told him to stop. There was a camp stool nearby, but he did not dare sit down.

He could hear a lengthy conversation take place. At one point the Colonel exclaimed:

"You don't say!"

The conversation was largely a murmur of voices to him, but he did hear the Colonel say:

"He says that? He claims that?"

Then: "Dressed how?"

More murmuring, then:

"Indian. An Indian? You say he looks like an Indian?"

The conversation went on and on.

Three officers came out of General Middleton's tent and engaged in animated conversation. First one noticed Jack and had trouble drawing his attention back to business; then another. Finally all three were staring at Jack with undisguised curiosity. They finally returned to their conversation but continued to steal glances at Jack.

Jack began to feel foolish and uneasy. He stood alone and suddenly found himself wishing a uniformed guard had been left with him. The conversation with Colonel Trubshaw seemed to be going on forever. He must be telling him everything from beginning to end, thought Jack.

Suddenly the flap on the big tent was thrown back and an imposing figure emerged. Jack recognized him immediately.

It was General Middleton.

Jack had seen him once or twice back east. He had also seen him when he reviewed the troops at the passing out parade. Jack would have recognized him anywhere. He wore his red tunic with two rows of brass buttons down the front and gold braid on each shoulder.

The stout General wore his hair short now, but not his moustache; it was the same great walrus affair of yore.

Now he was puffing on a big cigar. When he spoke he removed it from his mouth and gestured with it.

Someone must have mentioned the Indian near Colonel Trubshaw's tent for he turned and for several seconds, gazed at Jack. He was about to say something to the other officers when he was halted by the re-emergence of Lieutenant Richards from the tent.

"Private Holden," said the Lieutenant, "The Colonel will see you now."

Then he saw Jack looking toward the General and his companions. He went over and spoke to them briefly. Jack heard the General say: "Oh really?" and turn to look at Jack with renewed curiosity.

"Inside Private," said the Lieutenant, when he had returned, "and look smart about it."

Jack was paraded before the Colonel. He almost forgot himself and shot off a salute. He stopped just in time, remembering that you do not salute when in mufti.

Lieutenant Richards had come in behind Jack. He took up a position near the entrance and waited. The Colonel was seated at a collapsible desk. It was covered with papers upon which rested a pen. Several rolled maps were scattered on the floor nearby. An orderly had made up a military cot over to one side. A barracks box stood at the foot of the cot and a change of uniform hung against the tent pole.

Apart from this there were no other effects or furnishings in the tent except two folding chairs. The Colonel did not offer one to Jack.

"Well," said the Colonel, "Finally decided to come back, did you?"

Not a promising beginning thought Jack.

"No, Sir. Well, yes, Sir," he said, not knowing quite how to answer such a question.

"The Lieutenant here has told me all about your alleged adventures. Sounds far fetched to me. What do you say?"

"It is true, Sir."

"Kidnapped!"

"Yes, Sir,"

"Outlaws!"

"That's right Sir."

"Learned Indian."

"I did Sir, some."

"All right, say something. Speak some Cree."

"Sir?"

"You heard me."

"Yes, Sir."

"Well?"

"Yes, Sir. What would you like to hear Sir?"

"Tarnation son. I don't know. Anything, say anything!"

Jack felt not only embarrassed, now he felt foolish as well. He blushed, but, thankfully, no one could see it beneath the charcoal and dirt on his face.

"TAN-SAI TAWOW."

The Colonel just looked at Jack.

Standing at attention, attired in the Indian breech cloth, leggings and shirt and two feathers in his headband, he looked stupidly at the Colonel. A gulf of silence separated the two.

Finally the Colonel spoke.

"And what does that mean?"

"Those are words of welcome, Sir, of greeting," Jack was not extremely confident of his Cree. He hoped that he was right.

"Say something else," commanded the Colonel.

"NITAHKOSIN," said Jack.

"Yes? What does that mean?"

"'I am sick', Sir."

"You're sick?"

"No. 'I am sick', Sir."

"You're not sick?"

"No sir, I am not sick. It means 'I am sick'."

The Colonel turned to the Lieutenant and said irritably, "He's confusing me, Lieutenant."

"Private Holden, what is the word for 'beaver'?" said Lieutenant Richards.

"AMISK," said Jack.

"Brown bear?"

"Muskwa."

"Muskrat?"

"Wachusk."

"Rabbit?"

"Wapoos."

"Skunk?"

"SIKAK."

"Fish?" said the Colonel, getting into the act.

"KINOSEW," said Jack.

"Buffalo," said the Colonel triumphantly. "You must know the word for 'buffalo'."

"PUSKWAW MOSTOS," said Jack.

The Colonel sat back with a look of satisfaction.

For a few moments he contemplated Jack. Then a look of concern crossed his face.

"But Lieutenant," he said, "How do we know he's not making this up. Do you speak Indian?"

"No, Sir," said the Lieutenant.

The Colonel became skeptical once more.

"Lived with the Indians too, did you son?" He asked this with a smile on his face.

"I did, Sir. Yes, Sir."

The Colonel simply shook his head as though Jack had just claimed to be Napoleon.

"The Lieutenant says that you claim there may be a spy, a saboteur in our ranks."

Jack glanced at Lieutenant Richards.

"A saboteur, a spy. Either or both, Sir. The Lieutenant reported the conversations I heard. I just drew conclusions, perhaps others would draw different conclusions."

"Yes, he did report the conversations you claim to have overheard from the 'outlaws'," he said sarcastically, placing emphasis on the last word.

"Enough with this interview," he said finally.

"You're on charge. "Desertion under fire." The whole matter was referred by me to General Middleton. It was his view that there was no other proper course. He gave the order and in the army we all obey orders."

He paused for a moment. Then he added, "even you, Private Holden!"

"Yes, Sir, I understand, Sir," said Jack. He spoke this with more bravery that he felt.

"Lieutenant!" said the Colonel.

"Yes, Sir?"

"Private Holden is under arrest. Take him out of here. I'll arrange a detail for guard duty."

"Yes, Sir," said the Lieutenant. And as he was about to take Jack out the Colonel spoke again.

"And Lieutenant, clean him up. He's dirty."

"Yes, Sir, anything else, Sir?"

"No. Oh, yes. Get him out of that ridiculous outfit and back into khaki. He's still in the army. For now, at least. For how long we don't know."

This last humiliating remark was directed at Jack. After all his efforts to do his duty, this was the result. He had been misunderstood all his life. He loved his country. He had been faithful and loyal. He tried to warn the Colonel of sabotage. He knew it might save lives, even his comrades. But his reputation from home had followed him to this remote patch of wilderness, a spot unmarked on any map, and his own Colonel refused to believe him.

After they stepped out of the Colonel's tent Lieutenant Richards said, "This way," and directed Jack through a maze of other tents to a small tent at the back of the small tent town.

"In here," said the Lieutenant. "Consider yourself under close arrest. I'm taking your parole that you will not escape. You heard the Colonel. Guards will be posted shortly. Until that I trust you, Jack."

"I never did have any hope of persuading him, did I, Lieutenant?"

Lieutenant Richards hesitated to answer. Solidarity of command and loyalty were important to the proper exercise of military authority. He looked at Jack. He knew Jack was loyal. He knew Jack had placed his complete trust in him. Jack believed in him and believed in the fairness and justice of his country and its army. He has been my friend, thought Lieutenant Richards. Now he needs me.

"Jack, I can see now that there never was any hope of persuading the Colonel. I should have known that before. The Colonel jumped to the wrong conclusion despite all my efforts. He reported to General Middleton and they decided what to do. Now they're both committed. They could look foolish if they changed their minds after advertising your desertion in the army all over the west on wanted posters."

"Wanted posters?"

"Yes, Jack. You didn't know?"

"Well, now that you mention it, I remember. A peddler showed it to me. It said that the army would pay twenty-five dollars for information leading to my arrest and conviction."

"Yes, that's what the poster said. I saw one too."

"I know someone who dearly wanted to collect on that. I should have let him."

"Don't talk like that, Jack. It's not over yet. You have friends. I'll do all I can for you. Don't get discouraged."

"Thanks Lieutenant. Lieutenant, tell me one more thing."

"What's that, Jack?"

"What's the penalty for desertion?"

"Desertion under fire?"

"Yes."

"Execution by hanging!" said the Lieutenant. Then he turned and left.

CHAPTER FORTY-FOUR

THAT NIGHT was the worst night of Jack's life.

He had been a prisoner of outlaws, then a prisoner of the Indians. He had begun the day a free man. Now, in the evening of the same day he was a prisoner again. And this time of his own people. He had been steadfast in his loyalty. The bitter irony that he of all people should be suspected of desertion was simply too much.

That night he went to bed exhausted. Even to think of all that had happened in that one day fatigued him. Every ounce of his energy had been spent. Every emotion wrung from his body. Yet he did not sleep soundly. He tossed and turned on the narrow camp cot, his mind in a turmoil.

When eventually he did slip into sleep it was a light slumber and his mind continued to struggle with all the conflicting emotion within him.

As he slept he saw the dawn. He rose. He carefully put on his uniform, ensuring every button was polished and shining.

The guard party came to a halt on command outside his tent. The flap was thrown back and the officer commanding the guard entered.

"They're waiting. Are you ready?"

When will I ever be ready for this, he thought. But he nodded his assent.

"Outside," ordered the officer.

Jack stepped outside. The two man patrol stepped smartly to either side of him. On another command the party marched away.

One scene faded into another. He sat now in front of a court martial panel. He was alone. Opposite him sat General Middleton looking splendid in full scarlet dress, as usual. To the General's left sat Lord Melgund; to his right, Major Lawrence Buchan. These officers too were attired in all their military finery: scarlet tunic, brass buttons, gold braid, campaign ribbons, gold piping, lanyards and swords.

They spoke and conferred, but all was a blur for Jack.

Then the august Major-General Frederick D. Middleton, C.B. Commander of the North West Field Force turned and looked down upon Jack and spoke, his great moustache quivering with every word.

"We have heard the evidence. Evidence which points to only one conclusion; desertion of your comrades in arms while under fire."

"Do you have anything to say in your own defence?"

Jack tried to speak, to tell them he was not guilty. His mouth worked, but the words refused to come. He writhed in anguish.

He saw the General turn to Lord Melgund. He's too ashamed to speak, he seemed to say. Major Buchan merely shook his head in resignation that one such as Jack could even have found his way into military uniform.

The General turned once again to Jack.

"Nothing to say. That, at least, does you credit. You refuse to cavil. You refuse to defend what so clearly is wrong. For that, and that alone, you deserve congratulations. But for nothing else.

"You have committed the most heinous act it is possible to commit in the military. To run, to abandon your comrades when under enemy attack is the very height of cowardice and betrayal. It is deserving of the severest condemnation."

He paused. The three officers glared down at Jack. He was dimly aware of other troops in the room. Some along the sides, others behind. He could hear their murmur of approval. Then the General spoke again.

"You have been found guilty of desertion in the face of the enemy. Do you have anything to say before I pass sentence upon you."

Once again Jack found he could not speak. The words reverberated in his head. I am not guilty. I was loyal and I am loyal now. I love my country. But I was kidnapped and held prisoner. I did not desert. I would never forsake my friends, not under fire, not ever. But these words never found their way through his lips. It was as though he were paralysed and unable to speak.

"Incredible," said Major Buchan. "Even now he refuses to make an apology."

"Fap," was the only thing heard from Lord Melgund.

"Nothing to say," said General Middleton. "A pity, really. But I must do my duty. An example must be set."

He looked down at Jack and slowly shook his head from side to side as though to say how sorry a thing it was, indeed, for matters to come to such a point.

"It is the sentence of this court," he said in a loud firm voice, as he brought his head up high, "that you be taken from this court to the scaffold on the high banks of the Saskatchewan River, and on that scaffold you be hanged by the neck until you are dead!

"And may God have mercy on your soul!"

There was a loud commotion in the courtroom when these words were uttered. Jack was roughly turned around and with a guard party of ten, marched from the room into the early morning light.

It took a moment for his eyes to adjust, but when they did, he saw it. A huge twelve foot high scaffold standing on the bluff of the river. A staircase led from the ground to the platform, upon which rested a massive super structure. Reaching out from this was a stout wooden arm from which dangled a long, heavy hemp. At the end of the hemp was a noose.

All of this Jack could now clearly see against the dim grey light in the early morning sky.

Slowly he mounted the steps. Each step up shortened the minutes he had to live. He reached the last step; then the platform. He turned around and looked out over a sea of faces. He recognized many. He saw his whole troop standing there, mouths open, in silence. As a matter of fact there was no sound at all coming from all those people. That struck him as strange.

Then he saw Tom. Tom took a step forward. Jack shook his head and Tom stopped.

Jack turned back. He was surprised to see a man standing on the scaffold with him. This man did not wear a uniform. He wore a black hood, only his eyes could be seen.

"Over here," said the man, pointing to a square on the platform.

Jack stepped over and the hooded man put his hands on Jack's upper arms and moved him this way and that until he was perfectly positioned.

Then he held out another hood.

Jack refused the offer. He could not bear to lose one second. He would look upon this sweet world to the end.

Even as he thought this the noose was roughly brought over his head and down around his neck. The rough hemp scratched his forehead. Then the long thick hangman's knot was brutally pushed down until it was stopped by the base of Jack's skull. The rope was tight around his neck now. It was rough and pricked his skin.

Automatically Jack's hand began to move up to ease the scratching hemp. It was roughly whipped down behind his back where it was tied to his other hand.

A priest appeared at his side.

"Do you have any last words?" asked the priest.

Tears welled up in Jack's eyes. He shook his head from side to side.

The priest began to read in Latin.

I can't understand, he thought. Why not in English so that I can...

The thought was never finished. The bottom fell out of the floor and suddenly he was plummeting down, down.

He waited for the hemp to tighten, the knot to hit.

Instead, he heard his name, at first dimly and then louder.

"Jack, Jack," said the voice.

"It's Tom," thought Jack. "Help me Tom."

He was being shaken roughly. "Jack, Jack," said the voice. "Wake up."

A shock of relief hit Jack.

"Wake up Jack," said the voice more urgently.

"Wake up. You've been having a terrible nightmare."

Jack opened his eyes. Above he saw Tom smiling down at him.

"It's all right Jack. It was just a dream. Wake up. You've been thrashing around. Your cot tipped over. You'll be all right."

A wave of relief and gratitude washed over Jack.

It was all a dreadful dream.

"I'm alive," he said. "I haven't been found guilty yet. I'm going to live."

"Darn right," said Tom. "We haven't begun to fight."

CHAPTER FORTY-FIVE

THE TWO chums were overjoyed to see one another. Tom had heard of Jack's adventures. Lieutenant Richards had told most of the men in the troop. But he made Jack relate the whole story again. Jack did, this time leaving out nothing. Tom's interest increased when he heard about One Feather.

"Lieutenant Richards never told us that," he said.

"He couldn't. I didn't tell him about One Feather."

"Why not?" he asked Jack. "If he had that information he may have been more persuasive with the Colonel."

As soon as he asked the question, he knew the answer. Jack merely looked at him and said nothing.

"Never mind," said Tom. "You did the right thing! How could you know you would fall into Indian hands."

"I guess things were pretty rough back at the train."

"Naw. Not really. There was some pretty hot gunplay. They pinned us down for a while. But we just hung in there and they soon gave up."

"Lieutenant Richards. Did he…" began Jack.

"Not for a moment, Jack. Not for a moment did he think you had deserted. He was sure something had happened, but not that."

"Not Duffy Durrel though. Right from the beginning he was hollering desertion. I think he was scared though, and the guys in our troop thought he was doing all that yelling to divert attention."

"Duffy Durrel," said Jack. "I never would have thought it. He's always been so friendly. A good Ranger too. He's always fussing over his pony. He was currying his horse the night this all started.."

"I brought you something to eat," said Tom, changing the subject. He handed a mess tin to Jack, along with some canned beef and biscuits.

"Did you have any trouble getting in here?" asked Jack, between mouthfuls. He found he was ravenous. He realized it had been a long time since he had eaten food with which he was familiar.

"None," said Tom. "I don't think they're restricting visitors. Anyway I know the guard. He's a friend of mine from the 90th."

"The Lieutenant told us about your report that there may be spying and sabotage."

"Yeah," said Jack. "I don't think Colonel Trubshaw believed that either."

"He should," said Tom. "Some mighty odd things have been happening around here."

"Lieutenant Richards told me," said Jack.

"Think it might be Captain Howard?" asked Tom.

"The Lieutenant doesn't think so. How about you?"

"I don't know. The only other person who might qualify for the description 'bluecoat' is Yank, and I can't believe it's him. He's sure been a good trooper."

"It might help us if we could find out just who 'bluecoat' is. It may not prove I'm innocent, but it may cause the Colonel to think again about whether I might be telling the truth."

"I guess I've missed quite a bit. How have things been going?"

"Not too bad," said Tom. "There's been some grumbling. Some are saying the General should not have split the command."

"I heard about that even before I escaped. I gather Gabriel Dumont couldn't believe his good fortune at having to take on only half the force. Travel…my Indian captor found it quite amusing."

"Yeah. Well, he sent French's Scouts, the Winnipeg Battery, the Royal Grenadiers and about eighty Teamsters all over to the west bank under the command of Colonel Montizambert. Lord Melgund went along as Chief of Staff."

"I gather some got across in time to lend a hand but others didn't."

"That's right. And we could have used all the support we could get. The General kept the 90th Battalion, and the rest of us on this side. Colonel Houghton stayed with him as Chief of Staff. Everyone thinks Colonel Houghton tried to persuade the General not to split up, but…"

"I think Dumont's scouts were watching every move of the General all along the way."

"I'm sure they did. There was plenty of room for them to hide and manoeuver. All along the east side of the river are coulees, bluffs, ravines and bush everywhere."

"I gather they were pretty well dug in," said Jack.

"They sure were. You saw the huge ravine. They were dug in all over its face. Plenty of cover. Boulders, willow, birch."

Though Tom and Jack visited most of the day, a few other members of the troop and friends in other units also dropped by. Everyone had his own story to tell.

The enemy had been spotted about nine in the morning. The troops on the east side of the river were quickly deployed in a wide arc facing the ravine.

The 90th had carried most of the action and experienced the heaviest casualties. The Grenadiers had been ferried across the river and thrown into the line late in the battle. By then the enemy were already in retreat. The Grenadiers had boosted morale, however, and the entire front made a final determined drive.

The enemy executed a withdrawal under cover of a feint and suffered few casualties. The casualties of the militia were quite heavy. It was all over by two thirty.

Jack heard post mortems aplenty. It was the first battle experience for most of the men. They talked excitedly about the blast and screech of cannon, the acrid smell of cordite, the shouts and cries of men fighting and dying, and the terrified shrieks of horses. He heard about the heroes and the cowards, the stoic bravery of the gravely wounded, the sounds, the sights, the smell of battle.

Most of the men were impressed with the tactics of the enemy. They took great care, always, to maintain cover and move only under covering fire.

There was a great deal of criticism of the General. Why did he divide his force? Why did he hesitate to order a general advance? Why did it take so long to order the Grenadiers across the river?

Tom was more amused than impressed by the General. He thought he was a total ass.

To the general amusement he described Middleton as he rode up and down the line giving advice and commands. First they were to keep their heads up. Then down. The General had received a ball through his hat, and as he rode he held the hat in his hand and pointed to the hole, all while bawling to the men about his close brush with death.

Tom did an imitation of the General in action for each new visitor. The merriment of his audience encouraged him to embellish the tale with each retelling, producing much laughter and great guffaws.

Jack laughed along with the rest, but deep inside he suppressed a hint of envy. He had been on the eastern edge of the right flank of the militia. He and Lieutenant Richards had seen little action.

They did however, see the rebels gallop off in retreat.

"General Middleton says they're better bush fighters than the Maoris in New Zealand. They're hell fire for fighting," said Tom. After a moment he went on:

"Everyone's talking about Captain Forrest and the premier's son."

"Who?" asked Jack.

"Captain Forrest. Of the 90th. He and MacDonald really pressed the final counter attack. Forrest got his hat shot right off his head. He's got the hole to prove it. Miracle he survived."

"What MacDonald?" asked Jack again.

"Didn't you know? Sir John A's son. He's a Lieutenant with the 90th Battalion. We thought for a time he'd been killed yesterday, but he turned up all smiles and chuckles and full of stories about how he ran the bottom off the rebs.

"He's a nice fellow. At first everyone thought he'd be stuck up, being the Prime Minister's son and all. But he's not. He's just a regular guy. Everybody likes him.

"Middleton's always strutting when he's around. Hoping the son will report his fine manful military bearing and all that. Lots of the men in the 90th have noticed, and have been laughing behind the General's back.

"Not Lieutenant Hugh J. MacDonald though. A proper loyal officer he is. Nobody faults him for it though, he's so well liked."

The company came and went for most of the day. The guard outside apparently had no instructions to prevent visitors.

Jack guessed the time to be about five in the afternoon. The sun shone low in the sky. He had been kept so busy with visitors that he could hardly believe the day was nearly gone.

He did believe it though, because he had not eaten since the canned beef and biscuits that Tom had brought him. He was hungry again. So when he heard voices just outside the tent he assumed it was someone bringing him supper.

To his surprise it was Lieutenant Richards who entered the tent.

"Evening Jack," said the Lieutenant.

"Evening, Sir," said Jack, rising respectfully.

"How are you making out?"

"Fine, Sir, thank you."

"Someone will be along shortly to fetch you some grub. I just thought I'd drop by to let you know that there will be a military funeral tonight at sunset. By general order all hands wishing to participate are to parade over by the high bluff no later than six thirty o'clock."

He looked at his pocket watch.

"About an hour and a quarter from now."

"But Sir, I'm…"

"That includes you Jack. The order specified all who wish to take part."

"Thank you, sir."

"It looks like we've had heavy casualties. Ten killed. As many as thirty-six wounded. Some quite seriously."

"The doctors are doing all they can but I don't doubt there will be more burials tomorrow."

The Lieutenant paused. Then he shook his head sadly, and rose to go.

"Lieutenant," said Jack.

"Yes."

"Before you go. Where is the bluff, where the ceremony is to take place?"

"Just south of the Quartermaster's Head Quarters. He's planted himself and his supplies right near the river bank. About fifty yards south of the ammunition wagons. Tom knows. He'll show you the way.

"Let me know if you need anything Jack," said the Lieutenant. Then he turned and slipped out of the tent.

Promptly at six thirty the men fell in.

Jack had not quite realized just how large the North West Field Force was. Even with some men absent, either on duty as pickets on the perimeter of the encampment or guarding military supplies or the horses or otherwise, there must have been close to one thousand men present.

They formed up in a large open meadow. It must have been ten acres at least.

The regimental Sergeant Major stood facing the troops. The officers also faced the men, each opposite his own unit.

Jack fell in with the Rangers. Next to him was Tom. The Rangers were to the right of the 90th Battalion. All the men faced west, into the setting sun.

To his left, but many yards away near the river bluff, Jack could see the bodies of the dead laid out in white canvas shrouds, next to open graves.

So far from home, thought Jack, never to return.

The sun was brilliant in the west. It bathed the army in an ochre light. The figures of the officers looked dark against the evening sky. Beyond them Jack glimpsed the river. Its waters looked in turn dark and threatening and then gold and crimson, reflecting the far horizon.

"Attenn...ha," called the Regimental Sergeant Major.

The sound of military boots coming together rippled down the ranks.

"Right...dress!" he ordered.

The heads of one thousand men in rank and file snapped smartly to the right. Arms shot out. There was a shuffle of feet as the enormous body of men moved almost imperceptibly to even out the ranks.

"Eyes...front," he called, and all arms snapped down as heads smartly turned forward.

Now, not a man moved in all that multitude of men.

Suddenly a band struck up a slow military dirge.

Jack thought about his friend, Gunner Cook. How ineffably lonely and depressing to be buried here, far from friends, family, familiar things. To be buried under prairie sod that may not know another human step for a hundred years. He choked up and mentally shook at the thought.

The bandsmen stopped then and the Chaplain began to speak. He was far over to the left near the bodies and closer to the Royal Grenadiers. Jack found it difficult to hear, even though the Chaplain was speaking in a loud voice.

"God bless these boys...Brave soldiers...have mercy on their souls...forgive their enemies..."

"Man that is born of woman hath but a short time to live...

"...Commit their bodies to the grave...souls to the mercy of Almighty God... knowing that in his infinite mercy..."

Then the Chaplain began to recite the Lord's Prayer, and as he did the entire Force, unit by unit, began to pray with him:
"Our Father who art in heaven,
Hallowed be Thy name.
Thy kingdom come.
Thy will be done on earth,
As it is in heaven.
Give us this day our daily bread,
And forgive us our trespasses
As we forgive our trespassers,
And lead us not into temptation,
But deliver us from evil:
For Thine is the Kingdom, and
The power, and the glory
Forever.
Amen."

After the prayer the Chaplain led the men in singing 'Oh God our help in ages past', and Jack listened to the deep resonant voices. The words drifted in and out of his consciousness as he thought about the dead, their families so far away, his own family and his trials and adventures far from all that was familiar.

"Oh God our help in ages past,
Our hope for years to come,
Our shelter from the stormy blast,
And our eternal home.
Sufficient is Thine arm alone,
And our defence is sure.
A thousand ages in Thy sight
Are like an evening gone,
Short as the watch that ends the night
Before the rising sun.
Time, like an ever rolling stream,
Bears all its sons away,
They fly forgotten, as a dream
Dies at the opening day.
Oh God, our help in ages past,
Our hope for years to come,
Be thou our guard while troubles last,
And our eternal home."

When the men had finished the hymn the Chaplain intoned:

"At the going down of the sun,
And in the morning we will remember them."

At that point a private in the 90th Battalion, which had suffered the gravest losses, stepped forward and read the names of the dead:

"Lieutenant Swinford,
90th Battalion.
"Private Hutchinson,
Number One Company
90th Battalion.
"Private Ferguson,
Number One Company,
90th Battalion.
"Private Ennis,
Number Four Company,
90th Battalion.
"Gunner Demanoilly,
A battery.
"Private Arthur Watson,
School of Infantry.
"D'Arcy Baker,
Mounted Infantry.
"Gunner Cook,
A Battery.
"Private Wheeler,
90th Battalion.
"Gunner Ainsworth,
A Battery."

As a military detail stepped forward and began to lower the bodies of the dead into their graves, a bandsman stepped forward and played taps.

After all the dead had been laid to rest General Middleton asked for two minutes silence.

All the men of the North West Field Force bowed their heads in silence. As they did so the sun slipped down below the horizon.

"Company-y-y-y…" shouted the Regimental Sergeant Major, bringing the men back to attention.

Jack brought his head up, ready for the order to dismiss.

But it never came.

A terrific explosion filled the air.

The whole assembled force quaked, as though hit. Jack felt the earth shake beneath his feet. He flinched as the shock wave of the blast hit the right side of his body.

Discipline disintegrated.

Jack turned in the direction of the blast. Huge flames were leaping into the sky from the Quartermaster's compound.

"The caissons!" shouted Jack. "Someone's sabotaged the ammunition wagons."

Cries and shouts echoed in the night air. Confusion reigned.

"Indians," shouted someone.

"Where the hell were those pickets?" shouted another.

Men ran back and forth without purpose. Shells exploded and rocketed into the dark sky. Fuses blew, casting grotesque shadows that flickered and disappeared. Bullets whined and buzzed overhead.

"It's an attack," someone shouted.

"Attack."

"Attack."

"Take cover."

"Down."

"Bring up those rifles, men."

The entire force, trained in war, had either taken cover or had flattened themselves against the earth, seeking protection.

Lieutenant Richards had immediately dropped to the earth taking cover the best he could in the field. He crawled northward and found himself next to Tom and Jack.

"What's happened, Lieutenant?" said Tom.

The explosions had subsided now. Only the occasional burst and whine of bullets could be heard.

"I don't know," said the Lieutenant. "That sounds like forty-five calibre rounds to me. Our Winchester ammunition."

"Or Snider ammunition," said Jack. "Either way it sure sounds like our stuff."

"I think you're right, Jack," said the Lieutenant. "Those huge blasts sounded like nine pounder shells going up."

The three men looked northward, across the tall grass covering the verge of the river bluff.

"It looks like only one wagon's afire, Lieutenant," said Jack.

The Lieutenant gingerly raised himself on all fours. He peered across at the compound.

"I think you're right Jack. But not for long. The Quartermaster has lined all the caissons up. The closest one to the wagon that went up is only ten feet away."

"It's a wonder it didn't blow already," said Tom.

"I'm damned if the concussion alone wasn't enough to set it off," agreed the Lieutenant.

They listened to the crackling of fire as the caisson burned. Behind them conversation hummed. The men remained down as though paralysed.

"It must be like tinder, that caisson. Ready to go any minute," said the Lieutenant.

"What'll happen?" asked Tom.

"If that goes the rest go up too. Like dominoes. Our entire munition reserve right there. If that goes it's the end of the North West Field Force. For now anyway. It will take months for resupply."

"The Lieutenant saw a shadow move at his right elbow. It was Jack. He was on his feet. Crouched low.

"Get down, Jack. For God's sake. Get down!"

"Somebody's got to stop that ammunition from going up," said Jack.

"You can't do anything Jack. No one can. Get down."

"I'm going to Lieutenant."

"No Jack. You'll get yourself killed, sure."

"There's some think I'm a dead man now, Lieutenant."

"Jack," shouted the Lieutenant in one last desperate effort to stop him.

"Be seein' you," shouted Jack over his shoulder as he ran toward the burning caisson.

"It's going to go up any minute," finished the Lieutenant in a small voice trailing off into nothing on the thin night air, as Jack raced over the grassland.

"What's that man doing," shouted a voice. The Lieutenant felt sure it was the voice of Colonel Trubshaw.

"Runnin' to hell," said another.

"Crazy," said a voice.

"What can he do? What can one man do?" added a voice.

Jack ran toward the burning caisson. His feet moved faster than they ever had before. His hands were pumping up and down. His lungs felt as though they were about to burst.

He kept his eyes on the burning wagon ahead of him. Thirty yards. Twenty-five yards. Twenty yards.

A blast now and it's all over. I'll disappear. He could imagine the fiery explosion, the blast of hot air smacking the front of his body, punching the air out of his lungs as it lifted his body up and backwards and over the Lieutenant and Tom and over the troops.

Ten yards.

He ran on.

And suddenly he was there.

He ran to the tongue. He bent to lift it. It would not budge.

The ammunition is blasted away, he thought. It can't be that heavy.

Then he saw that the blast had driven the end of the tongue into the soil.

He ran to the carriage wheel, grabbed a spoke and started to push.

Suddenly he noticed someone pushing at the other wheel.

"Tom."

"I think you need some help," said Tom. "Heave."

The two put their shoulders to the spoked wheels and braced themselves against the earth. They strained with all the force they could muster.

The caisson merely rocked backward a moment. As soon as pressure was released it fell forward again.

"I can't stand this heat," shouted Jack. "Once more. It's now or never." He could feel the intense heat singe the hair on his arms.

"Heave," said another voice. This time it was Lieutenant Richards.

And this time the caisson rolled back.

"Take it by the hitch," shouted Jack. "Less heat."

The three ran to the hitch at the end of the tongue. In a moment they had the caisson rolling to the bluff and over.

"The one closest is liable to go up any minute," said the Lieutenant. "It's like tinder. It's got to go too."

The three ran to the second ammunition wagon. They began to heave on the wheels. The enormous weight of the unspent ammunition made it seem like tons of steel rotted deep in soil. It seemed unmovable.

Then miraculously it began to move.

Yet another soldier had joined them and put his shoulder to the wheel of the wagon.

It moved ponderously to the edge of the forty foot bluff.

At first a lip on the edge stopped it. Then, ever so slowly, it tipped over the edge, the hitching tongue flipped up violently as it went over backwards.

The four men watched it go down for a split second.

"Get back. It's hot. Any impact will send it flying," shouted Lieutenant Richards.

As he finished an enormous explosion burst below them. The earth seemed to jump as the men flattened themselves against the turf only inches away from the lip of the precipice.

The noise hurt Jack's ears. He heard nothing for a moment, then only monotone ringing.

It subsided just as he heard the Lieutenant shout:

"Get back. The earth is beginning to cave."

Jack stood. He felt dizzy and drunk. The earth shifted crazily beneath him.

He ran after the others away from the river. Then he fell again as more explosions ripped the air.

He looked back. Great plumes of fire rocketed into the sky. More explosions and bursts.

The ground seemed to shake forever.

The four men sat there, too stunned to move.

After an eternity the flashing stopped. The pounding of explosions stopped. The earth settled down.

Just the crackling of brushfire could be heard in the silence.

Then a cheer went up and almost a thousand men descended on them. They laughed and shouted.

Just before he was engulfed, Jack saw that the fourth man helping was "Yank" Smith.

Where did he come from, thought Jack. I didn't see him at the burial parade. As a matter of fact I haven't seen him since the night of the ambush.

CHAPTER FORTY-SIX

THE FOLLOWING morning he could scarcely believe yesterday's happenings. Here he was, still confined in the tent. Still a prisoner.

For a long time he lay on the cot. He listened to the sounds of the camp all around him. Voices engaged in earnest conversation. Sharp high pitched laughter. The clanking of mess kits as the men prepared for breakfast or washed up after breakfast.

The smell of frying bacon filtered through the flaps of the tent and little fingerlets found their way to his nostrils.

What I wouldn't give for a cup of hot tea and several rashers of bacon with some hard tack, he thought.

His mouth began to water as his hunger rose. He quickly changed his thoughts. No telling how long before breakfast.

His mind turned again to the pleasant events of the night before. He remembered them clearly, as though they were happening right now.

The men descended on the four of them with a rush. For a moment Jack had thought he would be crushed. But suddenly he found himself thrust up, above the crowd. He came to rest on the shoulders of his comrades.

Men shouted his name. They cheered. Somebody lit a torch and soon there were a number of torches as the men paraded the heroes back to the campsite.

For heroes it was. Jack turned and saw Tom and the Lieutenant too had been hoisted up and were carried along in the parade.

Above all the laughing and shouting he heard someone speak his name and then use his nickname 'Canada Jack'. He cast his glance to the left and found that someone from his own unit was talking intensely to an officer. He recognized the officer at once. It was Colonel Grasett, Commanding Officer of the Royal Grenadiers. He was unable to hear the conversation, but before he was carried out of earshot he heard the Colonel exclaim, "Close confinement? Custody you say? Ridiculous!"

The torchlight parade disintegrated and then dispersed as the men reached the tent compound. Jack did not see Tom or the Lieutenant again that night. He quickly made his way back to his tent.

Jack passed a good part of the morning in pleasant reflection of the evening before. It was almost noon when he finally received something to eat. When he had finished he settled down to wait out the long hot afternoon in the tent. It was two o'clock when he heard footsteps outside.

"Halloo there," said a voice. A shadow passed between the sun and the tent. The flap flew open and Tom came in. His face was wreathed in smiles.

"You won't believe what's going on," he said.

"It looks good, whatever it is," said Jack as he watched Tom's face. "What is it?"

"Well sir, you're not going to believe it. I hardly believe it myself."

"Colonel Grasett of the Grenadiers has gone to bat for you."

"What do you mean?" asked Jack.

"Well, when he found that the men who saved the munitions depot was in custody he darn near flew into a rage! He refuses to accept that a man who could do what you did would desert anybody. He's telling anyone who'll listen what nonsense all this is."

"How do you know all this?" asked Jack.

"Well it's all over camp for one. Also, Lieutenant Richards was over to see him. They had a long talk. I guess the Lieutenant told him your whole story. He's quite impressed.

"Unlike certain others, he believes what happened to you.

"You've got a powerful ally there Jack. He's well liked by all the men. Not just his own battalion.

"He's quite disgusted at how the battle here was handled and makes no bones about telling people his views."

"Yes, but how do you...?"

"The Lieutenant."

"Yes? The Lieutenant what?"

"Well he told me Jack. He told everybody in the troop as near as I can figure. Colonel Grasett thinks that when the Royal Grenadiers finally made it over to this side all gung-ho and fresh and wanting to charge the rebels they should have been given their head. Might have stopped the rebels right here. Right now."

"There's a lot of criticism of the General. They can't understand why he held back."

"What do you think?" said Jack.

"I don't know, but I think Colonel Grasett does. He thinks the General behaved ridiculously. Riding back and forth telling the troops to keep their heads up, then telling them to keep down.

"The rebels sure know how to fight. None of this phony gallantry for them. They keep down. You never see them in battle. The best you can do is fire at the puff of smoke from his rifle, hoping he's still there after he shoots. It's a different style of fighting says Colonel Grasett. There's nothing gallant or noble about exposing yourself unnecessarily, he says. The rebels don't give a damn about such stuff.

"They'll be back to fight another day, he says."

"The General…"

"The General. Hah!" interrupted Tom. "He's still talking about how fine his men were. How brave to expose themselves unnecessarily during battle. He still thinks that's the way to fight."

"What does Colonel Grasett say?" asked Jack.

"Hogwash, that's what he says. Hogwash. That's no way to fight this war."

"Colonel Grasett is not alone, I gather. Colonel Van Straubenzie of the General's own staff and Captain Hague agree with him."

"Colonel Grasett thinks the General is too concerned with impressing his English Lord."

"Who…?" said Jack.

"Lord Melgund," said Tom. "The General's second in command. Colonel Grasett says the General spends most of his time mincing around in front of the Prime Minister's son…"

"Lieutenant MacDonald?"

"Yes, Lieutenant MacDonald. Hoping he's going to report back to his father the fine military bearing of the General."

"Too much time concerning himself about what MacDoanld and Melgund think and not enough about tactics."

"Where did you get all this information?" asked Jack.

"From Lieutenant Richards, I told you."

"Well, where did he get it? How did he get it?"

"Colonel Grasett asked the Lieutenant to accompany him when he went to speak to the General about you."

"The General had his friends there, as usual. But Colonel Van Straubenzie was there. So was Captain Hague."

"Apparently Colonel Grasett and the Lieutenant could hear the General defending himself even as they approached the headquarters tent."

"The Lieutenant was quite surprised at the scene when they entered."

"There was the General denying he had exposed himself unnecessarily to enemy fire. He claimed it was necessary to inspire confidence in green troops and green officers."

"He called them 'green'?" Jack asked.

"You bet he did," answered Tom. "He said if he'd had 'regulars' he would have taken a position in the rear, planted his flag and sent his orders."

"And then he said something that raised a lot of eyebrows."

"What was that?" asked Jack.

"Apparently he said that it wasn't necessary to prove his bravery, at least, not in England where he's known."

"Had anybody accused him of...?"

"No one," interrupted Tom. "No one had suggested he wasn't brave."

"An odd comment," said Jack.

"Darn right it's odd. The Lieutenant said there were a few smiles when he said that. Then the General added that they would all have been scalped if he hadn't exposed himself as he did."

"That must have pleased the officers as much as his 'green officers' comment," said Jack, shaking his head.

Tom grinned widely, then he went on to describe the General's excuses for delay in pursuing the enemy. With nearly forty wounded men on his hands he could not advance. The long awaited river boat, Northcote, was not even within a hundred miles of the camp, so the wounded could not be evacuated down river. The wounded could not be moved to Saskatoon for that was a two day march away. Neither could they be taken by wagon to Clark's Crossing, a trip of one day, for the doctors had advised the General the trip over rough roads may result in more fatalities. Neither did the General think they could be left for that would necessitate leaving an armed guard and medical assistance. He felt he could spare neither from his Force.

"He blamed the wounded?" asked Jack with a puzzled expression on his face.

Tom looked at Jack and nodded in reply. Jack merely shook his head and smiled.

"All this in his high falutin' way," went on Tom. "The officers were fit to be tied. Even the Lieutenant was shaking his head in disgust. And you know how careful he is not to show any disloyal thoughts."

"But what about me? What did Middleton say about me?"

"Well, I've got good news and I've got bad news," said Tom.

Jack mockingly grabbed Tom by the throat and pretended to choke him.

"Wait, wait. Before you add anymore to your offences," said Tom, fending him off.

"The good news is that you're going to be released."

"And?" asked Jack.

"The bad news. Well, the bad news it that they won't drop the charges. You're on open arrest.

"The General conferred with Trubshaw and Melgund and then announced this "compromise" as he called it.

"Colonel Grasett told the Lieutenant the General was just saving face. Anyway you should get official word some time later today."

"Well, it's an improvement anyway," said Jack.

"There is one other thing, Jack. Sorry to have to tell you this, but better me than Trubshaw."

"Come on Tom. Out with it."

"Colonel Trubshaw has insisted that you not serve with the Rangers. He says it would be bad for morale."

"What am I going to do, fight as a unit all by myself?"

"Our troop is to help Lieutenant Hugh MacDonald refit the Northcote, if she ever gets here. He's been assigned from the 90th to Middleton's Navy." Tom laughed at his own joke.

"As soon as that's done you're seconded to the Midland Battalion."

"Midland Battalion?"

"That's right. The Midland Battalion will be arriving on the Northcote."

"I expect someone will be coming down to the tent later on to tell you about all this officially."

Jack looked crestfallen.

Tom watched him for a few seconds. Then he spoke again.

"I've some more good news."

"Yeh?"

"Yeh, I'm going too."

"You?"

"Yeh."

"How did that happen?"

"I told the Lieutenant that I'd better go along or you'd get lost again, and he okayed it."

At that they both rolled back on the cot laughing.

"I'm surprised the General relented at all, with Colonel Trubshaw and Lord Melgund having his ear."

"That Ponce," said Tom with feeling.

"Ponce?"

"Yeh. General Ponce. He'll listen to his friends Colonel Tubby and Lord Dandy all right. Except when Lieutenant MacDonald is around. He can't do enough to please him. Hoping Lieutenant MacDonald will bring back good reports to his daddy, the Prime Minister."

"Makes me wonder if Lieutenant MacDonald had something to do with winning your release."

"General Ponce," said Jack and they both broke into laughter again.

"Did you know that General Ponce thinks he won a big victory here the day before yesterday?"

"Nobody else does. Three or four to one. Heavy artillery, newest weaponry, even Martini-Henry rifles in addition to Sniders and Snider-Enfields. All this against poorly armed rebels, with no military training, shooting home made shot. And even that they're short of."

"And he thinks we may have fought the decisive battle."

"Apparently the Ponce is giving it as his opinion we may not have another major engagement with the rebels. We won it all here."

"I'll bet Colonel Grasett doesn't buy that," said Jack.

"Or Colonel Van Straubenzie or Captain Hague," added Tom, "but Lord Dandy does and that's all that counts with him.

"There's a lot of talk amongst the men about the rebels. A lot of sympathy.

"They've come out here and worked the land. Built some fine little homes. And they can't even raise a farthing by way of mortgage on their land because the government's not going to allow them title."

"Not fair is it?" said Jack. "They're the ones who have suffered the hardships of frontier life. They are the ones who live on the land and farm it.

"Seems only right they should have some say as to how the land should be held, how title should issue."

"I understand the government has mostly ignored their claims and grievances," said Tom. "Criminal really."

"They shouldn't ought to have revolted though," said Jack.

"That's Riel though," said Tom. "If it weren't for him stirring up the locals there would be no revolt. No war."

"If it weren't him it would be Dumont and if it weren't Dumont, someone else. It's hard to blame them. But they shouldn't have rebelled or taken to arms," said Jack.

In the middle of the afternoon, Tom stepped out to fetch some "government biscuits" and tinned beef. He returned and ate with his friend and then was back and forth the rest of the day.

Jack had other visitors. He was now a well known figure in the camp although not universally liked; the views of General Middleton and Lord Melgund being well known.

But this did not dissuade others.

At about three in the afternoon Jack and Tom were interrupted by a completely unexpected visitor. Captain John French.

Captain French had begun his military career with the militia in Dublin, Ireland. He soon moved to Canada. In 1873 he found himself in Toronto. He was offered the position of Inspector in the North West Mounted Police.

After serving for many years as a Mountie on the great plains he resigned and settled with his wife and children on a farm. He knew the West well, however, and with the outbreak of hostilities on the prairies he raised a small contingent of experienced frontiersmen: French's Scouts. He was not embarrassed to take his intelligence information on the enemy from wherever it could be found.

He questioned Jack closely and at length about his exploits on the plains.

Jack felt pleased that Captain French took an interest in what he had to say.

Colonel Boulton, who had raised Boulton's Scouts also dropped by. Again Jack was happy to tell this experienced frontiersman everything he knew about enemy strength, intentions and movements.

Others dropped by. Some to offer a word of encouragement. Others merely to have a look at Jack, the man on whom so much attention was focussed.

Jack was polite and friendly to all, even the curiosity seekers.

Even Colonel Grasett, Captain Hague and Colonel Van Straubenzie dropped in for a few moment. Each offered congratulations for the heroic deed in saving the armaments and munitions of the force.

Tom pointed out to Jack as each of them left that in addition to best wishes, each expressed optimism for Jack's future.

Lieutenant Hugh MacDonald stopped by to add his "Well done" to the many others that afternoon. He knew that Jack would be helping with the refitting of the Northcote. He mentioned this with a twinkle in his eye just before he departed.

"I still think he may have had something to do with your release," said Tom.

"Poor guy," said Jack. He was referring to the bad case of erysipelas from which the Lieutenant was suffering. The bacterial infection had covered most of the right side of this face below his nose. It looked like raw beef.

"It must be painful," said Tom.

"He won't be shaving for a while," said Jack.

Toward nightfall that same day Lieutenant William Henry Lacy came down from Colonel Trubshaw's headquarters to tell Jack that he should consider himself no longer under close arrest.

"Don't be misled," said Lieutenant Lacy. "Charges have not been dropped. You still must answer for your dereliction."

"He hasn't been convicted yet, Mr. Lacy," said Tom.

132

"This is none of your concern Private. You will kindly keep your views to yourself. We have no interest in them." He sniffed pompously as he said this.

Then he turned back to Jack.

"Let me tell you Private Holden, that you have only been released so that you can do your share along with every man jack in this army."

"No reason for you to laze around after so many casualties, a manpower shortage and so much to do."

"Did Colonel Trubshaw tell you to say that or is that something you added for your own benefit?"

The Lieutenant ignored Tom and spoke directly at Jack: "That comes straight from headquarters.

"You are to report to Colonel Trubshaw tomorrow at four in the afternoon. Alone," he added, turning to glare at Tom.

Then he turned and disappeared through the flaps of the tent.

"What a phony," said Tom. "No wonder he's a favourite of Colonel Tubby!"

CHAPTER FORTY-SEVEN

JACK AWOKE the following morning and looked up at the roof of the tent. For a moment he forgot he was no longer in confinement. Then he looked over at Tom sleeping peacefully.

It's still a tent, I'm still in the army and I'm still on charge, he thought. All this is true but I feel different.

The bugles blew reveille and within moments Jack and Tom had stumbled out of bed and down a lane of tents to the company "hygiene facility". A washroom, thought Jack, can become anything in the imagination of Colonel Trusbshaw.

About sixty men milled about washing and shaving.

It was a crisp morning but many wore no shirt. Their galluses hung down around their breeches. They groaned and complained about everything, especially the early hour.

"We ain't going nowhere. Why do we have to get up so early?"

"Hurry up and wait. That's the army's motto."

You could see steam rising from the basins and each breath expelled a small cloud.

Here and there a murmur of conversation could be heard and now and then a quiet chuckle.

After ablutions the men repaired each to his own tent to finish dressing.

As soon as Tom and Jack were finished they walked down to the mess tent where dozens of men stood in line with mess kits in hand waiting to be served by the camp cooks.

As Jack approached he could see the cook sweating over the makeshift grill. He worked without looking up, picking rashers of bacon from the grill with a fork and dropping them into the extended mess kit.

The perspiration trickled down his forehead over his face and cheeks, then onto the bottom of his chin where it collected. Any sudden movements from "Cookie", as the men called him, shook a globe loose, flipping it on to the hot griddle where it exploded.

The two soldiers collected bacon, hard tack and tea and then returned to their tent where they ate in silence. Tom and Jack continued to sip their tea after finishing their meal. When the tea was finished they washed their mess tins and utensils and hastened over to the temporary parade ground for general inspection.

Out of the corner of his eye Jack could see other companies and battalions forming up for inspection. A few more minutes and he and Tom heard the usual.

"All present and accounted for, Sir."

"Thank you, Sergeant Major," said Colonel Trubshaw. "You may dismiss the men. But remind them to check for orders of the day."

"And also to see to it that all military equipment is cleaned and polished and ready for spot inspection at any time throughout the day.

"Yes, Sir," said the Regimental Sergeant-Major, saluting the Colonel.

Then, as the Colonel departed with the other officers, he repeated the Colonel's 'suggestions' to the troops.

"Parade...dis...miss," he called.

The entire company of enlisted men did a smart right turn and then broke ranks.

Tom and Jack walked through the centre of the camp in the direction of the Quartermaster's compound. They passed row upon row of canvas tents. There were soldiers moving about everywhere and in every direction. Some wore red tunics, some green and some black. There was a variety of head gear too: wedge caps, pill boxes, pith helmets, peak caps, astrakhans, helmets with pikes and some without.

Jack recognized a few of the men, but nearly all recognized him immediately. They waved at him, smiled at him or called out greetings to him. "Good show," and "well done" were the most frequently heard remarks.

Some even ran over to shake his hand.

There were many officers about the camp. Jack and Tom were kept busy saluting. Everybody seemed to be busy doing something.

A few men from A battery were "Gee-hawing" a team of horses into place in order to move a nine pounder. The pair seemed reluctant to back onto the gun and lifted their hind legs gingerly as if about to step on the carriage.

Boxes and equipment seemed to be scattered everywhere, in no particular order.

Tents were being struck and others erected for no apparent reason.

"I hope somebody's in control," said Jack, surveying the apparent chaos. "I hope somebody is organized, knows where everything is and where it is going."

They passed teamsters grooming their horses. Several were hitching up transport wagons.

They gave a wide berth to the hospital tents for subconscious reasons. Some of the wounded were loitering around outside waiting to see the doctors.

Little was heard from the seriously wounded while loud groans could be heard from those who were lightly wounded.

Just east of the ammunition wagons and caissons lay the corral. Tom and Jack went by to tend to their ponies.

Cloud was pleased to see Jack. He stroked her head and when he stopped she nudged him until he did it again. He fed her some oats by hand and then placed a feeder in front of her full of oats. He gave her a good brushing as she ate contentedly.

As they left the corral they passed the Quartermaster's cattle corral. There were many horned and dehorned steers there.

A shot rang out in the tranquillity of the early morning.

It startled them both. They turned to see that an animal had just been killed. Several men stood by sharpening knives, getting ready to butcher.

"Fresh beef tonight," said Tom.

134

"I'm hungry already," said Jack. "I hope they roast it over open pits."

The two men made their way over to the scene of the blast the night before. A huge crescent gaped on the bluff above the point of the blast.

Over to the left they could see tiny wooden crosses collected in a small group along the ridge of the bluff.

How lonely they look, thought Jack.

The two did not walk over to take a closer look.

That afternoon they walked over in the direction of the battle several days before. Other soldiers wandered over the ground in silence. Occasionally one would exclaim to his companion: "Look here" or "look what I've found."

They roamed over the rifle pits the enemy had dug into the face of the ravine and over its rim.

"It's a wonder we killed any," said Tom, when he saw how they had been fortified and hidden with clumps of earth and logs and brush.

They had heard that many rebel horses had been killed. They found them far up the ravine. Jack stopped counting the bodies when he reached thirty-five.

On their way back they passed Lieutenant Colonel Van Straubenzie's staff tent. He was one of the General's senior staff officers. Once again Tom was a fund of information.

Over a lifetime the Colonel had seen service throughout much of the empire and the world. He had fought in India in 1849, in the Crimea during the war with Russia in the fifties and later in the Chinese war. He had been mentioned in home dispatches three times for courage in battle. He had been severely wounded early in his career, a wound from which he suffered still.

What impressed General Middleton most, claimed Tom, was not his extensive military experience but the fact the Colonel was a brother to the commander of the famed Light Brigade of the Crimean Campaign, Sir Charles Van Straubenzie.

The old soldier emerged from his tent to stretch his legs and take a breath of afternoon air just as the two passed him by.

They threw him a respectful salute. Being without head gear he did not return the salute, but he nodded pleasantly.

Then he noticed that Jack was one of the men. He broke into a wide grin and said, "Good afternoon soldiers."

He was getting old. Grey streaked his beard which fell below his neck. Two enormous moustaches twisted down below his shoulder line on either side of his face. His hairline had receded considerably giving him a high forehead.

His eyes crinkled when he smiled at them.

Though he had no cap he wore his tunic and a large immaculate tunic jacket over that. It was decorated with brass buttons and gold braid in swaths across his big chest. From his left shoulder sweeping across his chest to his right waist was a sash in several colors. It seemed to be the one thing about the Colonel Tom did not know.

Jack teased Tom about this lapse in his knowledge.

"I can't tell you about that," said Tom. "But I can tell you this: That's a soldier who could lead this man's army to victory."

"He looks old Tom. I'm sure he's a great old soldier, but I'll bet he's seen better days."

Jack wondered if the old man still suffered from the wounds he received in Indian thirty-six years ago, and he wondered too at the Colonel wearing his great coat in the warm late afternoon sun.

As he had been ordered, Jack showed up promptly at four in the afternoon for his interview with Colonel Trubshaw.

The Colonel was not present. Jack reported to his adjutant Captain Henslow. He occupied the tent adjacent. He was seated at a make shift table processing papers.

Jack marched in, saluted and informed the adjutant that he was reporting for his interview with the Colonel, as he had been ordered to do by Lieutenant Lacy.

"Yes, yes, yes," said the Captain. "Can't you see I'm busy?"

Jack stood there at attention. He did not know what to do.

After a minute or two the adjutant looked up again from his work.

"Well, what do you want? He said this as if Jack had not already spoken.

"I'm supposed to see the Colonel, Sir."

"Well he's not here. Can't you see that?"

"Yes, Sir."

"Well?"

"Well, Sir, I…"

"Listen soldier. He's off to see Colonel Van Straubenzie at General Headquarters. He's trying to organize a chukker or two of polo while we wait for the Northcote to arrive. He's left me with all these papers, all this work."

"I'm sure you're very busy, sir," said Jack.

"Yes, I am busy. Now, all I can suggest to you is that you step outside and wait for the Colonel to return.

"I can't do anything for you here and you're interrupting my concentration."

"I'm sorry, Sir. Yes, Sir!"

Jack saluted, executed a smart about face, and exited the tent.

Then he waited for the Colonel to return. It appeared to Jack as though the testy disposition of the Colonel had infested his entire staff.

It did not seem that long before he saw the Colonel puffing along toward his headquarters tent. Lieutenant Lacy and another Lieutenant were in tow.

It did not surprise Jack that Lieutenant Richards was not with them. He would hardly have polo on his mind with a war going on, wounded fighting for life under the surgeon's knife and brave men lying lifeless under lonely crosses on the nearby bluff.

Colonel Trubshaw brushed past Jack and headed for the open flap of his tent.

"I should have known it," he said in disgust, as he worked at removing his white gloves.

"Damned old fool has no class."

"Yes, Sir," said Lacy as he trotted along beside the Colonel.

"No class whatsoever. Imagine, refusing me."

"I should have spoken directly to the General. That man has class. He would have heartily approved."

"Good for morale I shouldn't wonder."

"What's wrong with a bit of fun while we wait for the Midland Battalion and that damn gatling."

"Tarnation! Lord knows when the Northcote will arrive.

"Plenty of work to keep the men busy. Plenty of officers to keep an eye on 'em too."

They had entered the tent by now. The Colonel was still fuming, however, and Jack could hear every word that was being said.

"Insult to injury," exploded the Colonel again.

"Lacrosse indeed. And not for officers. For the other ranks. Gad."

136

Jack could almost hear him shake his head in disgust.

"Imagine, old Van Straubenzie thinking that officers should work and their soldiers play.

"I think he's getting confused in his old age. Or maybe this is something that he learned in Afghanistan. Perhaps that's how they do it in India."

Then the Colonel abruptly changed the subject.

"What does he want, outside?" he asked, referring to Jack.

"You asked me to order him up for this interview, Sir," said Lieutenant Lacy.

"Did I! Oh, yes. Well, give me a moment. Then send him in."

After several minutes, Lieutenant Lacy appeared in the entrance and motioned Jack inside.

Used to the capricious nature of his leader, Jack made sure he marched in smartly. He saluted the Colonel, then stood rigidly to attention.

The Colonel, now seated at a desk, did not order a "Stand easy" as was the military custom. Instead he began to lecture Jack.

"Right from the outset I knew your kind. You've shown yourself to be just like I was warned you would be.

"In that sense Private Holden, you've never let me down.

"All this damn fool nonsense.

"And now with your little bit of theatrics at the ammunition depot you've got half the North West Field Force as true believers.

"Well I'm not. Never have been, never will be.

"And I'll tell you another thing. Freddie Middleton isn't either. Neither is Lorn Melgund. You won't work your ways with them and you won't work your ways with me.

"The charges stand, as far as I am concerned. In the final result it's up to me if the matter is to proceed and on that point I am resolute.

"It's a sad state of affairs at which we have arrived that a son of Cobourg, one representing our fair little corner of Canada should so disgrace his community.

"Well I won't have any more of it.

"The steamer Northcote arrives soon.

"When it does it will be refitted on General Middleton's personal orders into a gunboat."

"A highly useful idea if you ask me.

"I have volunteered Baker Troop to lend assistance to Captain Sheet, the skipper, for the refitting.

"Lieutenant Richards will be with you, but you will be under the immediate orders of 'Hughie'…uh…uh…I mean Lieutenant Hugh J. MacDonald.

"He has been reassigned from the 90th to temporary duty on the Gunboat Northcote and will supervise the refitting.

"The only reason I'm telling you this is to let you know that after that little bit of work you are no longer a member of the Rangers. Understood?"

"Yes, Sir."

"I would cashier you now if I could but I cannot.

"I blame the acting Judge Advocate for that. His advice to Freddie. Apparently you are entitled to a trial or court martial before sacking…"

"Thank you, Sir."

"But cashiered you will be. I will see you sacked."

"What happens to me after I finish duty with Lieutenant MacDonald, Sir?"

"I don't much care, so long as you are not with my outfit. But I understand that

Colonel Williams may be asked to take you. The Midland Battalion arrives on the Northcote. Perhaps they'll take you in."

"Sir?"

"Yes, Private, what is it?"

"Everything I've reported has been the truth. None of it is daydreaming, none of it lies."

"We've been through all of this before, Private Holden. And you know my view.

"Anything else you wish to say?"

"Yes Sir. All I've ever tried to do is serve my country and my unit. And to make both proud. I've done my best to do my duty, Sir."

"Well your best has evidently not been good enough. You've failed!"

Jack said nothing in reply to this. He merely stared straight ahead in accordance with military practice and awaited dismissal. It came immediately.

"When the refitting is complete Lieutenant Richards will have fresh orders for you. Check with him."

"Yes Sir."

"And in the mean time let me give you one last piece of parting advice."

"Sir?"

"No more screw ups, no more tall tales, no more false heroics.

"If not for yourself, then for us, your former comrades in arms. And if not for us, then for the folks back home.

"Now dismiss."

As unfair as it all was, and as much as he knew it was unfair, Jack could not help but feel humiliated when he left the headquarters tent of the Canadian Military Rangers.

That night a great fire was lit in the centre of the camp. As Tom and Jack had hoped, huge slabs of beef were seasoned with salt and pepper and layed open to the fire. The scent of roasting and charring beef permeated the camp and surrounding area for miles.

Jack smelled the cooking beef and his mouth watered. He was hungry again. Was it the fresh air or was he always hungry like this?

A four ounce tot of rum was ordered to be given to each man. The ration was to be issued to the soldiers by unit. Jack and Tom left their tent and made haste to arrive at the place allocated for the Troop well before the ration was poured.

Although most had dropped by to visit as individuals when he returned, it was the first time he had been with his Troop as a group except when on parade. As he strode up there were friendly hellos from many of them. Then an embarrassed silence settled over the men.

For a moment he did not understand. Then he realized what had happened. They know the Colonel has refused my return to active duty with them, thought Jack.

It was evening. The setting sun cast long shadows from the men. Some of them sat around a small campfire. Others moved about. Many were engaged in low conversation.

The tents not far away also threw shadows. But already, inside the tents, lamps had been lit and you could see figures flash up and down the canvas sides.

Jack was conscious of life in the encampment beyond Baker Troop and its campfire. Other companies and platoons had also organized small parties and lit other campfires. A shout was heard, a cackle of laughter and then a burst of laughter as one group enjoyed a joke.

A camp clown, thought Jack.

Sandy McCallum came over to say a few words of greeting to Jack. But he spoke in a low voice, as though he were at a funeral.

Then Jack heard a familiar voice.

"Chack," said Kurt Schmidt, "I haff decided to join the North West Mounted Police."

"Really," said Jack, waiting for the explanation that was sure to follow.

"Yes," said Kurt. "I will choin the Mounted Police."

"Tell him why," shouted Bo Sandford.

"You're not going to believe this," said Sandy McCallum.

"Because of ze uniform," said Kurt. "A splendid uniform."

"Tell him what you told us," said Crutch. "Come on," said Horace Busby.

There was a murmur as the men waited.

"Well," said Jack. "Why?"

"Well," said Kurt, "actually the pike."

"The pike?" said Jack. Now he was puzzled.

"Ya, the pike," repeated Kurt.

"Ya, the pike, Chack," imitated Crutch. "Ze pike in ze helmet."

At this the whole of Baker Troop broke into uproarious laughter.

Suddenly the ice was broken. All the reserve and embarrassment dissolved. The men of Baker Troop called out to Jack across the campfire and laughed. Some came over to shake his hand and clap him on the back.

It was like old times back at the training depot.

In the buzz and hum of voices Jack could still hear Kurt trying to explain to anyone who would listen. He was all seriousness.

None of the others paid him the slightest heed until Jack spoke to him again.

"I'm sorry Kurt, I didn't catch what you were saying."

"You iss a good man Chack. You always were a friend to me."

"Thanks Kurt."

"Vat I was sayink," said Kurt, "Iss that a uniform iss very important."

"Of course it is Kurt," shouted Langford Hughes to the general amusement, "especially to you Germanic people."

Kurt drew himself up in dignity at this remark, but otherwise ignored the comment. He went on, then as if he were talking only to Jack.

"The Cherman people yess," he said. "They know the value of a gut uniform. It does impress you know. And a good helmet worth the name alvays has a pike in the top."

"That's so you can lower your head and charge," shouted Higgins.

"And stab the enemy to death with your head," added Tubby Mills.

Uproarious laughter followed this comment.

Kurt, however, plunged on undaunted.

"A gut uniform hassits uses. Preachers vear uniforms of a kind. Policemen, firemen, chudges undt even barristers vear vigs in Court."

"Now hold on a minute there chum, you're talking about the Empire now." This was said by Tubby Mills in mock seriousness. "Vigs indeed."

"Vell iss it not so?" asked Kurt. He did not wait for an answer.

"Ze English do not know anysing about how to make a proper uniform. In Chermany even ze headvaiter hass a uniform more resplendent than a Cheneral in Canada.

"Ve know how to make a uniform and I don't mind admitting ve like uniforms."

There was a general round of good natured laughter at this. Then Kurt went on:

"Ve like our uniforms it iss so. I haff ein cousin in Austria. Ze border guards zere haff very fine uniforms. He wrote hiss examen to be a border guard. He passed. He iss now an Inspector of Customs and iss quite happy. He hass a fine uniform."

"Ya Kurt, tell us another one," said Horace Busby.

"It iss true," insisted Kurt. "That vass my muzzer's brozzer."

"Hiss name is Alois Schicklgruber."

"Shick...what?" exclaimed Tubby Mills. "There is no such name."

"Schicklgruber," said Kurt.

It was too much. The whole Troop erupted in riotous laughter.

Things were back to normal, thought Jack.

CHAPTER FORTY-EIGHT

THE NEXT few days fell into a routine much like the first day. A great deal of time was put in by the troops in cleaning and re-cleaning military equipment. The soldiers were assigned one duty after another, carrying, shining and moving. They were given extra drill and some were given little pep talks from officers who felt they had learned much from very little action.

In the afternoons, when the resourcefulness of the officers failed, desultory efforts were made to organize the men for informal games of lacrosse.

But of all these, one thing was constant. The camp was abuzz with excited discussion of the skirmish that had taken place and the battle that had yet to come. Each soldier had his own private adventure to relate. Many were true tales of heroic action.

They discussed their sympathy for the rebels, the arrogant indifference of the government and that 'damn Riel'. Most of them felt that Riel was the immediate cause of the uprising.

The officers were discussed too. Not before their faces, it is true, but in private.

They could not understand the failure of General Middleton to give the order to charge the enemy when it was clear he was in retreat. They could not understand why he did not order an immediate advance to prevent the enemy from regrouping and preparing for the next assault.

They did not see why it was necessary to wait for the Northcote. They had supplies aplenty, thanks to Canada Jack, and they had more than enough troops. What need was there to wait for the arrival of the gatling gun and the Midland Battalion.

They were divided on the issue of Middleton's Navy. They had heard of his orders to refit the steamer into a gunboat. Scuttlebut such as this swept through the ranks at an enormous rate.

Many thought it was a good idea. A large number of men laughed with glee at what they considered 'such nonsense'. They even dubbed the new gunboat to be "the Steamer Nonsense".

'Middleton's Navy', however, became the generally used public reference to this scheme of the leader.

The men had settled in to await the arrival of the sternwheeler not happily. But they had settled in.

CHAPTER FORTY-NINE

ON THURSDAY morning at eleven o'clock Jack and Tom were once again cleaning their rifles. They had spent the earlier part of the morning in drills. They had just returned from the temporary firing range where Lieutenant Richards had arranged for a bit of target practise.

It was already hot. The sun had driven away the moist air of early morning, and now shone brilliantly. Finding it too hot to work inside the tent Jack had stepped outside with his rifle.

Suddenly the sound of a whistle split the air.

Jack looked up from his work.

The whistle sounded again. This time it moved up an octave, half way through, into a screech.

"What is it?" asked Tom from inside the tent.

The whistle blew again. Twice this time, in rapid succession.

"Northcote," said Jack. "The wait is over. Northcote is here."

Tom and Jack left the tent and started over to the river bluff. Hundreds of others had the same idea; some running, some walking and others sauntering. It seemed as if the entire camp was on the move, headed over to the river bluff to witness the arrival of the Northcote. People ran ahead of them on either side. Jack and Tom suppressed the urge several times, but finally, they began to run too.

Jack felt silly running to the bluff, as though there were only a limited number of seats available to watch the arrival.

As he ran the last few steps, Jack saw the ridges of the bluff lined with hundreds of men from the various units.

He and Tom edged their way forward until they had an unobstructed view. The east bank of the river was much higher than the west bank. They had a commanding panorama not only of the broad sweep of the river to north and south, but also of the plain stretching into the blue grey morning mist of infinity in the west.

The turgid river surged past them many feet below. It was a powerful current, moving swiftly from the south.

A heavy growth of cottonwood, grey willow and poplar covered the steep embankment. About thirty-five feet below a broad shelf jutted out forming a natural landing. It ran along the embankment for little more than a hundred feet. On either side of it the bluff dropped precipitously to the river's edge.

Jack could already see some uniformed personnel carefully making their way down the side of the bluff to the landing below.

The whistle screeched again and Jack looked up the river to his left. It curved gently to the west about a half mile away. A heavy growth of trees and brush covered the far side of the river all the way to the bend, and beyond he could not see either the river or the Northcote. Further up, the river took a long gentle turn south east. From that point he could see the river meander for many miles into the distant murky blue haze in the south.

Suddenly the Northcote poked its prow around the tree shrouded peninsula on the far bank. A cheer went up from the soldiers. The Northcote sent up another long screeching blast of its whistle. Two white gulls, startled by the blast, flapped their wings and rose into the warm summer sky from the green grassy verge of the river's edge. They wheeled in tandem making a wide sweeping arc across the river in the direction of the east bank.

Jack realized he was looking down at the birds. He could hear the stir of excitement ripple all the way along the bluff, occasionally interrupted by exclamation, as the ship emerged.

"Ain't she a beauty."

"Look at her."

"How graceful."

She had cleared the tree cover on the far bank and now sailed in full view of the men. Against the muddy color of the water with its green and yellow reflections from land, she gleamed white except for two tall black smoke stacks toward the bow. Both of these belched thick black smoke that curled and billowed and flowed high above the ship toward the stern.

Two cranes jutted impudently into the air over the bow. The low chalky hull swept back only feet off the water line to the stern of the boat. There, churning mightily, was an enormous paddle wheel. A silver rush of water tumbled toward the turbulent surface of the river in the wake of the ship.

The boat foredeck was crammed with crates, and cords of wood were piled high along her sides.

A rail ran the length of the steamer on both the hurricane deck and the top deck. They were supported by fine white ornate lattice work which, from a distance, resembled the finest silver filigree. Jack could spot state room doors here and there along both decks.

All of this was surmounted by the pilot house. It was situated amidship toward the bow of the boat. It was white too but sported large windows on both sides and fore and aft. Jack could discern figures moving inside.

Lashed to the flagstaff on the bow end of the superstructure was the Union Jack. It fluttered proudly.

The vessel was jammed with the men of the Midland Battalion in their scarlet tunics. They lined the rails of two decks from stem to stern. They clambered over freight at the bow and crowded along the boat deck at water's edge.

As the Northcote churned abreast of the troops watching from ashore it gave off two more quick blasts of the steam whistle. A cheer went up from the Midland Battalion. Jack could see arms waving and hats rocking to and fro.

An echoing cheer rose from the men on the river bank. The cheer rose in crescendo to become a roar.

They were now an overwhelming force. Surely they were now invincible. In a curious way Jack felt sorry for the enemy in the battle that was soon to come.

The Northcote made a wide sweeping turn past the landing site.

With her white filigree and white superstructure studded with scarlet tunics everywhere, and all of this brightly reflected on the glassy surface of the water, she resembled nothing so much as a gargantuan crystal crown.

The ship looked huge as she churned in a wide clockwise arc in the middle of the river. Then, ever so ponderously, her stern wheel slowing almost to a stop, she edged slowly upstream toward the landing.

Then her port side nudged the bottom near the river's edge and she came to a shuddering halt. The red tunics aboard swayed forward slightly with the jolt, then settled back.

Deck hands shouted back and forth. Lines were thrown out and for the first time Jack noticed men on shore right at water's edge.

There was more shouting back and forth as the lines were secured and a gangway thrown across to land.

Immediately the ship began to disgorge red-coated soldiers. The men carried packs on their backs and rifles at their sides. The red line seemed to go on for hours. It wound its way across the gangway and up the short embankment to the landing. Then the soldiers began to make their way to the top of the bluff.

The men watching from above began to lose interest. Some wandered away.

Suddenly Tom said, "That's Colonel Williams."

Jack looked down.

"Over there," said Tom, "talking to Colonel Grasett and Captain Hague."

"Yes, I see them," said Jack. "Good looking officer. I wonder what they're talking about."

The officers talked for awhile as the Midlanders filed past and headed up the embankment. Occasionally one or the other of them gestured. Once Colonel Williams turned to call instructions to a sergeant who was still on board. The line of men was interrupted then, and military supplies were carried over the land.

"The only excuse the General has not to resume the march now, is the refitting of the Northcote. I can't wait to get started," said Tom.

Jack did not have to ask "get started on what", the march or the refitting. He knew the answer.

The march to battle.

CHAPTER FIFTY

IT WAS dusk. All day long the Midland Battalion had worked to settle in. Supplies had been hauled up the embankment piece by piece. It was back breaking work. The ship had now been offloaded of tents and crates and ammunition. Boxes and trunks and bags of all kinds were scattered around.

As the afternoon wore on order was gradually restored to the campground. Dozens of additional tents were thrown up and gear stored. All that remained to be removed from the ship was Captain Howard's gatling gun. It had been decided that a more suitable location could be found upstream for its removal.

The men had all been fed. Tom and Jack lounged in their tent. The flap had been thrown aside and as they spoke in low conversation they looked out into the twilight of eventide.

From far across the camp drifted the sounds of a harmonica. It played a sad dirge from the American Civil War. The tune was still popular with soldiers even though that war had ended twenty years before.

Then, over the evening air floated the strumming chords of a banjo. A happier mood, thought Jack. Men began to sing along. The voices were distant but they soon drowned the sadder strains of the harmonica. The two had not expected a visitor that evening. They were surprised, therefore, when they heard a voice just outside the tent.

"May I come in?" said a rich deep voice.

A man stepped through. Tom knew instantly who their new guest was: Colonel Williams, Commanding Officer of the Midland Battalion.

"A-tten Shun," said Tom with brisk military precision.

Jack and Tom both leaped from the cot and stood rigidly to attention.

The Colonel looked briefly over the tent, then at the two young men standing before him.

"As you were," said the Colonel.

The two young men relaxed somewhat, but remained standing.

"May I sit?" asked the Colonel, gesturing to a camp stool.

"Yes, Sir," said Jack. He ran over to pull the stool over from the tent wall.

"Thank you," said the Colonel taking a seat.

"Please, relax, both of you," said the Colonel again.

The two still did not sit but shifted uneasily on their feet. Finally the Colonel said, "You were seated on the cot before I came in. It would please me if you were to sit there again, so that we may have a little chat. It has been a long day. We'll all be more comfortable seated."

Lieutenant Colonel Arthur T. H. Williams was also a Member of Parliament. Jack felt odd that he should have such a visitor. The man could soon be his Commanding Officer.

The Colonel was without affectation. He made it a point to know by their Christian name each member of his Battalion.

His men had absolute confidence in him, knowing he would not ask any man to do what he would not do himself.

He was widely respected and liked throughout the whole of the North West Field Force. He was also widely believed to be their best tactician. This belief was shared by officers and men alike.

Colonel Grasett felt that an exception had to be Fred Middleton who constantly found fault with the tactics suggested by Colonel Williams.

The General was encouraged in his attitude by Lord Melgund who was clearly jealous of the Colonel's military skill. He looked down upon hoi polloi such as the Colonel. Though he was careful not to say so in front of Hugh MacDonald, he held elected politicians in low esteem. It appeared, in fact, that he held most people, other than himself, in low esteem.

He took no pains to hide his opinion of Colonel Williams. Every time the Colonel suggested a military maneuver to the General, Lord Melgund pursed his lips and raised his face to the sky. "Tuh," he said letting out air. Then he promptly turned away.

This always distracted the General who ran after the Lord solicitously each time, afraid he had offended him.

Now, he put the two young soldiers fully at ease. Although they remained respectful throughout, they had such an easy going chat that Tom had to stop himself from referring to General Middleton as General Ponce. Jack glared at him hard once, and the second time pinched him. Thereafter Tom remembered.

Colonel Williams was a tall robust man. He spoke slowly and distinctly. His hair was thick and brown. He wore long sideburns and a full dark brown regimental moustache. He had a high forehead, friendly brown eyes and an aquiline nose.

He looked smart and military in his red tunic.

Altogether he projected a benign yet correct impression.

The Colonel had heard about the explosion the night of the funeral and went to great lengths to compliment Jack on his quick action.

"It saved the mission of the North West Field Force."

"Thank you, Sir."

"No, Jack, it is I who should thank you."

"If it had not been for your pluck and courage almost our entire munition supply would have gone up with a bang."

"I don't need to tell you what that could have meant."

144

"It was a good show. I am not the only one who should be thanking you. I know I am not. I understand you have had quite a parade of well wishers over the last several days.

"I think you know I am referring to one who should have been over to thank you but has evidently not."

"I think I understand, Sir."

"I think you do."

"Anyone would have done it I'm sure," said Jack.

"There were almost a thousand men there that night. Only one man led that action. Not a thousand, but one."

"You showed real leadership, and we're proud of you."

Jack said nothing to this.

The Colonel then went on to refer obliquely to Jack's release from confinement.

"I'm just sorry it cannot be more for the present. But these things take time. I'm sure you understand."

"Yes, Sir, I quite understand." Jack looked the Colonel in the eye when he said this.

The Colonel chuckled knowingly. "I'm sorry it's not back to your old unit."

"That's all right, Sir."

"But you'll be of more use with my outfit. The Midland can always use another brave man like you."

"Then it's all arranged, Sir? I am seconded to the Midland?"

"It is, Private Holden."

"Thank you, Sir."

"I understand you're friends," he gestured to Tom. "I also understand you're both from Cobourg. That's not far from Port Hope you know. That's my home."

"That's right, Sir," said Tom.

"I've made tentative arrangements for you to come over too, if you like. Might as well keep as many of us together as we can. Would you like to do that?"

"You bet I would, Sir. Thank you, Sir!" said Tom.

The Colonel then went on to question Jack at length about his exploits after the ambush.

Like Captain French and Colonel Boulton he showed particular interest in any intelligence information about enemy allies, intentions and movements. Several times he pulled out paper and pencil and made a few notes.

He was keen to discuss the suggestion there may be spying or even sabotage. At one point he said, "This whole matter should have been given priority attention. There may still be time, but I doubt it."

After a time he rose. He thanked the two young men for their hospitality. He told Jack he should not be too disappointed or concerned that he would not be going back to the Rangers. "You know how Colonel Trubshaw is. Hell, everybody knows." He chuckled again. He told them they would both find themselves more than welcome in the Midland Battalion.

After this he instructed Jack to come by his battalion headquarters after the refitting to meet his staff officers. He would let him know about their respective assignments at that time.

He shook the hand of each of his new men. Then he left.

"He should be Commanding General," said Tom. "Not that Ponce."

"If anyone can win this battle for us it will be that man," said Jack.

CHAPTER FIFTY-ONE

THE COLONEL had no sooner departed than Sandy was at the door of the tent.

"No lounging about tonight fellows," he poked his head through the entrance. "Baker's going down to the Northcote to make a start right away."

"Oh no," exclaimed Tom.

"No use complaining to me soldier, orders are orders."

"Why tonight?" asked Jack.

"The Lieutenant wants to pack away as much reserve ammunition as he can tonight. Clear the decks so to speak. Get an early start on fortifications tomorrow."

"What time?" asked Jack.

"Seven thirty," replied Sandy. "Not much time. One half hour from now. At the landing."

He turned to leave then stopped and turned back.

"Oh, I almost forgot. Bring a bedroll. The Troop is going to kip on the boat tonight. That way we'll get an early start tomorrow."

Ten minutes after he left, Jack and Tom were out the door. They made haste and arrived at the landing with five minutes to spare. Lieutenant Richards was already there.

He told them to go right on board while he waited for the remaining several troopers to arrive.

Jack scrambled down the last few feet to the foot of the gangway. He looked up. The ship loomed large before him. It was now dark and lamps burned in the pilot house, and in the engine room and in several state rooms. Another several lamps lit up the forward deck beneath the long cranes. He could hear the moving river water burble and rush around the hull. It sounded cool, refreshing.

He and Tom walked up the gangway. They turned left and walked along the boat deck toward the light, up at the bow.

When they arrived they found most of Baker Troop already there and hard at work. Lieutenant MacDonald was there and the two saluted him.

"Good to see you men," said the Lieutenant. "Just throw your kit there for now." He pointed at a pile of bedrolls. "Both of you can give us a hand moving this ammunition below. We want it towed far from any danger of being lit by stray fire."

"Don't want to blow ourselves up do we?"

Sandy came up just then to take another box from the many stacked beneath the cranes.

"Just follow Sandy. He'll show you where to stack it."

The two men pitched right in.

Most of the ammunition was marked:
"Canadian Militia
9 Pound Shells
EXPLOSIVE
HANDLE WITH CARE

There were also many boxes of cartridges of various calibre, some for the forty-five calibre Winchester, a great deal for the Snider Enfield.

The men worked with a will. It was not long before Jack noticed the last member of the Troop had arrived. He was put to work along with the others. The ammunition

146

was carried through a forward companionway door, across a few steps to another door, through that door and down a flight of stairs. At the bottom a left turn was made. Another five steps, past the door marked "Boiler Room", and right turn down another short flight of steps. There the ammunition was deposited and secured. Well below the water line.

Jack had been working for about three-quarters of an hour when he emerged on the foredeck to find an impatient man in naval attire and peak cap standing there. He had greying curly hair which stuck out all around his cap. He wore long whitish sideburns. He was inclined to be stocky and had dark eyes that darted about as he spoke.

It was Captain Sheet, the skipper of the Northcote.

"Ease upon that line will you Lieutenant." This remark was directed to Lieutenant Richards. It was not so much a request as an order.

"Sir?" said the Lieutenant.

"That line on the port bow. It's much too tight. The current doesn't help. But we're much too tight with the shore line. Everyone's aboard now, so you tell me. No need to crush the portside against the shore line."

"It'll help me off tonight when we move upstream. I'm going astern to put a couple of turns on the paddle. When I do, pay out that line about eight feet."

There was more conversation but Jack did not hear it as he returned below with another load.

He felt the vessel shunt forward almost imperceptibly as he returned top side. Just as he stepped through the companionway door he heard a hoarse cry.

Twenty feet away stood Lieutenant Richards. He was screaming in agony. Jack took in the situation in a moment.

The Lieutenant's left wrist was crushed between the line and the gunwale. In a second Jack was at the side of the Lieutenant.

"A knife," shouted Jack. "A knife quickly, or the Lieutenant loses an arm."

The vessel was shifting to starboard. Somehow the Lieutenant, a landlubber, had permitted his wrist to come between boat and breastline while making ready to ease off. The boat had shifted to starboard and the line had snapped down like a savage trap. It held him like a vise. The Lieutenant was groaning in agony as the thick hemp line twisted down, grinding his flesh.

Suddenly, Yank was at Jack's side extending a knife to him.

He grasped the knife and cut hard with a sawing motion into the underside of the line.

"What the hell is going on down there."

It was the skipper shouting at him from the roof deck.

"Hand's caught," Jack said. "Got to cut the line before it severs his wrist."

"Oh well," was the only reply from the skipper. "I had to single up lines in an hour anyway."

Jack had no time for disgust at this callous reaction. He just kept sawing away. The hemp seemed as hard as iron, so difficult was it to cut. Soon, however, he had only two inches to go, then an inch. But, before he could cut the remainder of the line, it snapped.

Jack could feel the bow of the vessel subside to starboard before the second port bowline stopped her.

The Lieutenant's hand and wrist were a tangled mess of red blood, yellow gristle and flapping skin. Gobs of blood cascaded to the deck.

"Tubby," shouted Jack at Mills who stood transfixed in horror at the scene. "Get over here."

"Yeh, Jack?"

Jack was busy wrapping a handkerchief around the Lieutenant's arm. He knotted it, grabbed a thick pencil from the Lieutenant's pocket, placed it on the knot, and tied a second knot to secure the pencil. Then he turned the pencil several times to stop the blood from flowing.

"Get him up the surgeon's tent pronto. Double time. I don't care how you do it but get him there. Carry him if you have to."

Jack had dropped the knife when he applied the tourniquet. Now he looked down to retrieve it and give it back to Yank.

It was gone.

When Jack looked up he found the men had stopped working to watch the crisis unfold. Lieutenant MacDonald was standing next to them. He too was mesmerized by the grizzly scene.

Jack noticed that the only one who was not present was Yank Smith.

CHAPTER FIFTY-TWO

"ALL RIGHT men," said Lieutenant MacDonald, his voice shaking the men out of their lethargy. "The show is over. We have a lot of work to do before turning in. Let's get at it."

Mechanically the men resumed moving the munitions stores.

Jack had completed three more trips below. His muscles ached with the weight of the full ammunition boxes. He found that his knees threatened to buckle with each step down the stairway.

He was on his fourth trip when he noticed something strange. He had already made a left turn past the boiler room door when he realized it was ajar. It had been securely locked all evening long.

He completed his journey, quickly stowing the box of ammunition. Then he quietly made his way up the first flight of stairs. Instead of stepping through the companionway, however, he remained behind the door jamb in the shadows. For a few minutes he watched the door to the boiler room.

He was about to abandon his watch, thinking himself paranoid, when the door quickly opened and a man stepped out. He closed the door with his left hand, his back turned toward Jack. He moved up the stair so rapidly then, that he was gone before Jack could really be sure as to who it was.

Jack stepped over to the boiler room door, opened it, and slipped inside. He quickly descended the wooden steps. It was dark in the boiler room. Flickering reflections from the untended furnace cast an eerie glow.

For a long moment Jack looked around. There was something strange there, but he couldn't quite place it. One of the men from Baker Troop had just been here. He tried to figure out what it meant.

Then his eyes fell on the pale reflection of firelight dancing on some wooden boxes.

They were ammunition boxes. There must have been six of them.

All of them were stacked against the hot side of the boiler!

For several seconds Jack wondered what to do. The boxes may already be hot and ready to blow. Or it may take several hours before they went up.

He debated whether he should wait and try to confirm his suspicions as to who it might be that placed the boxes next to the boiler.

Then he heard the door to the boiler room close. He had left it ajar, just as he found it. He looked up through the gloomy interior. No light came from the direction of the stairway. He was sure then. Somebody had deliberately closed it.

He rushed up the stairway and grabbed the door knob. The door would not open. He pushed. Still it did not move.

Somebody had thrown the latch.

This time he heaved at the door. Then he threw his body against the door with all his might. It did not budge.

He looked down at the munitions. With every minute that passed they came nearer to explosion. Should he go down to move them or should he try to get help?

He banged on the door and shouted.

He kept up the din for several minutes. Then he heard voices outside the door and suddenly it was flung open.

Lieutenant MacDonald stood there. Behind him stood Tom.

"Quick," said Jack. Down here."

The three men went to work. First they moved all the munitions boxes across the room, well away from the heat of the boiler. Then they began to carry them up the steps and out of the boiler room altogether. Some of the boxes were hot to the touch. Jack felt his fingers singeing on the tinder hot wood.

It was not long before all of the boxes were removed. The three men then joined the remainder of the work party on the foredeck.

Lieutenant MacDonald was the first to speak.

"What were you doing in the boiler room?" This question was directed at Jack. Jack was stunned. He felt a surge of anger rise in his gorge.

"Sir?" he asked not quite believing the implications of the question.

"I asked," said the Lieutenant again, "What were you doing in the boiler room?"

All the men looked at Jack, awaiting his reply.

"Sir, the last time I passed the boiler room I noticed that the door was ajar. Previously it had been securely closed.

"I felt it was odd. Then I noticed one of the men coming out and I went down to investigate.

"When I tried to come out myself and make a report to you I found someone had locked me in."

"I did that," said Lieutenant MacDonald.

"You, Sir?" exclaimed Jack.

"Yes me."

"But...But..." started Jack.

"That door was supposed to be secure. Especially when moving ammunition. I locked the door."

"I thought..."

"Yes, I'm sure you did," said the Lieutenant. "Whom did you see coming out of there Jack?"

Jack levelled his gaze in the direction of Duffy Durrell. The Lieutenant's eyes followed. Durrell merely looked back at Jack steadily.

"Who was it Jack?"

"I'm pretty sure it was..." His voice trailed off. His father had once told him there was no such thing as 'pretty sure'. You were either sure or you were not sure.

"I'm not sure, Sir...I mean I don't know."

"All right. Enough of this. Someone made a mistake. Good job you spotted it

Jack."

"We're all a bit overtired. We have a big day tomorrow. Time we turned in."

The men then dispersed to the several small staterooms that had been assigned to them.

As Jack opened the door to his room on the portside of the hurricane deck aft of the pilot house, he thought about what had just taken place.

He felt sure it had been Duffy Durrell whom he had seen exit the boiler room. Or had he! Was it really Durrell? If so why had he not identified him to Lieutenant MacDonald?

I'm tired he thought. It could be anyone from the Troop. Hughes, Crutch, Busby, Bo, even Sandy. It could be Yank. It could be any of them. No. Not Mills. He was gone. And it certainly was not Tom. And it was not me. It could be any of them.

He flopped down on the bunk, too exhausted to remove his clothes. Any of them? No. The last thought he had was one of shame that he should suspect them all. He didn't. He did suspect...

Jack fell immediately into a deep slumber. He did not even hear the clank and hiss from deep within the bowels of the ship as the crew built up a head of steam to move the Northcote upstream.

CHAPTER FIFTY-THREE

HE DID not know what it was that had aroused him, but suddenly he was awake. The room was dark. He could hear the pounding of the engines and the wash of water from the paddlewheel. Now and then the boat trembled slightly. The Northcote was under way.

Was it the subtle movement of the vessel that had awakened him? Something made him uneasy. It was pitch black in the stateroom, but still he moved his eyes around slowly, peering vainly into the gloom. He did not move his body.

He sensed something unusual. Was someone in the room with him?

At once he saw the glint of a blade poised over his head and heard the quiet sound of movement.

He rolled toward the murky figure standing next to his bunk. The blade grazed past his right shoulder as he threw himself at his attacker. He hit with a thump and both bodies fell to the floor of the cabin. The knife clattered over the wooden boards.

For several minutes the two struggled in darkness. The man was quite powerful. Jack felt his head pushed back by the jaw. His neck pressed back against something firm. He's got a kind of hammer lock on me, thought Jack. His neck muscles strained with pain and he felt he was going to faint.

He struck forward but his blows did not land.

With a tremendous heave against his assailant he sought to break free. Suddenly he found himself catapulted off his enemy, his head striking a bench along the bulwark. In the blackness he saw only spiralling images of light from his own nerve endings.

A door slammed and he knew he was alone. He shook his head. He shook it again as he blindly groped to find the door. His hands searched desperately for the latch. He drew himself to his feet. As he did so he found the latch and threw open the door.

He looked to his right down the deck toward the bow of the vessel. No one.

He swivelled left, to the stern. Still no one. He stepped forward to the rail. All he saw was the relentless churning of the great paddle-wheel as it chopped its way through the black waters of the river. He heard metal pistons clang in response to steam pressure. He could also hear the splash of water not thirty feet away.

Suddenly he felt a terrific blow to the back of his head. It came from above. He fell forward. He thrust out his hands to break his fall, but there was nothing there but air. He felt his thighs graze the rail as his body tumbled forward into the black night.

His body hit the surface of the inky water. He immediately felt the frigid cold. Down he went. He held his breath. Down some more. He felt his body being swept along. Current? Undertow?

Then he remembered those churning blades. If one of those blades strikes, you're dead. It doesn't matter if your head is split open or you drown. Either way, you're dead.

Jack forgot his fatigue and shook off his initial surrender. He struck out with powerful strokes in the direction he hoped would bring him away from those relentless blades. Did he feel the undertow drawing him back or was that just the raging current?

Suddenly his face broke the surface.

He was three feet from the hull of the steamboat. It seemed to be racing by. The paddle wheels churned rapidly up out of the water. For a moment they seemed to pause at their zenith, then they came crashing down. Like a guillotine, thought Jack, as he drifted toward the slicing blades.

He redoubled his efforts, swimming away from the hull with all his might. He heard the blades come down. They seemed to strike the water just by his right ear.

Harder he stroked, faster.

The roar of machinery and water was louder now, so loud it sounded like a great rushing waterfall.

He felt the pull of the water rushing to meet the blades.

With his last ounce of energy he kicked and heaved his body forward.

Another stroke. Was he free?

Another stroke. He kicked hard.

And just as quickly as it had come, it left. The rushing sound dissolved. The tow in the water released him.

He turned to watch the Northcote plow on majestically in the night, oblivious to her former passenger.

His body quickly floated away. The speed of the ship seemed even greater than before. Then Jack realized he was being swept downstream by the current. If he didn't make an effort to reach shore he could soon drift to Batoche!

He swam with strong regular strokes in the direction of the east bank of the river. He couldn't really see it, but he knew it was there.

He swam with determination for fifteen minutes and then realized his feet could touch bottom. He stood. It was hard to hold his balance, so powerful was the current. He peered forward through the dark night and there before him was the shoreline.

Once more, with the help of Providence, he had come through.

CHAPTER FIFTY-FOUR

JACK HAD no idea what time it was. How long had he slept? He knew the events that sent him overboard and the desperate swim to escape death beneath the stern-wheeler seemed long at the time, but in reality took only minutes. But how long had the steamer been under way? Where was he?

He had crested the river bank some twenty or thirty minutes before. Then he struck out in an easterly direction believing traffic to or from the vessel would try to skirt the frequent ravines near the riverbank. Perhaps he would be lucky and could hitch a ride.

The darkness surrounded him and he wondered if chance could be so cruel as to throw him once again into the hands of the enemy. He shivered a little, but told himself it was the lingering chill from the frigid waters of the river.

He now realized how it had happened. How he had been propelled to almost certain death.

It was simple really. How could he have been so negligent? It would have been so easy for his assailant to step on to the rail outside the cabin and in jig time pull himself to the roof deck. No wonder he had disappeared so fast that he was no longer in sight the moment Jack opened the cabin door.

It was an easy matter, then, for him to swing down from the grillwork above with great momentum kick Jack overboard.

Jack shook his head in disgust at his own stupidity.

In a while Jack noticed that he no longer stumbled. He could see the ground. The sun had not risen but the pale soft illumination of early morning spread across the plains. The sun was just below the horizon on the east and about to burst upon a new day.

Cautious from his many days on the prairies, he made a mental inventory of protective bush and shrub, should it become necessary to hide.

Fortune smiled on him again, however, for it was not long before a rider appeared in the north. Or was it two riders? Jack remained motionless while he studied the approaching figures.

Even from a great distance he was able to discern that the rider was friend not foe. And as he drew even closer it was apparent that he had another horse in company.

Perhaps my luck has taken a permanent turn, thought Jack.

The rider, as it turned out, was none other than the fabled Captain Howard. He of the gatling gun.

Captain Howard was only too happy to oblige. Jack was most welcome to hitch a ride. The Captain was headed for the Northcote. The gatling gun was to be unloaded at the new landing before a nine pounder was craned aboard.

Jack threw himself with ease over the bare back of the spare horse and the two rode off.

The Captain was curious as to how Jack came to be out there in the middle of the lonesome prairie. Jack explained. The Captain listened intently to Jack's story. He shook his head several times. When Jack described his reluctant swim the Captain gave out a long low whistle.

"There have been strange happenings the last while," said Captain Howard. "None of them good. Some say it's sabotage. I don't know. I wish I did.

"I know this, if I were in charge of this man's army I would have investigated long ago."

Jack then told him about the kidnapping.

"I heard about that. That was you, was it?"

"Yes," said Jack. He went on to describe his last day with the outlaws, his eavesdropping, the conversation overheard.

"Bluecoat!" exclaimed the Captain. He did not look down at his own blue tunic. "Yes, as a matter of fact I heard something about this. Rumours. You know. I paid no attention. What's an army without scuttlebut?"

He stole a sideways glance at Jack. "I've given loyal service to the Canadians," he said obliquely. He did not say more, or ask Jack any questions. Jack waited, but none came.

After some time the Captain said, "Some say the Fenians are the ones to cause trouble for Canada. Play footsies with Riel. I don't know. There may be more trouble with American political zealots, if you ask me."

"What do you mean?" asked Jack.

"American expansionists," said the Captain. "They call it 'Manifest Destiny'!"

Jack was about to ask him to elaborate when the Northcote came into view.

"There she is," said the Captain. "Ain't she a beauty!"

And there she was. All snug up against the river bank. Jack had not noticed before but the high bluff had gradually given way to a kind of natural levee.

The sun had broken free of the rim of the earth and now sat like a crimson ball on the eastern horizon. The Northcote looked like a delicate white brooch, burnished in pink and gold.

CHAPTER FIFTY-FIVE

NOT LONG after the two men arrived Lieutenant MacDonald had turned out the men. Captain Howard and Jack joined them for a quick breakfast of tea and tinned beef with a side of government biscuit.

Promptly thereafter the men were ordered to go to work. Jack, however, was beckoned to one side where the Lieutenant could have a private conversation with him.

"What happened to you?" was his first question.

Jack explained.

A skeptical look spread across the face of the officer. Jack knew the look immediately. He had learned to recognize it long ago.

"It's true, Lieutenant," said Jack, imploring Lieutenant Hugh T. MacDonald, son of the Prime Minister to believe him.

"Jack, Jack, Jack," said the Lieutenant, shaking his head from side to side.

"Please Lieutenant, you've got to believe me. Look at my uniform. Would I take a swim in the river at night for pleasure? I'm telling you the truth." Once again Jack was pleading for someone not to believe the worst of him. Not to believe that once again he was absent without leave. Not deliberately. He had never been AWOL deliberately in his life.

"But Jack, such a story?"

"Lieutenant, feel here a minute." That's where I was hit. Oow," said Jack moving his head to the right slightly. It hurt.

"Only you have such adventures," said the Lieutenant noncommitally.

But when he drew his hand away from Jack's head there was blood on his fingers.

"I think you had better get a field dressing for that wound."

"And when Captain Howard goes back with the gatling you'll go along and report, forthwith on your arrival, to hospital."

Quite obviously Jack had been relieved of the detail converting Captain Sheet's vessel into a gunboat. He made his way through his mates busily working on deck, toward the pilot house where, he was told, a dressing could be found.

The men were busy erecting log barricades and other fortifications. Sacks were loaded with sand. There were laid strategically along the port and starboard boat deck and hurricane deck affording protection for marksmen aboard.

In the wheelhouse Jack saw mattresses piled against the stern wall. These would be thrown against the sides of the wheelhouse if needed.

After bandaging his wound he found his way down the next and returned to his cabin. He searched everywhere for the knife. It could not be found. The assailant must have returned for it. He was glad he had not mentioned that it had been dropped to the Lieutenant.

Jack joined Captain Howard on the foredeck where he was supervising the harnessing of the gatling gun to the tackle of the crane. Captain Sheets stood nearby and maintained a constant stream of invective. His main aggravation appeared to be the fortifying and arming to his vessel, but Jack guessed his real complaint was the conscription of the Northcote.

He muttered each time another sandbag was loaded aboard. "Weigh her down too much and she'll run aground on the first sandbar." Each time a nail was driven home into her gleaming white superstructure he winced.

Captain Sheets was not exactly gung-ho for battle.

The gatling finally was secured to the crane. Captain Howard and Jack left the vessel and took up a position nearby on the landing.

"All right men, heave," commanded Captain Howard.

As the men pulled back on the tackle the gatling lifted from the foredeck and rose about ten feet into the air.

Captain Howard waited patiently and finally the men were permitted to swing the gun over to land.

"Gently boys, gently," advised Captain Howard.

Slowly it was eased to the ground.

Before the armament was covered Jack had a good look at it. There were a number of barrels arranged in a circle and at the breech was a rather complicated looking mechanism.

Captain Howard briefly explained the gun to Jack while they waited for the remainder of the gatling equipment to be unloaded.

"The barrel is rotated in a clockwise manner," he said, "by turning this crank." He touched his fingers to the crank.

Jack ran his hand down the gleaming barrels of the gatling. "If I had a chance I'll drill you in its operations. It's powerful. It can fire more than a thousand rounds a minute."

"Wow!" exclaimed Jack.

"That's right," Captain Howard said proudly. "Raise the muzzle and you can lob shells, like a mortar."

"It's a pretty useful weapon," he concluded, patting the machine.

"I can see that," said Jack.

"We're selling them to governments all over the world."

"We?" asked Jack.

"Well, in addition to my commission as an officer in the Connecticut National Guard, I represent the gatling manufactory in the state."

Jack looked at the Captain. His hand caressed the barrels of the gun. He was tall and slim. His eyes had a kindly though somewhat sad look about them. He had regular features and wore full regimental moustache.

He was a handsome figure in his blue Yankee tunic with lanyard. But Jack found something incongruous about him that he could not identify.

Jack boarded Northcote one final time. He arranged to meet Tom later in camp at Fish Creek. He also wanted to bid farewell to his comrades and friends in Baker Troop. He shook hands with Bo and Sandy. Crutch slapped him on the back and wished him luck. The others merely waved and shouted joking remarks to him as they continued work. He was the first to leave the troop. He knew there were concealing nostalgic emotions so he laughed, waved good naturedly, then quickly left.

When Jack disembarked for the final time the gatling gun with carriage and limber had been hitched up and Captain Howard was ready to leave. Jack leaped on to the back of his horse and they were off.

The return trip was uneventful. Captain Howard was pleasant company. He was full of amusing anecdotes and experiences. He kept Jack well entertained. Jack found he liked the American a great deal.

It seemed that they arrived back at camp in almost no time at all.

After first helping to unhitch and stow the gatling, over the protests of Captain Howard who repeatedly urged Jack to be on his way, Jack finally left for the field hospital.

It was already three o'clock when he arrived. He reported first to a medical orderly who told him he should see the doctor who was still on duty in the hospital tent next door. When Jack entered he found himself at one end of a long tent on either side of which were lines of field cots with the casualties from the recent engagement.

The doctor was examining one of the wounded near the far end of the tent. As Jack walked between the beds he could see that the men bore mutilations to almost every part of the body. Not a few wore dressing around their heads. Some were heavily bandaged about the rib cage. Still others had large bandages on either leg or arm. Many of the bandages had bled right through and were soaked with blood. Some of the blood had caked and turned reddish brown. It looked to Jack as though many of the dressings needed to be changed and he wondered if the military command was short of medical staff.

As he reached the middle of the tent he heard his name called from behind. He turned. There was Lieutenant Richards, propped up on his right elbow, grinning at him.

"Lieutenant!" exclaimed Jack.

"Hello private," said the Lieutenant.

Jack went over to the Lieutenant's bedside. "How are you Sir?" "Fine Jack. I'll be fine. I guess I was in shock when Mills brought me in here last night. Sawbones there insisted that I stay in bed so he could keep me under observation for a few hours."

"How's your hand?" asked Jack.

"It's going to be fine, thanks to you. At first he thought he might have to remove it, but now he thinks it can be saved."

"How're the men?"

"Fine Sir. Working hard. They were hoping to finish by three. They may have already weighed anchor."

"Weighed anchor? You've become a sailor already, have you?"

"No, Sir I don't think so. I don't know if I'd make much of a sailor. The Northcote wasn't under way very long and they already had a man overboard."

"What?" Who?"

"Me," said Jack, with a grin.

"What happened?"

Jack then related what had happened the previous night.

He had just finished and Lieutenant Richards was cross examining him as to who might be responsible for these strange happenings when the doctor arrived at the Lieutenant's bedside.

The Lieutenant introduced Jack, and told the doctor he had been sent in from the field to have his head wound examined.

The doctor removed Jack's bandage then and there.

"You're going to live son. You have a nasty cut there. The blow must have split the skin. A couple of stitches and you'll be right as rain.

"Report to my surgery in the tent next door. As soon as I finish my rounds I'll fix you up."

The doctor examined Lieutenant Richards, told him he could pack his things and report for duty.

"Just be sure to check back with me for a change of dressing now and then. And be careful with that hand."

"Thanks doc," said the Lieutenant. He jumped out of bed and began to dress as he continued to talk to Jack.

"There have been interesting developments since I saw you last," he said.

"Yes, I guess I'm to be seconded to the Midland Battalion. I was supposed to check with you to get my orders but Colonel Williams already told me."

"He did?"

"Yes, Sir," Jack then told Lieutenant Richards about the visit of Colonel Williams.

When he finished, the Lieutenant, with a twinkle in his eyes and a smile on his face, said, "Tom, too?"

"Yes, Sir. Sorry about that Lieutenant."

"Don't be," the Lieutenant said with a laugh.

At first Jack was surprised, then he found himself somewhat resentful.

"That's what I wanted to tell you about," said the Lieutenant when he saw the look across Jack's face.

"What, what are you talking about." Now Jack's face took on a puzzled expression.

"The interesting development," said the Lieutenant.

"Colonel Williams came to see me too. Around noon."

"Oh yeah?" said Jack. He looked at his Lieutenant suspiciously.

"You're going to have to believe me Jack."

"There was a staff meeting this morning. Colonel Van Straubenzie was there as well as Colonel Williams, Colonel Grasett, General Middleton, his acting adjutant, a number of other officers and our own dear Colonel Trubshaw.

"Among other things, the General told them that a general order will be issued at eight tonight for parade at four tomorrow morning. We're moving out at five."

"You mean…?"

"Yes, Jack. We're finally going to march."

"I've got a feeling there's something more coming."

"Toward the end of the conference Colonel Trubshaw started to complain as usual."

"He had just learned that Tom had been shanghaied by Colonel Williams."

"With his usual petulance he said, ' You've got Private Holden. Lieutenant Richards is out of commission. Now you take Private Boulton too. You might as well take the whole Troop.' Colonel Williams broke in without pause. "All right," he said, "I accept!"

"Then Colonel Straubenzie spoke up before Trubshaw could draw his breath.

"That's all settled then," he said. Colonel Trubshaw nearly had apoplexy. But his friend "Freddy" said nothing. The General didn't interfere."

"You mean…"

"What I'm saying is the whole of Baker Troop has been assigned temporarily to the Midland Battalion."

"You…We…We're all now in the Midland?"

"You bet. And I wouldn't miss it for the world. Weal or woe, wound or no, I wouldn't miss it for the world."

CHAPTER FIFTY-SIX

JACK AND the Lieutenant parted company; the Lieutenant to discharge himself and Jack to attend to have several stitches at the back of his head. There was much to be done before the morning.

Although he was unsure that it was still required, as soon as a dressing had been applied Jack paid a visit to the headquarters tent of the Midland Battalion. It was a hive of activity. He reported to the adjutant, Captain Ponton.

"They've been quite busy," he said. "Plenty of planning to be done for tomorrow."

"That's all right," said Jack. "I quite understand. I can come back at any time that is convenient."

"No it's all right. They're just about to break. Why don't you go right in. The tent next door."

Jack stepped next door. The large tent was abuzz with voices. The entrance was open. Jack stepped right through and then waited by the door for an opportunity to present himself.

The first thing Jack noticed about the staff headquarters of the Midland was that everybody was very informal and friendly. Colonel Williams was listening respectfully to a submission being made by one of his Lieutenants.

Rolled maps were scattered everywhere; on chairs, on cots, even on the dirt floor and on top of a steamer trunk. One map was spread out before the officers on a camp fold-away table. It was weighted at the corners to prevent it from rolling up.

All of the officers listened intently to what was being said. Finally Colonel Williams spoke.

"That seems like a wise suggestion, Lieutenant Helliwell.

"Does anyone here want to make any comment?" Colonel Williams looked around and waited a moment or two.

"Fine then, we'll proceed as Lieutenant Helliwell has suggested.

"I think that covers everything. If there is no more business we can close down our shop for the day."

Again he waited to see if his staff members brought up any unfinished business.

There was no further word from the men.

"That does it then, gentlemen. It remains only for me to say thank you for your fine cooperation and assistance in planning this operation.

"In all probability we will engage the enemy tomorrow. I'm satisfied I have under my command officers and men as fine as have served our Sovereign anywhere in the British Empire. The men have been well trained and they are eager and ready for battle. I know that each one of you and every man in rank and file will acquit himself with honour.

"Canada can ask no more; I can ask no more.

"And I know that will be sufficient.

"Good luck to you all!"

There was a murmur of men's voices as the officers thanked the Colonel and shook hands with one another.

Some of the officers left to give final instructions to their units. However, many remained. Shortly, the Colonel's batman entered and began to decant tea from a silver tea set. This refreshment was passed around. When a cup was offered to the Colonel he looked up and spotted Jack standing where he had first entered the tent.

Immediately he beckoned to Jack to come over. Jack politely maneuvered his way through the press of officers dropping apologies and 'excuse me's' to ease his path.

"Sir," said Jack saluting the Colonel.

"Good to see you son. Take off your head gear and join us for tea."

Jack removed his pith helmet and placed it under his left arm. He accepted the proffered tea. Tea was not his favourite beverage and after taking several sips he discreetly placed his cup on the edge of the Colonel's map table.

"This is that remarkable young man that I've been talking about," he said to the officers surrounding him.

"Trooper Holden, I want you to meet my staff officers.

"This is Lieutenant Kenney."

Jack took the extended hand, shook it and nodded his head slightly in acknowledgement.

"Captain Bonnycastle of the 40th."

"Major Smith and Colonel James Deacon."

"Captain J. Leystock Reid, our Paymaster."

"Quartermaster Lieutenant Clemes, a good man for you to know."

"Battalion surgeons, Doctor Horsey and Doctor James Might."

Jack shook the hand of each officer. They all seemed so informal, so friendly.

"Perhaps you already met Adjutant Ponton next door. This is my other Adjutant, Captain Lazier of the 15th.

"He doubles as head of my intelligence section."

"Sir," said Jack as he greeted Lieutenant Helliwell.

"The Colonel has told me a great deal about your adventures Jack. May I call you Jack? We'll be working together a fair amount." Lieutenant Helliwell shook Jack's hand.

"Of course, Sir."

"Yes, Jack," said the Colonel. "What I have in mind is for you to be an informal member of my intelligence section."

"In addition to your regular duties, of course. Perhaps you've heard that your Troop has been seconded to serve as part of my Battalion?"

"Yes, Sir, I just paid a visit to Lieutenant Richards. He told me. He's discharged from hospital, Sir, and anxious to join the fray."

"Good to hear that. Another good man for the Midland." The Colonel paused for a moment, nodding his head, then continued: "I want you two to have a lengthy conference. I'd like to see you exhaustively debrief Jack." The last remark was directed to Lieutenant Helliwell.

"Right, Sir," said the Lieutenant.

"I want my right hand man in intelligence to have every scrap of information at his fingertips."

"We'll see to that, Sir," said Helliwell.

"Yes, Sir," added Jack.

"You'll spend a goodly amount of your time at headquarters," the Colonel said to Jack. "In addition to intelligence I want you for liaison.

"You're still part of Baker, though. You won't miss action.

"I think we can keep you busy."

"Thank you, Sir. I'll do my best," said Jack.

"My sixth sense about men tells me that you always have done your best."

This reference to the past surprised Jack, though he realized later, when he knew the Colonel better, it should not have.

"I know you're facing an ordeal that must worry you very much, and an uncertain future. But you're service here will enlist many new friends in your cause.

"And you have my assurance now, that I will do what I can for you."

"I can't tell you how much I appreciate this, Sir."

"Jack, you've earned it.

"I've got a feeling that the next few days will acquaint me personally with your character. Testimony like that can sometimes be of considerable assistance at a trial."

Jack felt a surge of gratitude to this man. He was so choked up he couldn't speak to thank him.

"I think it's time we dissolve our little tea party. We all have work to do in preparation for tomorrow.

"See to it that Jack here draws a revolver from stores," said the Colonel.

"I certainly will, Sir," said the Quartermaster, Lieutenant Clemes.

The Northcote returned right after dinner fully fitted out as a gunboat. Baker Troop disembarked. As soon as they returned to camp they learned of their reassignment as a unit. There was a boisterous reunion with Lieutenant Richards, Tubby Mills and Jack. Esprit de Corps soared.

The assignment to the Midland Battalion was very popular indeed.

After a late supper the men fell to with a will. Every weapon was recleaned, oiled and carefully placed with marching kit. The men groomed and fed the unit ponies down at the corral. There was much laughter and joking.

They're nervous thought Jack. And he wondered whether it was the same with troops the world over. Are they nervous the night before battle? These men are as good and as brave as any troops anywhere, he thought. Why should they be different in this?

That night the setting sun glowed with an intensity that Jack had never seen before. The clouds, ever shifting across its face, caused its rays to leap and dance and burst. The entire sky burned at the horizon in crimson, orange and yellow.

Like an enormous furnace in the sky, thought Jack. He wondered what the morrow held.

CHAPTER FIFTY-SEVEN

THERE WAS little sleep in the camp that night. The men were restless. Captain Howard and his gatling crew slept not at all.

The men fell in sharply at four in the morning. They did not need to be ordered to keep their voices down. The parade was subdued, even sombre.

As soon as all were accounted for the men were dismissed for breakfast. They formed up again, as ordered, at five in the morning.

Promptly at five thirty, one half hour later, the march north began.

Unlike others in Baker Troop Jack had slept soundly, so exhausted had he been. He heard none of the low nervous conversation sputtering from time to time throughout the night. And when reveille came, a silent reveille, for the bugles had been ordered into silence, Tom had to shake Jack to awaken him.

Once awake Jack was on his feet and making ready immediately. He was completely refreshed from a sound sleep. He eagerly looked forward to the day.

He and Tom were over at the corral well before the others. Cloud was happy to see Jack. She softly whinnied as he stroked her forehead and neck. Jack fed her some oats. When he negligently stroked her neck again, she playfully nuzzled him to tell him she wanted more oats.

It was strange for Baker Troop to fall in with the Midland Battalion, but they had little time to think about it. They were promptly dismissed for mess.

Jack and Tom walked their ponies over to form up in marching order. There was a great deal of good natured cussing from the men around them albeit in quiet tones. The horses complained, gently neighing and shaking their manes.

The morning was crisp. Each expelled breath created a small foggy cloud that immediately dissipated.

As the two men formed up the twilight of early morning gave way to the first rays of sunshine. The mood of the surrounding men moved up a notch, to modestly optimistic.

The order was quietly passed and the great contingent of men, machines and horses moved forward.

Cloud shivered once more and Jack leaned forward to give her a few reassuring words.

To Jack's left rode Tom on his chestnut mare. Ahead rode Lieutenant Richards. His left hand was still swathed in bandages. Strung out in twos behind Tom and Jack rode the rest of the Troop.

Though only an occasional word was spoken, the movement of almost one thousand men, many horses, wagons and artillery pieces raised quite a steady din: plodding hooves, slapping leather, creaking wheels, marching feet and muted orders and the rattle, clatter and jingle of sword, horse and harness.

The column moved north easterly now. The sun shone brightly. It was so low in the sky that when Jack turned his head to the right only slightly he was partially blinded.

The column moved ponderously forward.

Tom finally spoke.

"Do you think we'll see action today Jack?"

"I don't see how we could avoid it," answered Jack. "Batoche is their declared seat of government. It's their principal settlement. They can't do otherwise but defend it and it's not more than ten miles from our camp."

"I'm glad we're finally getting down to work," said Tom. Then the two soldiers settled once more into silence.

Moving in column was a slow process. Most of the troops were marching. To retain some semblance of order the troops were required to keep to their respective units. The whole column, therefore, moved no faster than the pace of the men afoot, marching. Jack found it mildly frustrating to be confined to a slow walk aboard such a fast horse.

The column had been moving in a steady course and it was difficult to see much farther ahead than Colonel Williams and his staff. He could see the black tunics of the rear ranks of the 90th Battalion shifting in unison from side to side as they marched forward. The Regimental Sergeant Major of the Battalion brought up the rear. He too was marching.

Immediately following the 90th Battalion were the officers and men of the Midland Battalion. Colonel Williams aboard his horse led the Battalion. Immediately behind the Battalion Commander rode his staff officers. Major Smith and Colonel Deacon rode together. Behind these two officers rode two more staff officers, Captain Ponton, the Adjutant and Lieutenant Clemes, the Quartermaster.

Then came the newest addition to the Midland Battalion, Baker Troop, with Lieutenant Richards riding his pony at the head of the Troop. All of the Troop was mounted. They were the only unit, apart from Boulton's and French's Scouts, that was mounted.

Jack turned in his saddle and looked through the slowly swaying lines of troopers toward the rear of the battalion. He could make out Lieutenant Helliwell, riding alongside Captain Lazier, of the 15th. Behind them marched the members of the Company. He could not distinguish officers and men of the Battalion beyond those two, but he could see the long lines of red tunics shifting and swaying in the bright morning sun. He knew also that the battalion surgeons, Doctors Horsey and Might would be in the column, mounted, and probably bringing up the rear.

After the North West Field Force had been marching for about two miles Jack heard an order being shouted, then repeated for each Battalion down the line.

Long before the order reached the Midland, he could see the column make a gradual left wheel and head west. Casting his eyes left away from the slanting rays of the sun it was easy, then, to distinguish the other units and their order.

Boulton's Scouts, about seventy-five of them, marched at the head of the column. All of them were mounted. Major Boulton rode alone at the head of his men.

Following the Scouts, Jack could see the blue tunic of Captain Howard, and immediately behind him the gatling gun with carriage and limber rolling easily along behind a team of horses. Three other men made up his small contingent.

There was a small gap behind the gatling gun. Then came the main body of troops from the Force.

Proudly at the head of the main body rode the General. His flag ensign rode to his left and a length behind. The standard for the Force fluttered lightly in the still morning air.

Other officers rode with the General. Although Jack could not distinguish them he knew Lord Melgund, Military Secretary to the General and Second in Command, would be one and Colonel Van Straubenzie another. Several others riding immediately behind, Jack did not know, but he did recognize Major Buchan, acting Field Adjutant.

After the Headquarters Staff rode Colonel Grasett and his staff. Then came the two hundred and seventy men of the Royal Grenadiers with Number One Company in the lead.

Suddenly Jack heard a shouted command: "Left...Ha...!" And the Midland Battalion began to make a slow left wheel. After some minutes Jack looked back to see the rest of the marching order.

Behind the three hundred and seventy-five men of the Midland Battalion trundled the two big guns of A Battery and their ninety-five officers and men. The Winnipeg Field Battery with two nine pounders and sixty men made up the balance of the artillery for the expeditionary force.

Behind the artillery came the hospital wagons and ammunition caissons and wagons.

And further back still, Jack could see hundreds of horses and mules and for food perhaps eighty head of cattle. All of them were being herded along by wranglers. This vast assemblage of men and animals at the end raised a gargantuan dust cloud that followed the massive column like an enormous tail.

French's Scouts rode the flanks of the force. They made frequent forays, constantly checking the terrain to left and right of the mighty column.

Soon after the formation had completed its turn to the west, Jack saw a rider gallop back from the General's staff. He conferred a moment with Colonel Williams and then made off once more at a gallop in the direction of the head of the column.

Shortly after, Major Smith turned in his saddle and called a few words back to Lieutenant Richards.

The Lieutenant turned and called to Jack.

"The Colonel wants you to ride with him."

"Who me?" asked Jack.

"Yes, you and Tom. Both of you. Look smart and report promptly. Let's show our new boss what kind of unit he inherited."

"Yes, Sir," said Jack.

"Yes, Sir," echoed Tom.

And the two troopers moved forward at a canter to take up positions on either side of the Colonel.

When Jack arrived he heard the Colonel muttering "…didn't he ask me that before. The time to ask, General, is at the planning session before the march. Not during the march."

Then the Colonel noticed his company had arrived.

Jack never learned what it was that the General had asked the Colonel, for at that precise moment he heard a blast on the whistle of the Northcote.

"What…?" exclaimed the Colonel.

Another blast.

"What the devil is that about now." Jack could see this was not a question directed at him. He said nothing.

Suddenly another order reverberated down the line. It came to the Midland. Major Smith turned in his saddle.

"Column…Halt!"

With a rattling of equipment the whole Battalion came to a halt. As the sound swept back through the units it vaguely resembled the sound of railway cars coming to a halt, one by one.

Jack craned his neck forward to see what was afoot. What he saw was that others were looking back. He turned to the rear and then he understood.

A Battery had unhitched a nine pounder, and in the finest quick order drill had limbered her up for firing.

"What in the name of…" started the Colonel. A blast from the artillery piece cut off his sentence.

"What's going on?" said the Colonel. The question was addressed to no one in particular, but this time Jack chose to speak.

"I think I know, Sir."

"You do," said the Colonel, incredulously.

"I think so, yes Sir. Lieutenant MacDonald of the 90th Battalion mentioned it to me, Sir."

Jack was about to go on but he could see the gun had been cleared, reloaded with a blank cartridge and ready for a second firing. He waited.

A gentle jump, a puff of smoke from the muzzle, another loud report.

"Lieutenant MacDonald is with the military on the Northcote. The whistling was a signal the ship is in position south of Batoche. I think that's what the Lieutenant said, Sir."

"And the cannon fire?" enquired the Colonel.

"Acknowledgement, Sir," said Jack.

"Tarnation," said the Colonel.

"And to let them know we're almost in position."

"And damnation," said the Colonel in impatient frustration. "And to alert the enemy of our position. If they were asleep before, they sure won't be now. This won't be a surprise attack, I can tell you that. Why the devil did he not tell the Battalion Commanders this little scheme."

"I don't know that it will make a lot of difference, Sir."

"What do you mean son?"

"Well those few shots we heard before we left camp…"

"Yes, some distance off."

"I don't think they were to fire at the Force, Sir. I think Dumont's Scouts were sending off messages."

"Of course, of our departure."

"I don't need to tell you, Colonel, that his Scouts have been watching us every step of the way."

"You're quite right, son. But do we have to give them any help.

"Damnation," he said again, after a pause.

Shortly the column again took up the march west to Batoche.

Jack looked at his watch. It was precisely seven in the morning. They could not be far away.

Though it was still early morning the sun beat down on Jack's back. The column ahead moved forward relentlessly. Tom rode on wordlessly at the right of the Colonel. Major Smith had fallen back a pace or two.

Jack glanced at the Colonel's face. It bore the look of grim determination. He will have some questions to ask when next he sees the Commanding General, thought Jack.

It was not long before irregular movement in ranks forward told Jack that the column had arrived at the outer reaches of the settlement.

The troops, on shouted orders, began to extend in skirmishing order.

Jack's Troop continued to move forward as the column seemed to melt to left and right. In several minutes Batoche came into sight. The Colonel reigned in his horse on a high ridge and held up his hand. Tom and Jack brought their horses to a halt on either side of the Colonel.

Major Smith passed the word for the Battalion to halt. A clatter of rifles and backpacks followed as the troops behind relaxed.

Jack found they were almost a mile from the river. Except for the occasional movement of troops or subdued command, it was a perfectly still morning. The prairie bathed peacefully in the sunlight. Jack could easily see the houses and building most of which nestled along the water. It appeared nearly all of the villagers lived on the near shore.

From the crest on which the Battalion had stopped the terrain gently descended to the west. Here and there a ridge or ravine interrupted this descent. Shrubs and a few trees also dotted the scene. From the south the river meandered in a wide sweep westerly to Batoche, then back again. And from north and south the steep east bank fell until, as it approached the village, it was quite low.

The silence of the morning was eerie and seemed to Jack quite unnatural. Perhaps ominous.

He was about to speak to the Colonel when a rattle of fire interrupted his thoughts.

The gatling!

Jack looked toward the right just in time to see the gatling open up once more on the nearest house. Captain Howard again stopped firing. No one left the house. Nothing seemed to stir in the peaceful village scene before them.

Jack then saw Major Boulton and his Scouts retire just as several men from A Battery ran a nine pounder forward. The gunners moved smartly under the eyes of the Commanding General and the staccato order of their Lieutenant.

"Common shell, percussion fuse -- load."

All along the bluff officers and men of the Field Force waited expectantly. Then came the command.

"Fire!"

The gun discharged with a bang and sent a puff of smoke forward. The gun recoiled. A whistling sound slipped through the silent morning air as the shell flew across the meadow. It landed on the second house with a loud explosion.

Several men jumped up from cover near the house and raced for the thicket beyond.

They were the first rebels the men had seen since Fish Creek. A small cheer erupted from the watching troops.

Shortly the two houses that had been fired on burst into flame.

There was still no other sign of rebel troops.

The burning houses stood about a third of a mile from the river. Midway between these two points were two more buildings, one of which appeared to be a church, the other a school.

A general order to advance with caution was issued. The Midland Battalion had extended in skirmishing order. Under the watchful eyes of Colonel Williams the Battalion moved forward, ensuring their flanks kept abreast of the units to left and right.

Now, in the distance, Jack heard a large explosion. The gun on the Northcote, he thought. Then a rattle of rifle fire could be heard. It too seemed to come from far away. They've sailed right on by Batoche, thought Jack.

Captain Howard and his crew of three had approached with the gatling to within close range of the church. Jack could see them stop and prepare the gun to fire.

Suddenly the door of the church flung open. A priest in a long black cassock emerged. Both hands were held high. In the left he carried a crucifix, in the other a white flag. He waved the flag energetically.

A party of mounted officers cantered forward. About ten other people poured out the front doors of the church. Half of them were men of the cloth. Jack learned later that all claimed to be prisoners of the rebels, but at the time he was very suspicious.

Suddenly the gatling opened up again, this time at the schoolhouse.

Again, only silence greeted this discharge. Still, no other rebels could be seen.

Jack could see General Middleton. He was well back, toward the crest of the hill, and waving impatiently at A Battery, which up until then had kept its distance. He motioned them forward with his right hand.

The gunners of A Battery jumped at the command of their Lieutenant and easily trundled their nine pounders forward and down the gently sloping land.

"Sir, I don't like it," said Jack to the Colonel. "In this whole village, not a single rebel. I don't believe it. We've seen only three and they quickly ran. As if to entice us forward. I don't like it," Jack repeated.

The Colonel watched the men of A Battery move their two nine pounders forward at a remarkable rate. The General was calling out compliments.

"Jolly good show men. Move right up there and give them a taste of power."

"Look smart about it, men," shouted the Lieutenant in command. He shouted loud enough for his voice to carry back to the General and his staff.

The infantry had advanced too, but the guns were well out ahead and still moving forward.

Colonel Williams shook his head from side to side.

"You're right, Jack. It looks ominous."

The two guns had now stopped. Jack could hear the Commander as they made ready to fire.

"Common shell, percussion fuse -- load!"

The men worked busily around the cannon. Again the command.

"Common Shell, percussion fuse -- load!"

"Bang" went the first gun.

"Bang", the second.

The guns recoiled, but almost before stopping Jack heard the orders again.

"Common shell, percussion fuse -- load!"

The Battery had begun to shell Batoche in earnest. Jack could see the explosion of shells across the river among the houses. Then several shells exploded near the homes along the east bank of the river and immediately women and children appeared, running helter skelter in a panic.

Now the General's voice could be heard between blasts from the cannon.

"Damn your eyes! Cease firing. Cease firing."

The chant was taken up by Lord Melgund.

"Cease fire. Cease fire."

Then the General spoke again. He spoke loudly, so that everyone nearby could hear.

"I gave precise orders. No one is to fire upon civilians. I gave meticulous instructions about that."

The cannon loading had discontinued. The panic stricken people down by the buildings at riverside continued to scurry in all directions.

Colonel Williams finally spoke again.

"Jack I think you should carry my advice to the General that our artillery is badly exposed. I think it should be pulled back."

"Yes, Sir, anything else?"

"No Jack, go to it."

But at that very moment a storm of shooting erupted. Bullets whizzed and zipped through the air.

Opposite the left centre position of the troops the enemy had abruptly appeared and now laid down volley upon volley of murderous fire. Screaming and yelling, shouts and orders competed with the report of rifles.

Horses cried in terror. One threw his rider and galloped right into the fusillade. Its legs suddenly crumpled and it collapsed only seven feet away from the rebel line.

Out of the corner of his eye Jack saw General Middleton's horse rear. The General grasped his saddle horn for all he was worth.

Colonel Williams was quick to react.

"Take cover. Men of the Midland take cover."

Major Smith rode along the line.

"Move back men. Be orderly, fall back to good cover, then stay put.

"Make your fire count men. Don't panic. No firing for the sake of shooting. Make it count.

"This is your chance. For Canada and the Empire. Make it count."

The Colonel noticed Jack hesitate.

"Too late for my message, Jack. Fall back to the crest. No use getting our ponies killed."

Jack already had his revolver out. He directed shot after shot at the rebel line.

Then Jack heard Lord Melgund's high pitched British accent.

"Ambush. We've been ambushed. Fall back. Retreat."

The absurdity of it struck Jack, but he had no need to suppress a laugh.

"Retreat," he heard his Lordship scream once more.

Jack and Tom followed the Colonel as he rode to a more protected site in a small depression. The bullets seemed to be whizzing and pinging right around their heads. Jack wondered if Lord Melgund was passing on orders from the General.

The men all along the line were pegging away at the enemy in the ravine. Twenty yards to the right an officer was in trouble. His horse snorted loudly, then it began to whinny. It reared back throwing the officer to the ground. The whinny turned into a shriek. Then Jack saw the side of the horse open up. Its hide peeled back from stirrup to hindquarter. Jack saw no blood, but for a moment he saw coil upon coil of purple blue intestine all neatly tucked in place. Then the horse came down hard.

A loop fell out. The horse stepped around in panic. More gut fell out. In horror Jack saw it coil around the hind foot of the panic stricken horse. The horse swivelled in fright. Will no one kill it? Can no one see, thought Jack.

He took careful aim with his revolver. He squeezed the trigger. The gun kicked. Mercifully, he saw the horse slump to the ground, dead.

The officer lay motionless on the ground not far away. Jack was unsure if he was wounded or gone.

"Stretcher bearer," someone screamed.

A pause. Then frantically the voice resumed like an incantation.

"Stretcher bearer, stretcher bearer, stretcher bearer." On went the voice. It was difficult to see from whence it came.

Screams rent the air. Groans from the wounded nearby lent a chilling background to the pop and rattle of gunfire.

Only moments before, or was it years, the valley glistened peacefully in the early morning sunlight. Now a haze had settled over the battlefield. It grew thicker as the minutes passed. The acrid smell of gunpowder grew more biting.

The men moved about and fired without direction.

Colonel Williams, his staff officers, Jack and Tom had all dismounted by now. The Colonel and Major Smith were busy issuing and transmitting orders. All were pouring gunfire at the enemy line.

It appeared that gunners from A Battery were struggling to retreat with the two nine pounders.

"We're in trouble down there," said Colonel Williams inclining his head in the direction of the guns.

"We'll lose those pieces to the rebels if we're not careful."

The infantry opposite the guns had been thrown into some confusion. They offered no covering fire to assist the efforts of the gunners to extricate the guns. Seeing this the rebels could charge at any moment.

"Another ten minutes and we'll have those guns turned on us," said the Major, tersely.

Jack waited no longer. He leaped onto the back of Cloud and raced off along the right flank of the line. Bullets zipped by his head. Jack tucked himself down beside Cloud's neck and prayed that his pony would not be hit.

Twenty yards away he could see the gatling. It stood silently in a small declivity. Captain Howard, quite visible in his blue tunic, struggled with the machine.

As Jack approached he saw the lone gunner assisting the Captain jerk back and to the left. He was still spinning as he hit the earth. Jack saw the Captain stare dumbly at his fallen gunner then turn his attention back to the gatling with furious zeal.

A red coat rose to his knees right before Cloud. Then he slumped to the ground just as Cloud streaked into the sky far above his lifeless body.

Down came Cloud. Jack reigned her right in the same fluid movement and then reigned her up and vaulted off right at the edge of the pit.

"Off you go," Jack shouted at Cloud above the cacophony of the battlefield. He gave Cloud a good slap on the rump and she made off for safety at a gallop.

Jack ducked into the Captain's protective pit.

"The guns," shouted Jack over the din. "We've got to save the guns."

The Captain looked over to the Battery now threatened by the rebels.

"You bet soldier. Just you give me a hand here and we'll bring hell down on their heads."

Captain Howard threw several cocking mechanisms back. He fiddled momentarily with the magazine.

"You fill this, Jack. And for the rest, well, that's my job."

"But keep those bullets coming."

"Yes, Sir!" said Jack. He seized the magazine and made ready.

The Captain grabbed the crank and began to turn it. With a terrific roar the gatling jumped into action.

"Down there," shouted Jack, pointing to the rebels nearer to the guns.

"Take that you devils," shouted the Captain. He swivelled the gun and cranked the handle without stopping. The gun sent up a deafening din as bullets raked the ravine concealing the enemy.

The gun poured out wave after wave of gunfire without ceasing. It's as though a thousand men militia had just come to the rescue, thought Jack.

Jack fed magazine after magazine into the infernal fighting weapon. The very volume of firepower seemed to intimidate the enemy. The rebels were now fearful of poking their heads out.

"Come on fellows," shouted Jack in encouragement to the men as they struggled to make an orderly withdrawal.

The battery, now shielded by covering fire, worked heroically, slowly withdrawing to safer ground.

"Attaboy Yank," shouted someone in the confused battlefield.

"Give 'em hell," shouted another disembodied voice.

"Take that and that and that," repeated Captain Howard over and over again as he cranked the handle and showered the enemy with venomous fire.

"I think they're clear now, Sir," shouted Jack over the roar of the gatling. The battery was now safely ensconced, well to the rear of the line of infantry.

Jack had a commanding view of the battlefield and though he paid constant attention to his duties at the gatling he could see the Grenadiers move into position on the right centre flank, beyond the church. There they began to extend in skirmishing order. This provoked an immediate barrage from the rebels.

The gatling gun apparently was considered a major threat to the enemy for it came in for constant attention. Bullets whizzed by their heads and into the earth around, kicking up small sprays of dirt.

"Captain, I think they're using their sharp shooter on us," said Jack. The officer took no notice but cranked the gun feverishly, pouring withering fire on the enemy line.

It was then that Jack noticed members of the 90th Battalion take up positions nearby. They began pegging away with Martini-Henrys. Sharpshooters, thought Jack. Good show!

Brief confusion following the initial encounter with the enemy had soon given way to order and military discipline. A ragged front had developed. Jack could see a company of Midlanders, far to the left, next to the river bank. On their flank he saw tunics of the 90th Battalion. As he ran his eyes further right along the line he saw Grenadiers and then more men from the 90th, elements of the Winnipeg Field Battery and finally a motley array of other units holding the extreme right flank.

Fierce fighting now raged all along the line.

Captain Howard, on receiving a signal from a major of the 90th Battalion, shut down the gatling.

"Pack up Jack," he said. He was crouching quite low. It was the first time Jack had seen him exhibit the least concern for enemy fire.

"We're moving over there," he pointed off to a position to the rear of the left centre of the line.

"In here soldier and lend a hand," he shouted to an infantry man.

"Yes, Sir," came the reply.

The three men manhandled the gatling into motion and soon it was careening across the uneven battlefield. Bullets flew everywhere. One hit the metal plating of the gun with a loud whack. Jack could feel the tremor down the length of the gun. At one point he was on the verge of grasping the barrels to turn the gun.

"Don't touch that unless you want to cook your hand. It's hot as hell," shouted Captain Howard.

The gun was quickly re-emplanted and soon was rattling off fire again. The new recruit departed for his unit.

Jack was surveying the field when he noticed the haze had increased dramatically. He turned to see heavy smoke curl from a ravine to the rear. He heard the crackle of fire and then noticed flames leaping in the tall dry grass. The fire raced down the length of the ravine. Choking fumes drifted toward the infantry and for several moments fire threatened to engulf the gatling.

Far to the right more grass was burning. Smoke from guns and fire swirled low along the contours of the battlefield. For a long time the fires continued to burn. Sometimes the smog grew so thick it was difficult to take aim with any confidence, but the gunfire hardly seemed to abate.

The big guns had continued to fire sporadically. They seemed to have settled into a pattern. A 'thump' from a far cannon, a long pause, a 'bang' from a nearby cannon. Then the far battery set off another blast. Jack thought he could feel the earth tremble now and then with the blast of cannon shot, but he could not be sure if it was imagination.

And always the command:

"Common shell, percussion fuse -- load." A pause. Then: "Fire!"

This was repeated over and over again. Jack heard it sometimes dimly over distance and sometimes loud and near. He wondered if the enemy could hear it too. He was sure they could.

The crack of exploding shells could be heard too. I'll bet they snug right down into the ground when they hear those shouted commands, thought Jack.

During a rare respite for the two men, taken only to allow the barrels on the gatling to cool and reload magazines, a fresh order was received: fall back. In some places the line would move only a hundred feet; in others several hundred yards. It was not a retreat, but an attempt to consolidate and rationalize the front and place the men in more secure positions.

The maneuver was made in orderly relays. One section laid down covering fire while the neighbouring section executed the strategic withdrawal.

Captain Howard and Jack moved back with the rest of the line. After the gun was again in place and ready to fire, Jack looked at his pocket watch. He was aghast. It had seemed like a whole day had passed. His watch, however, told him it was only fifteen minutes before noon.

In disbelief he looked at the sun. Shining through the haze of battle, it confirmed the time. It was Saturday. So much had happened he could scarcely believe only two days had passed since the arrival of Northcote at Fish Creek Camp.

For no apparent reason, an unexpected quiet fell over the battlefield. This lasted several minutes. During the lull Jack surveyed the entire front. The black, green, khaki and red tunics seemed to be on the move all along the line. Some of the men stood and turned their backs with seeming indifference to the enemy. Miraculously, not a shot was heard. The line extended over a mile. The figures on the right flank appeared so small, they resembled toy soldiers.

Then the firing recommenced. Immediately a shower of ball, buckshot and bullets rained down on the men. The firing was answered with a fusillade from the militia that rose in crescendo with the gatling gun breaking in at the peak to a sustained barrage.

This savage exchange continued for almost an hour. Then far down the field, Jack saw about five enemy soldiers move up a small Coulee. They stopped and abruptly laid on withering fire with deadly accuracy at a troop of A Battery. Jack saw a gunner fall. Then two more fell. He saw the survivors retreat smartly, some Scouts helping with the artillery pieces.

Another temporary stillness settled over no man's land. Jack felt the relief to his ears from the constant assault of explosions. For many minutes Jack revelled in the relative quietude. Then, without warning a soldier slipped into the natural trench from which they fired.

It was Tom.

"The Colonel wondered if you'd care to rejoin the Midland," said Tom.

"He's not angry?" said Jack with apprehension.

"Hell no. Relax. The whole battalion saw what you did. The Colonel and Major Smith think you and Captain Howard saved our guns this morning."

"That's a relief," said Jack.

"I guess you didn't hear the little cheer your buddies sent up when they saw you and Captain Howard begin to fire."

Tom turned to Captain Howard and said: "Congratulations Captain. If you were Canadian you'd be in line for a V.C."

"Thanks trooper," replied the Captain. Then as an afterthought, "V.C. What's a

V.C.?"

"Victoria Cross. Don't you Americans know anything, Captain, Sir?" Tom said this with an impudent grin.

"Saved your hide again, did we?"

"With a little help from Canada Jack. Yes, I'd say you did!"

"How about it, Sir? Jack asked Captain Howard.

"No problem Jack. I'll manage. Lots of applicants for your job. The men are fascinated by my little killing machine.

"You just run along and enjoy yourself."

"Yes, Sir."

"And Jack."

"Yes?"

"Thanks."

"You bet, Sir, anytime."

Quiet on the battlefield continued. It was as though the orgy of battle had exhausted both guns and men. Both sides were content for the nonce with the occasional token shot.

The troops seized the opportunity to rest in place, under the late afternoon sun. Sentinels were posted to sound the alert if necessary.

CHAPTER FIFTY-EIGHT

THAT NIGHT was one of the worst Jack had ever known. There were no comfortable camp cots. Neither were there tents, at least, not for other ranks. There was simply hard cold ground in the chill night air with only a bedroll for warmth. Campfires had been strictly forbidden.

But sleep was impossible anyway, since the enemy continued his sniping until dawn.

The troops had been gradually withdrawn from the line, unit by unit, under intense covering fire. About a half mile back a makeshift zareba had been thrown together using sod, logs and sundry equipment. There the men took shelter for the night.

And precious little shelter it proved to be. For under constant enemy fire there was many casualties. And effective retaliation was impossible; the enemy kept well concealed.

Further to the rear a paddock had been rigged by stringing rope in a wide circle through a sparse stand of poplar. Cloud and hundreds of other army ponies and mules and livestock were kept there.

Jack lay on his back thinking about the day's events. He looked up at the stars. The haze of battle had lifted and they were so clear and close he felt he could reach up and pluck them out of the black night sky.

Tom was not far away. He made no sound. Jack hoped he was sleeping. The rest of Baker Troop and Lieutenant Richards were also nearby. Cries could be heard from the direction of the hospital tents, even though they had been placed well to the rear of fortifications. Occasionally a muffled scream could be heard as surgeons toiled in rough conditions to extract a ball or bullet and to suture and bind.

The respite in the field had not endured. As evening approached sporadic enemy fire began, and soon both sides were once again pegging away.

The Northcote had proved to be of little value as a gunboat. Her frantic whistle could be heard from time to time. Intense far off fire could also be heard. Perhaps she was a useful diversion and drew marginal fire power from the battlefield.

Late in the afternoon the Scouts had captured a prisoner near the corral. Under interrogation he had claimed that the enemy in the field east of the river numbered merely several hundred, that Dumont's entire army, including Indians, was fewer than five hundred. This news swept through the camp like wildfire. The General and his staff were rumoured to have dismissed the claim as unreasonable and untrue.

Jack had been called to a brief meeting in Colonel William's headquarters tent. Lieutenant Helliwell was also present. As Jack entered they had been discussing Lord Melgund. This conversation ceased immediately and Jack did not hear what was said. Then they turned to the information obtained from the prisoner. After some discussion Jack was asked to offer an opinion.

Hesitantly at first, but with growing confidence, Jack launched into a review of probable enemy strength and disposition. He knew that the priests and civilians liberated earlier had provided information similar to that of the prisoner. Jack had enjoyed as good a view as anyone of enemy action that day, and because of his earlier adventures he had a better idea than most of those present of Indian contributions to rebel strength. But mostly he just flew by the seat of his pants. As he spoke he could see that he held everybody's respectful attention, even that of Colonel Williams.

As Jack lay there and remembered the meeting he felt very satisfied at his performance. I just know the Colonel was impressed, he thought. Absolutely! And why not!

Suddenly, he realized the conceit of his thinking. A wave of embarrassment swept over him. And then, in the darkness, he blushed.

With no little effort he forced his thought back to the meeting. For a time there had been animated discussion of the points he had made, with much give and take in which he had participated. Then after a time, Lieutenant Helliwell raised the matter of enemy logistics and reminded the Colonel the priests had said that the rebels did not have a great deal of ammunition. An extensive discussion of enemy resupply problems ensued.

Soon after discussion turned to other matters. Jack's presence was ignored and he listened in fascination. Apparently the General had been very surprised and somewhat discouraged at the fierce defence by the enemy. He had actually pondered withdrawal to Fish Creek, to await reinforcements. Only the entreaties of Colonel Williams and several other officers, appalled by the very idea, averted such an order.

Then someone raised the danger to the men from the possibility that the enemy may try to panic the livestock in the paddock, causing them to rampage through the zareba. Extra pickets were ordered for the area.

After this they discussed the morale of the troops, a topic upon which everyone present seemed to have an opinion. Ready as they were, the troops were frustrated and tired. Why no order to storm enemy positions? They felt like sitting ducks on the line, but it was just as bad in the zareba, with the enemy taking pot shots, then disappearing. And the rest they had earned never came. When the enemy was not sniping, the men were busied improving the defensive perimeter and loading ammunition. Even superiority in supply had turned to disadvantage: in the absence of regular munitions, the enemy was firing buckshot, nails and crude, home cast slugs, causing vicious wounds.

And worst of all, a feeling now pervaded the camp that the enemy had out-performed the army. Morale was not high.

Finally Major Smith noticed Jack was still present. He was dismissed, although the meeting continued. Jack was grateful because he was aching with exhaustion in every part of his body.

He and Tom had opened a tin of beef about an hour before. They had consumed that and some hard tack cold. Without fire they were unable to make tea. Tom had gone to sleep immediately thereafter.

Just before he drifted into uneasy sleep Jack wondered whether the General would order a full scale attack in the morning and decide the battle with his overwhelming number.

CHAPTER FIFTY-NINE

BUT THE command never came.

Jack had just shut his eyes, or so it seemed, when Tom was nudging him awake. Not a word was said. As Tom turned his attention to his kit, Jack groggily looked at his pocket watch. Then he looked up. The sky was beginning to break.

"It's only three thirty!" he exclaimed.

"I know," said Tom without looking back. "Parade at four. Our leader wants to make a speech."

Jack was too fatigued to enquire, but he assumed that meant, could only mean, the General.

The two ate in silence. Here and there they could hear muttered curses.

"Bloody hell," complained a cranky Grenadier. "The General ain't got no consideration, none at all." The soldier was standing, yawning and stretching as he said this.

"Don't he know I need my..." But he never got a chance to finish his sentence. At that moment a shot range out from a thicket only a hundred feet from the zareba. The shell zipped by the head of the Grenadier who ducked and quickly cowered with his companions.

Another shot far off. Silence had fallen over the area. Tom and Jack heard loud jeering from the direction of the shooting. Then galloping hooves.

Baker Troop fell in promptly, as ordered. Tom took a position on Jack's right. Darkness had departed by this hour and the first glint of sunshine touched the officers in front of them as they brought their troops to order. It was cold and the men shivered.

"I'm freezing to death," muttered Tom, "every bone in my body aches."

"Quiet in the ranks," called the sergeant major.

Tom was silent for only a moment. The sergeant major reported to Colonel Williams: "All present and accounted for, Sir."

"Fine Sar'n Major. Give them the standeasy. Let's get this over with quickly."

"He doesn't like this," said Tom, barely above a whisper.

"Not surprised," answered Jack without moving his lips. "Rather dangerous."

"What the...," began Tom. He said nothing more, just watched open mouthed as a soldier trotted out with a small box, setting it down to make a small podium for the General. With a bounce to his step the General mounted the box.

"Will you get a load of this," said Tom as the General began to speak. Lieutenant Richards turned to glare at the ranks. Tom fell silent again.

The General lavished praise on the men for their performance the previous day. Then he began to heap praise on the officers and admonished "every man jack" of them to pay strict heed to orders, "keep down", "don't offer tempting targets".

172

He went on in this vein for several minutes until Tom could contain himself no longer. In a voice that could be heard several ranks away, he blurted: "That blathering turnip, for this we stand here like twits."

Absolute silence fell. Not a man stirred. The General, with a puzzled expression on his face, had stopped in mid-sentence. For a moment he looked up and down the ranks. Quite evidently at a loss as to what to do, he lamely concluded his speech "…move to the front, sit tight; I'll have the artillery pound them into submission."

As soon as the General left the scene the officers had a brief conference. Jack heard several angry voices. The men were not happy with another day like the last. They were ready for battle, not another day holding the line. And this mood did not improve when they were moved back up to the line. They found they had been ordered into a position several hundred yards to the rear of the line the previous day.

As promised by the General, the nine pounders opened up on the enemy.

Much had been learned of their defensive preparations. Slit trenches had been dug in a wide sweeping arc facing the crest from which the militia had first seen Batoche. Westerly another such crescent of rifle pits had been placed, and so on the west in the direction of the village. Small coulees and deeper trenches connected each fallback position of the enemy, to enable him to retreat or advance under full cover.

These positions now were under intense intermittent bombardment.

The militia made efforts to advance as the artillery cease-fire was ordered, but immediately the guns fell silent enemy troops threw out a barrage of fire all along their outer defenses, forcing the militia to withdraw.

Several times, early in the day, as the cannonading recommenced, rebels leaped from their rifle pits and fled in apparent panic. Fearing a trap, headquarters had ordered no pursuit. The suspicions were well founded. After a few more attempts without result, to entice the militia into hasty advance, the ploy was dropped.

Around noon Baker Troop had been ordered into the line to relieve the left flank of A Company of the 90th Battalion. Jack found that he was sharing a rifle pit with Kurt. He enjoyed the company. Kurt chattered incessantly. Everything was stated in the most deadly earnest fashion. Yet he often said some of the most absurd things, as on the day he discussed the German passion for uniforms. Jack often found it difficult to discern if Kurt was serious, or simply putting him on.

The relentless sun beat down roasting Jack's shoulders and flooding the valley before him. He could see the ragged line of brightly coloured tunics winding off to his right over rolling fields. When he cast his eyes forward, toward the enemy, however, there was nothing to be seen. Jack had heard plenty from the veterans of the force. They sensed a new type of warfare was being born, and that the enemy was showing the way.

The field around, in which the militia had carved their pits, was not virginal prairie turf, but land that had been cultivated. The soil was fine and light. The least movement threw up tiny clouds to eddy and swirl, then seep into every crevice of clothing, down the collar and up the nostrils. In addition to the heat, Jack now felt gritty and filthy. He was loathe to move for when he did he raised more dirt. And there would be no bath that night. Only another dangerous, ever watchful evening at the ramparts.

The fighting, so intense during the morning, had by now settled into a war of attrition, with sporadic fire from both sides up and down the line. Both Jack and Kurt got off the occasional shot, Kurt between muttered commentary.

Then, toward three o'clock, Jack experienced a grisly incident. It was Sunday, and

Kurt had maintained a constant stream of complaint that there had been no church parade that morning. He hated church parade, Jack knew. Nevertheless he kept up a babble of invective, blaming the enemy, amongst others, for this serious lapse in military custom.

As he spoke he continually turned to face Jack, often rising slightly in the process. Jack could see that he was exposing his profile. He presented a perfect target to a rebel marksman with a Winchester forty-five. But no matter how often Jack warned him he always forgot himself.

"It vass all arranged," said Kurt in his most solemn voice. "Colonel Trubshaw and I haff been zecretly practizing. The Gheneral knew about it. He had vaved ze rule forbidding officers to fraternize viss ozzer ranks."

Jack listened, but kept his eyes trained forward. He could see a rebel in fur cap glide forward and disappear in a trench opposite. He corrected his thoughts: all he could see moving was the rebel cap. Desultory fire from near and far punctuated Kurt's nonsensical patter.

"He knew Trubshaw and I vere going to zing a duet at church parade today."

Jack did not see Kurt bob his head up as he finished his story.

"As a metter of fect, he vas chealous as hell. He vanted to make it a trio."

Jack suppressed a chuckle. At this precise moment a shot range out. A puff of smoke appeared where, only moments before, he had spotted the rebel.

Kurt's rattling conversation had stopped. There was only silence for a moment. Then Jack heard an odd sound from Kurt and he turned to look at his friend.

"Ch…k. Ch…k." It was a noise more than a voice. It came from Kurt's mouth, not from his throat. Kurt was white as a sheet. For a moment Jack could not see what was wrong with him. His eyes were wide with terror. He seemed to be choking and clutched frantically at his throat.

Then Jack saw what had happened. A forty-five calibre bullet had passed clean through Kurt's throat making a hole in his windpipe as large as a little finger.

Kurt was in shock. He was breathing fast, and every time he expelled a breath a spray of bloody droplets spewed out on either side of his throat.

Jack pulled Kurt down, well out of sight of enemy rifles.

Kurt gurgled, and began to breath faster. He grasped Jack's tunic with his hands and started to claw at him.

He's drowning, thought Jack. Here in the middle of the prairie he's drowning. Drowning in his own blood.

"Kurt, listen to me," said Jack in a loud stern voice. "You're going to drown to death unless you staunch the bleeding into your lungs.

"I want you to ram your index finger through your throat. Right through so I can see the tip at the other side.

"Do you understand?"

Kurt looked at him dumbly.

"Listen to me Kurt. Your life depends on it. Put your finger right there, like this." Jack lifted his left hand and made a jab into the left side of his own throat.

"Do you understand?"

Kurt nodded.

"Then do it. Do it now!"

With his right hand Jack grabbed Kurt's left arm and steadied it. Kurt poised his index finger at the hole in the left side of his throat.

"Now push. Push hard."

Kurt pushed. The tip of the finger disappeared.

"Push again," said Jack. He lifted Kurt's elbow and began to push it.

Now the finger travelled up to the second knuckle and stopped.

Kurt shook his head. He could not find the hole on the other side.

"Kurt you must. Hurry."

The look of terror in Kurt's eyes grew.

"Stretcher bearer, over here. Wounded man."

Then Jack screamed.

"Medic!"

He raised himself as far as he could with safety and screamed again. From a distance he heard a faint reply.

"Coming. Keep your shirt on, we're coming."

Jack once more turned his attention to Kurt. Now he could see the end of Kurt's finger poking out from the right side of his throat. The tip was red with blood.

It seemed like hours before the stretcher bearers arrived. Jack could see they had come at great personal risk. As they moved across the terrain the enemy kept up sustained gunfire. Many times they had to leap for cover.

They gently lifted Kurt onto the stretcher. Just before they moved him out he grasped Jack with his free hand and squeezed. Tears formed in his eyes. He tried to smile, but could not.

His breathing was laboured. It sounded more like wheezing.

As they left Jack wondered if he would ever see his friend alive again.

Jack was now alone in the rifle pit. He found he missed Kurt's idle rambling. In the absence of this diverting conversation Jack's mind wandered. What had Colonel Williams been discussing about Lord Melgund at the staff meeting last night? Why had the topic of conversation change so abruptly when Jack arrived? Jack was not surprised to hear that morale among the troops was low. He had heard plenty of discontented rumblings himself. And last night was nothing compared to this morning after parade. The men did not want to hear advice about caution, keep you heads down, the artillery will do your job for you. Sure, there was plenty of respect for a wiley enemy, but to a man, they wanted to hear the order to charge. They knew the danger, but they preferred attack over attrition. Lying in the fields by day and huddling in the zareba by night and providing a target for continual sniping was not a prospect to which they looked forward. A turkey shoot, thought Jack. Another day of this and the officers will have trouble on their hands.

The men had heard that the General had considered withdrawal to the main camp at Fish Creek. This had caused much merriment and caustic innuendo among the soldiers. Having just advanced to the battle scene, it struck them as ridiculous that they should now retreat to await reinforcements. The idea of waiting out the enemy in the hope he could be starved out, or that he would run out of ammunition, struck them as equally ludicrous. The men knew that during a siege they would be constantly harassed and gradually picked off by the enemy.

The General should keep such strategic options to himself and his staff, thought Jack. Everyone would be better off for it.

Jack wondered how Kurt was faring. That morning before parade Jack had passed the hospital tents. Not far away a grave digger was at work. Jack knew it was for Gunner Phillips of A Battery. He had been carried from the field badly wounded, only to die later. There would be no time for a military funeral. They could not even choose a burial spot. He had to be interred within the zareba.

How many more graves will be dug, Jack wondered, before military action ended.

When Jack was relieved and returned with Baker Troop to the zareba late that afternoon the first person he saw was Tom. Tom was relaxing against a wagon wheel not far from the location where the two had bedded down the previous night. Jack was surprised to see him already back in the zareba.

"One of the stretcher bearers got winged in the shin," explained Tom. "I replaced him. I was flabbergasted to see Kurt in the stretcher."

"He was hit bad," said Jack.

"That he was," agreed Tom. "We ran him over to the doc as quick as we would. He was in awful shape. Having a terrible time drawing breath. He wheezed. You could hear the air forcing its way around his finger. His face was turning blue. But he wouldn't pull out his finger."

"He was afraid to drown, I guess," said Jack.

"Well it didn't make much difference in the end."

"You mean...?"

"Yes he died about forty minutes after we brought him in. The doc tried but there was nothing he could do for him."

"Poor Kurt," was all that Jack could find to say.

"He's going to be buried tonight. A grave is being dug for him right now. Next to Gunner Phillips."

"In the zareba?" asked Jack.

"That's right. No way they can bury those two outside while fighting continues. Risk too many lives."

"Two?" querried Jack.

"Yes two. Kurt and Phillips."

"But I though Phillips was buried this morning?"

"They had to pull the burial detail out for duty on the line. They never got him down. Both go down tonight."

CHAPTER SIXTY

ALL THE members of Baker Troop were present when Gunner Phillips and Kurt Schmidt, swathed in white canvas, were lowered into the earth.

"From ashes to ashes and from dust to dust," intoned the Chaplain. Jack listened to the few words spoken hastily for his fallen comrade. As soon as a brief prayer was said the men were ordered to disperse. It was dangerous, even within the zareba, for too many men to be congregated for any significant period of time. It was too tempting a target for enemy sharpshooters.

As Tom and Jack walked back they passed by the front of the corral. Occasional shooting could be heard. The horses were uneasy and skittish.

Near the gate a burly wrangler tried to subdue an enormous grey mottled stallion while two other men looked on. He had managed to lasso the horse, but now it balked and reared at the end of the rope. All three men snarled directions and shouted curses at the animal, which only served to excite it further. Suddenly the animal reared up with a shrieking whinny and then began to walk backwards on shaking hind legs, pulling the wrangler along.

Until that moment the other ponies had stepped about, keeping well away, but now they scattered at a run.

Jack realized how real was the danger that the animals might stampede.

Other men were seen engaged in further improving fortifications. They worked away with pick and shovel and busily piled up dirt and sod. The zareba perimeter was three feet high and growing.

"It looks like General Ponce intends to settle down for a while," said Tom. "Next thing you see he's going to be throwing up a drill shed."

Jack smiled. He welcomed Tom's irreverent comments. Anything to take his mind off the gloomy burial detail.

They passed the hospital tents. Jack heard the "zip" sound of a bullet. It was difficult to know if it were twenty feet or twenty yards away. He heard another distant shot, a pinging, then a thud as a bullet struck wood. A tree trunk I hope, thought Jack.

As they skirted around the medical tents they could hear the conversation of the medics at work. The groans of the wounded could also be heard.

Jack knew then that there would be many more men laid to rest in the prairie wilderness before the fighting was over.

"Did you hear about Captain French?" asked Tom.

"French's Scouts?"

"None other."

"No, what about him?"

"Colonel Williams has asked General Ponce to put the Captain up for a V.C."

"Really, a Victoria Cross? What happened?"

"Well, they were under massive fire. Captain French ordered a withdrawal. But just as they were pulling back one of their men, Cook, I think, got it in the leg.

"He raised one hell of a row. Shouting for help. 'For God's sake, Captain French, don't leave me here.' He was shouting that his leg was broken and he couldn't walk.

"With bullets flying all around the Captain sauntered back like it was a Sunday stroll, threw Cook on his shoulders and carried him back.

"His whole unit saw it. He sure is something."

They moved on in silence through the zareba. Some of the men, bone tired from the day under fire, relaxed or slept. Others worked under the watchful eyes of officers. They were refilling ammunition boxes, cleaning rifles and doing a hundred other things that need always to be done in military life.

As they approached the area assigned to Baker Troop they saw that most of the others had arrived before them.

"Have you heard the lastest?" called Sandy in not quite a shout.

Tom and Jack sat down. Jack rested his back against a wagon wheel.

"You're not going to believe this," continued Sandy.

"Don't tell me. Let me guess," said Tom. "Dumont has surrendered." There was quiet laughter.

"General Middleton has decided to retreat to Fish Creek after all," offered Bo. There was more laughter.

Then Sandy continued.

"No. That's not it but you're close."

"Come on Sandy," said Tom, "give us a break."

"Is it good news or bad news?" asked Tubby Mills.

"Now there's an intelligent question," said Sandy.

Tubby smiled.

"Quite surprising really, quite surprising," continued Sandy.

The smile quickly fell from Tubby's face.

"Enough," said Tom. "What is it?"

"Well, it seems that Lord Melgund has departed our company."

"What do you mean 'departed our company'? He never was 'our company'," said Hughes.

"He left."

"What?"

"He did what?"

"He's left. He's gone. He's no longer here," said Sandy.

"When?" asked Jack.

"Yesterday. At about four in the afternoon."

"I'm surprised you didn't know that Tom continued Sandy. "Generally you know everything."

"Where's he gone. What for…?" began Jack.

"Well, it seems that yesterday, for some time, people thought he had gone to the camp at Fish Creek. It looks like we may be the last people on earth to hear about this."

"Why?" asked someone.

"Now that's the interesting question," said Sandy.

"Yeah, well answer it. Stop futzing around," said Bo.

"At first," said Sandy, drawing out his story for all the effect he could muster, "it was rumoured that he and the great chief had an argument."

"Who?" asked a voice.

"Middleton, you dope," said Tom. "General Ponce. Our great leader himself."

"Yes, General Middleton," said Sandy. "And if you guys can shut up a minute you can learn something."

Someone gave Sandy the raspberry. There was a lot of laughter and jeering. Then Sandy spoke again and the razzing subsided.

"Then word was passed that he had gone to fetch reinforcements," went on Sandy.

"I'd believe that," said Tom. "Did you hear what General Ponce was supposed to have said yesterday? I mean after he was persuaded not to gallop all the way back to Fish Creek."

Tom slowly looked around at all of his friends. When he had everyone's undivided attention, he put on a falsetto voice with a vague English accent. "I can make this place impregnable, and we can keep pegging away at them. I haven't enough men to charge their position!"

Laughter greeted his imitation of the General.

"Not enough men!" snorted Tom. "What does he think we are? A bunch of his bloody sepoys. Pukka Sahib General thinks he's still in India."

There was more laughter. Then Sandy spoke once more.

"It seems that none of the above is correct reason for departure. It seems that Lord Melgund has permanently retired from the battlefield."

"What?"

"Permanently?"

"Lord Melgund, Military Secretary to General Fredrick Middleton has left via Humboldt, for Ottawa. Something about a previous appointment in London," finished Sandy.

Raucous laughter erupted. After a time it settled down somewhat. Tom's voice could clearly be heard over the laughter.

"Poltroon."

"What?" asked Higgins still laughing.

"Lord Poltroon."

"Lord Poltroon!" echoed someone.

"General Ponce has lost his Poltroon," said Tom. "Not platoon, gentlemen. His Poltroon."

The laughter erupted all over again.

That night more men were wounded. A private in the Grenadiers, craving a smoke before turning in, was struck in the face by a sniper's bullet as he contentedly drew on his pipe. He died instantly.

All casualties were in the zareba.

CHAPTER SIXTY-ONE

MONDAY MORNING arrived. The third day of battle. At parade in the dim early light of dawn the officers gave their instructions for the day's action. The orders called for more of the same. Keep down and let the artillery bombardment continue.

The General, swagger stick in hand, paced up and down in front of the troops as plans were announced. It was then the men knew. There would be no assault on enemy positions. The General would either starve the rebels out, or bomb them into submission. A process that might take months, if it happened at all.

Tom, like the other men, was disgusted by developments. But unlike some he did not become sullen or stoic in the face of orders he deemed obtuse.

For a few minutes they waited for the Lieutenant.

"Keep you chins up lads," said Tom with a touch of pomposity. "He'll starve those devils into submission."

"Even if it takes a year," Bo added unhappily.

"It probably will," put in Sandy.

"Don't worry, he'll bomb them all the way to China. But he can't do it by doomsday; it's gonna take him a few days more."

The men laughed nervously. A few cast anxious glances around, afraid officers would overhear.

"Our fearless leader, the Lord High Poohbah General Ponce, needs reinforcements," went on Tom.

"Maybe Lord Melgund did go to fetch help," put in Bo.

"That's right," Tom shot back. "He's fetching the Light Brigade, what's left of 'em!"

Gloomy laughter greeted this remark.

"No really," said Bo, when the laughter subsided. "Maybe he did."

"He's gonna really beef up his command," said Tom. "He's bringing in the Bengal Lancers and the Army of the Potomac too."

"The whole British Army," chimed in Higgins, getting into the act.

"Absolutely!" exclaimed Tom. "We'll have men so thick up here we won't be able to lie down. We'll have to stand shoulder to shoulder, all night long. Our sheer number will just frighten the rebels to death. We won't have to fire a shot."

At this they all broke into laughter.

"Pipe down!" a voice barked. An officer standing thirty feet away glared at the members of Baker Troop.

"With this bloody lot, I'll bet he yearns for sepoys and the good old days at Lucknow," muttered Tom, making sure he had the last word.

The general mirth, unsmothered by the officer, only fully settled down when

Lieutenant Richards appeared. Immediately the men were serious and attentive as he gave them their personal detail for the day.

Shortly thereafter they were marched off for another tour of duty at the front. Just before they left however, Tom grabbed Jack by the shoulder.

"Stick with me today," he said.

Jack looked at Tom but before he could speak the order came: "Move out!"

The column had moved rapidly, but Tom managed to hustle alongside Jack.

"I have something I want to show you," he said. Jack had no time to ponder this enigmatic statement.

Baker Troop, along with the rest of the Midland Battalion, reoccupied their trenches on the extreme left flank. Tom and Jack settled in together.

The sun climbed wearily in the sky, indifferent to the figures below.

Jack kept a careful lookout over the rim of the trench. He could not see movement, but he did hear the regular far off pop of rifle fire, and near at hand the occasional report from close fire. Neither of them did much shooting, Jack for lack of targets of opportunity, Tom for lack of interest. He jabbered on, moving about the trench to point out things of interest.

Toward noon they both saw Colonel Williams lead a column of men forward under cover of a ridge near the river. Several minutes later gunners wheeled two nine pounders into the position secured by the Colonel.

"For God's sake, Colonel," said Tom, peering over the top of the trench, "what do you think you're doing? I thought you were told to sit tight. Damn fool doesn't know any better."

Jack chuckled quietly. He knew Tom admired the Colonel.

"I guess he's frustrated," said Jack.

"I'll break that man," said Tom, in a vague imitation of the General. "What does he think he's doing, fighting a war?"

Across the field they heard the command: "Fire!"

A terrific blast, the gun recoiled and several suspenseful seconds later an explosion blew in the side of the longest building in the village.

"Rebel H.Q., I'll bet," said Jack.

Then faintly they heard the command to reload. The shelling continued for some time.

All along the line the rattle of gunfire could be heard as the battle heated up. Jack and Tom kept low and after about an hour things seemed to settle down somewhat.

Tom took the opportunity of relative quiet to munch a bit of hard tack. Jack took his helmet off and slowly raised his eyes to ground level. There was no sound at all now as he scanned enemy trenches for signs of life. It must be dinner time, he thought. For a long time he lay there, stretched out on his stomach, watching for movement.

Then suddenly he felt Tom's hand on his left arm.

"Don't move," said Tom.

Jack froze.

"We have a visitor."

A strange sensation coursed down Jack's back.

"This is what I wanted you to see."

Jack started to turn.

"Slowly," said Tom, squeezing Jack's arm, "you'll scare him."

Jack turned. Tom was lying flat, his head rested just beneath the rim of the trench. Jack's eyes followed the gaze of Tom's eyes to a mound of earth at the rear of the pit.

Sitting there, absolutely motionless and staring back at them was a gopher.

"My friend," said Tom. "He visited on and off all day yesterday."

Moving carefully Tom threw a piece of hard tack two feet to the right of the animal. It blinked, but made no motion. The two men watched as though entranced. The gopher blinked again, then darted for the food. It munched away oblivious to the audience.

Several more times Tom threw tack to the mound of earth. Each time the gopher retrieved it, then perched happily on its haunches eating with his two friends.

"He must like it," said Tom. "He ate my whole dinner yesterday."

The gopher had stopped nibbling now. He blinked twice, then stared at the two prone figures.

Suddenly the crack of a Winchester broke the silence and the gopher catapulted backwards.

Tom threw himself across the trench to find his friend. Two feet down the far side of the mound he saw the decapitated body of the little animal. For a second it shivered stiffly, then twitched once, then lay still. The head was nowhere to be seen.

"Damn! Bloody hell!" he shouted.

"Tom." shouted Jack. "Get down!"

Tom felt the powerful arm of his friend around his waist and felt himself being hurled back, to the bottom of the shallow trench.

For a long time he sprawled there speechless. He stared at Jack with glassy eyes. He was very quiet for the remainder of the afternoon.

At sunset the Midland Battalion was withdrawn from the line. As Jack entered the zareba he immediately realized something was amiss.

He and Tom made their way over to their sleeping kit, deposited their rifles and ammunition pouches and hungrily ate some cold beef and biscuits. Only when he had finished did he realize what it was that was different.

Except for the dull metal clank of mess kits the place was completely quiet. There was no conversation, no good humoured joshing. The men ate in silence. A few shuffled about without apparent purpose.

Jack walked over to the centre of the camp, near the hospital tents, to fill his canteen. As he approached he could hear the pitiful cries of the patients and the terse conversation of doctors.

He had almost reached the water barrel on a wagon nearby when he practically stumbled on what appeared to be discarded rags. There was a wide row of them. Then he saw, in their midst, a solitary white face staring patiently at the evening sky. He felt a surge of revulsion, then unreasoned fear. He stepped quickly around the bodies and over to the barrel. He opened his canteen, picked up the dipper and was about to use it when he heard: "I wouldn't, if I were you soldier."

Jack swung around. At first he could not find the source of the voice. Then he did. A figure toiled away near the fallen. He was sewing canvas shrouds over bodies. Jack had not seen him at first because he wore dark tattered civilian clothes and worked in silence at the end of the row.

"It'll make you sick," explained the voice.

Jack dropped the dipper. The water was contaminated!

He beat a hasty retreat.

As he dropped down beside Tom he described what had happened.

"I'm not surprised," said Tom, when Jack had finished, "lots of the boys have dysentery. And they go anywhere. Either they can't make it to the latrines or they're afraid to move around too much.

"As a matter of fact the place is a pig sty. Trash all over, dung, dirt. The bloody dirt, it's into everything and the place stinks. Can't you smell it?"

There was no need to reply. The stench hung over the camp like an evil cloud. It had for several days.

In the silence that followed Tom's remark Jack sensed something else. The first tentacles of fear had found a foothold. Not fear of battle. The Midlanders, the Grenadiers, the 90th, all of them, to a man, they were ready, even impatient, for action. The fear that gripped the camp was that of a senseless, idle death in the zareba from a sniper's bullet.

For two nights and three days the men had lived under the threat of death from enemy snipers. The troops were demoralized. Enemy tactics were beginning to take their toll.

The officers saw all of this.

Colonel Williams decided to do something about it. He quietly summoned a private, informal conference at Battalion Headquarters, a conference that was strictly unofficial. A number of prominent officers, one being the General, were conspicuous by their absence. They had not been invited to confer.

CHAPTER SIXTY-TWO

JACK HAD just settled back with Tom to enjoy a little rest when a messenger arrived. It was Colonel William's batman. Would Trooper Holden attend forthwith at the Colonel's headquarters tent?

When Jack arrived the meeting was already in progress. All of the Colonel's own staff was present. Colonels Van Straubenzie and Grasett were present as was Captain Hague. It appeared to Jack that almost every fighting unit in the camp was represented.

Colonel Van Straubenzie was seated behind the only desk inside the tent. Colonel Grasett and Captain Hague had pulled chairs up to the desk. Other officers were seated as well and some were lounging at the sides of the tent.

Colonel Williams was on his feet speaking in earnest confidential tones. When Jack entered the Colonel merely nodded to him then continued to speak. Jack was aware that many noticed the nod of acknowledgement.

But their attention was focussed on the Colonel.

"You have seen the deteriorating conditions of the camp," he was saying. "The filth, the squalor. We have plenty of ammunition and plenty of food. No problem there. There is a real danger our water has become contaminated. The medics are advising that we boil it, but you know the standing orders regarding fires at night. We could fetch water from the river, but only at great and constant risk.

"But it's really the state of mind of the men that most concerns me. They've been ready for real action for several days, but the Commanding General seems content to wait, and perhaps, starve the enemy out. How do we know what his present supplies really are? Will they carry him to next Sunday, or for a month of Sundays."

"We cannot be sure he is not being resupplied from sources to the west here," put in Colonel Grasett.

"I think I've made all of you aware of the intelligence on supply that young Jack has given me," said Colonel Williams. "We have no way of knowing that that kind of resupply will not recommence. Indeed we cannot be sure it is not taking place at this present moment."

"The information from Trooper Holden should have been placed under immediate investigation," said Captain Hague. "Another grave omission if you ask me."

"Gentlemen I don't hold with the leadership view that we can starve the rebel out," said Colonel Williams. "I don't agree that we can successfully lay seige without very grave risk to ourselves; much greater than the risk of alternative action."

"It seems more like we're the ones under siege," said a voice from the back.

Gentlemanly laughter greeted this remark. Colonel Williams joined in. Then he went on.

"I have done my utmost to convince the General to order decisive action. With the influence of Lord Melgund no longer a factor, Colonel Van Straubenzie has tried to convince the General to move. We have tried everything. Colonel Van Straubenzie is the most experienced officer amongst us. I don't need to tell you his record. He has seen action all over the world under renowned leadership. His own experience in command is without equal, if I may say so, Sir." He turned deferentially to Colonel Van Straubenzie when he said this.

"Colonel Van Straubenzie has been unable to secure any assurance from the General that an order for attack may be forthcoming in the future. I said 'may' gentlemen, not will!"

"I have done my best gentlemen," said Colonel Van Straubenzie. He looked impressive in his great greying beard and red tunic. "He has grown impatient with me. He no longer wishes to hear my advice."

"I have told him that our numbers alone should give us confidence, if not our armament. But he lacks assurance about enemy strength." Colonel Van Straubenzie looked at Jack and smiled when he said this. "He scoffs at the figures.

"I am satisfied he will no longer listen to reason. He hears only his own lackeys and 'yes' men. I think something must be done."

There was a murmur of approval among the men. Colonel Williams interrupted. "I merely wish to say one thing. The responsibility will be mine and mine alone."

There was negative response to this suggestion. Colonel Williams finally had to hold up his hand to gain the floor once more.

"No. No. That's the way it must be. There is no profit whatsoever in sharing around the responsibility for what must be done.

"That is not the reason that you were asked to join our little discussion. Not at all.

"There is no need for more than one person to take the responsibility. If it should fail it will rebound to the detriment of only one person. It need be no other way; that's the way it should be.

"Each of you has indicated support for this course in private. I wanted you here together today to assure each of you that you are not alone in your views. I also wanted you here to assure myself that my course is the wise and proper one. And to seek your confidential support."

"Considering what must be done," interrupted Colonel Grasett, "I think the time for action has come. We have no more time for talk."

"This will take some hours," said Captain Hague. "I don't believe we have the luxury of further discussion.

"It is my suggestion that Colonel Williams consider himself authorized to take whatever steps he may deem necessary to bring about our purpose."

The remarks of Captain Hague were obviously approved by every man present. Several officers said "Hear, hear". One or two said "Amen."

"Thank you gentlemen," said Colonel Williams. "And thank you for coming. Now if you will excuse me we'll get right to it. We're in a spot of trouble and we should jolly well deal with it head on."

Colonel Williams went to the exit of the tent to shake hands with the officers as they left.

When Jack appeared at his elbow he took him gently by the arm and said, "Not yet, son. I'd like to speak to you privately. There is a little something I'd like you to do for me."

Jack went back in and waited. He knew something momentous had happened, but he was not sure what. Captain Hague's manner of speaking carried more meaning than his words.

When the last officer had left the Colonel told his orderly they were not to be disturbed. He dropped the tent flap and returned to his desk.

"Sit down Jack," he said. "This may take a few minutes."

Jack sat at the desk opposite the Colonel and watched his hand move swiftly across pages of stationery.

In the light of the oil lamp on the desk his hand cast a long shadow. From time to time the Colonel frowned deeply as he considered how to express his thoughts.

Finally with a flourish, he signed his name, folded the paper, placed it in an envelope and sealed it. He looked up at Jack.

"I don't need to tell you how confidential all of this is."

"No, Sir," said Jack.

"Good. I was sure you would understand."

"I am going to ask you to do something for me. It is not an order, but a request. You may refuse, if you wish, for any reason. I will not ask you why.

"No one else will ask you either, since no one knows that I am making this request of you."

"I understand, Sir."

"What I want you to do is to take this message and to deliver it to the nearest telegrapher for transmission. The nearest telegraph is several miles distance. Unfortunately on the west bank of the river."

"What about Clark's Crossing, Sir?"

"Too far. Too much time. Too many hostiles and too risky."

"Yes Sir."

"Will you do this for me?"

"Yes, Sir."

"Thank you Jack."

"Sir, I just want to serve my Queen and Country. I know that's what you're asking me to do."

"I'm glad you feel that way Jack. I knew you would.

"I would like to tell you what is in that message but I will not. It is better for you that I do not. I'm sure you understand."

"I do, Sir. When do I leave?"

"Right now, son. There can be no more delay. Let nothing stop you. That message may be more important than your life."

CHAPTER SIXTY-THREE

WITHIN THE half hour Jack was at the corral to saddle up Cloud. As he had approached, the foul air from the small paddock grew strong.

A wrangler opened the gate and Jack slipped in. He faced a wall of horseflesh. Fetid smells of fresh manure rose to assault his nostrils. A bay mare began to urinate in front of him. Pungent vapours from the splashing liquid filtered up to the miasma that hovered over the animals.

The nervous ponies moved constantly.

"Cloud," called Jack. "Cloud," he called again, louder now.

More than six hundred animals milled about. This is no way to bring her out, he thought.

He edged toward the gate and whistled.

One wrangler looked at him as if he were crazy.

He whistled again. Shortly, he could see a white pony picking her way through the throng of horses.

Within minutes Jack had her watered, fed and saddled.

And then he was off.

Jack had cleared the zareba about twenty minutes before. He had startled the pickets but they waved him on when they saw his tunic.

He knew that his shortest path was south west. But in that direction he could expect enemy snipers. Instead he took a wide sweep in an easterly direction turning in an arc to the southwest hoping to outflank the rebels.

Cloud galloped as if grateful to be free. She charged with abandon down coulees and up the other side. She whisked him with precision and an unerring eye around trees and bushes.

In the gloaming Jack, too, kept a watchful eye. I cannot wait forever, he thought. I must have cleared the enemy by now. Then it's straight west to the river.

Cloud suddenly slowed, causing Jack to grab the saddle horn to brace himself. At that moment he saw riders off to the west, at about two o'clock. He pulled Cloud to a halt behind a sparse growth of trees and waited.

Indians. About seven of them. Travelling north. Reinforcements, thought Jack. Then he wondered if he knew any of them.

He waited a long time for them to pass out of sight. Cloud grazed quietly.

It was dark when he started out again. This time he rode with a reckless determination. Darkness would cover him. Anyway, there was no more time to lose.

He heard Cloud's steady harsh breath with every gallop. Then abruptly they were headed down. The moon peeked from broken clouds about the west bank of the river and threw a glittering silver path across the black water. Once again Cloud came to a quick halt. The shining path now ended at her feet. They were there.

The moon disappeared once again. The river was so dark it was almost invisible in the night. But Jack could hear the rushing swelling waters as they coursed every northward to the sea. The gurgling trickle at water's edge sounded cold. Jack braced himself for the swim. He leaned forward to give a few reassuring strokes to Cloud's neck. She too would feel the shock of cold.

Jack knew he had lost many minutes waiting for the Indians to pass. He had no more time to lose.

Come on Cloud. The words formed in his mind but not in his lips. Instead, the only sound heard was a click. Was it a hoof against a stone or was it the sound of metal? A Winchester being cocked, perhaps?

"How do you do, stranger? Going for a swim?"

The voice bore a strange accent. He had heard it before. French. Of course, French. This was the enemy. Rebels.

Jack did not move. He and Cloud froze. The voice said something more. This time in French. Another voice answered. Were there two of them? Maybe more. Then the first voice spoke again. This time it was a command.

"Turn around soldat."

Jack began to reign Cloud to the right.

"Slowly soldier boy. Take it easy. Do not startle my pony. I have a finger on the trigger."

Ever so slowly Jack reigned Cloud around to the right.

Not twenty feet away were three mounted men. All of them were armed with Winchesters. All three rifles were pointed at Jack.

Jack groaned inwardly. Not again, he thought. Not a prisoner again!

CHAPTER SIXTY-FOUR

"LES MAINS," shouted the second speaker.

Jack looked at him stupidly.

"Les mains, les mains," he shouted again.

Jack continued to look at the shouting man. "Your hands, English. He wants you to raise your hands." It was the first man speaking. "Unless of course you yearn to feel a cold steel bullet between your lungs and your heart."

Slowly Jack raised his hands. The shouter wore a buckskin jacket fringed down the sides and arms. It was heavily beaded across the chest. He was black haired and though he was not Indian he had dark skin and black eyes. He was thin, and even sitting on his pony looked tall. The other two were also dark. They too wore buckskin. One wore a bandana across his forehead; the other a scarf or sash around his waist. These two were mounted on dark mangy cayuses.

The shouter now savagely kicked his horse. The animal jumped forward with a start then walked a few more steps. He shouted something to his two companions. They too moved forward.

"Qu'est-ce que vous faites ici," said the shouter.

Jack made no reply. He must know I do not speak French, thought Jack.

But if he did know it made no difference.

"Parlez!" commanded the shouter.

"You had better answer him, English. He has an itchy trigger finger."

"But I don't speak French," pleaded Jack.

"What's he asking?"

"What are you doing here? What are you up to?" translated the rebel with the sash. He seemed the most amiable of the three. "What are you doing at the river?"

Jack's mind flashed back to his mission. Time's awasting, thought Jack. What can I do?

"Fouillez-le!" commanded the shouter.

The amiable rebel gave a slight kick to his pony and started again to move toward Jack.

The message! I can't let the enemy have the message, Jack thought. In a flash his shooter was in his hand blazing away at the shouter. Jack was surprised, for the amiable rebel fell simultaneously. Jack fired his revolver and the third rebel pitched forward.

Stunned, Jack looked around. How had it happened?

He had fired only two shots, but three men lay dead at his feet.

"Put your gun up soldier," cried a voice back in the trees. "Unless you want to join your friends." Then Jack heard a long low familiar chuckle.

"Tom!" he exclaimed.

And Tom, mounted bareback on a grey gelding, walked his horse forward out of the trees.

"Howdy pardner," said Tom.

"How the…" began Jack.

"Just good scouting old fellow," said Tom. "I could hear your friend shouting half a mile away. Figured there was trouble." Tom inclined his head toward the shouter.

The body lay almost entirely in the water. It moved and Jack's hand grasped the handle of his revolver. But it was only the current tugging at the shouter, trying to take him away.

"But why…What are you doing here?"

"Came to fetch you."

"But I can't return. I must go on. I have orders."

"Your orders are cancelled."

"You spoke to…"

"Colonel Williams, yes," said Tom.

"You know about…"

"The note, yes. But only that you carry it, not what it contains. The Colonel told me that much."

Jack took the sealed message out of his pocket and looked at it.

"The Colonel said he wants you to read it. He said that he owes you that much. Whatever that means. Then you are to destroy it and forget that it ever existed."

Jack opened the envelope and removed the message. It was addressed to the Honourable A.P. Caron, Minister of Militia, Ottawa, Canada. For two pages the Colonel recounted accurately the condition of the troops, and strength of the enemy, the readiness of the men and the refusal of General Middleton to give the order to attack. All the information discussed at the meeting, and more, was related in the letter.

Jack turned to the last page. He read it with deadly fascination: "The General having refused repeatedly to order the attack, it can only be assumed, in all the circumstances related above, that he has suffered a temporary loss of nerve or will or, giving him the benefit of every reasonable doubt, a temporary mental incapacity.

"It is my advice, as one of Her Majesty's loyal officers, that he be removed from command pro tempore. It is my further advice that the senior officer present, Colonel Van Straubenzie, be appointed the officer in overall command of your North West Field Force. He has the confidence of officers and men alike and will swiftly bring the situation here to a successful conclusion.

"On a personal note, I would like to add that I alone am responsible for this telegram. Though I say confidently that an overwhelming number of officers in the field concur in my views.

"It remains only for me to say that if I do not hear from you in reply by telegraph, we in the field must assume that you have been unable to transmit a message through enemy lines. In such emergency circumstances and assuming it to be in the best interest of the nation and in accordance with the unexpressed wishes of government, we, the assembled officers in the field shall remove General Middleton from his command, forcibly, if necessary, and turn it over to one chosen by common consent as the most fitted therefore.

"By the grace of God, and In humble obedience to Our Gracious Sovereign, Her Majesty Queen Victoria.

Your obedient servant, Colonel Arthur T.H. Williams

Officer Commanding, Midland Battalion"

Jack folded the message. For a long time he simply stared at the ever flowing river. If that isn't mutiny, he thought, that's as close as you can come without being hanged.

Then he ripped the paper into a hundred pieces and let them flutter into the turbulent current.

Just as the message disappeared from view the current dislodged the body of the shouter, sweeping it away toward Batoche.

"I'm to bring you back immediately," said Tom. "You're to report forthwith to Colonel Williams."

"Do you know what's happened?"

"Not really. Something about some plans for tomorrow that General Ponce has confided to the Colonel."

"Action!" said Jack. "We're finally going to see real action."

"Maybe," said Tom. "But the Great Pukka Sahib General Ponce did not take this humble sepoy into his confidence. If he's going to attack, though, he'll have to tell the Battalion beforehand. I hope someone explains that to him."

"Maybe the General will prove us all wrong," said Jack with a laugh. "Anyway, I think we should be on our way."

"There is one other thing I want to tell you before we go," said Tom. "Bad news I'm afraid."

Jack looked over at Tom.

"It's Lieutenant Richards."

"Is he…he's…he's?" began Jack.

"Not dead, no," said Tom. "But badly wounded. He may not live."

A long silence followed. Lieutenant Richards had not only been the officer commanding Baker Troop, but had been Jack's friend. He was also one officer who had been unswervingly loyal. He had believed in Jack without reservation. A deep sense of grief welled up in Jack.

"How did it happen?"

"He was in the zareba. He and Sandy were talking. Sandy says they were talking about Captain Brown being killed."

"Captain Brown?"

"Yes, he was killed today. He was with Boulton's Scouts. I guess Captain Brown was a good friend of Major Boulton. The Major is very upset."

"What happened?" said Jack once more, interrupting Tom's discursiveness.

"Well, the Lieutenant had become a good friend of Captain Brown too," said Tom defensively. "They were talking about that when suddenly the Lieutenant turned white as a sheet.

"Sandy thought he was just upset about the death of his friend. But then his eyes looked really strange. Sandy says the pupils got really large.

"He asked the Lieutenant if he was ill. The Lieutenant said he though he had been hit. He put his hand in his jacket. When he brought it out it was covered with blood.

"It was only afterward that Sandy remembered hearing the crack of rifle fire just before the blood drained from the Lieutenant's face.

"It's amazing isn't it? He never felt nothing. He didn't even know he was hit."

Jack made no reply. He merely kicked his heels into Cloud and made off at a gallop.

CHAPTER SIXTY-FIVE

IT SEEMED that in no time at all the two were back in camp. Jack headed Cloud over to a wrangler, who smelled as bad as the corral, and then hurried on to report to Colonel Williams. The Colonel was conferring with Major Smith when Jack entered. When the Colonel saw Jack he excused himself to the Major and stood up.

"I'm glad Tom caught you. I was afraid it would be too late."

"I was held up, Sir. A small party of Indians riding north. They didn't see me, but I had to wait for twenty or thirty minutes before they rode out of sight."

"Did you...?"

"I took care of that little matter, Sir."

"Oh, Tom told you. Good."

"May I ask what happened, Sir, or rather, what's going to happen."

The Colonel looked over to Major Smith. The Major inclined his head every so slightly.

"I think I can. I think you should treat this as confidential, though. Until further orders, or course."

"Yes, Sir."

"The General has let it be known he intends to made a reconnaissance in some strength far to the north-east of our outermost right flank. His plans are to leave here at nine tomorrow."

"I don't know if I quite understand, Sir."

"Quite simply put son, the consensus seems to be that the General will be placing himself so far beyond militia lines as to be incommunicado.

"Sir?" said Jack with a question in his voice.

"Unable to communicate. In such circumstances, according to military law, the senior officer in the field may assume temporary command of the forces."

"You mean...?"

"Colonel Van Straubenzie should be de facto commanding officer at about nine forty-five tomorrow.

"He, Colonel Grasett, Captain Hague and I have agreed upon an attack tomorrow, contingent upon this event. Captain Hague has identified the weak spot in enemy defences. It's all set.

"And none too soon. We've had another bad day."

"I heard. Lieutenant Richards."

"Yes, Tom told you that too, did he? Well that was one of the reasons for the order to report promptly to me. He was hit in the chest. I understand he is not expected to live. But he's conscious. I expect you'll want to run along to see him. I'll let you do that in just one minute." "First, we have another piece of business."

He paused for a moment. Then he went on.

"We've had a bad day today. Nine killed; thirty-one wounded. I'm afraid

Lieutenant Helliwell, our Battalion Intelligence Chief, was one of them. Wounded in the shoulder. He'll have to be replaced. Then there's the problem of Baker Troop. They're short a commanding officer."

Jack looked with apprehension at the Colonel. A smile spread across the face of Major Smith.

"I've considered all possible alternatives. A replacement must be made without delay. Tonight, as a matter of fact."

"Sir…"

"Let me finish, Jack."

"I've decided a field promotion is the only rational option open to me. I have the unanimous concurrence of Battalion staff and, ill as he is, Lieutenant Richards himself made this recommendation.

"As of now you are promoted to full lieutenancy. Effective immediately you are ordered to assume command of Baker Troop. You are also expected to make yourself available for consultations as Midland Battalion Intelligence Chief."

"Sir, I…"

"Major Smith has some rank insignia that you'll require. Now I expect you'll want to get over to visit Lieutenant Richards."

"Thank you, Sir."

"You've earned it son. Congratulations."

"Congratulations, Lieutenant Holden," said Major Smith.

"Thank you, Sir."

"We'd better put these on tonight," said Major Smith. "You won't have time tomorrow." He passed Jack the insignia. Jack looked at the flashes for a moment. Then the Major awkwardly pinned them to Jack's tunic, finishing with a comradely clap on the shoulder.

"Gentlemen," said Jack, stepping back several paces. "Now if you will excuse me…"

"You may leave, Jack," said the Colonel. "You have many things to do, I'm sure.

"And tell Lieutenant Richards we're all praying for him."

"Right, Sir. Thanks again Colonel."

"Better run along son. I wouldn't want you to be late.

"One other thing," said the Colonel as an afterthought. "We have a staff meeting tomorrow morning at five. I'll expect you to be there."

"Sir!" said Jack. He saluted. Then he turned and left.

CHAPTER SIXTY-SIX

ONCE MORE Jack made his way across the camp to the hospital tents. The usually fetid smell of the camp had disappeared with the cool crisp evening air. Jack could scarcely believe all that had happened in just a single day.

As he entered the hospital area a private passed him. His left arm was in a sling, but he snapped off a smart salute to Jack nevertheless.

For a moment, but only a moment, Jack was taken aback. Then he quickly recovered and returned the salute.

A medical orderly directed Jack to the correct hospital tent. Jack noticed the number of such tents had grown.

A doctor coming out of the tent met Jack on the way in.

"Whom do you want to see Lieutenant?"

Jack found it odd to be addressed in this way.

"Lieutenant Richards, doctor."

"Richards, yes. He's on the right about five beds over."

"He's very weak. Don't keep him too long."

"How bad is he doctor?"

"He has a nasty bullet wound in the chest. It obviously did not hit his heart or he wouldn't be with us now. But it must be right next door."

"We're going to probe for it tonight."

"Will he...survive?" asked Jack.

The doctor looked at Jack for a long moment before he answered.

"You look like a man who doesn't want to hear fairy tales."

"Give me the truth, doc. I want to know if this is the last time I will ever speak to my friend."

"To be absolutely frank with you, Lieutenant, it looks very bad for him. The bullet is lodged near the heart. Very few men survive such a wound."

"But we'll do our best for him. The rest is up to the Lieutenant and to Providence."

Jack entered the tent and, once again, walked slowly between the rows of cots looking for the Lieutenant.

He found him one third of the way down from the entrance.

The Lieutenant's eyes were closed as Jack approached the side of the bed. For some moments Jack simply stood there looking down at his friend. Lieutenant Richards was very pale. At the same time his forehead looked damp. He was covered to his neck with a heavy blanket. His breathing was so light Jack could barely hear it.

The Lieutenant must have become aware that someone was there. His eyelids fluttered. Finally his eyes opened. He looked at Jack.

"Hi Jack," said the Lieutenant. His voice was so small Jack had to bend lower in order to hear it.

"Hi Sir."

"It's not 'Sir' anymore Jack. You are a Lieutenant, too, now. I'm no longer your commanding officer. Didn't Colonel Williams tell you?" This small speech had exhausted him and Jack spoke quickly to end further exertion.

"He did a..., ah, he did, and he told me it was on your recommendation."

The Lieutenant smiled faintly.

"It feels funny. I mean, I don't know what to call you. If I don't call you 'Sir' or Lieutenant what...?"

"Call me by my name."

"Your name?"

"Yes, my first name, John."

"Your name is John, Jack, the same as mine?"

"John, yes. Didn't you know that?"

"I guess I didn't, no."

"Jack there is something I want you to have. Can you get it for me? Sandy brought it over. It's under the cot."

Jack reached under the cot and brought up an officer's sword in its scabbard.

"But you can't...you're still an officer..you'll get well...I can't..."

"I want you to have it Jack. Whatever happens to me. Even if all goes well I won't be back in uniform for many months.

"I just want you to have it. I feel like a brother to you, Jack."

"Sir...I..."

"John," corrected the Lieutenant. "Remember we're brother officers now. It's John."

"Yes, John. I can't…"

"Don't refuse me Jack. It's yours."

Jack could see that to protest further would only place greater strain on his friend.

"Thanks John. I'll treasure this and our friendship all the rest of my life."

Tears welled up in Jack's eyes as he said this.

The Lieutenant's hand found Jack's wrist and close weakly around it. The hand was cold and clammy.

Jack tried to speak but could not.

"It'll be all right, Jack. I'm a fighter. I'm tough. You know me. I'll be all right."

Jack nodded. Finally, he found his voice. "The doc warned me not to stay too long. I'd better get out before they throw me out."

The Lieutenant smiled faintly again, then released Jack's wrist.

Jack stepped back from the cot and threw his friend a salute.

"Get some rest now."

The Lieutenant nodded almost without moving his head.

"I'll see you tomorrow, John," said Jack. Then he quickly turned and left. He was openly weeping now, and he did not want his friend to see.

CHAPTER SIXTY-SEVEN

WHEN JACK arrived the next morning for the Battalion staff meeting, he found that the Colonel had not yet returned from the conference with the General and his staff officers.

Jack was soon put at ease by the other officers. Each one made a point of coming over to congratulate him on his promotion and to offer a few words of encouragement for the recovery of Lieutenant Richards.

He had stopped at the hospital tents on his way to the meeting. The Lieutenant had survived the operation but was unconscious and in very low condition. The doctor held out little hope that he would live. Jack was not permitted to see him.

Finally Colonel Williams arrived. He was clearly in a state of suppressed anger. Normally he was so even tempered. Jack had never seen him like this. The entire staff snapped to attention when he entered.

"At ease gentlemen," said the Colonel as he removed his gloves and threw them down on the table.

"The conference this morning will be brief. The reason is simple. The orders for today are to proceed as we have done for the last two days.

"Yesterday, as many if not all of you know, I asked for and was refused permission to charge the enemy."

"I did not make that request today. Therefore, I suppose you could say that we have made some progress. We have not been refused permission to charge the enemy today."

The men burst into laughter at the Colonel's attempt to wry humour. The tension in the room evaporated. When he spoke again, however, the men fell silent. All attention was focussed on the Colonel.

"I have some news on the General's planned foray." He flicked his eyes from Major Smith to Jack, then to several other officers in the room. "It will not be as extensive as first announced. He will make the reconnaissance but does not plan to move very much beyond our right flanking position. He will probe north and west from that position."

Jack was now watching the face of Major Smith. The Major must have felt Jack watching for he turned his head right and looked back at Jack. He slowly moved his head from side to side. Then he turned back to the Colonel.

"I know the men have reached the limit of their endurance with this little game of hide and seek. I know you must wonder if the General staff really have the measure of the mettle of the troop under their command."

"But there you have it. There is little that can be done."

"I should like to add one small piece of advice."

The tentful of officers was so quiet now Jack could hear his neighbour breathing.

"You shall all do your duty, of course. I would expect nothing less from you. In moments of battle, however, situations will sometimes arise that do not permit consultation with higher authority. In such emergency circumstances, the responsibility of an officer is to use his common sense and to do his duty as God has given him the light to see that duty.

"Never doing anything, of course, against which an order has specifically been made. Ha...hem," he coughed somewhat, holding his closed hand up against his mouth.

There was a murmur amongst the men. Jack wondered if they knew what the Colonel was saying. Indeed, he wondered if he knew.

But he did not have to wonder for very long. The Colonel issued a few more specific directions then dismissed the officers. He asked Jack, Major Smith and several others to remain. Jack noticed that all of the officers remaining had been present at the meeting the night before.

"I don't need to tell you gentlemen how dismayed I was by the news this morning," said the Colonel.

"I met briefly and privately with Captain Hague and Colonels Van Straubenzie and Grasett after the conference."

"A grim lot we were, I can tell you."

"We all know the men are fed to the teeth with this infernal waiting...this... this..." He groped for an adequate word to express his disgust without defamatory insubordination.

"Delay? Procrastination?" suggested Major Smith.

"Yes, procrastination," agreed the Colonel. "They're demoralized, but at the same time aching for action. They're ready for the offensive."

"Colonel Van Straubenzie had made it clear, however, that he cannot do anything in the circumstances. The General will at no time be incommunicado. Consequently, any act of the kind discussed would be mutinous."

"Is there nothing that can be..." began Major Smith.

"There is one possibility," broke in the Colonel, "and that depends upon events."

"Colonel Van Straubenzie has indicated that it may well be dereliction of duty for an officer not to exploit an opportunity, if such an opportunity presents itself."

"And if the facts on the ground are changed, so to speak," said Major Smith, "what then?"

"Nothing was said directly, but Captain Hague has assured me that if an officer of ingenuity sensing a target of opportunity has committed troops, there can be no doubt whatever that Colonels Van Straubenzie and Grasett would lend immediate support."

"They would be confronted with a fait accompli, as it were, and there would be little time for staff meetings, there would be time only for action."

"I see…" said Major Smith.

"I think we have said enough," said the Colonel.

Jack saw another side of the Colonel. For the first time, he was ill at ease. "You gentlemen know your duty."

"Good luck to you."

The remaining officers drifted off. One or two had a final word with the Colonel. Jack was the last to leave. The Colonel grasped his hand. Then he put his arm around Jack's shoulders and spoke to him as he walked him to the door of the tent.

"This is your first time in command under fire. You have an excellent Troop, one of the best. You'll do just fine. You're the most resourceful officer on my staff.

"Good hunting."

As Jack left the Colonel he had the strange feeling that he had just been given a special assignment.

Things are different in the officers' world, thought Jack. He wondered if he would ever get used to it.

CHAPTER SIXTY-EIGHT

TUESDAY MORNING passed much the same as Monday. The troops in the line of skirmish exchanged desultory fire with the almost invisible enemy. The nine pounder guns fired occasionally.

It was one o'clock. The sun was brilliant and hot overhead.

The 90th Battalion had retired and was being retained as reserve. Grasett's Grenadiers held the right flank. Along the left flank stretching all the way from the river bank to the centre was the Midland Battalion.

Baker Troop occupied rifle pits about three hundred yards from the river. On either side other units of the Midland could be seen, the sun reflected on their bright red tunics.

To the immediate left of the rifle pit occupied by Jack and Tom lay the rifle pit shared by Sandy and Tubby.

These two men, watchful and hot, lay there expectantly. Expecting what, they did not know. Perhaps it was only their impatience they felt. Impatience with grinding out yet another futile day in the trenches.

But in these feelings they were not alone. For all along the line the men felt as they did.

Jack carefully checked his revolver to ensure every chamber was charged. He loosened the strap of his pith helmet. Then he removed the helmet altogether and ran his fingers through his hair. He ran the back of his hand across his brow, replaced the helmet again with his left hand, and adjusted it until it felt just right.

It was not pleasant in the rifle pit. Not only was the afternoon hot, but the least movement raised small clouds of choking, gritty dust. He felt filthy. Dirt found its way into everything.

Jack looked across toward the enemy lines and beyond. The fawn coloured rolling fields yielded to dun coloured depressions. There really was little brush or tree cover. He looked back at Tom. He was glad to have Tom with whom to share the trench. Alone, Jack knew, his mind would dwell on Kurt or Lieutenant Richards or the doubt that hung like a cloud over his own future. It was much better to have Tom there and listen to his reminiscences about home. A place so far away and so long ago it seemed sometimes to be unreal. But Tom made it real again. For a long time they talked of Sarah and of her father, Mr. Tuttle. Tom wanted to know whether she had been writing to Jack. Jack told Tom that a number of letters were waiting for him when he first returned to the unit. Then Tom wanted to know if Jack had written to Sarah about his experiences on the plains.

"Some," said Jack, smiling back. "The rest will have to wait 'till we get back. If we ever do, the way things are going here."

"Do you remember when we used to play pirates, on the lake?" asked Tom, abruptly changing the subject. "The wars we used to stage. I never thought you and I would be part of a real war."

"Do you remember the rafts we made?"

"I sure do. Especially the huge one with logs beneath and the little shack for a superstructure."

They both smiled in silence at the memory.

"You were skipper," said Tom. "I will always remember the way you looked on the raft."

Suddenly he sat bolt upright to strike a noble pose.

"This is you..."

Crack. A rifle shot interrupted his sentence.

"Down damn it," said Jack.

Quickly Tom was down again.

"Watch it Tom, for God's sake," said Jack, looking over the lip of the trench. "That's how Kurt got it."

There was no reply from Tom.

Jack glanced over. He saw no movement.

He looked a second time. This time fear seized his whole body.

"Tom," he said.

Still no response.

"This is no time to kid around, Tom."

Tom was only five or six feet away. When he still lay there Jack slowly made his way over. He was careful to keep his head down.

All at once he knew Tom was not kidding. The fear seemed to rise in his gorge and choke him. He had trouble breathing.

He pulled at Tom's shoulder. Tom rolled over to his back.

"Tom," said Jack in a frantic voice. "Tom!"

Tom's eyelids opened and his gaze settled on Jack.

Jack's eyes brimmed over with tears. He shook his head from side to side as his lips silently said "No" "No" "No".

"I should have kept down. I should have known better." Tom spoke in a very feeble voice. His voice grew even fainter. Jack leaned forward to hear what he was saying.

"I guess I won't be going home again," said Tom. He tried to smile but found he could not.

"Yes, yes, you will, you will," assured Jack. Then Jack raised his head. He shouted.

"Stretcher bearer."

He looked at Tom. A large red stain spread rapidly on his khaki tunic.

"It's too late, Jack."

Jack, still shaking his head, took Tom in his arms. Then he screamed again.

"Stretcher bearer!"

"...Don't waste...look at me." said Tom. Jack looked at his friend.

"I love Cobourg," said Tom. "I know I'm not going back."

He paused for a time, then he spoke very quietly. "It's lonely out here."

Now he looked beseechingly at Jack.

"Stay with me," he said. Then his body relaxed. His life had gone.

Slowly and gently Jack laid out his friend. As he did so his own body was gradually suffused with intense emotion. He became possessed with anger. All of his pent up frustration mingled with his outrage over this one senseless, useless killing. Something exploded within him.

He began a wailing lament.

Then, from the depths of his being started a primeval cry. It rose through his powerful lungs to his throat. The muscles on his neck stood out in thick chords. Then a hoarse roar erupted from his lips and rolled out across the battlefield toward the enemy.

Suddenly his revolver was in his hands.

"Youuuuuuu Baaastaaards!"

Then again "BAAAASTAAAARDS!"

He vaulted from his pit and began to charge the enemy lines. His rage was so intense he was oblivious of enemy bullets whizzing and zipping by him. He charged on, screaming.

The scream from Jack hit Baker Troop like an electric charge. It was the final call to battle. The command they had been awaiting for three days. The order to attack.

To a man they rose with their rifles and charged after their young Lieutenant, all of them screaming for vengeance.

The charge of Baker Troop ignited the entire Midland Battalion. All along the left flank the red tunics could be seen advancing on the double in a ragged line toward enemy trenches.

Jack was now aware that the whole of the Midland Battalion was charging forward. In front of him, not seventy yards away, a head popped up. He saw a rebel taking careful aim. Before he could get off a shot Jack brought up his revolver and let off two rounds. He felt the kick of the gun in his hand. The face of the rebel turned red and then disappeared beneath the rim of the rifle pit. Jack could still see the glint of sunlight from the metal gun barrel dropped by the rebel.

A cheer and shouting came to him from the distant right. He glanced over. The entire right flank was on the move. The Grenadiers were charging too.

Jack was dimly aware of the big guns shelling the enemy. The ground seemed to tremble with each blast. He heard the whistle and scream of shells overhead, then the deep crash as the fuse set off the explosion. Bullets whined and whistled in every direction. There were shouts and screams and curses. Then, more far distance cheering.

All along the mile and a quarter front the troops were on the move. Even the 90th had now joined the charge, and far off on the right flank of the charging line the General set upon his horse. He did not appear to understand what was taking place. He cried out: "Why in the name of God don't you cease firing?"

But the men charged on, Colonels Van Straubenzie and Grasett leading the cheers as they moved forward.

Soon the General's cry had subsided to a muttered oath.

Jack mounted the mound of earth before the first line of rifle pits. Suddenly he stood looking down into a pit holding three men. One swivelled, about to fire on

Jack, but a simple shot in the breast dropped him to the floor of the trench. The other two scrambled over the back of the pit and began to run. Jack remained standing on the small parapet, in full view of all. He took careful aim and dropped one runner in flight. The other vanished. He had reached the second string of trenches.

For the first time Jack realized how exposed he was. He jumped down into the safety of the trench. He heard the tumult of the battle raging over his head, the shouts, the ping of bullets. Then, for the first time he became aware of another sound: the scream of wounded men, the pitiful agonized cries for "stretcher bearer".

Jack looked down at the twisted lifeless shape of the man who had tried to kill him only a few moments ago. Then he saw a red tunic flash past above him. He heard the faint call for a stretcher. Then another call, this time much closer.

"Men of the Midland," cried a voice, "fix your bayonets." It sounded like Colonel Williams. It was quite near.

Then a far off voice echoed the order. "Fix...bayonets." It was Major Smith.

Both orders were given on the run. Jack heard the erratic click of metal as the men in the charging battalion struggled to comply with the order.

Another volunteer flashed by above. Jack leaped out of the trench to follow.

A light haze now drifted over the field. It filtered the afternoon sun.

Twenty-five yards ahead and to his left an officer of the battalion stumbled and fell. His sword catapulted three times and came to rest on a mound of earth protecting a rifle pit. Jack saw a rebel poke forward from his cover and seize the sword.

The officer was on his knees now and fumbling desperately for his revolver.

The enemy planted his two feet on the ridge of earth in front of the pit and raised the sword high over his head with both his arms.

Jack stopped jogging forward, took careful aim and let off a single shot just before the sword descended. The bullet caught the rebel high in the chest and threw him back and out of sight. He must have been thrown back into his rifle pit, thought Jack.

The officer finally released his revolver. He looked back as he drew it.

It was Colonel Williams. He waved and smiled.

"Attaboy Jack. Bit of a close one there," he called. Then he resumed his attack.

Jack pressed on too.

Sandy and two others from Baker had their hands full dead ahead. It looked like hand to hand combat. Jack raced forward. A confused struggle was in progress all over a large rifle pit.

Sandy had run through the thorax of a rebel with his bayonet. Miraculously, the man was not dead but had mounted a furious defence against his assailant. He had a firm two fisted grip on the bayonet and would not release it.

"Fire, Sandy, fire!" shouted Jack. Sandy did so, simultaneously yanking on his gun. The body easily jolted off the end of the bayonet.

Then Jack noticed Tubby on his back fighting fiercely to keep a knife from plunging into his throat. Jack fired. The knife fell from the offending hand, narrowly missing Tubby's ear.

"Jack," shouted Tubby. "Thanks Jack."

Jack had no time for reply. Crutch and a rebel were locked in combat over a Snider rifle. Both had a firm grip on it. They teetered on the edge of the pit.

Before Jack could act Tubby had seized the knife and with a blood curdling scream plunged it into the back of the enemy.

Another rebel leaped from the pit and began to run.

"I got him, Jack," shouted Sandy. He took aim with his rifle and dropped the fleeing man before he could again find cover.

Acrid smoke filled the air. Hand to hand combat raged everywhere. Shouts and screams rent the air.

Through all this melee a rebel walked unmolested into the face of the charging militia. He moaned and cried alternatively. He was clutching his abdomen with his large hands. Then Jack saw that he was holding back his own entrails. Abruptly, the man fell to his knees. He looked as though he were about to pray. Then a dark hole opened in his forehead and a rivulet of red ran down between his nose and his left eye. Then he collapsed forward.

Jack had no time for revulsion. He charged forward into the confusion. Black tunics mingled with red. Men of the 90th joined the Midland Battalion. Muskets and rifles pounded forth fire and smoke, knives flashed and slashed. Men shouted and cursed and called for help. The fallen lay about in ridiculous posture. Many were wounded, more were dead. One rebel, out of ammunition, swung his shotgun back and forth at an officer with a sword, preventing his advance. Another rebel rolled over the earth locked in hand to hand wrestling with a disarmed Midlander. Several times Jack tried to take aim with his revolver. Each time his comrade came up into his sights. Jack finally holstered his revolver and unsheathed his sword. He took five steps forward. Just as he did so a knife flashed in the rebel's hand. He was about to plunge it down into a helpless soldier. Jack brought his sword down with a vicious slash at the wrist of the rebel. The rebel looked in horror at the stump where only a moment before his hand had been. He tumbled forward covering his victim.

Jack waded onward into the fighting mob. He sliced again and again. Now he had the revolver in his left hand and sword in right. He hacked his way as though moving through a jungle. He saw men with skin hanging in ribbons, men with bloodied arms and faces and some men missing arms altogether. Time and again he saw soldiers stamp their feet down hard on the chest of a dead rebel in an effort to remove a bayonet.

The tumult of battle seemed to have reached a peak. Then suddenly, the din subsided. There was no more struggling.

"They're running," shouted a voice.

Jack looked ahead through the smoke of battle. Sure enough the enemy had taken flight.

A cheer went up, then another. Then rolling cheers ran all along the front and rippled back again.

Some men took after the fleeing enemy. Others dropped to one knee to take pot shots at their tormentors of the last four days.

Still others turned their attention to the wounded and dying.

The Battle of Batoche had ended.

PART SIX

TRIAL

CHAPTER SIXTY-NINE

MORE THAN six weeks had passed since the charge at Batoche, but it proved to be the decisive battle of the campaign. Resistance had been broken. Other battles were fought and extensive mopping up operations continued, but the rebellion had already been crushed. Though Gabriel Dumont escaped to the United States, in the following days Louis Riel was captured and imprisoned in Regina.

Regina was a modest little town far to the south of the seat of the uprisings. It boasted a dusty main street of one storey commercial buildings fronted with hitching posts and boardwalks. Small dwellings surrounded the centre of town. They were arranged in boring but regular rectangles. Nearby the town was a small water course more resembling a slough than a creek. In late summer it became covered over with a forbidding brownish green sheet of algae. This small body of water, stagnant for a good part of the year, exuded a most offensive odour. Occasionally the wind carried this smell across town. It caused weaker men to wretch and the fair sex to become faint.

A detachment of North West Mounted Police was stationed there. The town also boasted a livery stable, blacksmith shop, dentist, doctor, three churches, an undertaker, a chemist and a Court House. This unprepossessing little town had started life with the unpromising name, Pile O'Bones. The source of this indignity was the rodent ridden mound of buffalo bones bleaching under the summer sun down by the creek, the site of ancient Indian slaughter-pounds. The uncommon name had only been changed three years before, with the arrival of the railroad.

Regina also had a jail, located in the police barracks. It was in this jail that Louis Riel and Lieutenant Jack Holden were imprisoned. Mr. Riel was charged with high treason; Mr. Holden with desertion under fire. At the time, apart from the occasional drunk held overnight, they were the only two prisoners.

Jack occupied a corner cell. It was a small room only nine feet deep and seven feet wide. There was small barred window at the back. It was about five feet from the floor. Jack found he could rest his chin on the sill while he gazed out. The front of the cell also had bars, otherwise it was open to a hallway running off to the left.

The cell was furnished with a crude iron cot over which had been thrown a tattered mattress. The mattress had a musty smell. It bore large stains where unknown fluids had dried years ago. Under the cot was a chipped enamel pot. A small wooden stand stood by the bed. A basin rested on the top of the stand, a pitcher beneath on a shelf.

In the hallway, which ran the length of the building, stood a table. Often a constable sat at the table reading or playing solitaire.

The only other regular prisoner, the revolutionary and Jack's former enemy, occupied a cell at the opposite end of the hallway. Jack had as yet not seen Mr. Riel who was absent a good deal of the time, occupied making preparations for his trial. He consulted long hours with his counsel. Sometimes these consultations continued right up to the cell door and Jack could hear excited last minute instructions in French just before the cell door clanged shut.

Jack found himself with many idle hours on his hands. Apart from two half-hour regular exercise periods, one in the morning and one in the afternoon, his time was spent in the cell. He was allowed visitors, he wrote letters and he began to develop a friendship with the guard constable in the hallway.

He had plenty of time to remember and reminisce. In his mind's eye he could still see the glint of sun on steel, the flashing swipe of sword. He could hear even now the torrent of gunfire, the rumble of cannon, the cries of terror and the cheers of troops in victory. And the astringent smell of cordite in the air lingered even now in his nostrils.

The exultation of victory in battle had surged through his body. He had felt that it, too, would linger. But that was not to be.

The militia had quickly overrun the entire settlement. Enemy who had not taken flight attempted to surrender. Many of them were mercilessly bayoneted. Jack had reacted with revulsion and pleaded with his brother officers to have this stopped. Though many ignored his plea, many more acceded to his wishes for Jack had become the man of the hour, sharing glory with the Midland Battalion which led the charge on the rebels.

He was cheered everywhere. His advice was solicited. He was patted on the back by all who passed him by. His hand felt as though it had been shaken a thousand times, and perhaps it was.

He was, in all, the most admired officer in the entire North West Field Force.

Colonel Williams, Jack and a few other officers and men had discovered a dungeon in the main house at Batoche. One of the men had heard a pounding from beneath floor boards in the main salon. A trap door was discovered and released. When it was thrown back six people emerged. Some had been captive for months. They were pale and looked quite sickly. One had a shock of red hair. He did not appear to have been a prisoner of the rebels for very long. He was swarthy and looked quite vigorous. He also looked vaguely familiar to Jack. For a moment Jack thought he saw a look of recognition flash across this person's face. Then Jack dismissed the idea.

There was great merriment among the newly freed prisoners, and immense gratitude. Some had believed they would never survive with their lives. There was a lot of embracing as these men expressed their thanks.

Only two men remained aloof. One of these was the red head.

Colonel Williams then took a party to make a thorough search of the remaining buildings in Batoche. No other prisoners were found. Indeed, no other rebels were found.

It was late in the afternoon when the men heard the screech of the whistle on the Northcote.

All activity came to a standstill as many of the men drifted down to the river landing. There they watched the steamer as it hove into view. It was an impressive sight. It had appeared from the right, chugged along to a landing in the lee of the current just before the river bent. There was more whistle blowing from the steamer and a great deal more self congratulatory cheering from those aboard as well as those ashore.

The excitement was still running high and the men continued to exchange amusing and hair raising stories of their adventures. The Northcote had passed the approaches of Batoche under heavy enemy crossfire from both sides of the river. So intense was the shooting that the "Northcote Marines," as they dubbed themselves, were

200

convinced that the main body of enemy troops had been deployed along the river above and below the town. After running several miles down river, beyond enemy fire, they set anchor against the current and a debate ensued. Lieutenant MacDonald asked Captain Sheets to steam upriver to engage the enemy once more. The Captain categorically refused. When the Lieutenant pressed, the Captain became adamant, hinting that he had instructions from the "highest circles" not to expose his vessel again. There was a lot of good natured debate about this, the men not quite knowing what to believe. Finally the topic was dropped as men turned to fresh stories.

There were many casualties. Colonel Williams asked Jack to supervise his Troop in aiding the medical corps to load the wounded aboard the Northcote for evacuation south. The few former prisoners of the enemy who wished to embark with them would also be assisted aboard after the wounded were first looked after.

In addition many other militia units toiled at the landing. Some were off-loading ammunition and other supplies; others worked to prepare the vessel for a dangerous trip south. The landing was scattered about with boxes and sacks of supplies as the Northcote was readied for departure.

It was dusk. The sun had slipped down behind the starboard side of the Northcote. Someone had already begun to light lamps in the cabins along the port side.

This was the scene, then, when the exaltation of the day turned to ashes in the evening.

General Middleton had approached the landing with a small party. They were all mounted. They drew their ponies to a halt right in front of Jack and his Troop.

"There he is," said the General.

Jack was embarrassed. The General was pointing at him. Out of the corner of his eye he could see "Red" and the other prisoners. They were ready to board and they were watching.

Then the General spoke again.

"Arrest him," he said simply.

"What is this?" somebody in the crowd said in a deep, loud, stage whisper.

"You heard me," the General snarled to an aid. He impatiently motioned a Lieutenant in his party forward.

"Sir," said Sandy. "Why do you have to arrest our Lieutenant?"

"Yes, yes."

"Why?"

"What's this all for?"

All this from the men standing nearby. There was a general murmur of approval at this polite opposition.

The General's Lieutenant hesitated.

Then Sandy spoke again. He was very respectful, but he spoke with deep conviction.

"This is the man who led the charge, General. Were it not for him we'd still be eating bullets and dust in them trenches."

There was loud and uneasy chatter from the men. Their mood had turned surly.

"He's our man," shouted someone from behind.

"Canada Jack carried the whole battalion," shouted another.

"Well," disagreed a third, "the whole damn militia."

A cheer went up. Many laughed, but tension filled the air.

At this point Jack saw the crowd threaten to become a mob. He quickly spoke up.

"It's all right. I'm sure the General has his reasons. Like a good officer I do my duty."

"As you should--and get back to work."

That seemed to quell the mood of the throng. Jack quickly made his way over to the General's party and surrendered himself.

Jack was taken into custody that night. No one had any information as to why the General had changed his mind, why Jack's parole was not continued to the end of the campaign of the prairie. Most of the men in Baker Troop felt it was simply envy or resentment of Jack for leading the charge.

Colonel Williams had found a more ominous and perhaps more dangerous reason.

He had learned that the intention of the General was to move Jack south to Regina, that the march would begin early the following day.

He visited Jack that night.

Jack had been locked in a room of Batoche house, the largest building in the settlement. A lamp burned at the table. A guard had been placed at the door. The Colonel had some difficulty gaining admittance. Jack knew this because he could hear Colonel Williams taking great pains to persuade the guard.

The Colonel and Jack had visited for about half an hour when discussion turned briefly to the reasons for the arrest and then to Jack's future.

"What happened, Sir? Why did he revoke my parole before the end of the campaign?" Jack was bewildered. The Colonel felt compassion for his brave young officer.

"We'll never know for sure, I suppose, but I think I know the reason."

"Did you ask him, Sir?"

"Yes, I did Jack, but he almost refused to see me. Then, when he did, he pretended to have no reason. He was visibly angry with me. He did not look at me and scarcely spoke when I asked him questions."

"What do you think's wrong, Sir?" asked Jack with a sinking feeling in his stomach.

"What I think is wrong has less to do with the charge against the enemy than with that which he believes preceded it."

"I don't understand, Sir."

"I think he got wind of your little trip last night. Major Smith is convinced that he knows Captain Hague, Colonel Grasett, Colonel Van Straubenzie and I have been meeting and that we met again last night. He must have heard of your gallop to the river, put two and two together and…"

Jack looked at the floor and shook his head in silence.

"He has no proof of course. And even if he did have some he would avoid confrontation with me. Because that would involve Colonels Grasett and Van Straubenzie. He would not want to find himself set against the three Colonels who commanded the soldiers at Batoche."

"Especially Colonel Van Straubenzie. He has too many years of exemplary service and is too well connected."

"No, he would not want to involve Van Straubenzie."

"That leaves you. He thinks you are vulnerable. He's taking his revenge on you."

"My God!" was the only thing that Jack could find to say.

Then the Colonel said words that had buoyed Jack's spirits during all the weeks of captivity that followed.

"You have been like a son to me, Jack. I think I've told you that before, but I mean it, every word."

202

"I will never let you down.

"Count on it. I will be present at your trial to give character evidence and any other kind of evidence that may be required to win back your deserved honour and freedom.

"As long as I draw breath, you can count on me!"

The room in which Jack had been confined had one small window facing west. When the Colonel left Jack spent a long time at the window watching the crew making last minute preparations for the departure of the Northcote.

Finally Jack retired to a troubled sleep. He awakened with a start at five in the morning. Suddenly he knew why the red haired rebel prisoner looked familiar.

He was Mr. Benson's messenger to "bluecoat".

Jack raced to the window. The Northcote was gone. Gone too, was Jack's ticket to exoneration and freedom!

CHAPTER SEVENTY

JACK DID not leave for Regina that next day. No explanation was given, but the departure was delayed for twenty-four hours. He learned at breakfast that the internment of Tom, Captain Brown and others was to take place that day. Divine Providence had granted this last opportunity to say farewell to his friend.

With a little intervention from Colonel Williams, Jack received three hours parole in order to attend the service.

Hundreds of men stood about the zareba. They talked in hushed tones, a respectful distance from the dead. Jack stood alone amidst the men.

Then, without spoken orders, the soldiers began to fall in, unit by unit. A subdued command and the parade dressed itself.

Suddenly, muffled drums began to beat and the units started a slow march toward the river. Jack followed the shifting swaying ranks of red tunics ahead of him. Then a band began to play a slow mournful dirge.

They came to a halt beneath a high bluff on a small plateau with a commanding view of the mighty river. The last resonant strains of music seemed to seep into the prairie turf and drift off across the glassy surface of the water.

Jack felt the first faint stirring of a breeze. The leaves of a nearby willow rustled. The white shrouds of the dead fluttered softly.

As the regimental chaplain began to pray, the bodies of brave soldiers were committed to the grave.

And there, under the shimmering sun, a grief stricken Jack said goodbye to his closest friend.

His burial place was not far from the battlefield. But Jack new when the armies had departed, their business finished, it would be desolate. How deeply Jack had grieved for Tom.

Thereafter events moved swiftly. With mixed emotions Jack learned that Baker Troop had been abruptly detached from the Midland Battalion, deactivated from battle service and detailed for garrison duty in Regina. For this too, there was no explanation, but the rumours were rife.

The detached Troop, along with a guard detail for Jack and sundry others, marched to Regina. The trip took a number of days but ended without incident.

Jack had been taken into custody by people who knew nothing of his service and seemed to care even less. He had been shunted into his present cell without ceremony and since then left pretty much to his own devices.

CHAPTER SEVENTY-ONE

JACK KNEW he faced the gravest crisis of his life. While he spent considerable time remembering the sometimes painful recent past, not for a moment did he lose sight of his predicament. For all his dreaming he was an active person too. He set to work immediately preparing for his defence.

In this he was greatly aided by Sandy and others from Baker Troop. In general they lent moral support. Sandy let him know that every single man had offered to testify on his behalf. But as the two examined the potential of this evidence it seemed to become less tangible with every passing day.

That is how it came to pass, after ten days of discussion, that Sandy told him it was high time to retain a lawyer. A barrister would, no doubt, need time to prepare. Already precious time had been lost.

Did Jack know the local lawyers? Of course he did not. Did he know any lawyers from whom he could obtain advice? He did. Only one.

"Hiran Tuttle."

"Who's he? Where is he?" asked Sandy.

"He's a lawyer from home," Jack answered bleakly. "He's from Cobourg. How can he possibly be of any help?"

"That's for him to decide. Let him know you're in trouble. Let him tell you what to do.

"Write him today."

"Even better, do both."

Jack did both that very day. He sent a long letter to Hiran Tuttle, Esq., Barrister and Solicitor, Cobourg, Canada. He had Sandy send a telegram to let him know a letter followed. Jack also wrote a long letter to his parents and younger brother. It was the most difficult chore he had ever had to do, but he told them fully about the serious trouble in which he now found himself.

When his hopes had been so high, how, he wondered, had things gone so wrong so quickly?

In near despair he waited to hear from home.

CHAPTER SEVENTY-TWO

JACK KNEW that the trial of Mr. Riel was scheduled to begin soon, despite pleas from the defendant for more time to prepare. He also knew his own trial was scheduled to follow immediately.

From the beginning Jack was given to understand that he would have a choice as to court martial or civilian criminal trial. He had chosen to have his trial in regular criminal courts because of an offhand remark of Colonel Williams that he would be "better off in the hands of civilian" and "you don't know who will sit on a Court Martial Board. General Middleton will have a say as to its constitution."

Without hesitation Jack had chosen to be tried by civilians. He now began to distrust his decision. He had not received further word from Colonel Williams. He did not know the whereabouts of the Midland Battalion. He had no means of writing to discuss his concern.

As doubts began to assail him and he did not hear from home he began to wonder if Mr. Tuttle had chosen not to become involved. All Jack had asked for was a little advice as to how to begin to proceed. Had his repute fallen so low that even such a humble enquiry would not be answered.

Jack and Sandy were on the verge of speaking to a local barrister when they received a telegram. It stated simply and succinctly:

"Received your enquiry STOP letter follows STOP good news STOP DO NOT DESPAIR STOP.

Sgd. J. Hiram Tuttle."

The following day Jack received the letter. He looked at the postal cancellation stamp. The letter had been posted twelve days before. It had been delayed en route.

The letter read:

"Dear Jack,

I will be brief. The reason for this should be apparent to you when you finish reading this missive.

My first advice to you is to make no admission or confession. If it should become evident that a statement from you would have a beneficial effect upon your case your solicitor will advise you accordingly. For the present, therefore, my advice to you is to preserve your confidences for your counsel.

I have canvassed the possibility of retaining for you a local barrister. Without exception they received their training here in Canada. (That is, unless one has gained admittance purely through local articles. In which case I would have no knowledge.) Regrettably, and also without exception I would have grave reservations about recommending any for your defence. The reasons are too lengthy for me to go into at this time.

I have concluded, therefore, that the only course open is for me to represent you personally. My law partner has generously consented to my absence for this purpose.

You need have no worry about fee. Contrary to what you might believe (along with 99% of the population) money is not the supreme motivating factor in a lawyer's life. Should you ever be able to pay me, fine. If not, that is fine too.

I have made arrangements to leave by train tonight. Time is of the essence.

I must close now, if I am to have sufficient opportunity to prepare for this long journey.

Before I do close, however, I wish to convey some good news.

Your reputation in Cobourg (indeed for miles around Cobourg) has been more than re-established. I will give you full particulars upon arrival. Suffice it to say that everyone here now believes that you did, in fact, witness a murder. The body has been found.

The feeling around town is that you have been not only exonerated, but greatly wronged. If you return this summer or fall I am satisfied you would be welcomed as a conquering hero.

I regret to tell you many here have heard about your present difficulties. Certain individuals have been very loquacious in letters from the front. I am sure I do not need to tell you who.

I am happy to say, however, that few believe you guilty. It is now up to you and me to vindicate their present faith.

I am confident we can do that without difficulty.

Yours affectionately,

J. Hiram Tuttle

Barrister and Solicitor.

Post Script:

I am bringing with me a surprise. I am sure you will be pleased. Be confident.

Yours,

Hiram T.

When Sandy came to visit that afternoon, Jack showed him the letter. His first comment was, "if that's brief, I wonder what long is like."

Next he said: "I wonder how they found the body?"

Finally he said: "I wonder what the surprise will be?"

They did not have long to wait for answers to these questions.

J. Hiram Tuttle, Esquire, Barrister and Solicitor, arrived the following morning.

CHAPTER SEVENTY-THREE

J. HIRAM Tuttle had been unable to notify his new client or his client's friend of an exact date or time of arrival. Neither the ticket agent back home nor conductors along the way would vouchsafe these facts to him; they did not know themselves. Therefore the lawyer, being of philosophic bent, placed himself in the hands of Providence and the railway, prayed every night to be delivered from Indian and outlaw and waited for his train to deposit him in the town of Regina, smack in the middle of nowhere.

When he stepped off the coach a hiss of steam greeted him. Then he turned to assist his travelling companion.

There was no carriage to meet the weary voyagers. Mr. Tuttle spoke briefly to the stationmaster. Then he picked up two heavy carpetbags and they began to walk. They did not have far to go to find what they were seeking. The train station was located in the middle of town, only a few doors from the Ritz Hotel.

Mr. Tuttle looked up at the weather beaten grey-boards of the hotel front. The sign had seen more prosperous days too. It read:

ITZ OTEL

Along the front ran a boardwalk. Two benches had been placed against the hotel. They were shaded by a porch roof that extended from the side of the building.

Two men sat together on the bench to the right of the entrance. One had ten day's growth of grey grizzled beard. He looked like he had not moved for days, but his eyes followed every move of the strangers in town.

The other person lounging on the bench was younger, perhaps twenty-two. Practising up, thought Mr. Tuttle. One day he hopes to be as accomplished a layabout as his companion.

"Anyone here like to make a quarter?" enquired Mr. Tuttle.

"Who wants to know?" asked the older of the two. Mr. Tuttle watched his lips. If he moved them it escaped his notice.

"Why, I do," answered Mr. Tuttle. With that the old fellow spit. A great brown strain hit the pole supporting the roof. It ran slowly down until the hot dry wood absorbed its lubricating moisture.

"What for?"

It was the younger man speaking now. He felt free to do so, having decided his companion was not interested.

"What fer do y'all have to do…for the quarter dollar I mean?"

"Take this note to a Private Sandy McCallum. He's at the militia barracks, I suspect.

"Fetch him or a reply and you can pick up your pay from the desk clerk inside." He nodded in the direction of the doors.

"Thanks Mister. I believe I will. Could use a good meal at Ma's Cafe."

He accepted the proffered note. He took a few steps, then he turned and spoke again.

"Hey Winkler! Do you think Charley'd mind if I used his cayuse. Have it back pronto."

"I'll let him know you'll be right back," answered the older man.

The young man slipped easily on the back of a horse standing at the hitching rail and made off at a slow walk.

The two travellers stepped into the hotel. The lobby was cool and dark. The floor was covered by a deep red carpet with ornate design. The walls were finished waist high in cherry brown mahogany wood. Above that was chintzy wall paper. Kerosene wall lamps had been placed strategically around the room. There were several wine coloured leather sofas in the centre, at either end of which stood an ashtray and a brass spittoon.

The counter was also a deep cherry brown mahogany. It had been ornately carved and panelled. Mr. Tuttle stepped over and rang a small desk bell for service.

A sallow faced old man with sparse white hair combed straight back, prominent aquiline nose and no chin stepped from behind a red velvet curtain and shuffled over to the counter.

"Yez?" he enquired. He looked at Mr. Tuttle and his companion through watery blue eyes. His voice was weak and he breathed heavily.

Mr. Tuttle quickly arranged for two adjoining rooms. The old man rounded the counter. He picked up the two bags. They barely cleared the floor before he dropped them.

"Let me do that," said Mr. Tuttle. The three disappeared up the stairway to the second floor.

Mr. Tuttle shut the door on the clerk. He turned to survey his room. The bedstead was brass. The bed looked deep and comfortable, though it sagged in the centre. He sat down. The bed creaked with his every movement. There was a small dresser, but no desk. He would have to speak to management about that. There was also a small cabinet on which stood a deep white porcelain basin. Next to it a cake of white soap rested in a saucer. These had been placed on an embroidered cloth which in turn covered the top of the cabinet. He opened the doors of the cabinet to find a pitcher. Under the bed he found a white enamel pot.

He could hear every movement in the adjoining room, especially the creaking of the bed. I had better not rest my body against the wall or I'll go right through, he said to himself. He gazed out the window. It was nearly opaque with dust, but he was able to see a few buildings outside. Beyond them he saw the flat prairie.

As a matter of fact everywhere he looked it seemed he could glimpse the horizon.

He washed quickly, removed his shoes and jacket and laid himself out for a brief rest.

The next thing he knew he was awakened by a rapping at the door. He opened it to find standing there a handsome young man with light brown hair.

"You must be Sandy McCallum," he said.

"How do you do, Mr. Tuttle?"

"That is I," said Mr. Tuttle. "Do come in."

The two men fell into earnest conversation. They found they liked one another and before the afternoon discussion ended they had become friends. Mr. Tuttle also learned almost everything that had happened to Jack since his arrest.

They only broke up their conference for supper in the hotel dining room. Mr. Tuttle invited Sandy to join him. It was only then that Sandy learned that Mr. Tuttle had company.

Sandy was formally introduced to Sarah Tuttle. She had come along to provide company for Mr. Tuttle on the long journey west. She had also come along to provide moral support for Jack at the trial.

Sandy knew Jack pretty well. He had become a close friend. Since the passing of Tom, Jack had confided extensively in Sandy, who now knew all about Jack's adventures after the kidnapping.

Sandy wondered what Jack would think when he learned of the presence of Sarah Tuttle.

It was not seemly for ladies to visit the jail. Sarah repaired to her room for early retirement. Sandy and Mr. Tuttle walked over to the police barracks.

Jack had difficulty controlling his emotions when he saw Mr. Tuttle. As much as he tried to display a maturity befitting a man of the world and an officer in the Canadian Army his gratitude kept spilling out. Mr. Tuttle told Jack how glad he was to see him and gave him numerous assurances that everything would be looked after, everything would come out fine.

Then Sandy, who could contain himself no longer, told Jack that Sarah had come west to be with him at the trial. Jack expressed delight. He told them that seeing her would give him one thing to look forward to at trial. As he spoke Sandy watched him and pondered whether he masked other unspoken feelings. Perhaps I'll never know, he thought.

The three men sat down to discuss the impending trial.

CHAPTER SEVENTY-FOUR

DURING THE following week all of Jack's daylight hours were occupied with trial preparations. Whenever Sandy was free from duty he lent assistance. When he was not required by Mr. Tuttle or Jack he tried to offer Sarah such diversion as Regina could provide. They took long rides into the countryside. He walked her around town and pointed out anything which he supposed might interest her in the slightest. He did this until one day when, in jest, she began to point out points of interest to him. He knew then he had exhausted his ability to entertain her further. It was just as well. Mr. Tuttle had almost concluded his discussions with Jack. Sandy began to spend more time with his friend to try to maintain his morale for the coming ordeal.

Late one afternoon Mr. Tuttle dropped by the jail to speak to Jack. He had just returned from studying the law books at the Court House Library.

He did not bother to have Jack taken to the conference room that they normally used. He merely had the duty guard admit him right into Jack's cell. His face bore a serious look. At first Jack thought he was merely tired, but as the conversation unfolded, Jack learned that it was not simple fatigue.

After half an hour of rather distracted conversation the lawyer set down the pen he had been holding, looked Jack in the eyes and abruptly dropped the subject matter under discussion.

"Jack I must tell you that I am greatly disturbed," he began.

"I thought there was something on your mind."

"I debated with myself as to whether I should tell you this…"

"I want to know…everything," said Jack. "The good, the bad…everything."

"I knew you would feel that way. Our whole relationship has been one of the fullest mutual confidence. Like you, I would have it no other way.

"As a matter of fact knowing my daughter's affection for you…and yours for her…ah…ahem…and your reputation having been fully restored back home… I…ah…have come to look upon you as more than a young friend in need of legal counsel…I…ah…well, I…ah…have come to look upon you as a son."

"As a matter of fact I had hoped that if matters were to proceed satisfactorily here…and if certain other events should take place…you might…you know I have no son…I thought you might one day like to enter articles with me. A life in the law is a demanding one, it is true. But it is also satisfying. Your future would be assured if…well, you know," he finished lamely.

"Sir, I don't know what to say. I'm flattered, honoured.."

"Of course I…"

"You need say nothing now, of course," he interrupted.

Jack looked at Mr. Tuttle's face. Could this be what's on his mind, he thought incredulously. Jack felt a mild sense of panic subside when he heard Mr. Tuttle's last words. My emotions are in complete disarray, he thought. Why did his words cause me to be so apprehensive. Or is it fear of the approaching trial.

Mr. Tuttle broke into Jack's thoughts.

"I'm afraid I digress. That was not the topic I came here to discuss tonight."

Jack was wondering as he watched Mr. Tuttle: what can my lawyer be thinking that he can raise such matters when I face trial on a capital charge in a matter of days. Does he hope to distract me, raise my morale?

"I paid a visit to the prosecutor this morning. Mr. Pynch. A fine man. Queen's Counsel."

When Jack looked at him with a question on his face, Mr. Tuttle hastened to explain.

"Well he's the Queen's Counsel too, of course. I mean the government prosecutor. But he's Queen's Counsel as well. 'Q.C.', as we lawyers say. Honorific, if you know what I mean."

Jack began to wish his lawyer would get on with his story.

"He showed me his file. Laid it right open before me, would you believe. I spent a good hour looking it over and discussing its fine points with him."

"He feels he has a pretty good case."

"Do you?"

"Beg your pardon?"

"I said, 'do you?'." repeated Jack. "Do you feel it's a good case. You're my lawyer. It's your opinion that counts with me. What is your opinion?"

The lawyer looked at Jack. He hesitated. Then Jack startled him.

"Put another way Mr. Tuttle, am I headed for a hanging?"

"No, no dear boy. It was not my intentions to suggest that."

Jack sagged back with relief. It did not last.

"I must say, however, that he does have a good case."

Jack felt he could have fainted. Mr. Tuttle continued to speak. Jack strained through the shock to understand his words.

"….a sworn statement by General Middleton. An affidavit. Of course, I gave him my agreement on that."

"On what?" asked Jack.

"The affidavit. As I just told you."

"An affidavit as to what? What did you agree to?"

"It is not an unusual procedure. It saves time at trial. Spares a fine officer like the General a court appearance."

Jack winced when he heard this.

Mr. Tuttle merely rattled on. He did not notice his client's reaction.

"But what is in the affidavit? To what have we agreed?" Jack asked once more.

"Your I.T.R."

"My what?"

"I.T.R."

"My Individual Training Record?"

"That's right."

"The one maintained by the Troop Commander, Mr. Richards?" Jack asked, hopefully.

"Oh no, my dear boy. That would carry little weight. The Regimental records. Maintained by the General's staff. They would be the only ones that count."

"Must we do that?" asked Jack.

"I have already done it. Don't worry so, young man. You have a lawyer here to provide advice." Be wise. Take the advice. You've heard the old adage: A man who defends himself has a fool for a client.

"I am experienced in these matters. Please believe me. Our little gesture will be appreciated by the General. That cannot but help. It will surely be appreciated by the trial Judge. It will save him hours on the bench. They always appreciate that."

"Mark my words, we will create a favourable impression all the way around. You'll see."

By now Jack's head was reeling. But there was more to come.

"There is one other matter which it is my duty to report."

"What?" Jack asked in a dull voice.

"The prosecutor has offered us a deal."

"A deal?"

"It's called plea bargaining, actually."

"Perhaps you'd better explain."

"Of course. As I've told you, Mr. Pynch is confident that he has an iron-clad case. He believes your reputation is such that no jury will believe you."

"My reputation?" Jack seemed no longer capable of reaction. His questions were asked in a dull monotone.

"Yes, your reputation." Mr. Tuttle seemed impatient and embarrassed all at once. "You know what I'm talking about, surely."

When Jack did not reply he plunged on.

"In a few words what I'm…he's referring to is the widespread opinion that you tend to exaggerate, to dream, make things up."

"Oh," said Jack.

And when Jack said no more he went on.

"Yes, well, he's offered to allow you to plead guilty with the iron-clad guarantee… he will put it in writing if you wish…to recommend mercy to the Judge. In fact he would request on behalf of the Crown, that the sentence of death not be imposed in this case."

"What would happen?" asked Jack.

"Well, ah, in that event, ah, the sentence would be life imprisonment in a penitentiary."

Jack's apprehension had been growing as he saw the direction in which the conversation was going. Now he exploded.

"You didn't agree did you? You didn't agree to send me to the penitentiary for life?" He stood, trembling, over his lawyer.

"No, no, no dear boy. Of course not. I wouldn't do that without discussing it with you in advance."

"Never, never, never. Never let me hear you talk like that again."

"I'm not guilty. Don't you understand. I'm not guilty. I will never plead guilty. I could never spend my life locked up."

Jack plopped down on his bed once again. The last outburst seemed to have drained him completely.

"Of course not, of course not," said Mr. Tuttle. He had been intimidated by the strong reaction from his client and spoke in a very small voice.

The two sat in silence for several minutes. Then Mr. Tuttle rose.

"I really must be off."

Jack looked up at Mr. Tuttle, then he, too, got up.

"I do hope we make some progress in establishing contact with Colonel Williams," said Mr. Tuttle. I can see that we are going to need his evidence badly."

"You haven't managed to…?"

"I'm doing my utmost. The Army is not exactly cooperative, you know." There was a tone of complaint in his words.

"I have written him" said Jack, "but as yet I have not had a reply."

"I'm not surprised, though. The Force is campaigning strongly in the north west. Sandy said that he had heard they've travelled up the North Saskatchewan River as far as Fort Battleford and have marched beyond."

"His evidence is essential. You might even say crucial, to our case. He's the one man of authority and prestige who has indicated a willingness to bolster your repute. From what I have managed to learn he's well liked throughout the Army.

"We need him badly, and we need him soon. The Riel Case began a number of days ago, as you know…"

"I didn't know," interjected Jack.

"I am told by Mr. Pynch that it is moving along swimmingly. That means we're up shortly."

"Find him, Mr. Tuttle. Please find Colonel Williams. He must be told the date of my trial. I know he'll be there!"

"As I told you son, I'll do my best."

Mr. Tuttle then left Jack to his thoughts.

That night and the following day Jack had many thoughts indeed. Most of them had to do with his lawyer. He questioned the wisdom of the steps taken on his behalf by Mr. Tuttle. He felt a pang when he realized he had failed to caution Mr. Tuttle to make no further deals or concessions without consulting beforehand. He resolved to instruct him in this at the first opportunity.

Furthermore, the personal discussion dismayed Jack. Not so much because of its nature, but more so for the context in which it had been broached. In the midst of a life and death issue he introduced an irrelevant matter, trivial by comparison.

It disturbed Jack not just a little, that Mr. Tuttle had not yet been in touch with Colonel Williams. He wondered what kind of effort had been mounted, if any.

For the first time Jack began to doubt the wisdom of putting his life in the hands of Mr. Tuttle.

CHAPTER SEVENTY-FIVE

THE INFORMATION that the treason trial was already under way aroused in Jack fresh interest in Mr. Riel.

Each night for the past seven or eight days Jack was conscious of a monotonous murmur of voices at the far end of the prison corridor. He was naturally curious. One evening Jack heard the sound while the guard was delivering a tray of food for the evening meal. He took the opportunity to ask the guard about it.

"Prayers," said the guard laconically. "He's saying 'Hail Marys'." The guard smiled at Jack and departed without further explanation.

The following afternoon the same guard returned to the bars of Jack's cell. There was no evident purpose for the visit. The guard was simply bored with long solitary hours and nothing to do.

Jack was surprised at his first remark.

"You're Canada Jack ain't you?"

"I've been called that," allowed Jack.

"I've heard about you."

"Thank you."

"Quite famous you are."

"You're very flattering," said Jack, always careful to be polite.

Just at that moment a brown and white dog came trotting up. It was a cocker spaniel. The dog stood by the guard's heel, looked up at Jack and began to pant.

"I've seen that dog around before. Your dog?"

"Shore is," he said again. This time the guard was beaming.

The dog walked over to the bars. Jack reached through and began to stroke its head. The dog first closed its eyes in ecstasy, then opened them to look at Jack in adoration.

"Actually, we've already met." Jack was referring to the fact that the dog had often trotted around to the cell. This had started at mealtime. The dog was looking for supper. But Jack was friendly and the dog had begun to visit on a regular basis.

Jack loved animals. Especially dogs. He particularly enjoyed the company of the dog now.

The guard had been watching the two of them. Finally Jack said: "What's her name?"

"Vicky," replied the guard. "After Her Imperial Majesty, you know."

"I see," said Jack.

"See here," said the guard. "From everything I've heard you ain't a bad sort. If you give me your word not to do anything funny, I'll let you out. We can talk."

"Do you play whist, cribbage?"

"I can play some. Not very well, mind you. And thanks, you certainly have my word."

"If you hear someone come, pop back in the cage. Wouldn't look good you know.

You can usually hear visitors long before they reach the corridor."

"Fine," agreed Jack.

"And one other thing."

"Yes?"

"You won't tell on me? I mean anyone. Not even your friend Sandy."

"Count on it. It will be just between the two of us."

Jack learned the name of his new friend was Izzy. They talked for long hours, playing gin rummy and talked some more. Izzy especially liked to talk and Jack listened for endless hours to his chatter.

They soon became good friends.

One morning, after Izzy and Jack had finished a round of gin rummy the talk turned once again to Jack's nickname. Izzy had heard that Canada Jack was renowned across the plains. He was curious how Jack came by that 'moniker' as he called it.

Jack explained. He tried to make it brief, but Izzy would not allow it. He prodded Jack. He was curious. He wanted to hear it all.

Jack was protesting, claiming that he was not that well known at all, when suddenly Izzy snorted good naturedly and said something which startled Jack.

"You is so famous. The rebel knows you."

"Who?" said Jack.

"The rebel. That cuss at the end."

"You mean…"

"I mean…You know who I mean. I'm talking about the rebel chief. Mister Louis Riel!" he said sarcastically.

"He knows I'm a prisoner?"

"Yes, he knows that.. He also knows your moniker."

"He knows I'm…?"

"Canada Jack. Sure he knows it. D'you doubt my word?"

"Well c'mon over and see for yourself." With that he scraped back his chair, stood up and motioned with his head for Jack to come over to Riel's cell.

Jack followed Izzy over to the far end of the hallway. All the cells on either side were in darkness. All, that is, but the one on the far left corner. A flickering glow spilled out between the bars. Izzy stopped and looked inside. Jack stopped beside his friend.

Sitting there on a cot, fingering a rosary, was a man of medium build. He did not look up at his two visitors.

"Hey reb, look alive, you got company." Izzy laughed quietly at his own unexpected gallows humour.

The man on the bed raised head and looked over to his right. Jack saw a handsome man of dark complexion. Mr. Riel did not smile, but neither did he look unfriendly. He was about early middle age. His hair was wavy, thick and dark, but it appeared to be receding for he had a high forehead. He parted it on the left and combed it back on the sides piling it thick above and behind his ears. His eyes were dark and though they looked indifferent and rather sad now, Jack was to learn that they could become intent or even fanatical when Mr. Riel became aroused by conversation. He had a regular, slightly aquiline nose. He wore a full moustache, almost concealing his upper lip. His face was not quite thin, with rather high prominent cheek bones. The shadows on his face indicated he may have a slight cleft on his chin and slight dimples on his cheeks.

Jack thought he was a striking man. He had heard that Mr. Riel may be fanatical, or even slightly insane, but sitting there calmly in his cell he looked quite normal.

"Guess who I've got here reb?" said Izzy in a slightly mocking voice.

Mr. Riel immediately turned his head away.

"I mean Mr. Riel," corrected Izzy. "Sensitive bugger, ain't he?" Izzy whispered into Jack's right ear.

"I want you to meet Canada Jack."

Mr. Riel's head pulled around again. He showed immediate interest.

"Canada Jack. Yes I've heard of you." He got to his feet and took the two steps to the cell door.

Jack took his hand through the bars. The two men shook hands. Riel's grip was firm and sincere.

"Well, I've certainly heard of you," said Jack. Both men laughed briefly at this comment.

"You've got what a lot of people want, you know that Jack? said Izzy.

"What's that?" asked Jack.

"To meet Mr. Riel here. Dozens of people have tried but they're not letting 'em in."

"Well I consider it doubly an honour, then, Sir," said Jack. He shook Riel's hand twice more, and vigorously before releasing it.

"It is I who should be honoured meeting you," said Mr. Riel. "You have quite a fine reputation on the plains."

"It's nice of you to say that, Mr. Riel, but you needn't."

"I mean it. Word of your exploits has spread like a prairie fire. Many of my Indian friends have mentioned you to me.

"Black Bear in particular told me that you were a great buffalo hunter. He admired you much for that."

"You know Black Bear?"

"Of course I do. But you will excuse me if I don't say more about him." He glanced toward Izzy as he said this.

"I do not know Black Bear very well, but I know his son Travelling Spirit and his daughter, One Feather," said Jack ignoring Riel's last comment.

"I know Travelling Spirit," said Riel nodding his head. "A fine young man. He will be a chief one day."

"Black Bear told me something about you and Travelling Spirit, but I do not recall exactly…"

"He was almost trampled by buffalo…" said Jack.

"Oh yes…and you saved him from being trampled to death. Now I remember."

The conversation went on for about twenty minutes more. Izzy finally tired of standing there. He asked Riel if he would like to have Jack visit with him inside the cell where they could both sit. Riel said yes and Izzy unlocked the door for Jack. When he walked in Izzy slammed the cell door.

"Well, I'm damned," said Jack after Izzy had left. "I think he's jealous that I have a new friend."

Both men laughed heartily at this idea. From that moment the two cemented their relationship.

Jack found Mr. Riel to be a well travelled man. The two were never at a loss for conversation. Jack took every opportunity to visit with Mr. Riel when not occupied with his own lawyer or entertaining Izzy. He always found Mr. Riel interesting, with one small exception: he did tend to go on a bit about Metis grievances.

Jack heard a lot about St. Boniface where Mr. Riel was born in a sod and log cabin. He also heard a great deal about Mr. Riel's mother. She was of Indian, Irish and French descent. Mr. Riel spoke often of this Indian heritage. Jack heard little, however, about the father and only later learned that he was a white man.

Life in a small frontier town had much to offer a boy. When he was not in school or doing his chores Riel spent his days with his friends hunting or simply roaming the prairie.

He was a good pupil, however, and when he was eleven he was sent off to Montreal to attend the Jesuit college.

There he soon showed himself to be a conscientious student, eager and quick to learn. But he longed for the West. Upon finishing college he promptly gave up the glitter of life in Montreal for life on the prairie. During his absence his parents had moved to St. Vital, a Metis settlement.

He joined them and for awhile he half-heartedly farmed with his father. But his real interest was politics. Three years after his return he led the Metis in their first rebellion.

Jack heard a great deal about that uprising. Although it took place sixteen years before, it was still big in his friend's mind.

In the following years Riel moved about the eastern States and sometimes visited Montreal and Quebec City. Then in 1879 he moved to Montana Territory. There he was married and appeared ready to settle down. Mr. Riel earned a living by teaching, but found the pay so meagre he hunted buffalo to supplement his income. He had many tales to tell of his buffalo hunting days. He also listened with interest to Jack's adventures in the buffalo hunt with the Indians.

He told Jack how he had rejected the request of the Metis from Batoche to return. They had persisted, however, "and...well...you know the rest." When he remembered this he shook his head and said, ruefully: "I should not have allowed them to persuade me. I had a good life in Montana."

Then he brightened as he told Jack of his "Bill of Rights." It called for deeds to Metis land, the building of community institutions such as schools and hospitals by the Government, the setting aside of lands for descendants of the Metis, agricultural assistance to the poor amongst them and greater assistance to the Indians. It called for other grants and advantages, but the boldest demand was for Provinces to be created from the North West Territories.

"I presented these requests a number of times," he said. "For the most part my pleading was greeted with silence and indifference. If only some of them had been agreed to..." but he never finished his statement. Jack never learned what would have happened.

He told Jack how he had been elected to parliament many years before, but had never been allowed to take his seat.

"How different things could have been," he said.

"One day all of these things will come to pass. Today we are treated like a colony. It may take a hundred years to throw off colonial domination from Central Canada, but it will happen."

"In one hundred years, I predict that. They may suppress the West for all of those years. If they do, it will all end in the year 1985. You and I will be very old then. That is reason enough to live. To see this happen."

Suddenly they both realized the gloomy humour of the remark. Mr. Riel began to laugh. He slapped Jack's knee. They both broke into gales of laughter. That brought Izzy back. He was miffed and sent Jack back to his own cell for the night.

Thereafter Jack and Mr. Riel spent many evenings together. When they were not reminiscing they traded information on the progress of their cases.

They became very good friends indeed.

CHAPTER SEVENTY-SIX

AT NOON, three days later, Jack was abruptly taken from his cell at the barracks to the Court House. It was expected the trial of Louis Riel would wind up early that afternoon.

Jack and his escort entered through a door at the rear of the building. He was deposited in a conference room adjoining the main court room. He was left there alone, except for a guard outside the door through which he had entered.

It was not long before he heard people moving about in the courtroom. Two o'clock arrived. A booming voice then penetrated the door separating the two rooms.

"Everybody rise."

Jack heard people shuffle to their feet. There was a pause. He imagined the judge taking the bench. Then the voice said.

"I declare this court reopened in the name of Her Majesty the Queen."

"Be seated."

Another shuffle as the assembly made themselves comfortable.

Thereafter, except for the occasional voice raised in exclamation, all he could hear through the thin door separating the two rooms was a low murmur of voices.

It was not long before Mr. Tuttle arrived. He was all out of breath. He had only just been notified that his client had been taken over to the Court House.

The first question Jack asked him was the same question he had asked him everyday for the last week: had Mr. Tuttle managed to contact Colonel Williams? The reply too was the same. "No, but I expect to do so shortly. Be patient. I will find him eventually. He cannot have dropped off the face of the earth." Mr. Tuttle slipped into a chair and the two men sat there at the conference table looking depressed.

After half an hour had passed, Mr. Tuttle rose and opened the door to the courtroom slightly. The voices could be heard quite clearly when he did so. He watched for a period of time, then he beckoned Jack over.

Jack looked into the courtroom. It was jam packed. They had a good vantage point. The judge sat on a high bench to the right. To his left at a counsel table facing the bench sat several men. To his right another table faced the judge. A lawyer was standing on his feet at this table. He was addressing the Court.

"Mr. Robinson," whispered Mr. Tuttle, "Counsel for the Crown."

Jack looked at the prosecutor. He was of average height and slim.

The hair on his forehead was thinning but he had compensated for this with a heavy growth of mutton chop side burns. He was dressed in a business suit. Though he looked pale and anaemic, he spoke in a rich voice. He was directing his remarks primarily at a group of men seated in a box along the wall of the court to the right of the judge and only a few feet away from him.

The jury!

Jack tried to concentrate on what the prosecutor was saying.

"...bitter desolation of many human hearts, and gentlemen, we must not allow ourselves for one moment to speak lightly of anything which necessarily involves these terrible consequences."

"If this scheme had succeeded, gentlemen, if these Indians had been roused, can any man with a human heart contemplate without a shudder the atrocities, the cruelties which would have overspread this land."

"Those who are guilty of this rebellion and those who have not a proper excuse, have taken the step upon their own heads, and they must suffer the punishment which the law from all time, and which the law for the last five centuries has declared to be the punishment of the crime of treason."

The lawyer shook his considerable mutton chops at this point, and placing great emphasis on the word 'treason', glanced for a moment toward the prisoner's dock before he continued.

"Now, gentlemen, the Crown in this case has a double duty to perform. In the first place, to see that the prisoner has had every impartiality and fair play and every consideration which it was in their power to give him, and which the law afforded him. Let there be no mistake about that. If this fair play has not been granted, if this trial has not been impartial, if we have omitted any part of our duty, all I can say is that the prisoner's life has been in our hands quite as much as in the hands of the learned gentlemen for the defence." As he said this he gestured with his open hand to the lawyers seated opposite. Then he went on to conclude.

"But, gentlemen, we have another duty to perform; we have the cause of public justice entrusted to our hands; we have the duty of seeing that the cause of public justice is properly served, that justice is done."

"I will leave this case with confidence in your hands.

"This Crown asks only what is just, and the Crown believes justice will be done. That is all the public and the community have ever asked and to that the public and the community are fully entitled and that they believe they will receive."

With these words he sat down. The jury had been watching him intently. As soon as he seated himself the whole courtroom shifted on their seats. There was a scraping of chairs. Then the Judge began to speak. He had a resonant voice that carried easily to every part of the large room. He spoke very slowly. So quiet was the courtroom that whenever he paused Jack could hear a quiet hum in the back ground. It was the sound of summer penetrating the dusty window pane.

"That's Mr. Justice Richardson," whispered Mr. Tuttle. "He'll be your Judge too. He's about to charge the jury."

"Gentlemen of the jury," began the Judge, "that this is an important case and will require your very serious consideration, there can be no shadow of doubt. The duties which devolved upon those gentlemen who had the prosecution in hand, are ended. They have called their witnesses, and you have heard what they have had to say; in addition to that -- and this is the only case in which it is permitted -- you have heard from the mouth of the accused what he has to say.

"The remainder of the case rests with yourself and me. My duty is to show you, to place before you as well as I can, what the law is, to refresh your memory as to the evidence which has been given pro and con, and then leave the determination upon that evidence to yourselves."

At this point the judge paused. He looked around his bench, then moved some papers about to get organized.

"Osgoode Hall man," said Mr. Tuttle, apropos of nothing. "Some time ago he tried a man for cannibalism."

"Imagine that! Sentenced him to hang." Then, after a pause, he added.

"You'll be fine with him."

Somehow Jack did not find this piece of news reassuring.

"I wish I had your confidence," he said. Privately he wondered how confident Mr. Tuttle would be if he were next to the dock.

"Good looking man too," added Mr. Tuttle.

Jack's mind worked for a moment to deal with this last statement. 'Goofy' seemed to be the only category for it. He had to admit, however, that the judge was an impressive looking man, seated up there on the bench.

The judge had started to speak again and Jack had no time to further concern himself with the behaviour of his lawyer.

"Now, the charge against the prisoner is, as I told you, a very serious one. It is the most serious one in the whole criminal category. It is the charge of high treason. In order that I may not be mistaken, that I may not misplace any words it will be right for me to read to you what high treason is."

The judge picked up a large black volume. He flipped over some pages. He said a few more words.

"The charge of high treason, which is laid against the prisoner, is that of levying war against Her Majesty in her realms in these territories. It is founded upon a very old English statute, one on which is based the whole law of treason, and which was passed in the reign of Edward III."

Then he began to read.

"When a man do levy war against our Lord the King in his realm, or be adherent to the King's enemies in his realm, giving to them aid and comfort in the realm or elsewhere, and thereof be provably attained of open deed by the people of their condition, that this shall be one ground upon which the party accused of the offence and legally proved to have committed the offence, shall be held to be guilty of the crime of high treason."

At this point the judge put down the law book and picked up another. This one was bound in tan cowhide.

"Now, in order to constitute the crime of high treason by levying war, a standard authority lays down this."

Then he began to read from the book: "To constitute high treason by levying war, there must be insurrection, there must be force accompanying that insurrection, and it must be for the accomplishment of an object of a general nature. And if all these circumstances are found to concur in any individual case that is brought under investigation, that is quite sufficient to constitute a levying of war."

Once again, he put aside his book.

"The charge upon which the prisoner is upon his trial is under that statute, that clause of the statute, and it charges him with levying war upon Her Majesty at the locality of Duck Lake, North West Territories; also at Fish Creek, and also at Batoche. Having refreshed your memory as to the evidence which was supplied on the part of the Crown, and which you have heard on the part of the defence, it will be your duty to say whether that has been proved or not. If it has not been proved, if the evidence has not brought it home conclusively to this man, he should be acquitted. If it has been brought home to the prisoner, then another question turns up which you will have most seriously to consider, is he answerable?

"My intention now is to read the evidence which has been taken. I feel it my duty to do so, from the way it has been given, and after I have read it, to draw your attention to it and to make a few observations that occur to me, which may be useful to yourselves in arriving at a conclusion. Before I read the evidence, I may remark that before the prisoner can be convicted you must be satisfied that he was implicated in the acts charged against him. It must be brought home to him, otherwise he is entitled to be acquitted. If you are satisfied that he was implicated in the acts in which he is said to have been implicated, he must as completely satisfy you that he is not answerable by reason of unsoundness of mind.

"You will recollect that there are two points which you must consider; first, was this man implicated, supposing him to be sane, in the acts charged against him? It is for the Crown to satisfy you upon that. If he was so implicated, are you satisfied, from what has been shown, that he is not answerable?"

The judge began to review the evidence. Jack and Mr. Tuttle stepped back as the latter let the door close.

"He'll be quite a while with that," said Mr. Tuttle. "I don't believe we'll make a start on your case today."

He left the room. Soon thereafter Jack was escorted back to jail at the barracks.

That evening Jack did not visit with Mr. Riel. Izzy told him that Mr. Riel did not feel up to having company. Jack understood. He did not feel like company himself.

He was dozing at about nine forty-five that night. Hammering had been going on most of the evening, rendering sound sleep impossible. Jack slowly became accustomed to the noise. He was on the point of dropping off to sleep when a loud but dull bang shot him out of bed.

"What the...what's that?" he called over to Izzy.

Izzy did not call back as he usually did. He shuffled over to Jack's cell before he answered. He had a sly grin on his face when he spoke.

"Don't you recognize the sound?" he asked.

Jack waited for the answer.

"That's the scaffold. The boys have been working on it all evening, hoping to finish up."

"But the bang...?" said Jack.

"That's the drop. The trap door. The entrance to eternal life." He chuckled at his own pathetic joke.

"But the trial's not even completed," said Jack, protesting.

"Ha," snorted Izzy in reply. "D'you think the jury is gonna let that reb go free?

"Like hell they is."

He shuffled off and left Jack to his troubled thoughts. With two capital trials taking place, the "boys" are bound to get some mileage out of their macabre toy, thought Jack.

He tried to sleep after that, but grim reality kept intruding into his consciousness. He could not relax. Sleep eluded him.

CHAPTER SEVENTY-SEVEN

IT WAS midmorning when Jack was returned again to the waiting room at the Court House. Mr. Tuttle was already present. The second door leading into the courtroom was ajar. Apparently he had found a comfortable place from which to follow the trial proceedings. He had a chair pulled over to enable him to watch as well as listen. As Jack entered Mr. Tuttle put his finger to his lips. Then he motioned for Jack to come over.

"The judge is winding up his charge to the jury," he said. "It won't be long now." Jack planted himself behind his lawyer. He bent his head slightly to catch the words of the judge.

"...That I propound to you as the law," were the first words that he heard. The judge droned on.

"If the evidence conclusively satisfies you that the prisoner was implicated in these acts or in any of them I may say, has it been clearly proved to you that at the time he committed those acts he was labouring under such defective reasoning caused by disease of the mind as not to know that he was doing wrong? If the evidence convinces you and convinces you conclusively that such was the case, then your duty is to acquit the prisoner on that ground, and you are required to declare that he is acquitted by you on account of such insanity."

There was a short pause after the judge said this. He nodded his head ponderously and with evident satisfaction. Then he reached for a glass of water. He took a long draught before he started again.

"I think I have reduced my remarks within the smallest possible compass. You have been kept close at this case since Tuesday morning, and I cannot conceive that any further remarks would be of any assistance to you. On you rests the responsibility of pronouncing upon the guilt or innocence of the prisoner at the bar. Not only must you think of the man in the dock, but you must think of society at large, you are not called upon to think of the Government at Ottawa simply as a Government, you have to think of the homes and of the people who live in this country, you have to ask yourselves, can such things be permitted? There was one point I intended to have mentioned but which has escaped me. You will bear in mind that the law of the land under which this trial is held was objected to on behalf of the prisoner, and he has a perfect right to object to it, but the law of the land was in existence years before he came into this country three years ago, that Act came into force in 1875, and the law which he is said to have broken has been in existence for centuries, and I think I may fairly say to you that if a man chooses to come into the country, he shall not say, I will do as I like and no laws can touch me. A person coming into the country is supposed to know the law, it is his duty. We have the law given to us and we are called upon to administer it. I, under the oath that I have taken, and you, under the oath administered to you on Tuesday morning, are to pass between this man and the Crown. If therefore the Crown has not conclusively brought guilt home to the prisoner, say so, say that you acquit him simply by reason of that.

"I have now concluded my remarks."

"Gentlemen of the jury, you will now retire to consider your verdict."

The sheriff was immediately on his feet. He shepherded the jurymen out through a door on which were printed the words "Jury Room'."

The Judge leaned over to the clerk. He said a few inaudible words. The clerk jumped to his feet.

"Everybody rise," he called. The entire assembly rose with a great deal of scraping of chairs and audible breathing.

The judge rose too and proceeded out of the courtroom.

"This Honourable Court is now adjourned," announced the clerk.

Mr. Tuttle rose too. He shut the door and dragged a protesting chair back to the table. "Might as well relax Jack. May take a while. Don't think so, but it might."

Jack sat again at the table. For a while the two men discussed Riel's trial. Mr. Tuttle had much to say about the charge to the jury. He thought it could have been tougher. He felt the judge had gone on too much about the possibility Riel might have been insane.

Jack knew that this had been the defence offered by Riel's lawyer. He thought what he had heard had been fair. He said nothing, however, as Mr. Tuttle went on chattering. He was definitely giving the judge a bad review. He did not think much of the prosecution either. Then he came back to insanity.

"Crafty isn't it? The lawyers claim that he is not guilty by reason of insanity. That is the official defense. The accused, however, claims he is not insane. If he is not insane then he must be responsible for his actions."

"Ergo the jury must think him to be insane to claim that he is not insane."

"Crafty," repeated Mr. Tuttle, shaking his head in admiration, "crafty".

For a while they discussed Jack's case. Mr. Tuttle told Jack he had still not had word from Colonel Williams. He had sent letters and a number of messages by telegraph. He had been informed by local militia officials, however, that the Midland Battalion had returned to Fort Battleford. He assured Jack they would shortly receive word the Colonel was on his way. Perhaps even tomorrow.

Loud conversation and more chair scraping alerted Mr. Tuttle that something was about to occur in the courtroom. He slipped over and opened the door.

"The jury is filing in," he said to Jack. "They must have reached a verdict."

Jack walked over to stand behind Mr. Tuttle and watch proceedings.

The courtroom was once again packed. The fetid air from the assemblage wafted into the small anteroom. The jury was seated. Some spectators were seated, others standing. The prisoner was already in the dock.

About ten feet away Jack could see a lawyer seated and talking in a stage whisper loud enough for everyone to hear. The lawyer had great dark circles around his eyes which made him resemble a raccoon. His hair was all crinkly curls combed straight back over his head. His large nostrils faced forward, exposed to all the world. His ears were also large and seemed to have an independent life, so far did they extend from his head.

He had a malicious grin on his face. It caused his lips to be drawn back from his teeth which were both bucked and gapped.

He evidently had a high opinion of himself. He carried on in front of the spectators. When he drew attention or a little laughter his exhibitionism only seemed to increase. He seemed to be teasing Counsel at the defense table. They tried to ignore him, but this provoke even greater excesses.

He had just said something which drew a ripple of laughter from a few people behind him. Then Jack heard him quite clearly.

"Mr. Riel is going to receive a suspended sentence," he said. With this remark he pulled the end of his tie over to his head which he dropped to the opposite side. Then he let his tongue loll out of his mouth.

The lawyers for the accused turned when he spoke, just in time to see his demonstration. They blushed deeply, but maintained their dignity.

"That's Mr. Pynch," said Mr. Tuttle. "The prosecutor in your case. Isn't he clever? Isn't he a card."

Just then the clerk entered.

"Order please," he called. "Everybody rise."

As one, the assembly stood.

The door behind the bench opened and Mr. Justice Richardson strode in. He took the bench with a flourish.

"I declare this court reopened in the name of Her Majesty the Queen," intoned the clerk. "You may be seated."

Everyone sat down. It took a few moments for the audiences to settle itself. The judge and his entourage waited patiently. Then the clerk looked at the judge. The judge nodded to him once.

The clerk stood and turned to face the jury.

"Here it is," said Tuttle. "Watch the faces of the jurors. If they refuse to look at the accused they're going to convict."

Jack strained to look at the faces of the jurymen. He was unable to see where they were looking. If anything they were looking into every part of the court room and at the prisoner too.

Finally the clerk spoke.

"The prisoner will rise."

The clerk paused briefly while Riel rose.

"Gentlemen of the jury, are you agreed upon your verdict?"

The jury foreman rose in response to the question.

"We are," he said.

"How say you, is the prisoner guilty or not guilty."

"Guilty," responded the foreman.

Jack could see Riel flinch slightly, as though he had been slapped. His face turned deathly white.

Again the clerk spoke.

"Gentlemen of the jury, hearken to your verdict as the court records it, you find the prisoner, Louis Riel, guilty, so say you all?"

In a chorus the jury answered.

"Guilty!"

Several of the jurors nodded their heads in the affirmative. Jack could see, just as Tuttle had predicted, that while the verdict was announced none of them looked at Riel. Now the foreman stole a quick glance at the prisoner and unexpectedly spoke again.

"Your Honour, I have been asked by my brother jurors to recommend the prisoner to the mercy of the Crown."

The judge responded.

"I may say in answer to you that the recommendation which you have given will be forwarded in the proper manner to the proper authorities."

The jury was then discharged.

Mr. Robinson then rose and addressed the judge.

"Does your Honour propose to pass sentence now? I believe the proper course is to ask the sentence of the Court upon the prisoner."

The prisoner was still standing. Jack could see that he was swaying slightly. Every eye in the court was rivetted on the prisoner in the box.

The judge then spoke.

"Louis Riel, have you anything to say why the sentence of the Court should not be pronounced upon you for the offense of which you have been found guilty?"

"Yes, Your Honour," answered the prisoner. He spoke in a quiet even voice.

Necks were craned forward in order to catch every word. There was a brief, almost inaudible discussion amongst counsel and court. Then the prisoner spoke up again, quite audibly this time.

"Can I speak now?"

"Oh, yes," said the judge.

Louis Riel began to speak.

Jack watched his friend begin his last oration before sentence was to be passed. He had recovered his composure. Though he rambled somewhat he seemed gradually to pull his thoughts together. He spoke in a clear firm voice.

"Someone's knocking at the door," said Mr. Tuttle. They both turned. Mr. Tuttle walked over to open it. Then he admitted a young man. Mr. Tuttle motioned for Jack to close the door leading to the court room.

"Here's someone who's been asking to meet you. I should have mentioned it before, but I suppose I was distracted by the trial."

The young man held out his hand to Jack.

"Let me introduce myself," he said, "my name is Harry Preston. I'm correspondent for the 'Daily British Whig'. Here to cover the trial."

The two men shook hands.

"My editor has asked me to write up some local color to add to my dispatches on the trial proceedings. I thought I was sending him enough, but apparently not."

"Some days ago I received a message by telegraph to look into the extraordinary stories that have been reaching home about a young soldier. Apparently he was kidnapped on his way to the front. I was instructed to investigate and send all information of his adventures on the great plains to my editor."

"I gather there is enormous interest in this young man. I further understand he's from Upper Canada."

Jack listened politely to his visitor. He wondered what he was talking about and wished he would come to the point.

"The point of all this," said Mr. Preston, as though he had read Jack's mind, "is that two days ago I learned that the subject of my search was here, in town, in custody, about to face trial for desertion under fire.

"I'm glad I finally found you, Canada Jack," he concluded.

CHAPTER SEVENTY-EIGHT

HARRY WAS probably the most confident person Jack had ever met. He was of average height and well built. With his dark brown wavy hair and regular features he was also quite handsome. He was both brusque and brash, dismissed opposition or hesitation as negative, and never took 'no' for an answer.

His one ambition was to work for the Globe newspaper. Jack soon learned that the editor, Mr. Murrow, had promised a position and a great future if Harry could prove himself in the field just once. Having found Canada Jack, Harry planned to do just that. He would write a series of articles around Jack's adventures. If Mr. Murrow accepted them, Harry would promptly resign the "Whig" and accept appointment as a reporter for the Globe.

Mr. Tuttle and Jack listened as all of this poured out of Harry. Harry had big plans. Obviously Jack figured largely in these plans.

The conversation eventually turned to the prospects at Jack's trial. Mr. Tuttle attempted to put in a word or two. He was waved off by Harry. Jack became reticent to discuss the trial in any depth. He even found himself reluctant to discuss his adventures on the plains with Mr. Preston.

It was then that Harry Preston played his best card.

"A great deal of information about you is going to be published and circulated as a result of the trial. In the nature of these things, trials, I mean, it's going to be of the negative kind. The case for the prosecution will most certainly blacken your reputation."

"D'you want your parents, your friends, acquaintances back home to hear all this as uncontradicted fact? What will they think of you?"

"Will you ever be able to rehabilitate your reputation in Upper Canada? Once again the damage is done, it's done! Almost invariably the damage is permanent."

"But the defense..." protested Jack.

Harry interrupted him.

"Yes, the defense." He looked at Tuttle then back to Jack. "Your lawyer will tell you that no matter how good the defense is, even if you win acquittal, the initial impression often remains."

"When you throw mud, some of it sticks."

"He's got a point there," Tuttle interrupted quickly.

For once Harry let Mr. Tuttle have his say. Then he played his trump card.

"A lot of lies, half truths and distortions will gain currency through the trial and the mouths of other people."

"If you want people to know the facts, if you want to be sure that people hear the truth, tell it yourself."

"What I mean is tell me and I'll tell the world."

"That makes a lot of sense Jack," interjected Mr. Tuttle once again. "Couldn't hurt the trial either, if people knew your case was to be sympathetically published."

Jack hesitated. He heard the bass hum of voices in the adjoining room abruptly end. The scraping of chairs told him a recess had been called. He had missed his friend Riel's speech to the jury.

Harry Preston was looking at Jack. He had nodded his head at Mr. Tuttle's remarks. Then he repeated the word "sympathetically" several times. Then added "from your point of view, of course."

After another moment of hesitation he said, "How about it? Do I have your cooperation?"

Mr. Tuttle nodded encouragingly at Jack. Finally Jack said, "What do I have to do?"

"A good decision," said Harry, clapping Jack on his shoulder. "All you have to do is make yourself available to me over the next four or five days or however long it may take. When you're not required by Mr. Tuttle, that is, or at trial. I'll interview you. You just tell me your story."

"I promise you, you won't regret this. You'll be a legend in your own time. Maybe for all time."

"Anything to help win an acquittal," said Jack. In his deepest thoughts he held out hope for only marginal benefits for his trial.

"Whether we can do much for you there is problematical," said Harry. "Let's hope it helps."

"What we can do is ensure your reputation doesn't suffer in the aftermath. On that score, it would be a big help if we win the case.

"What do you say about giving me a rundown? What do ya know about the case for the Crown? How do you see the defense unfolding?"

"We can do that, sure," said Mr. Tuttle, "but the defense will have to be confidential until we present it in court."

"I understand completely. Mum's the word on the defense 'till it surfaces in evidence at trial."

From that moment a relationship began between Jack and Harry that grew through confidence and became friendship. The lawyer and his client sketched the Crown case and the response that had been planned.

It immediately became apparent to Harry that the entire defense had been built around Colonel Williams.

When he learned that the Colonel had not been in touch with Jack and his lawyer he resolved to help.

"A newspaper is not without influence," he said cryptically.

Another rap at the door broke up the discussion. It was the deputy sheriff. Court was about to reconvene for the passing of sentence. That spelt the end of the Riel trial. Jack could be arraigned immediately afterward.

Harry promised to visit Jack that night and every night thereafter. He would obtain from Jack at night such information as he was unable to gather during the day in interviews and at trial.

It was only much later that Jack realized Harry had kept every promise he had made. Though his help at trial eventually proved to be minimal, he did a series of articles on Jack and that, along with extensive lecture tours that Harry undertook turned Jack's life into legend.

More important to Jack was the fact that Harry became a lifelong friend.

Jack was ushered right into the courtroom. He was seated before the bar with the deputy sheriff to his left and Mr. Tuttle to his right.

Riel was brought in. He was placed once more in the dock. The jury box was empty. The crowd shifted impatiently as they waited for the judge to make his appearance.

Suddenly the door behind the bench was thrown open. A clerk stepped out.

"All rise," he called. Everyone stood. The judge emerged and took the bench. "I declare this court open in the name of Her Majesty the Queen," announced the clerk.

"Be seated!"

With another scraping of chairs the assembly sat down.

Jack too sat down. He looked around the room. He noticed that not a single woman was present. He wondered if there was a reason for this.

The entire room fell deathly silent. The only sound came from the bench where the judge was once again rearranging books and papers. Then Jack heard an odd sound. After a few seconds he heard it again: "Ptoink," a long pause and then again, "Ptoink". It came from the right, near the wall. He looked over and saw a man busily chewing tobacco. A brass spittoon stood two or three feet away in full view. A rich brown viscous fluid slowly ran down the ball portion toward dark oblivion below.

The judge nodded to the clerk.

"The prisoner will rise," he commanded.

Mr. Riel rose slowly from his seat in the prisoner's dock. He placed his hands on the front and looked up at the judge.

Without preliminaries Mr. Justice Richardson began to speak.

"Louis Riel, after a long consideration of your case, in which you have been defended with as great ability as I think counsel could have defended you with, you have been found by a jury who have shown, I might almost say, unexampled patience, guilty of a crime the most pernicious and greatest that man can commit. You have been found guilty of high treason. You have been proved to have let loose the flood-gates of rapine and bloodshed, you have, with such assistance as you had in the Saskatchewan country, managed to arouse the Indians and have brought ruin and misery to many families whom if you had simply left alone were in comfort, and many of them were on the road to affluence.

"For what you did, the remarks you have made form no excuse whatsoever. For what you have done the law requires you to answer. It is true that the jury in merciful consideration have asked Her Majesty to give your case such merciful consideration as she can bestow upon it. I had almost forgotten that those who are defending you have placed in my hands a notice that the objection which they raised at the opening of the court must not be forgotten from the record, in order that if they see fit they may raise the question in the proper place. That has been done. But in spite of that, I cannot hold out any hope to you that you will succeed in getting entirely free, or that Her Majesty will, after what you have been the cause of doing, open her hand of clemency to you.

"For me, I have only one more duty to perform, that is, to tell you what the sentence of the law is upon you. I have, as I must, given time to enable your case to be heard. All I can suggest or advise you is to prepare to meet your end, that is all the advice or suggestion I can offer. It is now my painful duty to pass the sentence of the court upon you, and that is, that you be taken now from there to the police guard-room at Regina, which is the gaol and the place from whence you came, and that you be kept there till the 18th of September next, that on the 18th of September next you be taken to the place appointed for your execution, and there be hanged by the neck till you are dead, and may God have mercy on your soul."

Jack could easily see Mr. Riel. He received the pronouncement of death without a flicker of emotion. Of course, thought Jack, he knew what was coming.

The moment the judge had finished, two policemen helped Mr. Riel from the box and removed him from the courtroom.

They know his propensity to speak, thought Jack. They're not about to be subjected to another tour d'horizon by Mr. Riel.

There was a general commotion in the room. Some people got up from their benches and chairs and left the courtroom. Their interest in proceedings had ended with the removal of Riel.

The Judge brought his gavel down twice.

"Order. Order please," said the Judge.

"Let me remind you, court is still in session." He brought the gavel down hard a third time. The noise subsided.

"Mr. Pynch. Mr. Tuttle," said Mr. Justice Richardson.

The two lawyers rose obediently.

"We've had quite enough for one day. This being Saturday, the case of Her Majesty the Queen versus Lieutenant Jack Holden will stand over to Monday morning at ten."

"Thank you, Your Honour," said Pynch.

"Thank you," said Tuttle.

With that the Court rose for the weekend.

Jack was returned to his cell in the barracks.

CHAPTER SEVENTY-NINE

IT WAS Monday. The large clock on the wall of the courtroom gave the time as five minutes to ten. Jack was already seated in the prisoner's dock awaiting the opening of court.

Sunday had virtually flown by. Mr. Tuttle spent little time with his client, preferring to read his law books at the Court House library. Harry Preston and Sandy kept Jack company at the barracks. Harry seemed to be able to come and go at will. Sandy kept Jack posted on the happenings with Baker Troop and Sarah Tuttle. Sarah, he was assured, would definitely attend the trial.

Sure enough she was there. She had come over behind the dock and put her gentle white hand on the left sleeve of Jack's khaki tunic. Jack turned, surprised. They exchanged a few words. Both suppressed an urge to hug one another, it had been so many months that they had been apart. Then Sarah demurely took a seat not far away in the front row.

Of course Harry was present. It appeared that Harry had made himself at least a nodding acquaintance of half the townsfolk. They waved hello and some called out greetings to him. He smiled and waved back, calling many by their christian names or nicknames. Harry appropriated a seat to Jack's left immediately behind the box. Throughout the trial Harry always took the same seat. Even when he was not present, Jack noticed, the seat remained vacant in case Harry should arrive late.

The courtroom was gradually filling up. Some ladies had managed to come.

"It's not for lack of entertainment," whispered Harry into Jack's ear. "Those little ladies have taken a genuine interest in the fate of 'that handsome unfortunate young man'," quoted Harry. "I should know. I've interviewed a number of them. They're sympathetic."

Jack was grateful to know that some people sympathetic to his case were to be present at trial.

Just as this thought passed through his consciousness he got the greatest possible boost to his morale. The whole of Baker Troop filed in and took up seats in the first three rows.

But the biggest surprise, and the one that meant the most to him, was that the Troop was led by Lieutenant Richards. He came right over to Jack. The two friends shook hands vigorously and beamed at each other.

"I have been trying for weeks to find how you made out," said Jack. "You look great. Just great. How do you feel?"

"I feel fine Jack. Just fine. The doctors told me later that it was touch and go there for a while. But once the probe was over I seemed to spring right back."

He smiled at Jack.

"I am still swathed in bandages and I'm supposed to take it easy."

"I'm glad you made it," said Jack. "I never thought to have you subpoenaed. I thought you'd be too ill to attend. But I could sure use some help."

"But I did receive a subpoena," protested the Lieutenant. "I have it right here. Look."

Lieutenant Richards withdrew a legal document from inside his tunic and handed it to Jack.

Puzzled, Jack opened it and began to read. Then he stopped for a moment to introduce the Lieutenant to Harry. As the two exchanged greetings and the usual pleasantries Jack scanned the document.

He looked up at the Lieutenant stunned.

"But it says here you have been called to give evidence for the Crown," said Jack. A note of dismay had crept into his voice.

The Lieutenant took the document from Jack's hand. His eyes looked frantically over the page to find the sentence that assigned him as witness for the Crown. As he studied the document it was clear that he was as surprised as Jack. But there was no more time to discuss the matter. The clerk had entered the courtroom. The proceedings were about to commence.

"All rise," called the clerk with authority.

The assembly rose obediently.

Mr. Justice Richardson swept into the room and took the bench with solemn dignity.

"I declare this court open in the name of Her Majesty the Queen," said the clerk.

"Be seated please."

Jack, the lawyers, the multitude of spectators all took their seats.

When the courtroom had settled down the clerk picked up a lengthy sheet of paper.

"Her Majesty the Queen versus Lieutenant Jack Holden, Your Honour." He passed the indictment up to the judge. He turned back to Jack. "The prisoner will rise."

Jack stood to face the judge. In his peripheral vision he could see Mr. Tuttle at counsel table to his right. To his left sat Mr. Pynch. He saw the indictment handed back to the clerk. Suddenly the clerk was speaking.

"Are you Lieutenant Jack Holden, the accused?"

"I am," replied Jack.

"Lieutenant Jack Holden, late of the town of Cobourg, County of Northumberland of the Province of Ontario, formerly Upper Canada; you stand charged…"

Jack's eyes drifted from the clerk to the judge and around the courtroom – he could hardly believe this was happening … "eighteen eighty-five," went on the clerk, "in the North West Territories of Her Majesty the Queen's Realm of Canada, you did, notwithstanding your duty as a loyal subject of Her Majesty and in dereliction of your duty as a member of Her Majesty's North West Field Force under the command of Major-General Fredrick D. Middleton, B.C., the Commanding General hereunto appointed, unlawfully and wilfully desert, while under enemy fire, the command of Lieutenant Colonel Wilbert Trubshaw, to wit: The Canadian Military Rangers, contrary to Article Eight of the Queen's Regulations governing Her Majesty's Canadian Army and Militia, and contrary to the form of statute in such case made and provided."

He paused, lowered the indictment and addressed Jack again.

"How say you to the charge? Do you plead guilty or not guilty?"

"Not guilty!" said Jack in a firm confident voice.

"Empanel the jury," said the judge. Immediately the clerk was calling forth prospective jurymen.

Jack had been seated once again. The process proceeded with a swirl above his head. He heard Mr. Pynch speak briefly a number of times. On each occasion he said "stand aside." Whereupon the clerk called another venireman forward.

A full panel of jurymen was selected with ease. Mr. Tuttle had raised not a single objection. Indeed, up until that point in the proceedings he had uttered not a single word.

Jack heard Harry whispering at him from behind. He leaned his head back to hear what Harry was saying.

"What's going on," he whispered. "Not a word from Tuttle. Has he no questions? What if one of those jurymen is prejudiced in your case? Perhaps related to the General or his staff? Does he know? Did he even look into it?"

"Why are there no challenges from the defense?"

Jack moved his head slowly from side to side to let Harry know he had no answer for his questions.

"I don't like this," said Harry. "I don't like it at all."

Mr. Pynch was now on his feet. He was speaking rapidly to the judge.

"Your Honour, my learned friend, Mr. Tuttle, and I have agreed to waive opening statements.

"He has also been so kind as to agree to the filing of certain documents without the necessity of calling witnesses."

"We believe this will save considerable time. It will also avoid the necessity of having to subpoena several witnesses from as far away as Ontario."

The judge inclined his head toward Mr. Tuttle, who basked in the judge's approval.

Thereupon Mr. Pynch began to file his documents. Evidence of the Birth and present age of the accused. The document of enlistment of the accused. His Individual Training Record, his assignment to the Canadian Military Rangers. The Individual Training Record for the Rangers Unit prepared in the usual course by the adjutant under direction of officer commanding, Lieutenant Colonel Trubshaw.

The list went on endlessly.

Finally, Harry was pulling on Jack's sleeve.

"Did you hear that. He's agreed to allow the report prepared by Trubshaw. I cannot imagine that will be of any help to your case."

"I suppose he thinks if it had not been entered by agreement the prosecution would have called the Colonel. He would have given the evidence verbally. Perhaps he thinks it would be more damaging that way."

"I don't think you understand about trials, Jack. I do. I used to be police court reporter for the Whig back east."

"What do you mean?" asked Jack.

They could see Mr. Tuttle glaring at them, but Harry went on indifferently.

"If he is not called to give that evidence in person he cannot be cross-examined."

"You can bet his report contains all the biased information formed from his twisted opinions about you. Not to mention all that stuff from Cobourg which has not been proved wrong.

"Like I said, I don't like it. I think it stinks!"

A good deal of time had been occupied already that morning. Each time a document was marked as an exhibit, the judge halted proceedings while he perused the information it contained. Jack had watched the face of the judge when he read through Colonel Trubshaw's report. The judge had looked from the document to peer down at Jack. For a moment their eyes locked. Then he resumed his reading. When he satisfied himself as to the content of the affidavit, Mr. Pynch read it to the jury. Suddenly Jack was aware that Mr. Pynch was suggesting that the court take its noon recess. Jack looked at the clock. It was already twelve thirty.

No sooner were Jack and Mr. Tuttle back in the same anteroom they had occupied before than Harry burst in. He immediately lit into Mr. Tuttle. Mr. Tuttle nervously moved about the small room as though by doing so he could turn aside the relentless questions.

Nothing, however, could deter Harry.

"By refusing to allow those documents in without witnesses to prove them you could have forced them to call witnesses to help Jack."

"Who, for example?" said Mr. Tuttle.

"Well his parents for one. Don't you think they could have helped him?"

Mr. Tuttle did not answer. Harry went on.

"And the Individual Training Record. Trubshaw's report. How about that?"

"What about it?"

"You know what about it. If you had not agreed to that, Trubshaw would have to take the stand."

"He's not favourable to Jack. How would he have helped?"

"He could have been cross-examined," said Harry. He was barely able to conceal his anger.

"So?" said Mr. Tuttle.

"So you could have forced him to admit that all his opinions were bias flowing from opinions from Cobourg. Opinions that Jack exaggerates, that he cannot be relied upon for truth, that he's a dreamer.

"And that he lied, that he concocted a story about being a witness to murder."

Mr. Tuttle's lower lip trembled ever so slightly. Harry rolled on to a conclusion.

"All of which has been proven to be false," he fairly shouted at Tuttle. With that he stalked out of the room slamming the door behind him.

When proceedings resumed that afternoon Harry was not present. The prosecution resumed their work and presented more documentary evidence. The last document presented was the affidavit of Major General Middleton. Jack was embarrassed to hear the adverse opinion of his character read aloud to the jury. In a way he was glad that Harry had not returned from the noon break. It was bad enough that all his friends in Baker Troop, especially Lieutenant Richards, should be present to hear the views of the General. As Jack listened to Mr. Pynch read the document's contents to the jury he remembered that the General had been present to give evidence at the trial of Mr. Riel. Why could he not be present as well at Jack's trial. Is my life of lesser consequence than that of Mr. Riel, thought Jack. Was it beneath the dignity of a general to appear at the trial of a mere enlisted man? Repeatedly, as he listened to Mr. Pynch, Jack heard assertions that were unfounded, opinions which could be exposed by even the most inexperienced of lawyers.

As if he had read Jack's mind, Mr. Tuttle slipped over to reassure him.

"You'll see," he whispered in Jack's ear. "We'll gain a lot of favour with His Honour and the jury by not bothering them, contesting every piece of evidence."

He patted Jack on the arm.

"We have your evidence. We also have the evidence of Colonel Williams."

"Don't lose heart."

Just before the afternoon break Mr. Pynch concluded his documentary evidence. The Court rose for fifteen minutes.

Jack was alone in the anteroom. Mr. Tuttle had gone off for a cup of tea with Mr. Pynch. Jack ran his eyes over the hundreds of law reports behind the glass case in the waiting room. They were beautifully bound, with gold lettering on the red labels on the spine of each book. He was wondering what type of person would deliberately choose a life in the law knowing he must spend agonizing hours reading such boring material, when the door flew open with a bang.

Jack turned around. Harry stood there with a wry grin on his face. He shut the door quickly, at the same time asking where Tuttle was.

"Having tea, I believe, with the opposition."

"I'm not surprised. I wouldn't be surprised by anything from our learned friend," said Harry. He emphasized the words 'learned friend', mocking both Pynch and Tuttle in the process.

"What do you mean" asked Jack.

"I've been over to militia headquarters. I came directly from there. I learned some interesting facts."

"Like what?" asked Jack.

"Like our Mr. Tuttle has been given the run around. He's been up there several times. That's true. And he's been making enquiries about the whereabouts of the Midland Battalion.

"Trouble is he could have had the information weeks ago. He only got it when, yesterday?

"I got friendly with a corporal in the orderly office over there. He told me hints had been dropped that helping Tuttle was not conducive to army interests. We can guess where that comes from."

"So?" asked Jack.

"So Tuttle merely got put off from day to day.

"The corporal says he was so polite, some might call it meek, in making his requests for information, any information, he was easily put off.

"They just laugh at him down there. They have their own name for him."

"What's that?"

"Timid Tuttle."

It fit so perfectly both Jack and Harry couldn't help but laugh.

"If our obsequious little advocate had screwed up his courage and pounded the counter, he'd have got what he wanted days ago if not weeks."

"What can I do about it?" said Jack.

Harry simply shook his head.

"You could sack him," he said finally. "But who could you get to replace him."

"At this late moment, no one," said Jack.

"Right," said Harry. "So the question is: are you better off with no lawyer or with Tuttle? I vote the former."

"I don't know," said Jack, uncertain.

"It's your life," said Harry. "I think he's done more harm to you than if you had not had any lawyer."

At that moment Mr. Tuttle entered. He threw a brief hello to Harry, then turned to speak to his client.

Over the lawyer's shoulder where only Jack could see him, Harry mouthed "Good afternoon Timid Tuttle!"

When court resumed at three forty-five Mr. Pynch called his first witness.

"Call Lieutenant John Richards to the stand," he said. He turned and smiled at Jack.

When the Lieutenant had stepped into the witness box the clerk handed a bible to him.

"Take the bible in your right hand," he instructed.

The officer grasped the black book.

"Do you swear by Almighty God that the evidence you are about to give touching the matter in question in this trial will be the truth, the whole truth and nothing but the truth?"

"I so swear," answered Lieutenant Richards.

"Kiss the book," said the clerk.

"You may be seated if you wish."

The clerk then took his own seat at a long low yellow oak table running along the front of the bench. He began to stamp documents.

Mr. Pynch rose to his feet.

"Please give the court your full name Lieutenant," said Mr. Pynch.

"John Richards."

"And your address please?"

"Presently my address is with the militia, but …"

"I mean before. Your permanent address."

"Kingston, Upper…uh…Ontario."

"And I understand that you attended Royal Military College in that same city and you are a graduate of that institution. Is that correct?"

"Yes, Sir."

"Now some time ago you were appointed Officer Commanding Baker Troop of the Canadian Military Rangers?"

"Yes, Sir."

"That appointment was on the recommendation of Colonel Trubshaw, Commanding Officer of the Rangers. Is that correct?"

"Yes Sir."

"Now Lieutenant, are you familiar with the accused in these proceedings?"

"Yes, sir. Jack Holden," he paused for a moment then began to speak again as he gestured toward the prisoner's box. "He's one of my best…"

"Just answer the questions Lieutenant," interrupted Mr. Pynch.

"Yes, Sir," said the Lieutenant, somewhat deflated. He looked at Jack as he said this.

"How did you become acquainted with the prisoner?"

"He was an enlisted man. He was assigned to the Rangers for duty."

"We're speaking of the Canadian Military Rangers, not the York Rangers?"

"That is right."

"What you are telling the Court is that he was placed under your direct command. Is that not so?"

"Yes, Sir, it is."

"Just as you are, were, under the direct command Colonel Trubshaw."

"He was C.O. of the Rangers, yes."

"Now at some point early in the year you received an order from the Colonel that is relevant to these proceedings, did you not?"

"I did sir."

"Will you give us the particulars of this order?"

Lieutenant Richards then proceeded to describe how he had reported to the office of his Commanding Officer and had been told that Baker Troop had been selected for special duty. He described the details of the order.

"I show you what purports to be a true copy of the written order to which you have just referred. Do you recognize it?"

The Lieutenant took the paper. He perused it for a moment.

"It is, Sir," he said. He handed the document back.

"May we mark this as an exhibit Your Honour?"

"Yes, Mr. Pynch."

"Exhibit twenty-three," said the clerk. He took the document, stamped it, then made a notation on it with his pen.

"Not to get too technical, or go into military jargon," he looked at the jury. "We are not military personnel like you…you were ordered to ride shotgun, so to speak, on a military munitions train headed for the west. Is that not correct?"

"That's right. We were to guard the train and especially the cargo of military stores. We had other orders effective upon our arrival…"

"We're not concerned with those at this trial," interrupted Mr. Pynch once again.

"Now in compliance with those orders you did proceed with Baker Troop, and with the defendant as a member of this Troop…you did proceed west with the special military train…as ordered. Did you not?"

"We did, Sir."

"That brings us to the day in question. Tell us in your own words what took place at the ambush of the supply train."

Lieutenant Richards did so. He began with Jack's trip to the stable car, his alleged encounter with an assailant, the fight across the roof top of the train and the halting of the train. He was in the process of describing the hail of fire that peppered the defending Troop when Mr. Pynch cut in once more with his questions.

"Can you describe for us – give an impression of the battle that took place at the train? The intensity is what we'd like to hear about."

"I don't know how I could describe it better, sir. It was a hail of gun fire. It seemed to pour down on us from all along the tree line. We were pinned down. No question about it."

"And so you decided to take some step to obtain relief, is that is?"

"Partly, sir."

"What do you mean, partly?"

"I figured we needed some help – a diversion – in order to break out of the murderous position in which we found ourselves."

"Yes, go on."

"Well, that's the reason – one of the reasons for my order to Jack."

"We're waiting, Lieutenant. You said 'partly'. We presume there was another reason for the order."

"Well yes. The other reason is that the line … the railway line … was out with the blast. I knew the scheduled train would arrive soon. It had to be stopped too."

"I see. And so just what step did you decide to take in order to deal with these two problems?"

"I knew that we were not far from a small way stop … coal and so on … you know … for the steam locomotive. There's a detachment of North West Mounted Police there. There's also a telegraph there." The Lieutenant paused for a moment.

"Yes, Lieutenant, please go on. We're most interested."

"The way I figured, I could send a man over, send a message east to warn the stationmaster to stop the next train and have the same man bring back what help he could for a small diversionary attack and relieve our situation."

"I see. And for this purpose you chose to send …"

"Private, I mean Lieutenant Holden."

"Well Private would be satisfactory. He was a Private at that time was he not?"

"Yes, Sir."

"Now then you chose to send Private Holden. And did you communicate this order to him?"

"It wasn't an order Your Honour," said Lieutenant Richards, "It was a request."

"I beg your pardon," said the judge. He appeared startled to be addressed directly by the witness.

"It was not an order," repeated the Lieutenant. "I asked Jack…Private…uh… Holden to go for help and send a message. He agreed to go. It was unnecessary to order him to do anything…he was always willing…"

"Never mind making any speeches," said Mr. Pynch. "I'm sure Mr. Tuttle can do that for his client himself.

"So it was not necessary to make an order. That's very interesting indeed.

"I gather therefore that he was quite willing, to use your word, to leave immediately from the scene of the fighting, was he?"

The Lieutenant could see immediately, that he had made matters worse, not better, for Jack. His mouth worked. He was bobbing and weaving in the witness stand, when Mr. Pynch spoke once again.

"Never mind. You've already answered that question.

"Now the instructions, if I may call them that," Mr. Pynch looked up at the Lieutenant from the papers he had been sorting at the counsel table, "were for your messenger to immediately deliver his messages, and return with help, again immediately. Is that not correct, Lieutenant Richards?"

The Lieutenant's face turned red, suffused with blood at his frustration in dealing with Mr. Pynch.

"Well not…uh…ah…"

"Return <u>immediately</u>, was that not your instruction." He said this in very loud measured words.

"Yes," said Lieutenant Richards. He hung his head and looked at the floor.

"Did you see him immediately after his errand?"

"No."

"Two hours after?"

"No."

Three?"

"No."

"Three days after?"

"No."

"When did you next see Private Holden?"

"At the battle of Fish Creek," answered the Lieutenant in a very quiet voice.

"Speak up, sir," said Mr. Pynch aggressively, "let His Honour and the jury hear your answer."

"At the skirmish at Fish Creek," said the Lieutenant. He had raised his head and spoke in a loud voice. He did not look at Jack. Neither did he look at the jury. He merely glared at Mr. Pynch.

"Your witness," said Mr. Pynch to Mr. Tuttle, as he sat down triumphantly.

"If it pleases your Honour," said Mr. Tuttle, "It is nearly five thirty. The jury and Your Honour have had a hard day. I wonder whether we might now adjourn and resume tomorrow at ten."

"I think that is a sensible suggestion, Mr. Tuttle," said Mr. Justice Richardson. "This court stands adjourned until Tuesday morning at ten." He brought his gavel down, promptly rose and left the courtroom.

Mr. Tuttle stood there as pleased with himself as if he had just won the case. It was the first time he had made an oration in court and he had succeeded without any difficulty whatsoever. He could feel his confidence. Slyly he looked over at Jack and Sarah. He wondered if it showed.

CHAPTER EIGHTY

THAT EVENING Harry paid a visit to Jack. He had some news. When he arrived at the police barracks he found Sandy already there. They walked down to the cell together.

Harry was glad that Mr. Tuttle had not yet arrived, the news he had for Jack was not the kind he wanted the lawyer to hear.

"You know I have not been very pleased at the way your lawyer has been handling your case?" started Harry.

"Yes I know, but …" said Jack.

"I took the trouble to telegraph back east. I wanted to know a little bit about your eminent counsel."

"What did you learn?" asked Sandy. Jack simply looked at Harry and waited for the news. Something about Harry's manner told Jack the news would not be pleasant.

"Well, that he's not."

Sandy and Jack looked at him nonplussed. They did not understand.

"Well he is and he isn't. You know how he holds himself out as a Barrister and Solicitor?"

"Yes," chorused Sandy and Jack.

"You know that a barrister is a lawyer who pleads cases in court?"

They nodded.

"And a solicitor is one who prepared such cases occasionally, but primarily occupies himself with estates, wills, deeds and such like?"

They nodded again.

"Well, guess which our eminent counsel is?" Harry grinned wryly at his two companions.

Jack shook his head.

"Damn his eyes," swore Sandy.

"He is actually qualified as a barrister I'm told, but he's never practised in the courts since his admission to the bar. What do you think of that?" he concluded.

"More important. What should Jack do now?" asked Sandy. But Harry never gave an opinion in answer to that question. At that moment Mr. Tuttle's voice could be heard in the hallway.

These four conferred in Jack's small cell. None of them could stay for long. Mr. Tuttle wondered aloud about the rest of the Crown's case. Who would be the next witness?"

"I think I know something about that," said Sandy. "Pynch has tried to persuade everyone in Baker to give corroborating evidence. Everyone refused…"

"Good," said Mr. Tuttle.

"…Except two," finished Sandy.

"Who?" said Jack.

"Duffy Durell and Yank Smith," replied Sandy.

"How could the others refuse?" said Harry.

"I don't know, they just did," said Sandy.

"But they could have been subpoenaed," persisted Harry.

"I guess Mr. Pynch did not want to have that many uncooperative witnesses on his hands," said Mr. Tuttle.

For once, thought Jack, I hear a sensible assessment from my lawyer.

Just before the visitors left, Harry turned to have one more word with Jack.

"I didn't get a chance to tell you. I've already sent two stories about 'Canada Jack' to the Globe. Both have been accepted.

"So have I."

"Congratulations," said Jack.

"I'm now official Globe correspondent. One day it will be the greatest newspaper in Canada. I know it. Maybe our first national paper."

"I'm really pleased for you, Harry. But will they still want your stories about 'Canada Jack' if I'm convicted?"

Harry never answered the question. He knew that in the event Canada Jack were sentenced to be hanged the stories would arouse even more interest. But he did not have the heart to tell his friend.

CHAPTER EIGHTY-ONE

COURT RESUMED promptly at ten Tuesday morning. Mr. Tuttle began his cross examination of Lieutenant Richards.

"Now Lieutenant Richards, yesterday afternoon you gave evidence that you did not give Lieutenant Holden orders."

"That is right sir."

"It was necessary only to make a request of him."

"Yes."

"Why is that?"

"Two reasons Sir."

"Tell us about them."

"Well to begin with, one of the first things you learn at R.M.C...."

"R.M.C.?"

"Royal Military College, at Kingston."

"I see."

"One of the first things that is taught to an ensign is never to order anyone to do anything when a request will suffice."

"I don't believe the jury and I quite understand. Could you explain?"

"Let me put it this way, it's a question of leadership. A good leader does not need to give orders. You are considered a failure as an officer if you need to give orders to get things done."

"I don't see how..." began Mr. Pynch rising to his feet.

"The relevancy will become clear in a moment if Your Honour will allow..." Mr. Tuttle's voice trailed off.

"Please Mr. Pynch, exercise patience," said the judge. "We'll make more progress, faster, that way I'm sure."

"Of course Your Honour," said Mr. Pynch with feigned generosity.

"Thank you, Your Honour." Now Mr. Tuttle felt himself hitting his stride.

"You were saying there were two reasons...what was the second reason?" asked Mr. Tuttle.

"The second reason was Jack...uh, I mean...Private Holden, as he then was."

"Yes, go on."

"Well, he was the kind of enlisted man who was always more than willing..."

"I object Your Honour," said Mr. Pynch, jumping to his feet.

"That is character evidence. There is a proper way to introduce character evidence. I'm sure my learned friend knows that."

"What have you to say, Mr. Tuttle?"

"My learned friend introduced a great deal of character evidence, Your Honour."

"Referring to...?" said the judge.

"I'm referring to the evidence of character introduced through the I.T.R.'s at both staff and Regimental level. Opinion evidence of the most condemnatory nature, impugning the veracity of my client and implying other grave deficiencies of character, was allowed.

"I must say Your Honour that my client disputes the truth of this evidence. I now seek to repudiate these insinuations and erroneous conclusions and statement of fact through the testimony of this and another officer.

"Mr. Pynch," said the judge, with a question mark in his voice.

"It has always been my view of the law that the accused is entitled to lead evidence of a witness who testifies to the general reputation of the accused in the community. That is not what he intends to do now."

"But Your Honour," protested Tuttle, "all kinds of such evidence was introduced by Counsel for the Crown."

"He's referring to the reports from Colonel Trubshaw and the General himself, Your Honour. He himself consented to the admission of them as evidence."

A look of dismay crossed the face of Mr. Tuttle, as he realized the treachery of Mr. Pynch.

"I am afraid that reflects my view of the law as well, Mr. Tuttle," said the Judge.

Mr. Pynch gazed past the back of Mr. Tuttle directly into Jack's face. He grinned a malevolent grin.

"Would I not be allowed then, Your Honour, to cross examine this witness as to the general reputation for valour Lieutenant Holden holds amongst his comrades?"

Mr. Pynch was on his feet again. Once again he protested most strenuously.

"Your Honour," he said. "I feel sure it would be most helpful to the case that my learned friend wishes to make. One can be sympathetic with him." Mr. Pynch put his right hand at the back of his right hip, elbow extended, "but at the same time one must be faithful to the law, practise and custom.

"What he is proposing now, it is my submission, would be a most unfortunate development in the latter; practise and custom.

"It is my submission that it would be highly inappropriate to allow an officer of junior rank to call into question the judgment of superior officers. Not only superior officers, but his superiors generally."

"Do you have any case law to support your contention, Mr. Pynch?"

"Indeed, I do Your Honour. May I cite the United States of America v. Smythe, a case arising out of the recent troubles south of the border. It's on all fours, Your Honour."

"Do you have it here?"

"I do Your Honour."

"May I see it?" asked the judge.

Mr. Pynch passed his law book to the clerk, who passed it up to the judge.

"Are you familiar with this case Mr. Tuttle?" asked the judge.

"No, Your Honour, I'm afraid not. What jurisdiction, Your Honour?"

"United States District Court," answered the judge. "State of Connecticut."

"I have other cases I could cite, Your Honour. All of them agree with the position I have adopted."

The judge waved aside another law book proffered by the clerk. The jury looked at Mr. Tuttle with stoney faces. Mr. Pynch strutted. Now he had both hands propped on his haunches. He gazed about the courtroom, a smug look on his face.

Mr. Tuttle, by now, had descended so deeply into a state of panic that he was nearly catatonic. He felt someone pull at his sleeve. It was Harry. Harry whispered frantically into his ear. A look of relief swept over Mr. Tuttle.

"If I may make a suggestion, Your Honour – " said Mr. Tuttle.

The judge looked up from his reading. He was clearly annoyed.

"Instead of imposing upon Your Honour to canvas the law in open court I would propose standing this witness aside at the present time. He could be recalled by the defense at a later time.

"That would afford Your Honour time to refresh your memory in this area of law. It would also offer me an opportunity to review the cases and make my own submission for the consideration of the court.

"A splendid idea," said the judge, "simply splendid."

The nausea that had been mounting in Mr. Tuttle subsided. Once more he was pleased with himself.

At the moment it did not occur to him that he had only deferred the problem, not solved it. Neither did it occur to him that he had only the most tenuous grasp of what had taken place.

Neither did Jack have a handle on what had just transpired. He knew for certain, however, that part of his problem resulted from the rank of Lieutenant Richards.

Thank God for Colonel Williams, he thought. I have at least one defense witness who does not lack rank.

But he had no more time to ponder the problem. Mr. Pynch bore down relentlessly.

"At this time the prosecution should like to call to the stand one Donald "Yank" Smith," said Mr. Pynch.

"Donald Smith," called the clerk looking around the courtroom.

Jack watched Yank move through the rows of spectators, come through the gate and take the stand. In short order he was sworn and led through his testimony. The gist of it was his description of the night of the ambush, hell fire raining down and Jack's swift departure. When the Crown Prosecutor had finished, Mr. Tuttle got to his feet.

"You did not know, of course, that the defendant had been told to make all haste by Lieutenant Richards, did you?"

"No, I did not."

"It would not be unusual therefore, if such had been the request, for the defendant to 'go like hell', as you so colorfully put it."

"No, I suppose not," allowed Yank Smith amidst general laughter throughout the courtroom.

"Thank you witness, that is all." Mr. Tuttle again took his seat.

"The next witness for the prosecution will be Duffy Durell," announced Mr. Pynch.

"Private Durell," said Mr. Pynch after the witness had been sworn, "you are a member of Baker Troop and have been since before the outbreak of hostilities on the plains, is that not correct?"

"That is correct, sir. I joined the military last year, in the fall."

"I take it then, Private Durell, that you were a member of the Canadian Military Rangers when that unit was formed back in … back east?"

"Correct again, Sir."

Jack watched his short slim comrade as he delivered his testimony. He was led through training and embarkation by train for the west. As he described the ambush he looked confident, even aggressive. Something nagged at Jack as he listened. It was as though something were missing.

"…and so you were present," Mr. Pinch was saying. "You saw what took place when the fighting got heavy at the train?"

"That I did. I saw it all."

"Please tell us about it," said Mr. Pynch.

"The bullets were flying, I can tell you. We were pinned down by fire. Unable to move."

"The Lieutenant, Mr. Richards, he had Jack…Mr. Holden…excuse me…"

"That's all right…please go on."

"He had Lieutenant Holden go for help."

"And what happened then?"

"Why he took off, hell for leather, like I knew he would."

"Why do you say that?"

"What...sir?"

"Like you knew he would. Why did you add that?"

"Because I mean sir, I knew he would."

"That's what I am asking," said Mr. Pynch with just a hint of impatience. "What gave you that idea?"

"Because I seen Jack...uh...before, I was not seven feet away from him."

"When, precisely, was that Private Durell?"

"Just ten...seven...about...minutes before the Lieutenant called him over."

"Yes, go on."

"Sir?"

"Go on. What did you see? Describe to us what you saw."

The small wiry body squirmed now, as if reluctant to answer. Finally he blurted out a reply.

"He was white as a ghost Your Honour," said Durell. "There was beads of sweat and fright in his eyes...and ..."

"It's not true," said Jack in an audible whisper to his lawyer. "Not true at all," he repeated. This time he was loud enough for the judge and jury to hear him.

"Mr. Tuttle, please restrain your client. His turn will come." Mr. Tuttle had come over and put his hand on Jack's arm.

Then Mr. Pynch spoke again.

"That would be now, Your Honour," he said with satisfaction. "Your witness Mr. Tuttle."

Thereupon Mr. Tuttle launched into a brief ineffectual cross examination. His questions passed aimlessly from one subject to another. If anything they simply provided an opportunity for Durell to repeat his evidence in chief.

Suddenly, Mr. Tuttle concluded his questioning and sat down. Mr. Pynch stood up. He looked about the courtroom briefly before he began to speak. Jack could hear the relentless ticking of the big clock hanging on the wall opposite the jury box. He was aware that Mr. Pynch was once again preening but had not heard what he was saying until the very last sentence.

"That concludes the evidence for the prosecution, Your Honour."

"Thank you Mr. Pynch."

Jack was stunned. The hour had come upon them so soon, too soon. Where was Colonel Williams?

"Mr. Tuttle?" said the Judge, inviting Mr. Tuttle to take the floor.

Mr. Tuttle rose ever so slowly. He too was stunned by the abrupt end to the case for the Crown.

"Your Honour," he almost stammered. "The defense will be calling two witnesses. One of these is Lieutenant Colonel Arthur T.H. Williams..."

"Of the Midland Battalion?" asked Mr. Justice Richardson.

"Why, yes, Your Honour."

"Willie will be here? Why that's splendid. I know him well. We're old friends. He and I were fellow officers you know. I hold my Lieutenant Colonelcy too, you know."

"I have the highest regard for Willie...u...ah...perhaps...in the circumstances... Lieutenant Colonel Williams."

"We have been trying to establish contact with the Colonel for some time now. Recently we received word that his Battalion is in the Fort Battleford area."

"Two days ago I sent a message by telegraph to let the Colonel know that the trial was expected to commence shortly and requested that he confirm that he will attend to give evidence for the defense."

"Regrettably, Your Honour, we have not as yet had a reply, but we expect such confirmation at any time."

"Willie," mused the judge. "It will be good to see Willie again." Then he brought his attention back to matters at hand. "I expect that in the circumstances we can commence with your second witness."

"Yes, of course, Your Honour. I wonder whether, in view of the time, we might begin the case for the defense this afternoon?"

The judge glanced to his left. The clock read twelve fifteen.

"I think we could do that."

"If Colonel Williams should arrive in the meantime, I wonder if you would be so kind as to ask him to stop around to my chambers, Mr. Tuttle."

"I most certainly will," beamed Mr. Tuttle.

"Fine," said the Judge. "Adjourn court."

The clerk jumped to his feet.

"This court stands adjourned until two o'clock this afternoon." The judge had already left the room.

When Jack, Harry and Mr. Tuttle reached the anteroom, the lawyer could not contain his exultation.

"Did you hear that?" he asked. "Willie. He knows him well. Fellow officer."

"I knew things would work out for the best." This statement was made to Jack, but it was made for the benefit of Harry. Mr. Tuttle turned slowly to glare at the latter.

Harry merely picked up his hat and walked to the door.

"I hope you're not celebrating too soon," he said as he walked out. Mr. Tuttle, however, had not heard him. Once again, he was chattering about 'Willie', 'friends', and 'fellow officers'. He was fairly prancing about the tiny room.

CHAPTER EIGHTY-TWO

COURT RESUMED precisely at two o'clock.

"The defense calls the accused, Lieutenant Jack Holden, to the stand," stated Mr. Tuttle in a confident tone of voice.

After he had been sworn, Jack took his seat in the witness box. Thereupon Mr. Tuttle led Jack through the events of the last year of his life. It seemed more like a lifetime to Jack. He repeated his denial of desertion. He described his abduction and all of the extraordinary things that had happened since.

It took an hour but it seemed that in no time at all he had told his story and Mr. Tuttle was saying: "Your witness, Mr. Pynch."

Mr. Pynch rose from the table provided for Crown Counsel. He paced briefly, looked down at his notes, then looked up at Jack, grinned wickedly, put his hands on his hips and began to cross examine Jack.

"So it is not true that you deserted your comrades under fire."

"It is not true," answered Jack. "I was asked to go, to summon help."

"We know that," snapped Mr. Pynch peevishly. "But you did not return, did you?"

"But I did return," shot back Jack.

"Yes, but not before the gunfire had ended and you had enjoyed one fine long vacation, isn't that so?"

"It is not so. What I said today in this courtroom is the truth, under my oath."

"Your oath, indeed," said Mr. Pynch, his voice dripping with sarcasm.

"You would have us believe that promptly you took off by pony down the railway line you were taken into custody – kidnapped?"

"Not promptly, no. I said some miles down the track."

"And yet you left the area where the outlaws were pouring gunfire?"

"That's right. Under orders, so to speak."

"Would you have us accept that there was, in fact, a second gang. That they just popped up there out of convenience."

"I never said that, no. And I believe they were part of the same gang, as I've told you."

"Yes, under the command of a Mr. Beesly."

"No, not Beesly."

"Beetle Beesly was it not?" asked Mr. Pynch looking down at his notes.

"No," said Jack again, patiently, "Beetle Benson." He realized that Mr. Pynch knew perfectly well what the name was.

"And he was the same person – so you claim – as the individual wearing the trilby hat committing murder back in Cobourg."

Jack was not going to allow himself to become lazy or sloppy with his answers.

"He was the same individual, but he did not wear a trilby. It was a derby."

"Ah, yes," said Mr. Pynch. He chuckled quietly as if being told something quite amusing. "A brown one if I recollect."

Jack did not respond to this statement.

"Now as I understand your testimony, you were with this gang for weeks?"

"That's right."

"And putting aside the last day you were with them… May we do that Lieutenant?" he asked with mock respect.

Jack merely nodded in the affirmative. Pynch now paused.

"Putting that aside, you did not make one single solitary attempt to escape. Is that not so!"

"I…I…"

"Please answer the question – it really is quite simple." He repeated it. "Not one single solitary attempt to escape. Is that not correct?"

Mr. Pynch was no longer looking at Jack. He was looking at the members of the jury.

"There was no opportunity," Jack answered, somewhat lamely.

"No opportunity?" Mr. Pynch echoed with incredulity. "No opportunity?"

"My hands were tied to my saddle horn most of the time." asserted Jack.

"But your horse….what do you call her?"

"Cloud."

"Yes, Cloud. She was under the saddle, was she not?"

"Yes."

"Her legs were not hobbled."

"At night they were."

"Always?"

"Not always, no."

"Only occasionally," suggested Mr. Pynch.

"Most of the time," retorted Jack.

"Ah, but not all of the time. That is the point. Not all of the time. We've got it right now haven't we?"

"I think so yes."

"Thank you," said Mr. Pynch. "So tell me why, even though your hands were bound to your saddle, why did you not simply ride off?"

"I think the answer to that is quite obvious," answered Jack.

"Well then, answer it," said Mr. Pynch.

"Because if I had tried to do so I would have got a bullet in the back," said Jack angrily.

"But you did eventually ride off, did you not?"

"Yes, that's true."

"Do you have a bullet in your back now?"

"No."

"Oh! Did you have it removed?"

"No. I've never had a bullet in my back."

"Oh, I see, so you rode off and yet never got a bullet in your back."

At this point Mr. Pynch paused to allow his last statement to imprint itself on the consciousness of the jurymen. Then he quickly turned to another subject.

"Now we've heard a great deal about some great sojourn with the Indians."

Jack remained silent.

"I think we must have some latter day James Fenimore Cooper on our hands."

The jury laughed at this remark. Jack was not sure what it meant, but guessed that it was not a good sign.

"Anyway, to get on with this story…"

"It was not a …is not a story…" started Jack.

But Mr. Tuttle, miraculously, was on his feet objecting.

"My learned friend has used that expression to suggest that my client has told the jury and Your Honour a fairy tale, which is not true, Your Honour. I think he might at least use a more neutral word than 'story'."

"You're quite right, Mr. Tuttle."

"Please, Mr. Pynch, when asking your questions do not imply that the witness himself has used the expression 'story'."

"I did not think I had done that Your Honour, but I will try to be more careful in future."

"Thank you Mr. Pynch."

Two thoughts flashed through Jack's mind. First, that his lawyer had finally come to life. Second, that even from defeat Mr. Pynch pulled a small victory. He had the Judge thanking him.

"Anyway, as I was saying before that unfortunate interruption by my learned friend, according to your version of events, you were so fortunate as to rescue an Indian Princess from the hands of…"

"Your Honour," protested Jack to the judge. "I did not say Princess. She turned out…I later learned that she was the daughter of Black Bear."

The judge said nothing so Mr. Pynch rolled on.

"Yes, Black Bear. And you later saved the life of a little chief by pulling him from beneath the hooves of a stampeding heard of buffalo…"

This time Mr. Tuttle was on his feet objecting simultaneously with Jack's protest to the judge that he had never stated that Travelling Spirit was a little chief.

Mr. Justice Richardson threw down his pen impatiently.

242

"I think tempers are growing short. It's time for an afternoon recess. Clerk!"

The clerk rose and adjourned court for twenty minutes. Twenty minutes that would shake the defense to its very roots.

CHAPTER EIGHTY-THREE

AS SOON as Jack walked into the anteroom he knew something was wrong. He saw Harry standing there with a grim look on his face.

"What's wrong Harry?" asked Jack. At that moment Mr. Tuttle came into the little room.

"I'm afraid I may have some bad news."

"What's the matter?" repeated the lawyer.

"The name you mentioned was Williams, was it not?"

"Colonel Williams, yes," said Jack.

"To be precise," said Harry, raising a newspaper that he held in his hands to read a line, "Lieutenant Arthur T.H. Williams, Commanding Officer of the Midland Battalion."

"Yes," said Jack. "Why what's the matter, has…has…?"

"He's dead," said Harry. He threw the newspaper he had been reading down in front of Jack.

"Dead?" said Jack. "How could that be, was he killed? He was so young. He couldn't just die…I won't…"

"Read it for yourself," said Harry. "I just dropped by my hotel room on my way back after dinner. I found this newspaper. It must have been mailed before they knew I had resigned."

Jack spread the newspaper out before him and began to read:

DAILY BRITISH WHIG

LATE COL. WILLIAMS

His Illness and Death – His Presentment of the End of Life –
Battleford Funeral.

The Mail.

Pool Williams first felt the sickness which resulted in his death on Sunday, June 28, while at church parade. "It is only a slight attack of sunstroke," he said; "I shall be all right in a couple of days." But as the days passed he did improve. He came down to the press quarters on the North-West and with a kindly smile remarked to a journalist, "Well, it would be hard lines if I should be bowled over now, after passing unhurt through the whole campaign." On Wednesday morning he was not so well. He was nervous, and some trifling matters seemed to annoy him. Everything that could be done for him was done, but next morning he was unconscious, and in that state he lay until his soul passed away. He died without suffering or pain. The cause of his death was typhoid fever and inflammation of the brain. The fever was contracted from the damp ground on which he had been camping at Pitt. He was desirous of changing his quarters, but presuming that a homeward move would be made without delay remained, and died. When the ill-tidings became known – and how quickly bad news does spread – all the steamers, in Indian file down stream, hoisted their colours at half-mast. At night a graceful and deserved tribute to the lamented dead appeared in orders, which you have already received by wire.

HIS LAST DAYS.

Looking back at events, I am half inclined to think that this gallant gentleman had a foreshadowing of his end. He was as cheery as usual up to the hour he took to bed, but the disease has evidently been hanging on him for some time. On the last occasion that he and I had a long chat, some nine days ago, he was wondering what they were doing at Ottawa and whether the "boys" would all get back to their old employments on their return. A French-Canadian happened to be humming a tune near us. Williams asked him what he was singing, and the man said a French translation of Whittier's Hymn on the Red River. Williams said he had not heard that for years. I recited the well known words, beginning:

> Out and in the river is winding
> The links of its long red chain,
> Through belts of dusky pine-land
> And gusty leagues of plain.

When I reached the last two verses, he asked me to repeat them; so that he might learn them. I did so, and for hours afterwards (it was a bright moon-lit night, and we were sitting on the river bank) he kept slowly saying, as if in a reverie:

> And when the Angel of Shadow
> Rests his feet on wave and shore
> And our eyes grow dim with watching,
> And our hearts faint at the oar,
> Happy is he who heareth
> The signal of His release
> In the bells of the Holy City.
> The chimes of Eternal Peace.

At this time he said he felt a "weary feeling", and he was suffering from cold and headache; but I little thought the signal was so near. I am speaking by authority when I say that the officers and men entertained the very highest opinion of Col. Williams as a soldier. It was not merely the splendid dash and courage he displayed in leading the charge far ahead of all others at Batoche but his respect for and unfaltering obedience to orders, his unselfishness, his bright and cheery disposition, his gentleness, and above all, his chivalrous and old-fashioned idea of honor. The men – I don't mean the Midlanders, but the other corps – used to call Williams the "boss officer." They all loved him.

THE FUNERAL AT BATTLEFORD.

On July 5th, bright and early Battleford was reached. By ten o'clock the arrangements for the funeral of Col. Williams were completed, and shortly afterwards the cortege set out on its way. The Midland Battalion led and was followed by the 90th band. Then came the corpse, wrapped in a Union Jack and carried on a gun carriage, behind which was led the Colonel's saddled horse. The pall-bearers were Lt.-Cols. Mackeand, Otter, Grassett, Straubenzie, Montizambert, Ouimet, and Gens. Strange and Middleton. One company of the Winnipeg Light Infantry marched in advance of the 90th Battalion, behind them the Grenadiers, and for part of the way the 65th. Arrived at the fort the Midland were drawn up in …

Jack folded the newspaper. He could read no more. He covered his face with his hands. He was overcome with grief.

Harry looked at his friend with pity. Then he glared at Mr. Tuttle. His voice was hard.

"The hell of it is, he's been dead for days now. We should have known about this long ago…so we could plan…"

Jack put up a hand slightly.

"No Harry let's not get into blame. That can't help me now."

"Nothing can."

CHAPTER EIGHTY-FOUR

COURT RECONVENED. Jack once again was back in the dock. Voices swirled about him. He finished his own evidence hardly conscious of his answers. Vaguely he heard his lawyer waive recall of Lieutenant Richards. He was aware of Counsel making closing arguments but heard not a word.

He had seen a capital trial; he knew what was inevitably to follow. He had lost all hope.

It was late in the afternoon now. Mr. Justice Richardson was working toward his final words to the jury. Jack could sense the eyes of his friends, Sarah, all his comrades in Baker Troop, even Mr. Tuttle watching in despair as the case wound down to the fateful last words he had heard uttered to his friend Louis Riel.

Suddenly he heard a door slam open at the very end of the courtroom. Voices rose in excited whispers. Harry was raising his voice at Mr. Tuttle.

Jack had felt himself floating down, as though drowning in a deep lake. Now he stopped. Slowly his consciousness began to fight for the surface. He became aware that he could make out words once again. Miraculously he could make sense out of the words.

Mr. Tuttle was on his feet putting forth an eloquent plea for the case to be reopened. They had a new witness.

Could he have been mistaken, thought Jack. Was Colonel Williams not dead after all.

He looked over to Mr. Tuttle. Standing next to him was a man. The man looked vaguely familiar.

Mr. Pynch was now on his feet. He was pleading vigorously with the judge.

"…It cannot be done Your Honour. The Crown has closed its case. The defense, too, has closed its case. Your Honour has almost concluded your charge to the jury."

"It is my earnest submission, Your Honour, that this cannot be done."

The judge hesitated a moment.

Mr. Pynch plunged on with his clincher.

"It cannot be done, Your Honour. There is no precedent in law for such a procedure."

"No precedent you say?" exclaimed the judge.

"No, Your Honour. There is simply no precedent, at this stage of the proceedings, the defendant to reopen his case to call further evidence."

"Well, in that case, Mr. Pynch, it is about time that I made one. The defendant's application to reopen…"

His ruling was interrupted by loud enthusiastic applause.

"Order, order," said the clerk. The judge banged his gavel. The noise slowly began to subside.

"This is simply not done," said the judge. "I mean the applause. If you feel it necessary to demonstrate it will have to be outside the precincts of justice."

"Now where was I?"

"Application to reopen," prompted Mr. Tuttle.

"Oh yes. The defendant's application to reopen his case and call further evidence is allowed.

"Mr. Tuttle, proceed.."

"Thank you Your Honour," said Mr. Tuttle. Now finally, he was in command and he knew it.

"The defense calls David Ormsby Pratt to the witness stand."

The stranger standing by Mr. Tuttle's side took the stand. But he was no longer a stranger. Jack now remembered him. The 'remittance man' from Benson's Gang!

Events now moved at a relentless pace. Mr. Pratt was sworn. He testified to his birthright, such as it was, how he came to be in North America and how he had fallen into Beetle Benson's grip, just as Jack had done. Then he described Jack's capture and explained why he had been held.

Suddenly Jack was aware he was hearing facts he had never known about the gang and he was stunned all over again.

"What was the purpose of the gang," asked Mr. Tuttle.

"To seize and convey arms and ammunition to the rebels and their allies the Indians."

"When you say seize…"

"When I say seize I mean take – from whatever source and by whatever means. They were importing guns through a hardware and ammunition shop in Cobourg … And in other towns in Upper … in Ontario as well. Shipping them west crated as farm implements."

"That was the purpose of the ambush: to seize the arms in that munitions car."

"They may have succeeded too if their little helper had done his job."

"They had a man, a spy aboard that train?"

"Yes they did. He was supposed to uncouple the munitions car, but he failed. I think he may have been interrupted by our friend here." He nodded his head toward Jack.

Slowly Jack turned his head to look at Baker Troop.

"I am told he did a great deal more damage too."

"Objection," shouted Mr. Pynch. "This is irrelevant to these proceedings."

"Objection overruled," said the Judge without explanation.

"Please tell us how you know that?"

"Well Mr. Benson, when he failed to seize the train cargo and knew he could supply no more weapons to the rebels, sent a messenger north to advise the rebels and our little helper. Benson's messenger made contact with both. I know because he told me. Benson's messenger I mean. Trouble is, Riel became so furious he locked him up."

"The army released Riel's prisoners. The messenger was amongst them. He immediately ran for it."

"He came to find Benson, but Benson's dead. They're all dead. Those Jack didn't dispose of, I killed."

"Anyway he came to the rendezvous and found only me."

"That's how I learned Jack was in trouble. He saw Jack and recognized him immediately. Saw him arrested for desertion."

"I knew that was as phony a case as I've ever heard of."

"I just had to come and save Jack from the gallows. Jack'll know why." He turned and smiled at Jack. Jack could hardly believe his good fortune. He smiled broadly back at Pratt.

"I asked you before why…" began Mr. Tuttle.

"I just told you."

"I know. I mean why, why was Benson doing this? Money?"

"You mean the raison d'être of his little gang of outlaws."

"Yes exactly."

"Manifest Destiny."

"I beg your pardon."

"Manifest Destiny. Haven't you heard of it??"

"I think I have…" began Mr. Tuttle, but Mr. Pratt was not waiting.

"A fringe element across the border. Believe it's the manifest destiny of the United States to occupy the whole of the continent."

"Lunatics, all of them," he said dismissing them.

"But how? Mr. Benson…"

"Not Mr. Benson." corrected Mr. Pratt.

"I beg your pardon?"

"Not Mr. Benson. Captain Benson of the 7th United States Cavalry."

"The American Army operating in the Canadian North West?"

"Not exactly. Some of them were in the U.S. Army all right. Not all. And they were not acting under official orders."

"I don't understand," said the judge.

Mr. Pratt turned to the bench and patiently explained to the judge.

"They were a cell of the Manifest Destiny Committee that had infested the United States Army, Your Honour."

"I know the Army knew nothing about it. Mr. Benson told me that himself."

"They took their orders directly from the Manifest Destiny Committee in New York. Just a small renegade cell in the U.S. Cavalry. Like an infection, Your Honour."

The judge sat back, satisfied with the explanation.

"That would explain the code word 'bluecoat' wouldn't it?" asked Mr. Tuttle.

"That's exactly right," he replied. "'Bluecoat': U.S. Army colours."

"And can you tell us, witness, who this bluecoat is?"

Jack could feel the small hairs on the back of his neck bristle. He fought the temptation to turn around.

"Of course I can."

"And how is it that you are able to make such an identification?"

"Well for one, I'd heard him described so often I could pick him out of a fifty man line-up."

"You said 'for one'. Is there, per chance, another means upon which you rely?"

"There sure is."

"What is that, if you please?"

"He doesn't know it, but I saw him about a year ago in Montana Territory. He didn't see me but I sure saw him. He had a meeting with Mr. Benson and his military cell."

"I heard Mr. Benson instruct him to join the Canadian militia. A unit destined for western service."

Jack could hear a stir in the courtroom behind the prisoner's box.

"And did he..." started Mr. Tuttle.

"He did just as instructed, obviously. He's sitting in a Ranger uniform, just behind Jack."

"Ain't you Duffy Durell?" shouted Mr. Pratt, lapsing for a moment into western slang.

Simultaneously Durell jumped to his feet. He had a revolver in his right hand.

"Don't anybody move," he shouted, "or I shoot the judge."

Startled, the judge rose. A shot rang out and shattered the picture of Prince Albert to the left side of his head.

"Down, Judge," shouted Jack. The jurist dropped from view as Jack rolled to his left over the back of the box. He landed, then shot straight back and up. His head hit Duffy Durrell's chin just as Durell reached out to snatch Sarah for a hostage.

But his hand never reached her. The two men rocketed backwards into the spectators. Chairs scraped. People screamed and shouted.

Another shot rang out. This time it aimlessly hit a ceiling lamp. Shards of shattered glass rained down on the spectators.

The two men rolled on the floor. Chairs fell over, more screaming. Locked in this deadly struggle Jack was nevertheless aware of the absurd sound of the judge's gavel banging time and again on the bench.

Suddenly Durell's gun flew across the floor hitting chair legs as it went. Now Durell was on his feet. Somehow he had broken free. He was virtually vaulting across people and chairs, headed for the exit at the rear.

Jack charged after him like an enraged bull. People fell like tenpins.

Durell had cleared the last row of chairs. Not more than twenty feet stood between him and freedom. At that moment Jack hit him in the back, with the force of a locomotive and he lurched forward crashing to the floor.

Durell was agile and quickly rolled to his feet. Just in time for his jaw to intercept the full blunt force of Jack's large fist as it hurtled almost from the floor and headed for the ceiling. The blow lifted Durell off his heels and threw him once again to his back. He did not stop sliding until his head hit the wall at the back of the room.

CHAPTER EIGHTY-FIVE

TWO WEEKS had passed since the trial. It was noon and Jack was in the corral at militia headquarters saddling up Cloud.

It had been the most joyous two weeks in his life.

The morning following that night when Duffy Durell had been taken into custody, court had been called back into session. Lieutenant Richards had at last been recalled. He testified at length as to Jack's integrity. He described Jack's valour that flaming night at Fish Creek. Major Smith had appeared while the trial was still in progress. As soon as he had gone through Colonel Williams' personal papers he had noticed the correspondence about the impending trial. He remembered Colonel Williams had spoken of his pledge to Jack to testify at the trial. The major insisted on giving evidence. He described the Colonel's high opinion of Jack's integrity and valour. He described how Jack had led the charge at Batoche. He stated it was the firm view of the Colonel that it was that personal act of valour on the part of Lieutenant Holden that was decisive in the battle.

He added that being the senior battalion officer present, now living, it was his view as well. Finally, he read aloud the laudatory remarks in Jack's Individual Training Record of the Midland Battalion.

Throughout all of this, Mr. Pynch sat silently. He did not cross examine. He uttered not a word. He was thoroughly crushed.

The Major concluded his testimony. Without preamble the judge turned to the jury.

"Gentlemen of the jury, you have just heard character evidence without equal in English jurisprudence. Moreover you have personally been witness to the most heroic act ever displayed by any prisoner at any time anywhere on this earth.

"Notwithstanding all of this, Young Jack here has been vilified and abused beyond that which any young man should be compelled to endure.

"It is time to set matters right. Right for a community, which should tender amends, but most especially right for Canada Jack.

"It is an unusual course that I am about to adopt, but it is the only one fitting in the circumstances.

"I instruct you to bring in a verdict of not guilty. There is no other verdict, in my view, which a sensible jury, reasonably instructed, could reach."

The foreman of the jury shot to his feet.

"We ain't needing your instruction, Your Honour."

"We find the defendant 'not guilty'."

An outburst of shouting, cheering and applause shook the courtroom.

The judge banged his gavel and called loudly for order. When the crowd refused to stop, the judge threw down the gavel and beamed at Jack.

The clerk almost fainted when he saw what the judge had done. When he finally managed to subdue the demonstration the foreman rose in his place once more.

"We further recommend, Your Honour," he called out over the excited hum of voices, "that you convey to Her Majesty's Government that it is the recommendation of the jury that the accused be cited for bravery by the Parliament of Canada."

At that a fresh burst of applause shook the courtroom.

The judge had thanked the jury and then discharged them.

He congratulated Jack and discharged him.

The following day Mr. Pratt came to say goodbye to Jack. He saw Jack at the militia barracks where he was once again bunked in with Baker Troop.

Jack thanked him, then asked him about his plans for the future, now that he was free of the gang. He told Jack that Prime Minister Gladstone had invited him to enter politics. He was returning home with the intention of standing for Parliament. Jack wished him well, but inwardly he heard Tom's irreverent voice, "Politics. A suitable calling for a remittance man. Parliament moves up a notch."

Major Smith also came to say goodbye. Jack had requested that he be granted an Honourable discharge from the Army. The Major had arranged it. He surprised Jack, then, by telling him that Colonel Williams had long ago paid the Army for Cloud,

Jack's pony. "Most officer's own their own horses", the Colonel had explained. He had been too shy to tell Major Smith he loved Jack like a son and simply wanted to give him the horse that meant so much to him.

On Jack's last night Lieutenant Richards and the men of Baker Troop had given him a party to say goodbye. There were a good many of them who struggled to hold back the tears.

Now, Jack walked Cloud to the corral gate. Mr. Tuttle stood there with Sarah. Tears sparkled in her eyes.

Jack stopped to speak to them.

"You're sure you won't change your mind son," said Mr. Tuttle.

"I've given this a great deal of thought, Mr. Tuttle."

"I sure want to thank you for everything you did for me."

"It was nothing really," said Mr. Tuttle. He tried to sound nonchalant.

"It was my life, Mr. Tuttle. You saved my life. I will always be grateful to you for that."

Mr. Tuttle looked down.

Jack looked at Sarah. Neither spoke. He took her in his arms. They clung to each other for several long minutes.

When they broke off the embrace, Mr. Tuttle tried once more.

"I…We both would love to have you come back home. Sarah…," he stopped himself. "My practice is yours Jack…" This time he choked up.

Jack looked out over the great flat plain. He thought of Tom, lonesome under the northern prairie soil. He thought of Nance, of Magee, waiting. He thought of One Feather.

"I am not finished with the great plains," said Jack as he swung himself into the saddle. "I have miles to ride." He stroked the long muscular neck of his beloved Cloud.

"I have unfinished business here."

He tapped his heels lightly into Cloud, reigned her over, and rode off toward the distant horizon.

THE END.

ISBN 141203142-7

9 781412 031424